Creating Space for Shakespeare

SHAKESPEARE AND SOCIAL JUSTICE

Shakespeare and Social Justice addresses the relevance and responsibility of Shakespeare work and production to the practices, processes and goals of social justice. It addresses the significant teaching and learning, performance and practice, theory and economies that not only expand the discussion of literature and theatre, but also refocus engagements dedicated to creating positive social change.

Series Editors
Matthieu Chapman, SUNY New Paltz, USA
David Ruiter, University of California, San Diego, USA

Advisory Board
Bernadette Andrea, UCSB, USA
Chris Anthony, DePaul and The Shakespeare Center of Los Angeles, USA
Lezlie Cross, University of Portland, USA
Ambereen Dadabhoy, Harvey Mudd College, USA
Nandini Das, Oxford University, UK
Carla Della Gatta, Florida State University, USA
Sarah Enloe, American Shakespeare Center, USA
Ewan Fernie, Shakespeare Institute, University of Birmingham, UK
Coen Heijes, University of Groningen, The Netherlands
Peter Holbrook, Australian Catholic University, Melbourne, Australia
Farah Karim-Cooper, Shakespeare's Globe, UK
Baron Kelly, University of Wisconsin, USA
Lee Chee Keng, Yale-NUS College, Singapore
Regan Linton, Phamaly Theatre, Denver, USA

Forthcoming Titles
Multisensory Shakespeare and Specialized Communities
Sheila T. Cavanagh
978-1-3502-9642-8

Creating Space for Shakespeare

Working with Marginalized Communities

Rowan Mackenzie

THE ARDEN SHAKESPEARE
LONDON • NEW YORK • OXFORD • NEW DELHI • SYDNEY

THE ARDEN SHAKESPEARE
Bloomsbury Publishing Plc
50 Bedford Square, London, WC1B 3DP, UK
1385 Broadway, New York, NY 10018, USA
29 Earlsfort Terrace, Dublin 2, Ireland

BLOOMSBURY, THE ARDEN SHAKESPEARE and the Arden Shakespeare logo are trademarks of Bloomsbury Publishing Plc

First published in Great Britain 2023
This paperback published in 2024

Copyright © Rowan Mackenzie, 2023

Rowan Mackenzie has asserted her right under the Copyright, Designs and Patents Act, 1988, to be identified as author of this work.

Series Design: Tjasa Krivec
Photograph © Yevhenii Orlov /Getty and Joe Woods/Unsplash

All rights reserved. No part of this publication may be reproduced or transmitted in any form or by any means, electronic or mechanical, including photocopying, recording, or any information storage or retrieval system, without prior permission in writing from the publishers.

Bloomsbury Publishing Plc does not have any control over, or responsibility for, any third-party websites referred to or in this book. All internet addresses given in this book were correct at the time of going to press. The author and publisher regret any inconvenience caused if addresses have changed or sites have ceased to exist, but can accept no responsibility for any such changes.

A catalogue record for this book is available from the British Library.

A catalog record for this book is available from the Library of Congress.

ISBN:	HB:	978-1-3502-7265-1
	PB:	978-1-3502-7274-3
	ePDF:	978-1-3502-7272-9
	eBook:	978-1-3502-7266-8

Series: Shakespeare and Social Justice

Typeset by Integra Software Services Pvt. Ltd.

To find out more about our authors and books visit www.bloomsbury.com and sign up for our newsletters.

Dedicated to the actors in our prison theatre companies who have woven the magic we've created together and in memory of my late father, Mick Mackenzie

CONTENTS

List of Illustrations x

Introduction 1
    Social justice and social injustices 1
    Creative spaces 7
    Performance spaces 7
    Reflective spaces 9
    Mediated spaces 10

1 The need to break down silos 11
    Learning disabilities 13
    Mental health issues 15
    Criminal justice system 17
    Homelessness 22

2 Creative spaces 25
    Short-term projects 28
        Flute Theatre 28
        1623 Theatre 32
        Remand prison 34
    Medium-term projects 39
        Flute Theatre 39
        Romeo and Juliet project 43
    Longer-term projects 48
        The Gallowfield Players 48
        Emergency Shakespeare 60
        Blue Apple Theatre 63

Riding Lights Theatre – Acting Up! 65
Conclusion 68

3 Performative spaces 71
Demarcated spaces 77
   Out of Character 78
   Acting Up! 80
   Flute Theatre 82
   Firebird Theatre 85
Appropriated spaces 91
   Broadmoor Hospital 92
   Donmar trilogy 95
   The Gallowfield Players – *The Merchant* 96
   Emergency Shakespeare – *Macbeth* 107
Conclusion 117

4 Reflective spaces 119
Individual Reflections 125
   Internment camps 125
   Robben Island 129
   English prisons during Covid-19 133
Reflections on group dynamics 147
Conclusion 168

5 Mediated spaces 171
Journalism 179
Documentaries 186
Low-budget media 192
Written media 194
Conclusion 202

Conclusion 207

References 217
   Films and documentaries 217

Government and institutional policy documentation and data 217
Her Majesty's Inspectorate of Prisons Reports 221
Performance publicity content 222
Productions 223
Rehearsals and workshops 223
Shakespeare texts 224
Unpublished Interviews 225
Unpublished written content 226
Academic publications 229
Conference papers and key note speeches 247
News articles, journalism and social media posts 248
Podcasts and public talks 252
Websites 252

Index 255

LIST OF ILLUSTRATIONS

1. Emergency Shakespeare rehearsing *Macbeth*, HMP Stafford (July 2019). Photo: Monica Cru-Hall 26

2. 'Trance' one of *The Tempest* games at Centre d'Educacio Especial Montserrat Montero (March 2017). Photo: Flute Theatre 42

3. The Gallowfield Players logo designed following collaborative discussions and drawn by Michael, HMP Gartree (December 2018). Courtesy of Michael 49

4. Prospero and Ariel (Tommy Jessop and James Benfield), Blue Apple Theatre, *The Tempest+* Winchester Royal Theatre (June 2019). Photo: Mike Hall Photography 72

5. Emergency Shakespeare, *Macbeth*, The Visits Hall, HMP Stafford (17 September 2019). Photo: George Vuckovic Photography 109

6. Brody's initial sketch of the set design, completed during rehearsals in his Rehearsal Diary (June 2019). Courtesy of Brody 111

7. Wade (played by Mark) being arrested by HMPPS Custody Manager, Emergency Shakespeare, *Macbeth* (17 September 2019). Photo: George Vuckovic Photography 114

8	Richard's illustration of the two Dromios for inclusion in *The Comedy of Errors* Activity Packs during COVID-19 (May 2020). Courtesy of Richard 135
9	Brody's illustration of *A Midsummer Night's Dream* for inclusion in the Activity Packs during COVID-19 (April 2020), which won him a Koestler Commended Award, 2020. Courtesy of Brody 137
10	Richard's illustration of Henry V for inclusion in the *Henry V* Activity Packs during COVID-19 (June 2020). Courtesy of Richard 140
11	Brody's illustration for inclusion in the *Julius Caesar* Activity Packs (May 2020). Courtesy of Brody 142
12	Richard's illustration of Titania and Bottom for inclusion in the *A Midsummer Night's Dream* Activity Packs (May 2020). Courtesy of Richard 143
13	Brody's illustration of Banquo's ghost at the banquet in *Macbeth*, part of a comic book version he created during the pandemic (September 2020). Courtesy of Brody 144
14	Sketch completed by Brody during Emergency Shakespeare rehearsals for *Macbeth*, HMP Stafford (2 June 2019). Courtesy of Brody 148
15	Richard's drawing of the cast of *The Merchant* wearing masks, drawn during the COVID-19 lockdown and inspired by a cast photograph taken

at the Family Day performance (illustration – May 2020). Courtesy of Richard   152

16 Richard's illustration of Shylock, Portia and Antonio for inclusion in *The Merchant of Venice* Activity Packs (July 2020). Courtesy of Richard   153

17 Brody's illustration of *The Tempest* for inclusion in the Activity Packs (April 2020). Courtesy of Brody   156

18 Richard's cartoon of *Sycorax's Storm* (July 2020). Courtesy of Richard   161

19 Richard's pastiche of Shakespeare characters in *Sir John Falstaff in Looking for Love* (July 2020). Courtesy of Richard   163

20 Richard and Michael's sketches for costumes for *Sycorax's Storm* (July 2020). Courtesy of The Gallowfield Players   165

21 Brody's illustration of *King Lear* which he and I agreed was too macabre for inclusion in the Activity Packs (June 2020). Courtesy of Brody   167

22 Brody's cartoon-strip of *Othello,* Acts 1 & 2, drawn for inclusion in the programme for Emergency Shakespeare's production of the play, planned for 2021 (September 2020). Courtesy of Brody   169

23 Motif of The Gallowfield Players in character for *The Merchant*, drawn by Richard (January 2020). Courtesy of Richard 199

24 The logo for Shakespeare UnBard, designed and drawn by Michael, The Gallowfield Players (August 2020). Courtesy of Michael 204

25 The Gallowfield Players, crown from *Macbeth*, created from cardboard and silver paper by an inmate who is cell-bound due to age and ill-health. This has become symbolic of the work of The Gallowfield Players (October 2018). Photo: Rowan Mackenzie 216

Introduction

Social justice and social injustices

Social exclusion and marginalization affect millions of people worldwide: those on the periphery of society for a multitude of reasons including those with mental health issues, learning disabilities, substance misuse issues, criminal convictions and who have experienced homelessness. In contrast to this widespread marginalization – theatre generally and Shakespeare in particular are often seen as the epitome of culture, an activity enjoyed predominantly by the middle and upper classes. This book examines what happens when these two disparate worlds are combined. Shakespeare can alter the spatial constraints for those who feel imprisoned, whether physically or metaphorically, enabling them to speak, and to be heard, in ways they may previously have struggled with. Applied theatre is growing in popularity and reach but continues to focus on a singular marker of marginalization, such as, learning disabled theatre, prison theatre. Moving away from this binary segregation is important in a people-centred approach and allows cross-fertilization of artistic practices between organizations for the benefit of participants.

I write from the dual perspective of practitioner and academic and would hope that this book stimulates further consideration and discussion of the issues of ownership, communication and positive autonomy affecting those on the periphery of society. To further enrich the field of such work we need to be able to listen to those affected and to gather evidence from the perspectives of all involved. Drawing on a wide range of initiatives from around the world and from diverse organizations allows me to frame the conversations of identity, community and trust in a way which foregrounds our common humanity whilst acknowledging the individuality of each participant. I believe that this can offer new opportunities for development of dialogue within the field of applied Shakespeare which centres the person rather than their marker of marginalization.

Applied theatre defies simple definition; it is an umbrella term which covers a multitude of 'theatrical practices and creative processes ... that is responsive to ordinary people and their stories'(Prentki & Preston, 2009: p.11). Tracing the historical origins of such a non-homogenous discipline is complex but, as Prentki and Preston document, the practices recognizable as applied theatre have 'progressively gained currency throughout the second half of the twentieth century' (2009: p.11). The widespread nature of applied theatre includes (but is not limited to) theatre in education, community projects, work with those with learning disabilities, mental health issues, conflict resolution drama, work with those incarcerated, theatre with those who have experienced homelessness, dramatherapy, theatre in war zones and the aftermath of natural disasters, and work which has a social diaspora focus such as tackling racism or other inequalities. Academics such as Helen Nicholson have been instrumental in developing the genre of applied theatre which she describes as 'the gift of theatre' (2015: p.4), contributing a number of monographs and edited collections as this field expands in popularity at both undergraduate and postgraduate levels. Nicholson and Hughes acknowledge an 'ecology of practices' which are 'continually shifting and developing' (2016: p.4), and this book aims to contribute to the development of this richly nuanced and diverse field.

Boal's seminal text, *Theatre of the Oppressed,* significantly influenced the development of this field of work, encouraging theatre in which monologue is transformed by the actor into dialogue and 'theatre is action!' (2008: p.135). His description of theatre as discourse drew on George Ikashawa for the concept that 'the bourgeoisie presents the spectacle' (2008: p.120) whilst the oppressed are not yet sure of how their world looks and so they present unpolished rehearsal as they use theatre to explore their relationship to the wider world. Boal's concepts of image theatre (using non-verbal sculpting of the actors' bodies to create statue-like tableaus representing moments of oppression) and forum theatre (in which the audience are invited to 'intervene decisively in the dramatic action and change it') (2008: pp.112–17) have become ingrained in theatrical practice. They are an intrinsic part of organizations such as Cardboard Citizens who pride themselves on making 'theatre which activates change' (Cardboard Citizens website, 2020) as they offer a methodology of empowerment in which alternative narratives can be explored by actors and audiences.

Many of those who society ostracizes have experienced significant trauma and 'among socially marginalised populations experiences of individual and systemic discrimination may elicit particularly marked adverse consequences' (Matheson et al., 2019). For this reason I will draw on some of the developments in trauma-informed pedagogy such as the principles underpinning these approaches as defined by Substance Abuse and Mental Health Services Administration (SAMHSA). As Felitti et al. discovered in their *Adverse Childhood Experience (ACE) Study*, those who experience four or more categories of childhood traumas, such as abuse, neglect and severe poverty, are four to twelve times more likely to have addiction issues, self-harming and suicidal tendencies along with increased risk of poor health and obesity (Felitti et al., 1998: pp.245–58). This study has been instrumental in developing focus on the need to acknowledge trauma and to develop strategies which are able to alleviate some of the issues and avoid causing further distress. Trauma-informed approaches are becoming increasingly widespread across educational, carceral and therapeutic settings, and have influenced my own practice-based research methods.

Labels can be problematic and at times damaging, reinforcing issues of marginalization and stigmatization. Humans should view humans as such, not divide according to their educational needs or mental health. However, in the interests of clarity it has been necessary to ensure the reader's understanding of the people being cited is not compromised. To this end I use people-centred phrases such as 'person with learning disabilities', not because this is the defining factor about the person but it is important contextually within the book both to understand their situation and also the way in which they may experience judgement and prejudice.

For those within the prison system this labelling is even more problematic and there is a growing movement to define a new lexicon with which to discuss those in custody. Where possible I elect to refer to them as 'men', 'people' or 'actors'. Additionally, I refer to the male and female estate but within that estate there are transgender and gender-fluid individuals and The Gallowfield Players comprises fourteen men and a pre-operative transgender woman so in plurality I sometimes use the term 'guys' as they felt this to be a gender-neutral address they were comfortable with. Occasionally in order to make clear the distinction about whom I am writing it is necessary to differentiate staff or visitors from those incarcerated and at those times I use the term 'inmate' as this is the term agreed by the actors in both theatre companies as the one they personally find least offensive. All of the participants within prisons were anonymized in line with HMPPS and Ministry of Justice (MoJ) requirements, for security purposes and in the interests of protecting victims and their families. Each participant within prison was allocated a pseudonym, thereby protecting their identity whilst retaining their humanity.

The combination of Shakespeare with the inherent 'cultural capital' (Bourdieu, 1986: p.241) his works convey, the physicality of theatre artistry and the deployment of trauma-informed methodologies enable those who have struggled to find their voice, or for their voice to be heard by wider society, to articulate themselves in new ways. Cultural capital is a complex issue as Shakepeare can be seen to have been a contributory factor to marginalization of many communities through this inherent cultural capital. My work focuses on how this cultural capital can be inverted and exploited by marginalized communities within a people-centric approach. Many of the case studies included here appropriate and adapt Shakespeare both in the sense of his plays and what Bristol described as 'big-time Shakespeare' (1996) – the pastiche of power dynamics, themes and cultural capital which are attributed to his work. The appropriation undertaken in these case studies is often as a result of the community involved's lived experiences and a desire to appropriate Shakespeare to provide a wider societal cultural validity to these experiences through the medium of his works. Paul Prescott and Katie Steele Brokaw speak of 'leveraging the cultural currency of Shakespeare' (panel, 2022) because of the internationally recognized nature of his work and how this can be used to add validity to a range of contemporary issues. By appropriating Shakespeare's plays the marginalized groups I write about in this book are able to articulate issues pertinent to their own existence in a way which non-marginalized people may listen to more than if they simply narratized their own experiences.

To evidence the ways in which communication can encourage people to see things differently I borrow from Foucault's concept of 'heterotopia' as real places which act as counter-sites, 'outside of all places, even though it may be possible to indicate their location within reality' (1984). He developed the concept from the medical term for something which is *out of place* and used it to describe cultural spaces which are dislocated from expectation, which contradict and challenge the anticipated response. This book examines a broad spectrum of marginalized communities and the way in which both live performances and media depictions can alter public and personal perceptions about the limitations to which they may be subjected, either physically or through societal expectations. As Danielle Kassarate from MAWA Theatre Company describes, it is powerful for people who are marginalized and feel that their voices are not heard to be able to 'see people like themselves speaking Shakespeare, recognize themselves in the actors they see' (interview, 2022). This act of heterotopic challenge has an immensely empowering impact on people who have previously been ignored by the homogenous *wider society*.

Drawing on the wealth of material in existence, including the ever-developing field of audience reception theories in the context of both live and mediated performances, I attempt to navigate the complexities of how actors from marginalized sectors of society can utilize the power of theatre to challenge preconceptions related to the supposed limitations connected to their marginalization, yet also the need for their art to be critiqued objectively by audiences. Claire Bishop summarizes this in her assertion that:

> Value judgements are necessary, not as a means to reinforce elite culture and police the boundaries of art and non-art, but as a way to understand and clarify our shared values at a given historical moment.
>
> (2012: p.8)

There is a temptation for those engaging in work with marginalized individuals and communities, who are not themselves marginalized, to assume a mantle of superiority, to patronize (albeit unintentionally) those with whom they are creating theatre through the assumption that they are giving the gift of cultural achievement through this artistry. Jenny Hughes writes of the historical prevalence of these 'sanctioned cultural activities [which] can be understood as disciplinary impositions of middle-class respectability on the poor' (2016: p.44). I explore the media contribution to this colonialization of marginalized people in significant detail in Chapter 5 but the undertones of this attitude resonate more widely across pedagogical and faciliatory approaches to applied theatre. My own research is responsive to the accusation that some applied theatre assumes a form of colonialized superiority in which those facilitating the work seek to deliver charitable aims to those marginalized as they assert a value judgement of self-improvement (Loftis, 2019). The duality of role as practitioner and researcher is complex and whilst 'congruent with a much valued (and vaunted) rights-based social and political agenda' the nuances of balancing the competing priorities pose challenges (2016: p.29). Aldridge explores these difficulties and offers valuable insights into how to conduct this dual role with integrity, authenticity and ethical consideration as researchers endeavour to move participants from the tokenistic involvement of passivity to the emancipatory role they perform in social transformation (2016: p.156). This basis has underpinned my own research-as-practice and led me to encourage activism as the antithesis to passive appropriation of marginalized people working with applied theatre.

Focusing on spatial dynamics serves as a way of developing from the siloed cataloguing of marginalized groups which is prevalent in much existing research. This allows me to develop the principle of equal participation between people marginalized for differing reasons and to remove the seeming need for a primary marginalization marker (i.e. that a person either has learning disabilities or mental health issues or lived experience of prison or of homelessness, when in reality many people experience more than one of these). Instead the spatial dynamic allows me to consider people as individuals with their own complexities, categorizing their experiences rather than their existence. Within the chapters there is still overlap of the documentation of these case studies as people are not easily contained within boxes of any kind, and their experiences bleed across spaces they inhabit and each of us grows and develops based on our unique experiences and circumstances.

Creative spaces

The creative spaces of rehearsals and workshops are often where Shakespeare is explored by groups who may previously have felt that his work was not for them due to societal judgements. In this context I build on the concept of space as a socially constructed entity which is moulded by the activity undertaken by those inhabiting the place. Considering the intersectionality of space, time and power enable the development of positive autonomy, a term I have coined to encompass the freedoms developed within these programmes whilst acknowledging that total autonomy may not be possible or desirable for people with severe disorders or who are convicted of criminal activities. Longer-term programmes facilitated emotional growth and communication development through appropriation of Shakespeare's cultural capital and his multi-faceted characters. The work created a sense of community with its attendant emotional support network which thrived both in and outside of rehearsals. As Brody articulated, Emergency Shakespeare is 'a wonderful opportunity to express myself in a different way' (2019) and he identified the development of his communication skills during the first six months as significant. The element of temporality is important as it is through long-term interventions that significant developments can take place, where there is the time for mutuality and trust to develop and for peer support to become a central tenet of the work. A large proportion of creative work is focused on short-term projects although increasingly funding bodies are realizing the benefits of support in excess of twenty-four months to enable development of semi-permanent groups. This longevity of project is a key component in the potential impact across all of the marginalized communities I worked with.

Performance spaces

Performance spaces are filled with heterotopic potential, especially when they combine marginalized people and performances of Shakespeare. The concept of heterotopia has been developed by Marin, Hetherington and, recently, Tompkins in *Theatre's Heterotopias* where she outlines her concept that it is through the juxtaposition of constructed space and abstracted space that the heterotopia is seen and challenges perceptions (2014: p.27). My own definition of heterotopias borrows much from Tompkins's methodology in terms of the constructed space of the theatrical intervention (whether in a theatre or other location). This constructed space is the one of the play-world, asking the audience to suspend their disbelief and engage with the world they see enacted before them regardless of the level of realism ascribed by the scenery, props and costuming of the production. However, in the context of marginalized groups engaging with theatre the abstracted space is instead an abstracted concept; drawing on Bourdieu's notion of cultural capital and the groups' appropriation of Shakespeare. In the context of performative space I consider both the *demarcated spaces* of traditional theatres and *appropriated spaces*, often repurposed from primary functions as school halls, chapels and visits halls. Formal theatre spaces can add a sense of cultural validity to marginalized performances through what they represent, but can also be intimidating to some attendees in relation to the signifiers embedded within their primary function. There is clinical research which suggests that 'recognition of personally familiar places may share neural mechanisms with episodic memory retrieval' (Sugiura et al., 2015: p.183). Episodic memory retrieval 'includes the sensory, conceptual, and emotional experiences that define an event' (Shimamura, 2011: p.277), suggesting that when a person recognizes a familiar space they will automatically trigger emotional and conceptual remembrances from within that space.

Appropriated spaces retain signifiers pertaining to their predominant purpose which can be alternately beneficial or prejudicial for those attending a performance. They may have emotional connections, positive or negative, which are difficult to set aside during a theatre production. However, in both types of location there is the possibility for the performance to allow the audience to see the work 'as an alternative way of doing things' (Hetherington, 1997: p.viii) in which marginalized people are applauded for their artistic skill rather than judged for their *otherness*. The appropriation of Shakespeare by marginalized groups enables the participants to be seen differently, appreciated for their artistic abilities rather than ostracized by society for their differences. As one audience member described 'I forgot I was in a prison and was lost in the play' (anonymous questionnaire, 2019), evidencing the way in which this heterotopic combination enabled what Howard Barker described as 'braver theatre' which 'asks the audience to test the validity of the categories it believes it lives by' (1993: p.52).

Reflective spaces

In contrast to the public display of performances is the private and often solitary reflection on Shakespeare as a resource from which to develop resilience and personal agency. Michael described 'I reflect the beauty of what has been achieved, the taste of freedom that is so sweet – in pages – and escape the conflicted reality which is my life' (Michael, 2020) when writing about how he coped with the enforced isolation in prison during Covid-19. It provided 'a tether to the Gallowfield Players' community' which helped him deal with the mental health impacts of total separation from family and friends during this period, enabling him to draw on the knowledge that the work would recommence in the future.

Such reflections can provide emotional and cultural sustenance during times of prolonged isolation and/or trauma. It offers a mechanism by which those marginalized can pierce the surface of *otherness* and use this literary mirror of the imagination through which to reflect their own place in the world. Those involved drew from it a sense of continuity; they were able to mentally and emotionally connect with the theatrical engagements and creative experiences which preceded this time of significant dislocation from the community. This provided reassurance that this dislocation would be temporary. The sense of connection to a cultural history, identified as key to trauma-informed practices, is provided by Shakespeare for some during times of duress or segregation from their normal lives. This is differentiated when the reflection is personal and individual compared to when it also contains reflections of group activities undertaken, such as was the case with the prison theatre companies during Covid-19. The memory of the collective trust was embedded within the members of the theatre companies and provided them with additional social sustenance during challenging times, which went beyond Shakespeare's text to the support network of the group.

Mediated spaces

Media *presents* content of marginalized people engaging with Shakespeare, *presenting* both in terms of making it visible and also making it feel immediate and relevant to the social context of modern society. Against a backdrop of media and social media serving as portals to the world for many, and with increasing digitization of theatre and other artistic events, there is an ever-growing place for media depictions of artistic endeavours. However, as Todd Landon Barnes warns, the media presence can be exploitative, manipulative and driven by a commercial agenda (2020: p.14). It is imperative to consider whose voices are being heard in the media narration; often it is not those who are marginalized. Instead there is the inherent risk that it becomes an 'unwelcome intrusion. It is easy for trust to become dependency, for generosity to be interpreted as patronage, for interest in others to be experienced as the gaze of surveillance' (Nicholson, 2015: p.166). Through analysis of differing forms of media I identify best practices for mediated narration of these types of practices. I plot these forms on a spectrum from those most removed (news coverage) to those most closely linked to the actual practice (materials created by the participants themselves). Wherever possible the content should be defined and portrayed by or in conjunction with the marginalized people, ensuring that their perspective has centrality and the mediated output discourages manipulative or colonial undertones. Whilst frequently the voices foregrounded are not those of the community this does not have to be the case and through a combination of allowing people to develop their resilience, confidence and sense of autonomy it is possible to enable creative activism where those marginalized become centralized and their own perspectives can be shared, and more importantly, listened to.

There is richness in the breadth and scope of applied theatre with various marginalized communities; however, many of the projects and interventions take place disparately and much of the work is relatively ephemeral with practitioners often moving onto the next project without materials being archived in a way which would make them accessible for others.

1

The need to break down silos

The majority of applied theatre research exists in siloed consideration of specific groups, with little intersectionality across differing circles, although the read-across between those with mental health issues, learning disabilities, those who have experienced imprisonment and experienced homelessness is vast. Through encouraging a critical discourse which encompasses a broader consideration of these sectors of society my aspiration is that there will be positive implications for current and future work.

Statistics suggest that 25–40 per cent of people with learning disabilities also experience mental health issues, with many of them not receiving support for these issues due to 'lack of communication between mainstream psychiatry services and intellectual disability psychiatry services' (Mental Health website). Mental health issues amongst those incarcerated is four times higher than the general population of the UK with over 70 per cent of prisoners having two or more of the following – psychosis, neurotic disorders, personality disorders, hazardous drinking and drug dependency (Singleton et al., 1998). Despite this, it is estimated that reception screening upon imprisonment identifies less than a third of those with mental health needs (Brooker et al., 2002). Incidents of self-harm and suicide within the criminal justice system are widespread with the *Prisons Annual Report 2018–19* documenting a 15 per cent increase in self-inflicted deaths in custody in the male estate and 25 per cent increase in self-harm from the previous year, with over 45,000 instances logged in 2018.

Finding statistical evidence of the prevalence of learning disabilities within the criminal justice system is problematic due to differing assessment tools and a lack of comprehensive screening, but the Prison Reform Trust estimates approximately 32 per cent are borderline or have learning disabilities whilst 30 per cent have dyslexia and close to 60 per cent have 'severe deficits in literacy and numeracy' (Loucks, 2008). Whilst there is no evidence that people with autism spectrum disorder (ASD) are more likely to commit offences, 4–5 per cent of sentenced prisoners have ASD comparative to 1–2 per cent of the general population, highlighting a significant issue which is not yet adequately understood (Lewis, 2020). So widespread are mental health and learning disability issues with those convicted of criminal offences that new sentencing guidelines were implemented from 1 October 2020 to 'provide clarity and transparency around the sentencing process for this group of offenders' (*Sentencing offenders with mental disorders, developmental disorders, or neurological impairments*). The 2016 report on the joint inspection of prisons and probation found that 'over two-thirds of [short-term] prisoners need help with accommodation' (Stacey & Clarke, 2016: p.21) on release and lack of suitable accommodation is frequently cited as a barrier to successful desistance. The, admittedly limited, 'evidence base suggests that cognitive impairment amongst homeless people is common' (Oakes & Davis, 2008: p.326) according to one of the few studies conducted into this field. Given the intrinsic links between these forms of marginalization the development of positive communication methodologies needs consideration across the spectrum rather than focusing on one isolated reason for an individual being marginalized, ignoring the other contributory factors. This intersectionality adds a dimension not previously fully explored within academic research; taking a more holistic approach to marginalization and the inherent trauma it causes allows the potential for interventions to be created which are appropriate for a broader group of people. When academics, practitioners and policy-makers move to a position of dismantling the silos which exist between work for people with learning disabilities, mental health issues, incarceration and homelessness it enables cross-fertilization of creative practices.

Learning disabilities

Accurate figures on the number of people with learning disabilities are not readily available but Mencap estimate that there are 1.5 million affected people in the UK (based on extrapolation of various data sources, cited on their website). Global comparative data are not available as level of assessment varies significantly between countries. Clinical research into the use of drama with learning disabled people, particularly those with autism, articulates a

> belief that theatre may provide an ideal environment to teach a variety of core skills that children with autism often lack …. We hypothesized that children with autism would demonstrate improvement in social perception (memory of faces, the expression of emotions and theory of mind), skills and adaptive functioning.
>
> (Corbett et al., 2011: p.505)

The initial findings of this research were relatively inconclusive given the small group size (eight participants) and the lack of a control group, but a further study in 2015 using thirty-three children demonstrated that 'SENSE Theatre facilitated gains in memory for faces and social communication skills' (Corbett et al., 2016: p.669). Their work involved theatre games, role playing and improvisation, culminating in the group and their peer actors (same-sex and age as ASD participant) rehearsing and performing a 45-minute play. This study validated what many theatre practitioners have believed for decades, that drama improves communication skills for those with learning disabilities. The data gathering was extensive and included measuring independent play, facial recognition and social functioning compared to a randomized control group.

The 2017 Autism Arts Festival at the University of Kent provided one of the most notable evaluations of audience perceptions in the sphere of learning disabilities to date. This two-day event was designed to be 'an entire festival that was as autism-friendly as possible' and which one attendee described as 'autistic space' (Fletcher-Watson & May, 2018: p.406). The event also gave the organizers the opportunity to create a 'qualitative curatorial feedback model of evaluation' comprising of mixed-methods data collection (p.412). This data focused on audience experience, artists' experience and suggestions for future accessibility improvements for the arts. The project highlighted a number of developments which may help assuage the concerns of non-neurotypical attendees to events in the future, including plot synopses, sensory trigger lists and video trailers. As the authors note, these adaptations are not always available in theatres and live arts venues and their work may be influential in prompting the inclusion of these as the number of relaxed performances (productions adapted to avoid sensory triggers and provide pre-attendance information to special needs audiences) continues to increase. The findings resonate with the *Relaxed Performance Project* evaluation (currently the most comprehensive study of these performances) which states that 'preparation and information are absolutely key, if audiences know what to expect there is less for them to worry about' (Potter, 2013). The concept of issuing illustrated handouts to introduce the staff and cast ahead of the event is used widely by many companies who produce relaxed performances, including Flute Theatre, Firebird Theatre and Tell Tale Hearts.

There is a growing demand by disabled actors for them to be judged on the quality of their artistic outputs rather than assessed through the lens of their disability, as happened with the early examples of disabled theatre in the 1980s. Matt Hargrave theorizes that there are three schools of thought on the topic: therapeutic intervention, its diametric opposite – empowerment through the 'process of *communitas*' in which a group coheres around an issue to instigate social change – and the touring of semi-professional disabled theatre companies (2015: p.34). Hargrave identifies 'the perceived inability of the learning disabled performer to be the sole, autonomous author of work and the expectation that such a performer may require additional support to embody a role', but there is a desire for the work to be appreciated on its own merits more than it has been previously (2015: p.217). My article '*The Tempest+* from Blue Apple Theatre Company' aimed to foreground the artistic output rather than the disabilities of the company, considering the way their production unified Shakespeare's text with current socio-political concerns in relation to Brexit. In this book I examine the roles of disabled audiences and disabled actors, contextualizing them against the wider lens of marginalization, including examples of people who are learning disabled within the carceral environment as well as those outside the walls.

Mental health issues

In 2017 it was estimated that over 792 million people globally were living with mental health issues and the Covid-19 pandemic is believed to have severely exacerbated an already annually increasing issue (Dattani et al., 2018; Nochaiwong et al., 2021). Statistically, one in four people in the UK will experience mental health issues each year yet popular perceptions often remain skewed with 1/3 of the public thinking those with mental health issues are violent when in fact they are more likely to be victims of crime or to harm themselves than others (MHFA website 2020). The potential well-being benefits of arts were foregrounded when over £1M Economic and Social Research Council (ESRC) funding was awarded to create the MARCH Network conducting research into the mental health impacts of social, cultural and community assets (2018–21). Whilst James Thompson raises the valid consideration that 'the insistence that survivors "tell their stories" is a culturally particular approach that can become problematic if applied universally' (2009: p.49), across Western cultures the sharing of stories and dramatizations of traumatic events are widely accepted as having therapeutic benefits and it is on this premise that dramatherapy is predicated.

'Dramatherapy is a form of psychological therapy in which all of the performance arts are utilised within the therapeutic relationship' (British Association of Dramatherapists website), with the focus firmly on the therapy rather than the artwork. A large proportion of dramatherapy is based on devised work in which the participants enact problematic scenes from their own lived experience to resolve unaddressed trauma. There is a subtle yet important differentiation between dramatherapy and the therapeutic benefits of drama in its truly artistic incarnation. The former focuses on the participants' changing their own perceptions and relationships whereas the latter focuses on producing theatre whilst appreciating that personal development may be a by-product. Bessel van der Kolk's seminal text *The Body Keeps Score* examines a multitude of case histories of those who have suffered immense trauma and he is 'convinced of the therapeutic possibilities of theatre' (2015: p.330). He cites 'the life-changing process … [he] witnessed in a workshop run by actors trained by Shakespeare and Company' (van der Kolk, 2015: p.345) for war veterans in which *Julius Caesar* was used to build tolerance of intense emotions.

Sue Jennings uses the themes of Shakespeare as a medium to access previous trauma. Her 'innovatory dramatherapy project' utilized *A Midsummer Night's Dream* with patients at Broadmoor Hospital 'as a focal point for dramatherapy exploration' (Jennings et al., 1997: p.83). Each participant was assessed by numerous psychological tests during the six-month project. The lack of consistency of results was attributed to 'the multidimensional nature of assessing and treating the dynamics of any individual case' (1997: p.97). Despite the inconclusivity of the assessments the researchers asserted that 'there was no doubt from all concerned that there had been an improvement in self-image both individually and collectively' (1997: p.110). Jennings acknowledges the way in which using text-based drama, such as Shakespeare, serves as 'a means of dramatic distancing' (1992: p.17), allowing dramatherapy clients to explore themes in their own lives from a safe vantage point. Brenda Meldrum writes that Jennings 'believes that the roots of dramatherapy lie in the theatre and not in the clinic' (1993: p.68) and this is borne out by Jennings's own publications and interviews.

Jennings was also involved in organizing the Shakespeare performances at Broadmoor Hospital 1989–91, about which *Shakespeare comes to Broadmoor* was written, combining recollections from staff, actors, patients and others connected with the ambitious project. Murray Cox was the Consultant Psychotherapist at the Hospital from 1970 until his death in 1997. Cox and Thielgaard wrote 'of particular importance to Shakespeare's paraclinical precision is the range of different ways in which people relate' (Cox & Thielgaard, 1994: p.232) and they argue that the characters can be used as prompts within the psychotherapy process with patients, particularly those who may initially be resistant to engagement.

Mutative Metaphors in Psychotherapy cites Gaston Bachelard's quotation 'but the image has touched the depths before it stirs the surface' (Bachelard, 1964: p.xiii) as the central theme of their Aeolian Mode, in which the patient is able to be freed from the restrictive legacy of their past through narration. Cox and Thielgaard explore the metaphors within Shakespeare as pivotal to these opportunities through 'dramatic distancing', allowing an individual to use the words of a character when they struggle to articulate their own experiences and therefore to reflect through that lens. As Brody, a member of Emergency Shakespeare, with a history of mental health issues, explains:

> I can see why it's so easy to get caught up in the parts you play. As I am learning with Shakespeare so much of it is relatable or identifiable but you have to really break it down and feel it to be able to truly understand it.
>
> (2020)

For many marginalized people, the opportunity to reflect through a character allows them to at once explore that constructed role and also their own connection to the embedded emotions.

Criminal justice system

The prison system within England and Wales is structured differently from other countries and a brief description is necessary to ensure clarity and understanding, both operationally and culturally. There were 78,743 adults incarcerated as of 10 September 2021, 75,564 in the male estate and 3,179 in the female estate (with a prison population rate of 131 per 100,000 capita). This is in the context of global mass incarceration estimated at over 11.5 million people, of which over 2 million are imprisoned within the United States (which has the highest rate of 629 per 100,000 capita) (Fair & Walmsley, 2021). Youth custody figures are less readily available but there were an estimated 859 young people in custody each month in England and Wales in 2019 (Ministry of Justice, 2020). The English adult male estate has four security categories:

- **Category A** – Prisoners whose escape would be highly dangerous to the public or the police or the security of the State and for whom the aim must be to make escape impossible.
- **Category B** – Prisoners for whom the very highest conditions of security are not necessary but for whom escape must be made very difficult.
- **Category C** – Prisoners who cannot be trusted in open conditions but who do not have the resources and will to make a determined escape attempt.

Category D – Prisoners who present a low risk; can reasonably be trusted in open conditions and for whom open conditions are appropriate.

(Grimwood, 2015: p.4)

There are prisons to accommodate each individual category, although Category A prisons also house Category B inmates and when a person is re-categorized there is often a significant delay in their being moved to a lower security institution, meaning that there are often mixed categories in male prisons. Those people convicted of sexual offences are generally detained either in specifically designated prisons or Vulnerable Prisoner Units (VPUs), segregated from the main prison population. VPUs also house those at risk from the general population for other reasons such as the nature of their crime, severe mental health issues or those who worked within the criminal justice sector prior to conviction. The adult female estate has four security categories but these are not the same as the male estate and in practice the highest category in use is 'restricted status' with the majority being categorized simply as 'open conditions' or 'closed conditions' (Grimwood, 2015: p.9). Given the relatively low numbers of incarcerated women, multiple categories are usually accommodated within one prison as there are only twelve female establishments throughout England.

The beneficial effects of creativity for those incarcerated are widely acknowledged by the Ministry of Justice, practitioners, third-sector organizations and academics. Dame Coates, in her influential report, cited the importance of

> greater provision of high-quality creative arts provision, and Personal and Social Development (PSD) courses. Both improve self-knowledge, develop self-confidence and therefore help tackle reoffending.
>
> (2016: p.ii)

This report directly influenced changes to prison funding to enable Governors to engage non-core educational providers for activities such as music and drama sessions. The combination of the Prison Education Framework (PEF) in 2018 and the Dynamic Purchasing System (DPS) in 2019 was intended to 'enable governors to commission bespoke education in their own establishments'

(Ministry of Justice, 2018: p.13), although the reality of the implementation has been problematic with accessibility and functionality issues delaying tender processes throughout 2019–20. Ofsted and HM Inspectorate of Prisons announced in September 2021 that as a result of the lack of improvement following Coates's review a further Prison Education Review was to be conducted over the next twelve months. The recent review of reading education found severe issues in the lack of prioritization given to this fundamental skill by both prisons and education providers. It cites 'systemic barriers that prevent prisoners from receiving effective support to acquire or improve their reading skills' (Taylor, 2022).

Angela Sanders's review of *Leadership in Prison Education* also highlighted a number of issues and identified the need for consistency of leadership development but acknowledged the reduced budgets some establishments had suffered as part of the PEF implementation whilst the pressure to deliver tangible outcomes remained unchanged (2020: pp.28–31). HMPPS funded the development of the Intermediate Outcomes Measurement Tool to facilitate a move from anecdotal evidence to more formalized data collation across the topics of personal agency, well-being, impulsivity, interpersonal trust, motivation to change, hope, resilience and practical problems.

A recent *Bromley Briefing* cited the importance of purposeful activity to aid rehabilitation during custodial sentences and the ways in which 'arts, and informal learning […] allow people to engage and progress during their sentence' (Halliday, 2019: p.49). The Prisoners' Education Trust (PET) and Prisoner Learning Alliance (PLA) encourage dialogue and research through publications, conferences and seminars aiming to foster collaborations, partnerships and positive outcomes for those incarcerated. The PET 2019 report on active citizenship stated:

> We believe in creating a space in the prison environment where talents and qualities of people are central and prisoners can feel recognised as human beings, work on a positive self-image, develop their talents and strengthen their relationships with others.
>
> (Oglethorpe et al., 2019: p.5)

My in-prison theatre companies were founded on these principles and their longevity has enabled these spaces to be firmly established both during rehearsals and outside of formal engagement. Creative projects are frequently conducive to developing talents and positive relationships; 'participation in arts activities enables individuals to begin to redefine themselves' (Plant & Dixon, 2019: p.5), embrace positive engagement, self-management and individual autonomy.

Clean Break (founded in 1979 by two incarcerated women) and Geese Theatre (established in the UK in 1987 following the model of Geese Theatre US which began in 1980) are two of the most well-established prison theatre companies whilst dozens more exist across the world. Academics James Thompson and Michael Balfour's edited collections laid the foundations for wider interest in the topic over the last two decades. Thompson aimed to address what he identified as a lack of analysis of the 'real role' of prison theatre through provision of a forum for practitioners to explore 'theory, description, guidance, history and analysis' (1998: p.11). When he edited this edition Thompson was Director of Theatre in Prisons and Probation (TIPP). This publication contained a reflective essay from Cox about the Broadmoor Shakespeare project, the legacy of which was the 'establishment of dramatherapy as a professional enterprise within the broad range of psychotherapeutic initiatives' (1998: pp.209–13), the introduction of regular visiting theatre companies for performance, discussions and workshop facilitation and an initiative involving Geese Theatre within the Young Persons Unit. Balfour's book brought together writing from academics, practitioners, ex-prisoners and prison officers, acknowledging that the essays do not 'create a vision of the field that is complete and harmonious' (2004: p.9). The first chapter was an abridged reprint of Zimbardo's Stanford University Prison Experiment which was intended to further understanding of 'the basic psychological mechanisms underlying human aggression' (Haney et al., 2004: p.19), the results of which have become infamous for the marked aggression/submission which developed amongst equals within a matter of days.

Jonathan Shailor is both academic and prison Shakespeare practitioner with over a decade of experience facilitating theatre in Racine Correctional Institution. He edited *Performing New Lives* 'in part from [his] own desire to build a community of prison theatre artists' (2011: p.21). Contributions included programmes ranging from solitary confinement (Laura Bates's work with Larry Newton) to Jean Troustine's work in Framingham women's prison.

Rob Pensalfini's *Prison Shakespeare* attempted to survey the history of prison Shakespeare although acknowledged the disparate nature of the work and that it has 'emerged without a cohesive theoretical narrative' (Pensalfini, 2016: p.9). Primarily focused on Anglophone interventions but noting the proliferation of non-English speaking Shakespeare programmes in prisons across the world, Pensalfini also draws on Joe White's comments of the 'steady erosion, throughout the prison system, of opportunities for prisoners to become actively involved in the making of theatre' (White, 1998: p.183). Alongside a detailed case study of Queensland Shakespeare Ensemble's Shakespeare Prison Project, founded by Pensalfini, the volume also focuses on wider issues of the claims of this type of work and the specificity of Shakespeare's 'cultural status' (2016: p.214) as a methodology of validation of the inmate experience.

Ashley Lucas's *Prison Theatre and the Global Crisis of Incarceration* focused on 'why incarcerated people think theatrical collaboration enriches their lives' (2020: p.5). Lucas's perspective is heavily politicized regarding the issue of mass incarceration and this is reflected in the lexicon used. She contrasts those incarcerated with the 'free world' (2020: p.10) and argues that those in prison are no more in need of rehabilitation and empathy than any other group of people. She warns that to claim theatre 'makes people free or helps them escape' (2020: p.14) is inaccurate as it does not physically do so. Her work is predicated 'on the assumption that prisons are dynamic spaces where growth, learning and cultural shifts can be possible' (2020: 8), which is true but it is important to be cognizant of the way those spaces appear to many at the outset of such work.

Space within the prison estate is carefully controlled and tightly confined and as Rob (an actor with The Gallowfield Players) describes, 'in prison people can be very conscious of the idea of personal space' (2019) as they spend a lot of time queuing or bottlenecked around gates. Carceral space is a form of control, demarcated with heavy iron gates, through which the inmates can pass only with the approval of officers. Time is another form of control; they can move from one location to another only when permitted. Foucault explored the way in which prison space can be used to enforce dominance and submission in his book *Discipline and Punish* and other academics have written extensively on the physicality of prison space and carceral geography. Social power structures are complex and multi-layered, often influencing how individuals and groups feel within particular spaces – who has the right to be in a space, how the power dynamic within that space functions and whose agency is dominant. True creativity requires power to be owned by those who are working creatively and collectively; it cannot flourish in an environment of total subservience to another's agenda. This is evidenced by my theatre companies within the English prisons where:

> all involved have a sense of ownership of [the theatre company], a possessiveness over a beautiful organism that grows in unexpected and wondrous ways. There is a sense of responsibility bestowed on everyone involved to act in a certain manner; to promote the best 'us' we can be.
>
> (Michael, 2019)

Ownership and incumbent responsibility are a central theme throughout this book, allowing those involved to develop a positive identity from a sense of belonging to a community they are able to influence and shape.

Homelessness

It is extremely diffciult to obtain accurate figures for the number of homeless people as 'homelessness is recorded differently in each nation, and because many people do not show up in official statistics at all' (Crisis website 2020). In England alone Shelter estimates there to be in excess of 280,000 and internationally this figure is estimated to be over 100 million with 1.6 billion lacking adequate housing (Shelter website 2019). Those with lived experience of it 'can suffer from low self-confidence, self-efficacy and agency' (Iveson & Cornish, 2016: p.254). Homelessness is expected to increase as a result of the economic impacts of the Covid-19 pandemic. There are a number of theatre companies who work primarily with people who have experienced homelessness. Cardboard Citizens is one of the longest running, founded in London in 1991 by Adrian Jackson who used Boal's Theatre of the Oppressed in making theatre for and with people who have experienced homelessness (Chris Sonnex was appointed Artistic Director in August 2021 following Jackson stepping down). Nadine Holdsworth contextualizes:

> theatre would seem to be an irrelevance for those struggling from homelessness and statelessness but Cardboard Citizens combines a theatrical and social agenda to address citizenship-related issues for the homeless, refugees and asylum seekers through its use of Forum Theatre.
>
> (2014: p.135)

Their repertoire has been extensive, from devised pieces to Shakespeare and a critically acclaimed production of *Cathy* (a modernization of *Cathy Come Home*) in 2018. Michael Dobson reviewed their politicized version of *Pericles* as having the effect of identifying 'Shakespeare as a tool of oppressive state apparatus' within the construct that the audience were asylum seekers watching the play to 'contribute to [their] assimilation into British culture' (2004: p.272). Jackson himself stated, 'I really like *Pericles*, it's so flawed' (interview 2016) whilst explaining his decision to interweave this rarely performed Shakespeare play with migrant stories gathered during research and development. Cardboard Citizens' *Timon of Athens* failed to impress Dobson a few years later where he described the most interesting element being the annoyance of 'impecunious retired academics' (2006: p.314) being asked to wear coloured stickers denoting their income levels. In contrast Sonia Massai applauded the way in which the actors' own accents 'effectively punctured the patronising rhetoric peddled by the facilitators' (2020: p.45) in the motivational workshop setting of the production. The academic discourse surrounding Cardboard Citizens is focused heavily on the artistic and social-activist impacts of their work, rather than the social or personal effects on those participating in the creation of work.

Manuel Muñoz-Bellerin and Nuria Cordero-Ramos are social workers who conducted a devised project in Seville which they used to write about the social implications of theatre with those experiencing homelessness. The 'participants play themselves and put a spotlight on their stories, thereby exercising certain social and political rights' (2020: p.1624). Their methodology was heavily influenced by social work training, undertaking 'autobiography and one-on-one sessions' (2020: p.1620) to develop trust and encourage participants to share their narratives. It is clear that the power balance between participant and social worker was an unequal one, a colonial perspective that their involvement somehow improved the lives of those Barnes describes as 'self-defeating, self-marginalizing, failed individuals' (2020: p.24) for whom the arts held some emancipatory power. Muñoz-Bellerin and Cordero-Ramos's redemptive narrative is problematic and undermines the validity of the marginalized person, suggesting that in some way those who are homeless need to be healed or improved by those who facilitate theatre with them. My own practice in which equality of participation is central has been influences by a consciousness of the social injustice of such perspectives.

Embodying equality is the work of Théâtre du Bout du Monde which combined professional actors with people experiencing homelessness in a French version of *A Midsummer Night's Dream* in 2010. Isabelle Schwartz-Gastine wrote about the project which aimed 'to reach people who otherwise feel excluded from society for personal, medical or social reasons' (2013: p.2) and which was the culmination of a series of workshops held in local communities. As well as encouraging pro-social behaviours and offering the cast the opportunity to find relief from the challenges of their usual existence it made 'a valuable contribution to the already rich understanding of the play' (2013: p.2). Through 'adjust[ing] the staging to their participants' (2013: p.5) the directors were able to accommodate the abilities of the participants whilst relying on the professional actors to offer on-stage support with lines if needed. The project drew on the skills of all involved whilst avoiding patronizing or creating a sense of inferiority and a number of participants later became professionally employed in the field. Schwartz-Gastine affirmed that 'this is what can happen when the director believes in the ability of the cast to go beyond what they had thought were limitations: it was a dream come true' (2013: p.8).

2

Creative spaces

Whilst performative space is the public face of theatre where the audience engage with the actors, it is the rehearsal space where many of the most creative elements occur. Rehearsal space is 'often ignored' as it is 'part of the hidden domain of theatre production but can have a significant impact on the final production' (McAuley, 1999: p.70). Texts such as McAuley's and *Theatrical Heterotopias* contribute significantly to the development of the lexicon of theatrical space but notably focus on the intersection of theatrical endeavors and audiences. This chapter aims to centralize the importance of the rehearsal space in terms of impact on those working within it and how it can be used to facilitate effective communication, positive autonomy and emotional growth. For many people who are marginalized by society this creative outlet may give them an opportunity to speak and to be heard (two things not necessarily synonymous), to be 'given a voice, no longer shadows in the daylight but people once more' (Michael, 2019). Combining Lefebvre's concept of 'conceived spaces' (1991: pp.38–9) which describes how spaces are affected by the activities within them and the element of temporality to consider the embedding process which takes place over time, this chapter examines how creative spaces can become nurturing and safe. Subtly nuanced alterations in how a space feels can occur with even the shortest of interventions but repetition within a space enables development of its 'qualitative, fluid and dynamic' (Lefebvre, 1991: p.42) qualities which persist beyond the ending of the activity. Longer temporal opportunities allow those participating to form stronger interpersonal bonds and view their agency as being more firmly entrenched.

The majority of arts projects are short-term – typically a series of workshops or an intense few weeks to create a production. A large

FIGURE 1 *Emergency Shakespeare rehearsing* Macbeth, *HMP Stafford (July 2019). Photo: Monica Cru-Hall.*

proportion of funding is specifically for short-term projects with Arts Council stipulations that 'you should not rely on receiving support year on year from Project Grants funding to deliver your core work' (Information Sheet, 2018: p.3). However, there is added efficacy and impact in interventions which offer an element of permanence; this longevity allows emotional growth and positive autonomy to be developed more fully and embedded into the lives of those involved. Mark Rylance described that the 'plays created *catharsis* or healing or transformation' (Cox, 1992: p.27) when performed in Broadmoor. Whilst this can certainly be true for an audience the impact is magnified when someone engages with a play in rehearsal, requiring consideration of the emotional complexity of his characters and lines in a more prolonged and focused way. People consider alternative choices for the characters, and possibly themselves, which may not have previously been contemplated. My analysis of longer-term projects was enabled through working with stable groups, which facilitated the 'gather[ing of] empirical insights into social practices which are normally "hidden" from the public gaze' (Reeves et al., 2013: p.1365). Foucault argues that 'space is fundamental in any form of communal life; space is fundamental in any exercise of power' (Foucault, 1991: p.252) and through considering space and time it is also necessary to consider the impact of power.

Rehearsing Shakespeare enables the creation of positive autonomy, the development of a sense of personal freedom, whilst accepting that total autonomy may be unachievable. This is intrinsically linked to trauma-informed methods to enable participants to acquire the emotional space and opportunity to develop this positive autonomy. As van der Kolk writes, 'trauma by nature drives us to the edge of comprehension, cutting us off from language based on common experience or an imaginable past' (2014: p.43). People from marginalized sectors have frequently suffered significant trauma through their personal experiences, their physical, mental or emotional limitations or the stigma and prejudice experienced within society. Trauma-informed pedagogy identifies the need for consistency and 'creating community expectations' (Jennings, 2019: p.71) which can only be achieved and implemented fully through ongoing work rather than fleeting sessions. Speaking the words of Shakespeare, with his attendant cultural capital, offers people the opportunity to reconnect with language which trauma may have dislocated them from. Developing on from the consideration of trauma and the way in which it restricts an individual's access to language is the third element of this chapter: the way in which Shakespeare enables adults and children to find a method of communication which they were previously unable to. This in itself enables them to engage more successfully with others within society and can offer a range of long-lasting benefits including increased self-esteem, confidence, team-working and negotiation through empowerment.

To fully explore this intersectionality between space and time within creative locations this chapter is divided into short, medium and long-term projects, evidencing the more profound impact on emotional maturity, transferable skills and enhanced communication in long-term enterprises. Marvin Carlson's concept of theatrical 'ghosting' (Carlson, 2001: p.16) is particularly relevant to these longer-term projects. His writing is in reference to the text, which Barthes describes as a 'tissue of quotations' (1977: p.146), physical costumes, sets and props used in multiple productions which an audience may see. However, this ghosting also applies to the rehearsal space itself and the way the physicality of rehearsing imprints itself within the participants' minds affecting their ongoing perception of this social space. Many from marginalized groups of society may have seen engagement with cultural activities as being unattainable or outside of their sphere of reference, unrelated to 'their identity and culture' (Skelton, 2020: p.22). The act of creative playing can also become a positive and empowering method of communication. Anne Ubersfeld's 'scenic place' (1999: p.154) embodies the combination of the fictitious place of the play-world with the experiences of a specific group within society which is so relevant in rehearsal spaces. For many people this scenic place becomes a safe environment in which they can explore their creativity as a way of narrativizing their personal stories in combination with the cultural richness of Shakespeare's texts.

Short-term projects

I define short-term projects as one-off workshops, where participants engage, perhaps for the first time, with Shakespeare. Within a few hours they interact with a narrative, characters and dialogue from his works but often without significant context and perhaps no familiarity with the other participants or the person facilitating. In the context of trauma-sensitive methods of engaging marginalized groups this lack of familiarity poses some significant challenges. Few confident, well-adjusted adults would feel comfortable performing with a group of strangers so this is a demanding situation to place marginalized individuals in. This section comprises of three case studies; the first two involve special educational needs (SEN) children (one within a theatre space and one in an appropriated space) and the third in a prison with high turnover of incarcerated people. The SEN case studies fall within the 'therapeutic application of drama' (Hargrave, 2015: p.34) which is one of the prevalent modes of thinking about learning disability and theatre.

Flute Theatre

Flute Theatre's adaptation of *The Tempest* was first performed in 2016. Kelly Hunter describes in *Shakespeare's Heartbeat,* how she created these games based on the four elements of Shakespeare which Louis Zukofsky identifies as being fundamental – 'eyes, mind, reason and love' (Hunter, 2015: p.3). Individuals with Autism Spectrum Disorder (ASD) often struggle with a number of what would be everyday actions for neurotypical people, including eye contact and use of imagination (Senju & Johnson, 2009: p.1204). Hunter worked within a SEN school for two years developing the original set of games which drew their inspiration from *A Midsummer Night's Dream*, she then went on to create a further series of games based on *The Tempest* and has recently created a production of *Pericles*. *Shakespeare's Heartbeat* acts primarily as a manual on how the games should be facilitated to 'heighten the children's awareness of themselves and provide an opportunity to explore emotions' (2015: p.1).

The Hunter Heartbeat Method (HHM) was the subject of an Ohio State University (OSU) research project which focused on the repetition of the activities over a fourteen-week period. The study identified some improvements in facial recognition capabilities from the children but, in Hunter's opinion, did not do justice to other improvements in interactivity (interview, 2016). The findings published in November 2017, documented that 'results indicate measured skill improvement across the three measurement time points in the domains of communication, social skills, friendship skills, and facial emotion recognition' (Mehling et al., 2017: p.7). However, the caveat was noted:

> variable treatment response across individuals is common. Thus, although the effectiveness of a social skills intervention on a group level across multiple domains is compelling, it is of limited clinical utility in informing treatment recommendations for an individual child.
>
> (2017: p.7)

I attended two performances of *The Tempest* at The Orange Tree Theatre in 2016; the first group were children whose parents had booked individually and the second was a school trip. This theatre was an unfamiliar space, embedded with cultural signifiers such as the thrust stage, raked seating and lighting banks. Cultural signifiers provide non-verbal cues which convey meaning about the activities which take place within the location, a way of reading the space from the layout and objects which are visible. The *Relaxed Performance*

Project in 2013 engaged almost 5,000 people in exploring ways to make theatre trips more accessible for those with additional needs. The findings suggested that 'preparation and information is key [...] to make people feel comfortable and secure' (website). The *Project* advocates the production of visual guides depicting the layout of the theatre and what to expect to simulate a sense of familiarity. The Orange Tree Theatre issued a guide to this effect and one parent commented that 'the visual guide helped as my daughter knew who she was going to be interacting with' (questionnaire, 2017).

Few of the attendees had visited this location previously and upon arrival many looked uncertain in this unfamiliar space, populated with unknown people. One care-giver noted that 'starting off they were withdrawn, quiet and looked slightly worried/uncomfortable' (questionnaire, 2017) as they arrived into the theatre and were invited to form a circle on a floor-cloth of swirled blues and greens, around which six actors in basic costumes were seated. The circle created a conceived space within the theatre auditorium (demarcated by the floor-cloth and lighting) where the children were encouraged to explore their creativity. Hunter introduced herself to the children and began the Hunter's Heartbeat, patting her heart reciting 'hel-lo' and encouraging the children to do the same. This was then followed by 'throwing the face' where Hunter made emotional faces (happy, sad, angry) and 'threw' it across the circle to a player who then showed that exaggerated emotional face before 'throwing' to the next person.

The actors then commenced the games, which focused on the elements of eyes, mind, reason and love. When Miranda and Ferdinand first meet, Prospero comments that 'they have changed eyes' (1.2.444) which led Hunter to create the game 'Oh you wonder' where both participants made 'doyoyoyoing' (2015: p.166) eyes at each other by making circles with their thumb and forefinger and rapidly moving them, enabling the children to make eye contact with another person through a parodic, cartoon device. The actors engaged with the children to whatever extent they were comfortable with. Tricia Gannon who played Trinculo went over to enact this game with a teenage girl from the school group who was unwilling to remain on the floorcloth, preferring the fixed seating. During much of the session the girl engaged little, moaning loudly and stimming (exhibiting self-stimulatory behaviours) (Wang, 2018) but when Gannon made cartoon eyes at her she was rewarded with a giggle and the girl responded after a few attempts. Gannon demonstrated the importance of trauma-sensitive methodologies and what Patricia Jennings describes as having an 'awareness of the present moment with an attitude of curiosity and openness' (Jennings, 2019: p.121) through taking the game to the girl as she wasn't comfortable coming to join the other players on the floor.

The 'Teaching Caliban to speak' game required 'independence of mind from both players' (Hunter, 2015: p.141), being designed as it was to give them experience of being both pupil and teacher (Hunter interview, 2016). Miranda and Caliban sat legs apart with their feet almost touching whilst Miranda taught him the syllables of his name using vocalization and Makaton symbols before they progressed to 'sun' and 'moon', drawing the shapes in the air. Then the whole circle made the symbols and sounds of 'Ca' 'Li' 'Ban', enabling even the non-verbal participants to have someone mirror and encourage their efforts at communication. However, autistic academic Sonya Freeman Loftis challenges the appropriateness of this game when she notes that 'playing the game may evoke the frustration' (2019: p.265) that both neurotypicals and autistics experience in trying to communicate with each other. She also challenges the concept that 'HHM seems to function on the premise that autistic people have no prior language or culture that is unique to the autistic community' (2019: p.265), in what she perceives as a colonial interpretation of Caliban as an ungrateful disabled being whilst Miranda is gracious and able-bodied. Her perspective, that this belongs to 'the growing phenomenon of therapy/charity Shakespeares' (2019: p.258) is an important warning which has influenced my own practice.

Whilst Loftis challenges HHM for being 'firmly wedded to the medical model of disability', which focuses on 'treatment for autism over the need for social acceptance for autistic people', she does acknowledge the empathy and compassion of the work which teaches educators 'to assume the competence of autistic children' (2019: pp.257–60), a fact often overlooked. Sifiso Mazibuko, who played Prospero in 2016, explained 'it's never about the amount a child can do, but what they are able to get to experience'(Al-Hassan, 2016). One parent articulated benefits which included that 'after the performance my child was unusually very confident and initiated an in-depth full-blown conversation with one of the actors in a way I've not seen before' (questionnaire, 2017). The immediate positive impact on neurotypical communication for this child was significant although it is unclear whether this was a short-term effect which dissipated over time or had a longer-lasting impact.

1623 Theatre

Derby-based 1623 Theatre aims to 'give voices to marginalised people in response to Shakespeare' (1623 website) through community engagement including facilitating projects in Special Educational Needs (SEN) schools. Workshops facilitated by 1623 Theatre at Fountaindale SEN School involved participants with a range of complex learning disabilities, utilizing an appropriated space, not a theatre. Appropriation of existing space has the benefit of familiarity which can trigger 'episodic memory retrieval' (Shimamura, 2011: p.277), helping the children to feel comfortable in their known environment but also adds a challenge in them freeing their imagination in a place laden with codified meanings and connotations.

Prior to the children arriving into the space Artistic Director Ben Spiller created a nautical theme using a blue/green lighting-scheme, fabric lengths scattered in a circle to encourage tactile engagement from the children, sea-breeze room fragrance and a soundtrack of ocean waves. Spiller and I discussed the importance of preparation to differentiate the space from their usual experience of the school-hall and also to enable those who may struggle to understand the narrative of the story to engage using other senses. The children (some of whom were in bespoke wheelchairs or confined to bed) were escorted into the transformed space by their teachers/teaching assistants who positioned them in a circle as Spiller began to tell a simplified version of *The Tempest*. The soundtrack of the sea became louder and more violent as the story of the shipwreck progressed. Although many of the children showed little evidence of cognitive comprehension of the story they appeared to be actively listening as Spiller used dramatic voice skills to add additional texture to his tale. The children were encouraged to use the fabric pieces to make the motion of the waves; some were able to do so unaided by working in small groups to emulate the rolling surf. Others with less mobility or coordination were assisted by staff with the explicit intention to engage everyone, to some degree, in the multi-sensory experience. Throughout the hour-long session the children were encouraged to immerse themselves in the fictional realm of the narrative which altered the familiar space of the school hall into somewhere new and unexplored for a brief period of time. The children appeared to have forgotten where they were and instead allowed their imaginations to take them to the mystical land of which Spiller spoke. Whilst autistic people have long been believed to lack the ability to exercise their imagination, this assessment is being challenged by more recent research which suggests their imaginative ability exists but with differing manifestation and expression from neurotypical people (Shaughnessy, 2013: p.31).

The school hall was used daily for assemblies and lunch; it therefore had its own set of social constructs and would have asked of the children certain behaviours which would become routine throughout their attendance at the school. A 2019 *Urban Planning* article hypothesized:

> place is defined by an alignment of mental image, behaviour, and physical setting. A model within which mental image has an implicit temporal dimension where past experience is reflected in affective and cognitive responses to current physical settings.
> (Del Aguila, 2019: p.250)

Sally Mackey brings this understanding of space to bear directly on theatrical locations. She acknowledges the foundations of spatial theorists such as Lefebvre and de Certeau, who redefined the concepts of space and place, before making the argument that 'theatre animates space into place' (2016: p.109). This definition suggests that perhaps Lefebvre's representational space or social space which combines the mental with the physical could perhaps be more accurately termed *representational place*. This representational place was superimposed on the SEN school hall for only a brief time period; however, the transience of this appropriation does not undermine its validity. Theatre, by its very nature, asks the audience to suspend their disbelief and to engage with the performance unfolding before them. An audience watching a professional production are aware that they are actively engaging in the experience of the theatrical endeavour, that the stage moves the place from London to Venice or Arden. Whilst the children in this workshop may not have been so consciously aware of this mental shift of theatrical place they clearly chose to engage positively with the activities. For some of the children it was easy to see the joy they took from the experience, smiles and laughter evidencing their pleasure and the teachers commented on how they enjoyed the session. *Art for Art's Sake? The Impact of Arts Education* aimed to survey the field of educational arts interventions, and despite its shortcomings, the study identified that 'drama classes enhance empathy, perspective taking, and emotion regulation' (Winner et al., 2013: p.156) all of which are key elements of emotional development and positive communication abilities.

Remand prison

The third example of short-term projects differs widely in terms of participants, taking place in a category B male remand prison housing approximately 308 men. It has a 'short term transient population' (Clarke, 2018: p.5) with an average stay of only a matter of weeks, making it difficult to develop long-term activity within the establishment, and as a result, the majority of the workshops I facilitated there were discrete sessions. In the 2015 Inspectorate Report the establishment was deemed unsafe but the 2018 inspection noted the concerted efforts of the Governor and staff to address the issues, although violence and drugs continued to be problematic (Clarke, 2018: pp.5–7). My sessions were located in the small, windowless library which we repurposed into a place where debate and discussion could take place but which was not conducive to theatrical work. The cramped nature of the space posed challenges as there was barely room for the men to be seated and no hope of them being able to act with twelve of them in the two tiny inter-connected rooms. Unlike the 1623 Theatre events there was no possibility of sensory engagement and we were restricted to interacting with the text as a way of unlocking the potential power of Shakespeare.

Bridget Keehan (Writer in Residence, HMP Cardiff 2004–7) praised 'the value of [Shakespeare] specifically in prison – a sense of being validated, of cultural ownership – richness of language, being able to speak this beautiful language' (interview, 2016). This cultural ownership was evident even within a single session; the participants grasped the opportunity to feel that they had in some small way appropriated Shakespeare's work and made it their own. These individual sessions demonstrated a perception that the language was difficult to access and they were keen to use the themes of the scenes but translated into modern language which they felt was more reflective of their own vocabulary. For example, Iago's warning to 'beware, my lord, of jealousy! | It is the green-eyed monster, which doth mock the meat it feeds on' (3.3.167–8) became 'beware of jealousy, it eats you alive' and Othello's response 'oh damn her' (3.3.478) became 'it's over, she's burnt my head out' (workshop outputs, 2017). Although Thompson and Turchi 'caution against [...] translation-performance exercises' as they do 'not allow the class as a whole to grapple with the dynamism of Shakespeare's language' (2016: p.53), in my experience as a practitioner it often has a place early in a person's engagement with Shakespeare.

A two-hour workshop as part of the 2017 Talent Unlocked Arts Festival was attended by a mix of ages and nationalities and it became apparent that a number of the men struggled to read the text. During the session the group dynamic altered from disparate individuals to a collective with a common purpose as they became absorbed in their task of rewriting *Othello* speeches into modern parlance. Morey and Crewe write about the 'implication in a good deal of prison sociology [...] that men are [...] fearful of appearing in any way vulnerable' (Morey & Crewe – Maycock & Hunt, 2019: p.38), although they partially challenge this commonly held view with their research which included examples of some supportive, empathetic friendships within the prison system. For a number of the men English was not their primary language meaning they experienced difficulties reading the Shakespearean text or the modern translations derived by the group. Our session culminated with a table-reading of the created work, during which the inmate sitting closest to each of them would quietly read the words, enabling them to repeat them at normal volume as though reading. As well as enabling communication in a positive way this demonstrated a level of empathy (about the way the men may feel about being unable to read the text), emotional maturity and compassion, things often deemed to be lacking within the prison estate. I was surprised to see the men support each other so readily with the potential vulnerability of illiteracy in a short-term remand prison where many of them were unknown to each other at the beginning of the session. This contradicted my expectation of:

> the machismo of the prison environment, the tendency of prisoners to impugn signs of weakness and femininity, and the subsequent impulse for prisoners to 'mask' emotional expression and put on 'fronts' of bravado and aggression.
> (Crewe, 2014: p.396)

In a very short space of time the collective group transformed the space into a supportive one in which some fragile social bonds had been formed. The inmates were asked to complete short self-assessments pre- and post-workshop and they reported increased confidence in public speaking, oral communication, written communication and empathy to others. Questionnaire feedback such as 'these sessions develop communication skills', 'they bring people together' and 'it gives me a better understanding of life' evidenced the impact that even a single session had through allowing them to use dramatic distancing as a way of contemplating themselves and their situation.

I delivered a series of individual workshops in this prison including one focused on the scene between the Macbeths following Duncan's murder – a tense dialogue as the implications of their crime begin to infiltrate their consciousness (2.1.14–72). The men involved, including two who had attended the *Othello* session, worked positively and productively adapting the text into modern language. There were healthy debates about the meaning of the lines and the depth of emotion both characters would feel given the enormity of their regicide. One participant commented that he had learned he 'can challenge others from a mature point of view instead of criticism of the personality' – a significant emotional development in an environment where tensions frequently run high with violent consequences. The men asked for an additional session so they could 'give it a go acting it' (comment, 2018).

The additional workshop took place three weeks later, by which time only four of the group remained. I split them into two pairs, one taking the Shakespearean text and the other their translation. None of them had experience of acting and initially there were reservations about 'looking silly' in front of their peers (comment, 2018). Senior Public Health Lecturer, Nick De Viggiani writes that inmates are in a 'social environment in perpetual flux as "actors" jostle to acquire social literacy, legitimacy and status'(De Viggiani – Maycock & Hunt, 2019: p.192) and nowhere is this more apparent than in local remand prisons where inmate turnover is rapid with a high concentration from surrounding communities. This melting pot of local affiliations and tensions along with a range of accused crimes from theft to murder, coupled with ongoing addiction issues leads to potentially high levels of violence, as has been seen in prisons including HMP Birmingham and HMP Nottingham over recent years. So their trepidation about displaying any kind of vulnerability was understandable as it could have potentially led to subsequent repercussions on the wing.

We did an initial group read-through of each version before they split into their respective pairs in the two small library rooms. There was no potential to create any form of theatrical environment given the constraints of the space and I felt that they would feel uncomfortable playing drama warm-up games so we focused on the text they were using and the emotions they felt the characters would be experiencing as they addressed the enormity of their crime. Cox writes of the Shakespeare performances in Broadmoor:

> All psychotherapy undertaken at Broadmoor must [...] involve the confrontation with self in which a patient needs to move beyond Macbeth's understandable reluctance to face what he has done.
>
> (Cox, 1992: p.133)

This reluctance or emotional inability to face what Macbeth had done was discussed at length by the four men who explained the 'need to pretend it's not real' (comment, 2018) after committing a crime to retain some semblance of normality. This identification of similarities between their situation and Macbeth's was unprompted and demonstrated a deeper emotional connection to the work than I had anticipated. It was also the catalyst for them engaging fully with the business of enacting the parts as they worked tirelessly on refining and rehearsing their characters prior to performing for each other and myself at the end, in what, for a brief period, became a theatre space.

They created distinctly different characterizations: the Shakespearean version featured a belittled husband whose wife mocked him for being 'infirm of purpose!' (2.2.51). In contrast, the modern language adaptation had a more equal alliance where both recognized that they were 'bang to rights'. During the short debrief they acknowledged that skills gained from the session included 'a deeper understanding of Macbeth' and 'empathy of viewing others past my fixed point of view' (comments, 2018). This correlates positively with the findings of the pilot study conducted in HMP Winchester with Bear Face Theatre where learner self-assessments identified increases in empathy, confidence and impact on others, albeit using a devised rather than textual theatre project (Russell & Barton, 2018). In the workshops I facilitated, the character engagement was immediate and despite no attempt to create a stage area, scenery, costumes or props the space was altered by the work taking place within it, the staging briefly 'became real' (comment, 2018). Their attention to each other was total, a phenomenon rarely seen within the prison estate, evidencing the impact it had made on them. Unfortunately, due to the nature of the prison all but one had moved before my next visit and there was no way of following up whether they had retained any of this enhanced empathy after the session concluded. Bear Face Theatre's pilot study identified that 'sporadic attendance appeared to be a significant barrier to establishing a transformational learning environment and achieving deep learning' (Russell & Barton, 2018), which I would concur with from my own research experience of short-term projects in prisons.

Within a few hours in a rehearsal room environment it is possible to unlock some sense of engagement with Shakespeare and theatre, to open up new possibilities for people who may never have explored this type of creativity previously. The conceived space becomes one in which participants are able to explore their imagination and behave differently than they would usually do which alters the way the place feels for them. In a very short period of time people are able to begin to use the mechanism of dramatic distancing to at once reflect the character and themselves. One participant commented that he had found a deeper understanding of 'the outcome of crimes on the psyche' (questionnaire, 2018) from the *Macbeth* workshop. A parent who attended the Flute Theatre production noted her daughter was 'still talking about it and describing it as "amazing" to people she meets' (questionnaire, 2017). These can lay the foundations for marginalized people to develop their communication skills but a longer period of involvement is required to allow this to really embed on a social and a spatial level and for participants to develop positive autonomy.

Medium-term projects

Medium-term interventions, with a specified timeframe, offer a deeper opportunity for the creation of positive autonomy, a sense of community, enhanced communication and emotional development than individual sessions but there are issues relating to longevity of impact and the emotional toll experienced upon culmination. With projects which involve some level of recurrence there is the opportunity for the space to become more than simply a receptacle for the activity and for permeable symbiosis to take place wherein the space is altered in the minds of those involved by the Shakespeare they have created within it. Carlson argues that 'all theatre. ... is a cultural activity deeply involved with memory and haunted with repetition' (2003: p.11) and whilst he makes this point in reference to audiences at professional theatres this applies for those creating theatre too, in whatever location is available to them and over whatever time period they are able to work creatively together.

Flute Theatre

In 2017 a collaboration between Flute Theatre and La Kompanyia Lliure brought Hunter's adaptation of *The Tempest* into a Barcelona Special Educational Needs school, using the games described previously. This was the first time that the same group of children played the games in their school environment and then transferred this into the theatre, where their families were invited for a final performance. I attended rehearsals, workshops and the performance which enabled me to build rapport with the actors and the children and witness the development of relationships.

The actors worked with the children for three half-days, starting each session with the heartbeat circle and then moving into *The Tempest* games. These workshops took place in a large classroom used for creative activities, appropriated as a drama space. Windows along one side of the room provided abundant natural light whilst a large chalkboard covered the opposite wall.

The children were familiar with the space having previously used it for music lessons; the type of appropriated space which Bachelard described as 'felicitous space' (1964: p.28), the space of familiarity and homeliness where an individual can relax and feel safe. However, the subtle changes to the dynamics of the space were not without impact – the staff supporting the children sat at the side of the room and throughout the initial part of each workshop the children regularly looked to them for reassurance and affirmation. The children were encouraged to sit around the circle, demarcated with tape on the floor, with the actors dispersed amongst them. The ownership of the space was an interesting dichotomy as the school room was familiar to the children but the fact that the theatre company had come in and created the circle rendered it at once both recognizable and unknown to the children resulting in initial reassurance-seeking.

Gradually the children's focus shifted to the games inside the circle, although a number of them returned to their carers for periods of time. As the workshops progressed they began to develop trust, need less reassurance and engage more fully. Although there was no formal seating arrangement the participants chose to sit in exactly the same formation each session, gravitating to the same actors. This desire for continuity is human nature and is magnified for those with ASD. According to research, even those with high functioning ASD 'usually present with severe difficulties in social communication; behavioral inflexibility; coping with changes; restricted, repetitive, and/or stereotypical behaviors; and sensory processing disorders' (Ricon et al., 2017: p.1).

This tends to lead to people requiring a high level of consistency and routine within their environment to diminish distress and allow them to function comfortably. With those with more severe ASD this requirement becomes more prevalent and the majority of the children in this project had complex ASD. The need for the participants to have consistency of where they sat and who they engaged with was not unexpected but the preciseness of the group formation each session was noticeable. Many autistic people crave continuity and one of the boys asked actor Quim Avila directly: 'can we do this forever?' (comment, 2017), demonstrating how much they were enjoying the sessions and wanted them to continue.

The Barcelona production featured a more intense element of music and rhythm than its English counterpart due to the intrinsic musicality of the region and the company. Hunter herself commented on the added dimension the music gave (rehearsal notes, 2017); what in the UK was a way of interlinking scenes and signifying the end of a game became a much more integral part of the performative ambience in this iteration. This musicality culturally embedded the work in the Catalan region and made it more recognizable to the children as the familiar entwined with the unfamiliar. Whilst Josep Marti counsels against homogenizing any culture into a single entity, he does acknowledge that 'the use of Catalan in different music manifestations of the city constitutes an excellent sign for the social absorption of a given musical style as one's own' (2001: p.186). The game in which Ariel engaged the dejected Ferdinand and made him forget his grief for his shipwrecked father was started by Prospero's rhythmic sounds which brought Ariel to life and inspired him to interrupt the sighs of the young nobleman. When Ferdinand then stood to follow the 'beautiful music' it was accompanied by the percussion and vocal sounds of all participants and his response was a hypnotic dance as he followed Ariel's palm stretching his body towards 'th'air' and 'th'earth' (1.2.388). Many learning-disabled children have a limited range of movement and this game encouraged them to experience stretching, which was particularly noticeable with one girl (Dania), who initially demonstrated a very limited range of movement and verbal responses, sitting mutely hunched over. According to staff this was her usual state so it made it all the more inspiring to see her, during the subsequent sessions, unbend herself and start to use her body to take an active role in the games. She became confident enough to initiate a translated conversation with me during a break, evidencing positive autonomy and enhanced communication.

The second of the games using trances required the children to close their eyes and follow the noise of the finger-cymbals Ariel played as he led them around the circle. A number of the children struggled with keeping their eyes closed and trusting their aural capabilities without sight. Studies of autistic children suggest that their social concept of trust is developed differently to that of neurotypical children (Yang et al., 2017: pp.615–25). One particularly innovative response to this challenge of keeping her eyes closed for one child (Imma) was solved by the actress, Raquel Ferri suggesting she feigned sleep. She felt that in order to 'play at sleep' (Imma, 2017), she needed something to cushion her head, using her own sweatshirt during the workshops. On this basis she was happy to close her eyes and engage fully with the sounds of the game; however, during the theatre performance, she had no discarded clothing available. Ferri improvised by taking off her own waistcoat for her to use. Given the challenges that autistic children often find with changes to their routine or being confronted by the unfamiliar it was amazing to see her readily accept this unknown article of clothing and lay her head on it, testament to the trust she had developed in Ferri over the course of the interactions.

During the final rehearsal in the school a number of the children began drawing on the chalkboard during a break, collectively creating a sea-creature inspired by their interpretation of games on a desert island. This was unprompted by the actors or school staff and appeared indicative of the level of ownership they felt of the location at that time.

They sought no permission to draw on the board, feeling able to freely express their creativity in an embodiment of Ubersfeld's 'lieu scenique' (1999: p.155), combining the physical location of the classroom with the fictional realm of the theatrical island. This was significant both in their ownership of the space and the evidencing

FIGURE 2 *'Trance' one of* The Tempest *games at Centre d'Educacio Especial Montserrat Montero (March 2017). Photo: Flute Theatre.*

of their imaginative powers, a topic now being re-examined in the context of autism (Shaughnessy, 2013: pp.321–34). Their confidence and ownership of the space grew each session; they began to come into the space uninvited which demonstrated the way in which it had become a social space, not a location in which they did only as directed but one in which they felt empowered and emboldened to be freely inventive. Their appropriation of the space extended beyond the organized games as they took creative ownership of it. It was clear that the children began to become accustomed to a routine of theatre-making after only a few sessions and the actors continued to work voluntarily within the school for a period of time after Hunter left due to the children's enthusiasm.

Romeo and Juliet project

The second medium-term project was a collaboration between myself, HMPPS and Drum and Brass (a social enterprise working primarily on community music projects). Julie Maxwell (co-founder of Drum and Brass) and I agreed to run a series of four workshops inviting inmates to engage creatively with themes from *Romeo and Juliet*. Maxwell and I facilitated sessions with no pre-determined outcome in mind, to allow the men to respond to themes of dysfunctional families, forbidden love and gang allegiance. Recruitment was a challenge given the high turn-over in this remand prison where a large number of local gang members were incarcerated so access to activities was necessarily tightly managed. The group we worked with was formed of a number of rowdy younger men who were friends on the wing and attended together. Initially there was also a couple of older men, including a Peer Mentor, Derek, who had attended every session I facilitated in there as he had a love of Shakespeare. Peer Mentors offer support to other inmates for a variety of areas including inductions, functional skills assistance, access to education and support services.

Sadly, due to the raucous and frequently difficult behaviour of the younger contingent the older men decided they no longer wanted to continue attending after the second session. This decision was particularly sad in the context of Derek's passion for Shakespeare. Managing group dynamics is always challenging, exacerbated within an environment of incarceration and further so when the men involved have issues such as violent tendencies which have not begun to be addressed and ancillary problems such as drug dependency. Van der Kolk asserts that 'athletics, playing music, dancing and theatrical performances all promote agency and community' (Van der Kolk, 2015: p.355), which is entirely true but the creation of such community takes time, patience and resilience on the part of both the facilitator and the participants. With the length of this project and the complexity of the relationships within the group it was not possible to create a community where all felt comfortable and this concerned me deeply on a personal level. Whilst it informed my work across the prison estate in terms of the need for longevity of projects and the time needed for social cohesion within a group of people who have both inflicted and suffered deep-rooted trauma, as a human I felt sadness that this man no longer felt able to share the Shakespeare activities. In an attempt to compensate for this, I visited him each week outside of the group and we worked on a number of monologues he chose.

Maxwell wanted to use improvisational activities with Shakespeare as a springboard into creative exercises such as raps and spoken word performances which differs from my facilitation in other prisons. We used short pieces of text and the basic plot; then asked the men to respond using experiences from their own lives. The first session saw them in two groups writing raps based on *Romeo and Juliet's* prologue. Subsequent sessions focused on the gang dynamic between the two households and resulted in the creation of a short piece of theatre and a number of discussions around forbidden love and familial tensions. The sessions were held in a cramped room on the main wing which was inadequate for the activities; there was no space for men to work in smaller groups or to rehearse. This location made the sessions challenging as noise levels quickly became unmanageable if multiple people were talking and the furniture in the room meant physical movement was severely restricted resulting in the sessions having to be predominantly static. Much of the benefit of drama is that it enables those who may struggle with traditional education to learn in a physically active way; however, in this location there was no possibility of this. Prison aurality ethnographer Kate Herrity writes that 'sound is a powerful medium for emotion' (2019: p.1) and the combination of the high level of noise from the prison wing seeping into the room and the volume of their discussions within the room created a claustrophobic, tense atmosphere. Background noise outside the room made concentration difficult and when a fight broke out on the wing during one session the men surged to the tiny window to witness the spectacle and were unwilling to return to their seats for a considerable time. Whilst much of this book focuses on the creation of social space and how this can often make the location feel very different as participants engage with Shakespeare and each other, in this instance the oppressiveness of the room made this impossible to achieve to any great degree and likely affected the ability of the men to fully focus on the sessions.

There were undoubtedly some beneficial moments of these workshops, as demonstrated by Colin, whose criminal record began as a child, sparking a cycle of incarceration. He initially played the role of the class clown – making jokes to his friends, giggling at inappropriate moments and lacking any real sense of engagement. However, a couple of weeks in he began to engage more positively and to contribute well to sessions, admitting 'I never dare speak in group therapy, I go to the toilet when it's my turn, but here it's different' (comment, 2018). He explained his fear about such situations, suggesting low self-esteem and perhaps that his views had been previously dismissed or ridiculed; however, he enjoyed speaking the lines of Shakespeare and this helped him to find the courage for his voice to be heard in a group context. He contributed thoughtfully to the sessions and I witnessed him behave in a more mature manner as his confidence increased. He would often challenge the others in the group if they became too silly and was supportive of the facilitators in keeping the sessions on track.

Another younger individual who seemed to benefit from the sessions was Jack, whose behaviour was initially challenging but when we began to discuss the challenges of a romance where the families are feuding he chose to share his personal experience of this in relation to the mother of his child. They concealed their relationship until she was heavily pregnant, wanting to avoid attempts at coercing her into aborting the foetus. As I described in a book chapter:

> this level of emotional outpouring was not something I expected given the dynamic of the group but the others listened respectfully

and expressed their sympathy with him as he explained how the level of interference from the families ended their relationship and made his son's formative years difficult.

(Mackenzie, 2022)

He appeared comfortable explaining his experiences, linking them to the Montagues and Capulets in what was seemingly a turning point for him with his attitude being very supportive and positive after that outpouring. He became the one who engaged most positively with the sessions, although he was transferred before the final session.

The final session was missing another individual, Jamil, who was in the segregation unit. He incited much of the rowdiness which made others uncomfortable; a disruptive individual whose confidence often manifested as arrogance and who embodied the description Maycock gives that 'muscularity and size are key aspects of being seen as "hard"' (2019: p.70). Jamil alternated between antagonizing the other men and making inappropriate, suggestive comments to me, despite me frequently asking him to refrain. When the altercation described earlier took place he was the main ringleader in trying to leave the room to bear witness to, or perhaps engage in, the ensuing fight outside. On the third session he arrived clearly under the influence of some substance. His behaviour was more erratic than ever and he spent much of the session clearly disengaged from the work, trying to remove his clothes. This, combined with a number of other incidents, resulted in the Governor deeming it appropriate to remove him from the main wing and place him in segregation.

The *Romeo and Juliet* project delivered some benefits in enabling the opportunity for emotional development and developing transferable skills such as confidence, teamwork and empathy, all of which will be invaluable upon their release. As the 2017 thematic review of resettlement noted 'many prisoners needed substantial help before they were released' (Stacey & Coates, 2017: p.8) and often this is not consistently available across the prison estate. Interventions which help to equip inmates with the skills they will need on release to help with securing employment and dealing with the authorities and agencies they will interact with are extremely beneficial. Whilst there was a limited opportunity for the skills and benefits to be embedded, given the length of the programme, it gave them the opportunity to engage positively and to see the world a little differently, to 'grow a bit in confidence' (questionnaire, 2018). The outcomes were mixed with noticeable improvements in communication from Colin and Jack as they began to use the space to articulate their views and experiences in ways wider society deems appropriate, developing positive autonomy. In contrast to this Derek's decision that he was unable to tolerate the loudness and lewdness from some members of the group was a clear indicator that it was not a total success.

Medium-term projects create some form of consistency, allowing participants to get to know each other and the facilitators to some degree. Given that the majority of people feel inhibited when initially asked to act if they have not done so before, this familiarity with the people and surroundings can be extremely beneficial in building the confidence of those involved. The work in Barcelona showed the children developing a sense of agency within the rehearsal room and their bonds with the actors became more apparent with each session. The project within the remand prison was constrained by the space in which it was held and the results were mixed with some engaging positively whilst others chose to remove themselves (in the case of Derek), or behave negatively (in the case of Jamil). As Kristin Souers and Pete Hall counsel in their book *Fostering Resilient Learners*, 'we want instantaneous success' (2016: p.126) but we need to accept that often we must try a number of different strategies before one has the desired effect when working with those who have suffered trauma in any form. It requires time for people to develop trust and openness and to become comfortable in their surroundings, particularly if the rehearsal space may have previously restrictive connotations, such as a classroom or a prison location. The conceived space which offers freedom to explore creativity takes time to develop as participants become more engaged with the activities and they begin to feel the space is one very much entwined with their theatre-work. It is for this reason that longer-term projects provide benefits which are exponentially more profound and effective than short or medium-term interventions. Programmes which are ongoing in nature and where a supportive community can form and continue to nourish and sustain participants as they grow collectively and individually support growth in ways which medium-term enterprises are unable to fully create.

Longer-term projects

In contrast to the projects already discussed, theatre companies are more permanent in nature; obviously, individuals will join and leave over time but the company continues. This section considers theatre companies in prisons and those with learning disabled participants: one working with children and another a professional, adult company. Ethnographic research combined observation, questionnaires (where appropriate and taking into consideration issues around gathering feedback from learning disabled participants), rehearsal diaries within the prisons, semi-structured interviews and group debriefs to give as full an understanding of the work as possible. When writing about these projects I write in the past tense about specific productions and occurrences but in the present tense about the benefits of the work and the plans these companies have for the future. Whilst this can be difficult from a phenomenological perspective it accurately encapsulates their longevity and permanence. These are not discrete research projects which have ended, they continue to develop and thrive and will do so beyond publication.

The Gallowfield Players

In March 2018 I began a project in a category B prison of circa 700 male prisoners, predominantly convicted of murder. Her Majesty's Prison Inspectorate Report in 2017 noted

> 641 prisoners were serving a life sentence, and the remaining 63 an indeterminate sentence for public protection. Half of the prisoners were within the first few years of their indeterminate sentences. 90 per cent of prisoners (635 out of 708) were assessed as presenting a high risk of harm to others. One-third of prisoners were from a black and minority ethnic background and almost one in six were foreign nationals.
> (Clarke, 2017: p.7)

The Shakespeare project was approved for an initial period of six months but given the successful outcomes demonstrated within that time period it became a permanent part of the Reducing Re-offending work at the prison and it has continued to flourish. It

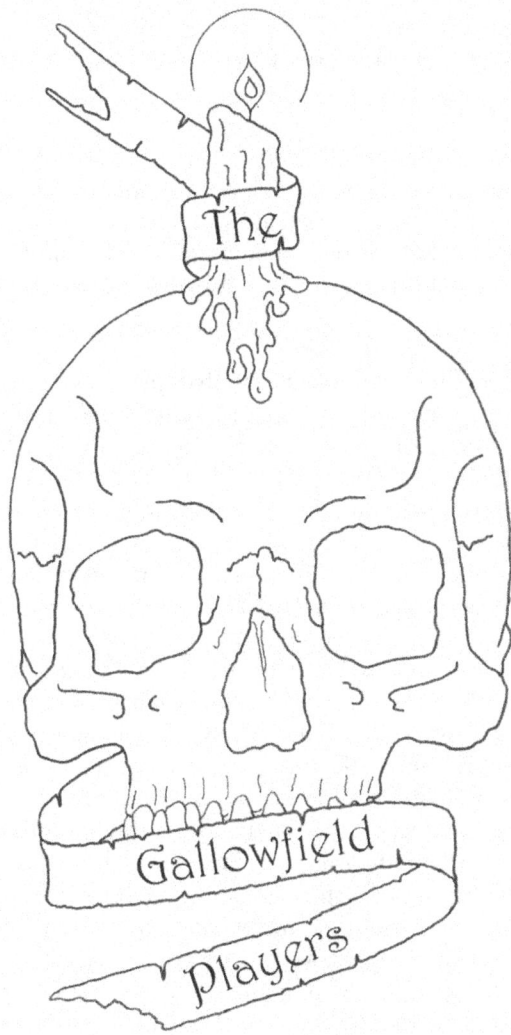

FIGURE 3 *The Gallowfield Players logo designed following collaborative discussions and drawn by Michael, HMP Gartree (December 2018). Courtesy of Michael.*

developed into a theatre company named The Gallowfield Players, owned collectively by myself and the actor-inmates.

Dame Coates in *Unlocking Potential: A review of education in prisons* stated:

> Education in prison should give individuals the skills they need to unlock their potential, gain employment, and become assets to their communities. It is one of the pillars of effective rehabilitation. Education should build social capital and improve the well-being of prisoners during their sentences.
>
> (2016: p.3)

My own prison work contrasts with organizations such as Marin Shakespeare Company who work in a number of California State Prisons and are more educational in nature (Marin Shakespeare website). The Gallowfield Players is not formal education; however, it is aligned with Coates's holistic vision of the provision of activities within the criminal justice sector and it has allowed the participants to unlock previously unknown potential. As one psychologist commented in feedback on the second production, an edited *Julius Caesar*, 'doing more practical education seems to be enjoyed more, you could tell it helped the men' (questionnaire, 2019). Coates's desire for inmates to 'build social capital' resonates strongly with my belief that this work enables people to find methods of communication and grow emotionally through their appropriation of the cultural capital of Shakespeare and the sense of achievement created through long-term programmes. Sam King and other criminologists deem social capital integral to the desistance narrative. Christopher Kay challenges the validity of the centrality attributed to this concept (arguing the assumptions made ignore fundamental nuances and present an overly homogenized perspective of people who commit crime) (2020: p.4) but it continues to feature heavily in the lexicon of desistance. Ben is an actor with The Gallowfield Players and his mother spoke to me of her surprise at his involvement in the group given that he 'had really struggled to learn to read and write' and had always been shy about public speaking (verbal feedback, 2019). Ben performed Mark Anthony with such authenticity that he reduced many of the audience to tears. It is testament to the powerful confidence he developed during the rehearsals that he wanted to play such an iconic role and did so with pathos and passion.

I was allocated the library for our rehearsals: a large, book-lined room with one door containing a small window onto the main corridor. This location was distanced from the Education corridor and I was told early on that being based in Education would discourage some inmates from engaging as many have negative associations with formal education. The library was a more neutral location, although it was described by Michael as 'a repository of knowledge closed to most of us most of the time' (2019). Michael described education as 'classrooms to sit and quietly absorb regurgitated lessons on nothing practically useful' (2019) and this was the initial impression I had of their expectations of the Shakespeare sessions. The first few inmates to join thought it was an educational discussion group and admitted to attending out of a sense of vague interest and a potential relief from the monotony rather than a desire to act. I have written in detail about the challenges of those formative months in my article 'Action is Eloquence' (Mackenzie, 2020). The creation of this group took time and persistence as asking men to embrace the vulnerability of acting was challenging in a location where being vulnerable is dangerous.

As we began rehearsing the room transformed from a windowless prison library into a creative space. A stage area was created by moving the tables to one side and arranging the chairs in a gentle crescent, with a central aisle and entrances on either side of the 'stage'. I always arrived before the actors and prepared the stage area so that they arrived not to a library but to a theatre. Rob reflected:

> each week it only takes a few minutes to transform half the library into our play area – I mean that in the sense of the play but also where we play and have fun.
>
> (2019)

The impact of this playfulness within the group cannot be underestimated – this is one place within the prison that the actors can set aside their protective personas and be themselves. Jennings asserts:

> play is a developmental activity through which human beings explore and discover their identity [...] Play encourages symbolic thought and action [...] In play we learn to create as well as to set limits; we learn about freedom as well as its boundaries.
>
> (1990: p.15)

Their communication with each other and with me developed significantly during the formative months and continues to do so. As they arrive each week many of them will initiate positive physical contact with each other in the form of hugs, a gesture unseen throughout the prison for fear of showing weakness or accusations of homosexuality. Research into the effects of life-imprisonment on young adults suggests that positive physical contact as commonplace as hugs or sitting side by side on a sofa can be beneficial to feelings of wellbeing (Hulley – book-launch, 2020). The actors are keen to share how their week has been and to enquire about each other's and mine in their identification as a 'family in this hostile place' (Wayne, 2019). The empathy demonstrated bolsters them and this stronger support network increases their 'well-being' whilst they are completing their custodial sentences and should equip them with tools for 'effective rehabilitation' (Coates, 2016: p.66) upon release.

The atmosphere within the room is often loud and jovial and the social space we have collectively created is 'safe and supportive'(Michael, 2019). During rehearsals the actors free themselves from inhibitions and try various ways of acting out their roles, thinking of ways to express the emotions of their character and looking for ways to balance pathos, humour and humanity. There is much written about the beneficial effects of playing as a creative outlet; Donald Winnicott argues that 'in playing and perhaps only in playing, the child or adult is free to be creative' and in this creativity 'the individual discovers the self' (1971: pp.62–3). Professor Ivinson specializes in learning for marginalized adults and children who have suffered personal, societal or intergenerational trauma. She describes that trauma-informed methods require educators to facilitate 'a pedagogy not about who [people] were in the past but opening up a passage into the future' (conference 2019). This future focus is important for The Gallowfield Players as they consider their eventual return to society, but it is grounded in the longevity of the company existence, allowing the development of deep bonds and trust. Wayne wrote in his diary the extent to which his 'confidence is growing and I feel comfortable with everyone in the group, the importance of being accepted for being me' (Wayne, 2019).

To return to the intersectionality of space-time-power which is fundamental to this chapter, the combination of the 'play area' of the library and the longevity of the theatre company has impacted on power and autonomy. It has enabled the actors to develop personal agency previously stripped away upon entering the penal system. Jason Warr states that 'the deprivation of autonomy is potentially the most destructive of the pains of imprisonment as it confers a direct assault on one's sense of self and erodes any positive notion of the self' (2016: p.593). Inmates are allowed to make almost no decisions affecting their daily lives which psychologist Craig Haney describes as 'infantilizing' (conference, 2002) and, over time, results in apathy or passivity to authority. The Gallowfield Players to some extent reverses this infantilization and within the group there is a respectful sharing of power. I minimize the distinction between us; we all drink from the same plastic prison-issue mugs, take turns directing the group and collectively make decisions. Agreement on how a play is to be adapted and developed is achieved through discussion and the inmates involved have developed positive autonomy and 'a sense of what life used to be like before prison' (Michael, 2019). The actors instigated monthly production meetings, submitted funding applications and created a company business plan. Significant trust has been nurtured amongst the group which has allowed them to be truthful and honest in how they feel about the work we do together. Keith wrote in his diary that rehearsals 'make me feel normal and it is a place I belong' (2019), a sharp contrast to the widespread sense of social and societal dislocation triggered by imprisonment. Rex Bloomstein has spent much of his career filming documentaries depicting authentic prison life and asserts 'trust is such a fundamental thing for people' (interview, 2019) in the context of positive prison relationships. It is common for one or more of the actors to assume a directorial role, offering their reflections on how a scene can be improved, employing Boalian forum theatre techniques to pause the action and suggest alternative interpretations (Boal, 2008: pp.1717–20).

Within the prison environment latent underlying aggression takes little to be ignited; a comment taken as an insult, a bump against another inmate or some perceived slight can provoke anger. Initially the actors would seek input only from me as the facilitator but they now seek and give their own opinions freely – feedback is meant for the purpose of improving the company and production. These positive developments equip them not only within the rehearsal space but with their interactions both within prison and, in due course, upon their release. They eagerly seek inspiration from recordings of productions, group discussions and reading they choose to undertake in their own time from a small library of books gathered from various sources. This collaborative directing at times means that the scenes may take longer to become cohesive as the multitude of shared ideas can be time-consuming and leads to debates; however, their voices being heard and opinions being given credence are vital. The positive autonomy is evidenced through diary entries which note 'it's come together, today it felt like we achieved, we did this together and we did it well!' (Michael, 2019) describing a *Julius Caesar* rehearsal months before performance.

Our repurposing of the library does pose challenges: from the mundane, such as the regular interruptions of inmates wanting to return books (the library is closed during rehearsals), to the more profound emotional connections which can be triggered. Michael is a highly intelligent, complex individual who arrived for rehearsal one day very distracted and struggled to engage during the early part of the session. During coffee-break he explained that in the library the day before he had suffered what he described as a Post-Traumatic Stress Disorder (PTSD) flashback when he saw someone who reminded him of a significant person in a past traumatic event. The effect was so severe that it made him shaky and blurred his vision and he had asked to be escorted back to the wing. For this reason, he was scared to attend the rehearsal but told me that he had done so to face his fear and because the group means so much to him. 'Being in here today has exorcised the terror of yesterday' (Michael, 2019) he told me, allowing him to tackle his Pavlovian response to the panic attack of the previous day. The trust within the group is crucial in enabling this type of trauma-informed conversation to take place and for him to feel confident in expressing his feelings, knowing that the group would be supportive.

Michael underwent a prolonged hunger strike in the summer of 2019 in protest about issues in the way he and his belongings were treated by the institution. This was a very difficult time for him and previous similar protests have resulted in violent outbursts. However, this time he continued to engage with the group throughout the duration and we spoke regularly about his physical and mental health. His deterioration was distressing for all involved and he was closely monitored with regular blood tests. In some rehearsals he was too weak to take an active part but continued to attend regardless and the other actors escorted him around the prison, carrying his bag when it was too heavy for his weak frame and ensuring he was accompanied in case he collapsed. He wrote in his rehearsal diary that 'without this to look forward to I don't know how I'd get through the week' (Michael, 2019) and he did not miss a single session even whilst faint from the effects of prolonged starvation. After several weeks his Personal Officer sought me out to tell me they had resolved the issues and he had agreed to eat again, but would not do so until rehearsal. Michael came in carrying a bag of dried mango and we sat together as a group whilst he ate a few pieces of the fruit and the importance of the symbolism of that resonated with me long after the day concluded. That act demonstrated the creation of a far deeper interpersonal solidarity than the rehearsing of Shakespeare. This social aspect of the group has continued to become more apparent during the years we have worked together.

This social cohesion was highlighted poignantly during a rehearsal in summer 2019. The previous week I had stressed to the group the importance of focusing on improving the current production so that they would be proud of their work (occasionally rehearsals deteriorate into silliness and puerile humour). A young actor, Wayne, had taken the message very much to heart and at this particular rehearsal was very short-tempered when the inevitable joking camaraderie came to the fore. His outburst was out of character and had clearly rankled with the group so I guided us to move on, intending to speak to him at the coffee-break about the cause. However, before I had the opportunity, Michael took him to one side for a quiet conversation, exploring Wayne's perspective and rationale for his outlook whilst balancing it with the overall need for the group to both produce theatre but to enjoy the process too. This engagement between the two diffused the tension completely. Whilst this may appear insignificant to people used to resolving disagreements with verbal dexterity, to witness this from two men both convicted of violent crimes was incredibly powerful.

At the end of rehearsal, when we sat in our customary circle discussing the session Wayne chose to apologize for his outburst, explaining to the group that he had taken my words too literally. The level of self-realization and confidence required to publicly acknowledge this showed emotional maturity which was not previously evident. Wayne was incarcerated at a young age and appeared emotionally immature when he joined The Gallowfield Players but his reactions began to demonstrate maturity, as this example exemplified. Detention is acknowledged to 'impair the normal course of adolescent development' (Allen – Jewkes et al., 2016: p.529) and those imprisoned at a young age can often be released in middle age with no external developmental experiences beyond their teens. The 'forms of social and relational maturation that long-term imprisonment denies' (Crewe et al., 2019: p.328) limit the ability of those incarcerated to emotionally develop and instead fosters harmful coping mechanisms which are detrimental to mental health. *The Social Impact of Custody on Young People in the Criminal Justice System* examines the way in which custody stagnates emotional maturity and limits 'opportunities to learn independence skills and develop resilience …. which are central elements to reducing recidivism' (Paterson-Young et al., 2019: p.135). However, the sense of agency, positive autonomy and emotional resilience which is evidenced within The Gallowfield Players suggests that some interventions can reverse this stagnated development.

This was encapsulated by an incident involving Dean in his first production (*The Merchant*) in January 2020 during additional rehearsals in performance week. It was very clear from the time he joined the company that he deeply resented any form of authority. During a seated session where we were running lines (the room allocated to us was too cramped for acting) he appeared disengaged and spent much of the time looking at a book when not directly involved in a scene. I had repeatedly asked him not to and when he continued I verbally snapped at him in front of the rest of the group. He did not retaliate and sat silently for the rest of the session but chose not to return that afternoon. Michael said that Dean had explained 'his head wasn't in a fit state and he would be back the following day', adding his own opinion (expressed in the spirit of openness fostered within the group) that I had been unduly harsh with my response. After reflecting on the comment overnight I realized my own tension about the production had resulted in me behaving out of character. When Dean arrived in the library I publicly apologized and asked him to shake hands, which he did. He later told Michael that it was the first time anyone had apologized to him in his life. Since then he has been noticeably more engaged with the group and during lockdown he completed every activity pack I sent.

The Gallowfield Players' sense of community permeates throughout the prison and although this will be explored more fully later it is worth considering briefly here as it effectively bridges the chasm between the work we do as a collective and their life for the remainder of the week. The 'creative place' The Gallowfield Players have conceived within the library is to some extent portable and is taken back to the wings with them as 'running lines has become so commonplace that it's normal for others just to ignore it or simply see it as an everyday occurrence' (Michael, 2019). The creativity permeates the prison because the social capital continues to flourish beyond the physical and time-bound confines of the session; they can access the support and emotional well-being that has become integral to the group at any time and place. 'Association' several times a week is an opportunity for inmates to socialize with men from their wing and the actors put this time to use discussing the play, rehearsing or working on amendments for scenes we have rehearsed that week. It is common for me to arrive at rehearsal to discover that a number of them have tackled a problematic piece of blocking or amended stage directions to improve the flow between scenes. During the Covid-19 pandemic they used their limited time out of cells to work on costume designs, programme content and script edits.

However, this permeation on the wings is wider than the actors; it is now common to hear Shakespeare quoted on the landings. The men trade Shakespearean slurs with others as a way of intersecting prison culture in which 'insults […] are usually brutal' (Michael, 2019). This appears to diffuse the underlying menace which is usually prevalent and to have brought an element of felicitous space to the prison. The jostling for supremacy on the wings cannot be overestimated as these men are spending decades of their lives away from their families and the distractions of work, leisure and daily living, leaving them with little on which to focus. Tensions frequently run high but this permeation of Shakespeare onto the wings can allow insults to have a more jocular meaning than they would otherwise. The inmates' adoption of phrases such as 'do you bite your thumb?'(1.1.42) (despite this not being a play we have worked on) demonstrates the extent to which Shakespeare has permeated the culture of the prison in unexpected ways and further evidence of the emotional maturity which is being fostered. Finding alternative ways to navigate and ameliorate interpersonal tensions which could otherwise escalate into violence is hugely beneficial within the prison overall.

This extract from The Gallowfield Players' *The Merchant* (an adaptation of *The Merchant of* Venice) addressing issues of racial and gender inequality demonstrates the ways in which the actors choose to use drama as a way of tackling social injustice and prejudice. Whilst waiting for her fundraising ball to begin the wealthy, philanthropic heiress Portia engages the Manager of the Belmont Hotel in conversation.

Act 2: Scene 1

MANAGER
>I work hard, in fact I am all self-made.
>So what should it matter that my skin is a different shade?
>Too dark for those who patronise this abode,
>Too light to fit in back home.
>I spend more time in boardrooms than on the beach
>Causing my pallor to appear almost bleached.
>What should it matter the colour of my skin?
>Surely it matters more what lies within?
>In here *[pointing to heart]* not all this *[gesturing to skin]*
>I am always other, something amiss.
>People see me and recoil in fear,
>Judging me purely on the clothes I wear
>And the shade of my skin.
>Why should I be judged by a different set of standards,
>Even when I prove them wrong and screw the bastards.
>As I succeed they recoil more
>Fearing a man like me who manages power.
>All because of the shade of my skin.
>So I succeed more, blaze a trail of hope
>In my wake provide thousands of jobs
>Why then do I receive such scorn,
>When in this world I have done no harm?
>The shade of my skin.
>I have built hospitals and schools,
>Yet I am always treated like a fool,
>Those around me blinded by the media propaganda
>Expecting someone of this colour to have a dangerous agenda.
>Seeing only the shade of my skin.

PORTIA
> I too have seen such behaviour,
> I, as a woman, must be a failure.
> 'Men will do it better than I ever could'
> But they don't do they or else they surely would.
> Stereotypes thrown at us because of race and gender
> Only serve to push us forward in our endeavours.

A Prisoners' Education Trust representative commented that 'I thought [the theatre company] was something that might seem small (a few hours a week) but was actually having this huge impact both for the men in the Players and the staff around them' (Reynolds, email, 2019). This is perhaps because it is not just the space that we have changed through the work we do: we have changed the people involved (I include myself in this process of transformation) and this has a wider impact on their interactions within the prison. They and I are not the same as when this project began; they often speak of the way in which they have grown, as Wayne succinctly describes 'I am proud to say that my identity has changed from being a Gallowfield Player' (2019). The trust the actors have created is powerful and allowed them to develop inner resilience which many felt they lacked previously. The importance of trust and positive relationships is one acknowledged by leaders within the prison service but is often hard to facilitate within this environment, yet with tenacity, perseverance and the addition of much humour we have achieved this within The Gallowfield Players.

After attending a rehearsal one visitor tweeted 'inspirational teamwork. They really care about each other and the stories they are telling together. Lots of big laughs, meaningful conversations and bear-hugs too. Life affirming' (Spiller, 2019). The company agree visitor invitations in advance and they continue to be themselves and work authentically, not feeling the need to perform a role as they frequently do within the carceral environment. There is a growing body of work considering the dynamic of audience engagement with theatre, including Theatre and Performance Research Association (TaPRA), the International Network for Audience Research in Performing Arts (iNARPA) and publications from Gareth White, Kirsty Sedgman and Ben Walmsley. McAuley describes the hidden nature of rehearsal space; it is the place where the actors work prior to sharing with external attendees. This raises the interesting question of how actors may be subtly different when an observer attends. To combat this, our visitors take an active role, whether reading in for an absent actor, leading warm-up games or giving directorial notes (depending on their own expertise) to remove the feeling of an assessing observer. Where initially the actors would have been reticent to engage, symptomatic of their shunning of the external world from which they feel excluded or marginalized, there is now an openness on their part to positively engage. They want academics and practitioners to see the work we are doing as they have a sense of pride in their creation and they also want the underpinning themes to be made available more widely within the prison estate to provide rehabilitative opportunities for others.

Emergency Shakespeare

This desire to disseminate and share rehabilitative culture is also prevalent in the second long-term prison case study, based in a category C male prison with 750 men convicted of sexual offences. Governor Lubkowski passionately adhered to the mantra of 'releasing citizens not offenders back into our communities' (2019) and proactively supported the provision of creative activities and the incumbent Governor who replaced him continues this legacy. Prisons for those convicted of sexual offences tend to have lower levels of violence and drugs than the general prison population but often have aging populations and staff are warned about potential manipulative tendencies. In March 2019 I was engaged to create an ongoing drama group as well as Ride-Out's short-term theatre projects which the prison already commissioned. The prison recruited a dozen men to attend the first session where I introduced the concept of how this programme would work. However, I was keen that the company was created by the men themselves, not a formulaic methodology of a replicable prison theatre company. Of the original recruits, a number decided that acting was not for them but those who continued recruited others, forming a group which spanned five decades of ages and multiple backgrounds and ethnicities.

We began with Macebth and rehearsals were held in the Visits Hall, a large, airy space in a separate building and which the men would have previously attended only for visits from friends and family (those who have maintained external contact as some have no visitors at all during their sentence and despite having been in the prison for years may never have seen the Visits Hall).

The latest Inspection Report for this prison noted:

> the relationships between staff and prisoners were generally good, with 85 per cent of prisoners saying they were treated with respect. However, the perceptions of black and minority ethnic prisoners of their treatment was less favourable.
>
> (Clarke, 2016)

Emergency Shakespeare included one Asian and two black men, one of whom, Mark, went on to play the lead role in the first production whilst a third black man was enlisted to assist with music for the performance. Racial tensions never became an issue with Emergency Shakespeare (or The Gallowfield Players which is also multi-cultural) and in 2021 we performed *Othello* which threw issues of race and racism into stark relief.

However, there were challenges to address; one individual in particular, Liam, antagonized the group with his assumed superiority on the topic of Shakespeare and his often-unpleasant comments to other members of the group. His interpersonal skills were evidently underdeveloped and he lacked the ability either to understand or to care that his behaviour caused anger. Both staff and inmates suggested that I remove him from the group but my opinion was that in the external world everyone has to deal with people they dislike and so expulsion would not be beneficial in preparing them for returning to the community. Patricia Jennings identifies that many who work with people who have suffered trauma make the mistake of 'ignor[ing] inappropriate behaviour' (2019: p.72) which I was keen to avoid by speaking to this individual about his challenging comments and requesting that staff address with him the consequences of his behaviour. He began to temper his outbursts, which would usually be over some imagined-slight or his antagonizing the group when a consensus had been reached which he wished to overturn.

However, generally the group worked well together and there were clear instances of emotional development and improved communication. One such example is Brody who, during the first few sessions demonstrated very challenging behaviours with an air of simmering anger which seemed likely to explode at any time. In one session he became 'frustrated' about the pace of the work and after verbally challenging me he 'switched off halfway through the session' (Brody, 2019). His demeanor worried me but I felt it appropriate for him to remain within the group and gradually over the weeks he appeared to relax and to enjoy the rehearsals more. However, it was not until he asked me to read his rehearsal diary that the full extent of what had happened during his involvement in the first Shakespeare production became apparent:

> A little over six months ago I was as close to suicide as I have ever been, I can't forget just how strong the intensity was. From there I nearly lost it completely as I struggled with my internal conflict. [...] It was whilst being on the medication that Mark suggested that I join the group. [...] Taking all factors in: gym, chilled working environment, counselling to help me understand, art, this group. Emergency Shakespeare has given me a way to express myself in another form, it's something I've wanted to do for a while. It has been a positive factor in the transformation of my thinking [...] So what does the drama group give me? I'm committed to it, I enjoy it. I know I can use the spectrum of emotions that I have struggled with for years now; especially within the group.
>
> (2019)

As Ivinson affirms 'the last thing we need to do when someone is in this meltdown is abandon them – we need to stand with them' (2019) and whilst she made this comment in the context of traumatized children it has the same validity with adults. Brody's diary entry demonstrates self-identified progress with communication through alternative forms of expression and in emotional growth with his articulation of utilizing the spectrum of emotions he has previously found problematic.

Another actor, Batu, described himself as 'severely autistic' (2019) and initially found rehearsals difficult, spending much of the first few months in near silence and when asked to speak his lines as Macduff would do so without any apparent emotion. He wrote in his diary 'on a personal level I struggle a lot with my words and actions' (2019) and though he attended every week he exhibited few external signs of enjoyment. He studiously avoided any form of physical contact when the scene required it and was often defensive when anyone commented on his scenes, seeing feedback as criticism rather than an attempt to help him improve. Difficulties interacting with others were identified as a superordinate theme in a recent study of prison experiences for those with autism (Vintner et al., 2020). My sense is that if the sessions had taken place over a short period of time they would have left him uncomfortable and without the opportunity to gain tangible benefits from the experience. However, during the six months of rehearsals for the first production he began to improve both in his acting (becoming more free in his movements and expression) and in his cohesion with the group. He initially presented as extremely introverted but he appreciated 'focusing on our actions and portrayal of emotions' (2019) and repeatedly wrote of his enjoyment and the support within the group as he developed and refined his emotional communication strategies. He used the felicitous physical and mental space of rehearsals to explore emotional expression which helped him communicate more successfully with the group and the wider prison population. He epitomized the description van der Kolk gives of his own child's growth when enrolled in drama classes: 'theater gave him a chance to deeply and physically experience what it was like to be someone other than the learning-disabled, oversensitive boy that he had gradually become' (2015: p.331). This appeared to be the case for Batu; his self-confidence grew to such a degree that he asked for a larger role in the second play. He began to make jokes within the group expressing a dry sense of humour which the others had not seen before and began to laugh at his own foibles in a group setting, demonstrating enhanced self-awareness and confidence. More recently he and Brody have become my Assistant Directors for the Creative Workshops programme I run for men who are not members of Emergency Shakespeare.

Blue Apple Theatre

Batu's experience resonates with the experiences within learning-disabled theatre companies where the benefits of communication, trust and autonomy are developed within longer-term initiatives. The first example is Blue Apple Theatre, founded in 2005, with the aim 'to challenge prejudice and transform the lives of people with a learning disability' (Blue Apple website). They have a strong agenda for addressing disability issues through their core company, outreach projects, research initiatives and advocacy work. They commissioned a Big Lottery Fund supported *Evaluation Report* on the impact of their work in 2019 which used self-assessment analysis tools to quantify the impact in a range of areas such as social networks, community participation, social skills and behaviours. The findings suggested 'positive improvements in members' confidence levels in accessing new places in the community and asking for help', 'member's social skills were beginning to increase through the drama-based games, activities, skills and experiences' and 'an increase in social network members' (Collard, 2019: pp.23–35).

I worked with Blue Apple Theatre as Shakespeare consultant on their adaptation of *The Tempest* in 2019. Artistic Director Richard Conlon edited the script and cast the play before they undertook a table reading and proceeded to rehearsals. The core members have been working together for many years so the group cohesion is strong and it is perhaps for this reason that the multiplicity of studios they used for rehearsals seemed to have little impact on their focus. This suggested that the specific physical space began to take on less importance once the social space of the group was embedded within the university campus.

The larger, non-core cast, many of whom required additional support, used the plot of *The Tempest* as a starting point from which to create new, improvised scenes based on their reaction to discovering they were shipwrecked on an island. Conlon's view was that this would give them the opportunity to be involved at a level they were capable of; for some this would be simple phrases whilst others created elaborate backstories for their roles. These new scenes reflected the plot of *The Tempest* yet gave the actors the opportunity to speak back to the political turmoil of protracted Brexit negotiations and concerns about Trump's behaviour. The play was organized so that the new scenes could be included for the performances in June 2019 but removed for the subsequent planned tour (which was indefinitely postponed due to Covid-19). The tour would involve only the core actors due to practical considerations of costs and the reality of touring for those members who are less independent and would have needed greater levels of care and support.

During rehearsals the non-core group was asked to imagine being the lowest echelons of ship's crew arriving on an unknown island and the scenes were then constructed from their responses. One girl responded to the turmoil in which she found herself with an outraged ebullition of 'scraps?' in response to the concern that when the nobility left the island those remaining would be forced to 'live off scraps'. In contrast, young actor Kym Nash created Sam Pigeon, a cabin boy who had previously endured a life of drudgery. Nash spoke about Pigeon's initial desire to achieve social mobility in this new world but that he then 'realises it's hard and he wants to go home' (2019). The environment for newer cast members to feel confident to express themselves was empathetically created through simple warm-up games, clear introductions of any new person or activity and the support of a team of dedicated volunteers. Nash described 'I just enjoy the friendship and the love the cast gives each other, even if one of us is feeling down, we're like a family' (2019). This description echoes the words Wayne used when describing 'the Gallowfield family' (Wayne, 2019). Whilst the locations and life experiences of these young men could not be more different, they have both suffered the trauma of marginalization and their references to the actors as family demonstrate a strongly bonded sense of community which transcends the physical, appropriated place in which they rehearse.

Riding Lights Theatre – Acting Up!

In contrast to Blue Apple Theatre rehearsals is the methodology of Acting Up!, the SEN youth theatre of York-based Riding Lights Theatre Company, directed by Kelvin Goodspeed. This company of eleven- to nineteen-year-olds rehearses and performs in the Friargate Theatre where in 2016 they performed their first Shakespeare, an adaptation of *The Tempest*. The small, black-painted theatre had a cave-like quality to it and by using the same staging from day one of rehearsals there was never the potential issue of transference and the added complexities which this can bring in terms of entrances and exits. For children with complex needs the movement to a new location can be disconcerting and impact on their ability to focus on the production whilst their senses are being bombarded with new aural and visual cues.

Patricia Jennings writes that trauma-informed teaching must 'at all costs, avoid responses that might trigger the students' feelings of powerlessness and fear' (2019: p.90). Goodspeed's decision to work in the same location throughout provided a sense of consistency which alleviated fear responses and encouraged the cast to feel comfortable in the space, developing a sense of ownership. Those with more complex needs required onstage assistance and Arial became a choral role with multiple individuals sharing his much-edited lines to allow the less experienced members of the group to experience speaking a few lines in their debut performance. There was also a conscious directorial decision to use props from the outset to facilitate familiarity with them, again reminiscent of Carlson's concept of theatrical ghosting (2001: p.11).

Goodspeed and Assistant Director Jenna Drury worked hard to balance the participant's spectrum of needs, from younger, largely non-verbal individuals to a high-functioning autistic young man (Tom) who played Prospero. The play underwent two edits – an initial, shortened text was handed out scene by scene as the actors worked through the story together (to avoid initially over-facing anyone with the full script), then additional cuts were made based on the cast's ability to perform each line and scene. A number of lines of the script were annotated with brackets signifying that the plot would continue to make sense if these were cut late in the process. Many of the lines were reduced to simple phrases or at times just a single word to allow the actors to embody their role where verbal communication was a significant issue. Scenes such as the one involving Trinculo, Stephano and Caliban at the mouth of Prospero's cave became very physical theatre with few spoken lines and focus directed to the spectacle of their theft of the garish garments. The actors performed an almost farcical comedy routine where they grabbed and dropped the clothing whilst running around in an apparently drunken state.

Tom memorized Prospero's lines in a single week but struggled with group interaction and became agitated if progress was slow. He usually sat apart from the group, listening to music as this appeared to calm him. Goodspeed told me that Tom had previously been prone to outbursts of temper; however, during the rehearsal process he became more willing to engage with the others and at times proactively helped some of the newer cast. One such example was Goodspeed's own son (Gary) who often needed assistance to be at the right place on stage. Tom calmly guided him through a scene and offstage with gentle physical contact, in much the same way as one of the volunteers would have done, a significant act as Tom usually avoided physical touch. Aversion to social touching is common for people with ASD (Croy et al., 2016: pp.491–6) and it was evident with both Tom and Batu. However, Tom overcame this aversion, demonstrating empathy, a desire to assist Gary and to make the play run more smoothly. Tom's level of self-awareness was apparent in the post-performance debrief where they were each asked to draw the outline of a person on flipchart paper and then to add details of the parts they had liked and disliked and how they resembled or differed from their character. Many of them took this activity at a superficial level, likening themselves to their character because 'I like to be silly' and 'I like to play music' (2016). However, Tom reflected that he had 'encountered antagonistic relationships in the past' and he offered the explanation that both he and Prospero found it 'difficult to engage with others, preferring to be loners than part of a group' (2016).

The enclosed space of the theatre in which they worked seemed to engage them in a creative process which resulted in a powerful adaptation of *The Tempest* but also appeared to have deeper benefits. There was a clear transition from the outside world of reality into the world of the play which was entered when the group entered the theatre space together. Massey writes of 'the sharp separation of local place from the space out there' (2005: p.7) which seems particularly resonant within the Friargate Theatre where the challenges of the external world are temporarily separated from the theatrical endeavours. The regular commitment of weekly rehearsals and the ability to develop their creativity appeared to allow some sense of family to develop within the group. There were occasional arguments and frayed tempers during rehearsals but an acceptance that everyone had a contribution to make and differences required resolution. They became more at ease within the space as time progressed and would often comment on the spatiality in relation to the play even when the stage was bare. This became their social space in which they felt comfortable and were able to focus on Goodspeed's mantra that 'your lines are your character's thoughts' (2016) rather than on feeling self-conscious or being distracted by an overload of sensory cues.

Conclusion

Shorter-term projects can sow the seeds for change but only those with a longer time frame enabled those seeds to take root and flourish. The key elements of emotional growth, positive autonomy, development of communication and the importance of trauma-informed methodology can be seen to some degree across interventions of all lengths. However, the very nature of developing consistent and robust processes by which marginalized groups can begin to possess positive autonomous power requires time. Whilst much funding for the arts is done on a short-term basis this limits the impact of work with marginalized groups, either through the delivery of stop-start work or an uncertainty of the future of projects which are continually seeking funding. As Mark (Emergency Shakespeare), who also undertook a two-week drama and dance project facilitated by Rideout (Creative Arts for Rehabilitation) commented

> there's a real low when a project finishes but when I went to my cell after our [Emergency Shakespeare] performance I knew we were starting again on Sunday and that made it all good – I could enjoy the buzz.
>
> (Mark, 2019)

Whilst it is problematic to attribute an individual's emotional growth or their increased communication skills to a singular source, given the complexity of human nature and the way in which we are all influenced by a myriad of experiences and external factors, my research evidences that it plays a part in imbuing participants with the desire and the ability to communicate.

Shakespearean scholar Ramona Wray challenges the evidence frequently presented of the efficacy of prison Shakespeare projects, stating 'prisoner statements […] are rarely interrogated and tend to be taken at face value' (2011: p.343). At an individual project level Wray's criticism has some validity, especially in the context that many of the accounts are written by practitioners with a personal involvement. Additionally, project continuation is likely to be dependent on funding which has to be secured from the reporting of achievement against certain success criteria. Resonating with this is Conlon's comment that many of those with learning disabilities will aim to please those facilitating the work by giving answers they think are being sought (Conlon, 2016). However, against this backdrop of personal testimonials and the inherent challenges of securing funding, wider conclusions can be drawn. The breadth of interventions with marginalized groups across all strata of society and the positive outcomes documented by practitioners, participants, academics and researchers cannot be dismissed as being without evidence. The study commissioned by Shakespeare in Prison which catalogued and coded immense amounts of data from rehearsals and focus groups provided perhaps one of the most detailed efforts to 'define and measure the direct impact of participation [...] on individual members' (Fisher-Grant et al., 2019). Whilst pinpointing the specifics of how and why these interventions are so successful is difficult, my own attempt to define the effects across the strands of emotional growth, positive autonomy, developed communication (all of which are underpinned by trauma-informed methodology) opens up new opportunities for dialogue in this area. The consideration of the impact of longevity on effectiveness is one which is rarely explicitly considered with these types of projects but it demonstrates the importance of the time needed for changes to take root and be nurtured as those stifled by societal expectation use the cultural capital of Shakespeare to make their voices heard.

3

Performative spaces

Without an audience, a performance is a rehearsal; audiences have an intrinsic, complex role to play in the live production of any work and this interaction between audience and actors is what differentiates live theatre from its filmed counterpart. Mark Rylance describes how a performance 'is a conversation really. If it is just a one-way presentation then it is dull. It is dead, it's got to be a two-way thing' (1992: p.31). This chapter explores the ways in which juxtaposition of Shakespeare's cultural capital with marginalized voices can create heterotopias in which the world appears differently from expectation; instigating changes in social perception. To draw on Tompkins's description of heterotopias enabling 'other possibilities for socio-political alternatives to the existing order' (2014: p.6), appropriating Shakespeare as their own enables marginalized communities to demonstrate their ability to take possession of cultural capital which is frequently denied them by wider society. Social exclusion is a negative experience and public performances of Shakespeare are often exclusive, an academic and social bastion into which the great actors and critics of the world are admitted. Peter Brook argued 'each line in Shakespeare is an atom. The energy that can be released is infinite – if we can split it open' (Brook, 1998: p.25). Traditionally that atomic power has been held and wielded by the middle and upper-classes but inverting the cultural capital of Shakespeare means it can be possessed and harnessed by those otherwise marginalized. Tompkins theorizes that between 'the concrete space of the theatre venue, the imagined locations depicted in that venue and/or the social context for the performance' (2014: p.16) the heterotopia is created. In this chapter the focus is on how these spaces and contexts

FIGURE 4 *Prospero and Ariel (Tommy Jessop and James Benfield), Blue Apple Theatre,* The Tempest+ *Winchester Royal Theatre (June 2019).* Photo: Mike Hall Photography.

intersect and the ways in which marginalized people engaging with performances of Shakespeare 'demonstrate the rethinking and reordering of space, power and knowledge' (Tompkins, 2014: p.6). The use of Shakespeare as a performative vehicle enables the creation of a heterotopia by engaging people through the use of his cultural capital and then revealing the unexpected through the way that capital is owned by marginalized people. This inversion of the cultural capital whilst at the same time drawing some validation from it allows marginalized groups to assert their rights to access culture but also challenges perceptions frequently held about those groups. I have divided performative spaces into two categories – demarcated space and appropriated space, as well as considering the composition of the cast and the composition of the audience.

By demarcated spaces I mean theatre venues with the intrinsic cultural signifiers which inspire expectations of the performance; it is the disruption of these expectations which gives the power of potential change to the heterotopia created. In contrast, appropriated spaces are locations with an alternative primary use meaning that the act of a theatrical performance disrupts existing embedded signifiers. A chapel, dining hall or visits hall becomes a place of theatrical performance, intrinsically altering the fabric of the location in the minds of those involved, often long after the performance has concluded. The space within which performance takes place, whether demarcated or appropriated also nuances the reception due to the cultural signifiers embedded within the location. The traditional theatre space of a purpose-built stage is *demarcated space*: it was intended for the purpose of putting on performances – carrying a series of cultural connotations and expectations, as examined by academics such as Keir Elam and Marvin Carlson in their work on theatrical semiotics. This demarcated space informs audiences about the type of event they are going to see, bringing either anticipation at the thought of a production or triggering anxiety regarding expectations and etiquette. The exception is people with more complex learning disabilities who may not be involved in the decision-making process to attend a performance (this decision often being made by caregivers) or comprehend the signifiers. Whilst those who are regular theatre-goers may find pleasure arriving at the theatre, many from marginalized groups may feel intimidated by the experience. They may feel that this is not for them, be uncomfortable about what to wear or how to act or be concerned that they themselves or the person they are accompanying will not behave in the way society deems appropriate for the theatre. What McConachie describes as 'our contemporary custom of engaging with performers through studied attention, emotional charged silences and occasional laughter' (2008: p.2) may be implausible, given marginalized audiences' mental health or their lack of experience of this mode of behaviour, or impossible, given their physical or mental impairments.

Marginalized groups frequently avoid the experience of attending a theatre, as outlined in the Arts Council 2016 Report which documented the 'ongoing concern about reaching out to audiences from different socio-economic backgrounds' and that 'only 6-8 per cent of [London theatre goers] identified as having a disability'. An increase in Arts Council grants for inclusive productions and initiatives such as *The Relaxed Performance Project* demonstrates a commitment to changing this reality but, as yet, the issues remain significant in encouraging attendance from marginalized groups. Demarcated space however, does serve as a validation of the authenticity of the experience; it adds additional cultural capital through performing in a space designed for this specific purpose. It also allows the production to utilize the trappings of theatre in the portrayal of the story, focusing audience emotions, encouraging 'joint attention' (Scaife & Bruner, 1975: p.265) or applying sensory muting as required.

In contrast *appropriated space* encompasses locations which have a primary usage other than theatre but have been repurposed for a period of time, however short- or long-term. Site-specific theatre became popular from the 1960s and has been influenced by Peter Brook and Deborah Warner amongst other directors, providing an opportunity to 'disorder, distort and circulate texts' (McEvoy, 2006: p.592). In recent years many buildings have been adapted to create theatrical locations for particular productions written or adapted for a specific site; Punchdrunk's *Sleep No More* being one of the most famous (an immersive adaptation of *Macbeth* where the audience 'create their own journeys through a film noir world' in the McKittrick Hotel, New York), with other notable examples including Shakespeare in Yosemite and Grid Iron's numerous works. Theatre critic Andy Field railed against the stretching of the term site-specific into a 'suffocating umbrella' (2008) encompassing all performances in non-theatre spaces. For the productions examined in this chapter the choice of setting is driven not by artistic design or site-specificity but by practicalities: an available room large enough to accomodate the performance. This pragmatic choice is one often required by schools, community organizations and prisons, where there is no ability to locate performances within a purpose-built theatre. This appropriation of familiar space creates a different dynamic, presenting simultaneously the recognizable and the unknown. The space familiar for its predominant purpose now asks the audience and performers to suspend these memories and inhabit the stage-play world. It provides a known locale which may ease the nerves of those fearful of new places; however, it requires those engaging to utilize a different set of cultural and behavioural signifiers within the space.

As well as types of space in which the performance takes place, this chapter considers productions across two axis – the performers and the audience. Recent decades have seen rising academic interest in the interaction between performers and audiences. Susan Bennett argues that before the turn of the century there was an:

> explosion of new venues, companies, and performance methods, there is a non-traditional theatre which has recreated a flexible actor-audience relationship and a participatory spectator/actor.
> (1997: p.18)

McConachie focuses on the cognitive impact of being a theatre audience member and the intersectionality between genetic cognition and cultural memory. He challenges the way theatre scholars have often likened 'audience experience to a version of reading', instead focusing on the 'spectator action and interaction' (2008: p.3). He brings the work of J. E. Malpass on the 'synthesis of experience, space, place, knowledge and humanity' into the context of theatre and explores the importance of the physical, social and cultural placing of the audience in a way which resonates with my practice-based research where common humanity is explored through Shakespeare (McConachie, 2008: p.132).

Walmsley's monograph puts forward an agenda for interdisciplinary audience research and his conclusion is that:

> performing arts audiences are brimming within untapped potential: as the very people who make performance manifest, they are the only people who can make sense of and confer meaning on art.
> (2019: p.239)

Audiences are non-homogeneous individuals often brought together solely for a production and each attends with their own perceptions and experiences. The notion of 'conferring meaning on art' is a complex one; each of us as audience-member has their own personal experience which will be reflective of emotional, sociological and physical baggage which we have acquired throughout life, although some commonality may be detected across audience responses to productions. Claire Bishop argues the 'desire to activate the audience in participatory art is [...] a drive to emancipate it from a state of alienation' (2012: p.275). In many instances of applied theatre the audience are asked to undertake a different role than in mainstream professional theatre, invited to engage in a slightly different way. The complexity of audience – actor – performance intersectionality becomes more pronounced and nuanced when it involves those from marginalized groups. Drawing on the heterotopic potential of inverting Shakespeare's cultural capital, people otherwise on the fringes of society are able to instead be appreciated for 'their creative talents, projecting their best selves' (The Gallowfield Players, audience feedback, 2020) and claiming ownership of their appropriation of his iconic works, whether as artists or audience-members.

The majority of theatre and performance studies focus on mainstream performances for mainstream audiences as these make up the majority of theatrical events with Arts Council research evidencing that '92 per cent of customers purchasing theatre tickets were white, 92–94 per cent did not identify as disabled' (Arts Council, 2016). However, my interest lies in events where marginalized actors perform for mainstream audiences, mainstream actors perform for marginalized audiences and marginalized actors perform for marginalized groups. Matthew Reason's argument about the impact of learning disability theatre is equally applicable across other marginalized groups, when he states:

> There is *something* about the intersection of audiences / aesthetics / learning disabilities / theatres that does *something* or asks *something* about the nature of spectatorship and our experiences of art.
>
> (2018: p.164)

He does not attempt to crystalize this *something*, acknowledging it not to be a singular entity as theatre makers and audiences are not homogenous, but he does assert that this type of theatre 'disrupt[s] the very fundamentals of theatre' (2018: p.173). He attributes this to the actors blurring boundaries of reality and fiction and to the audience being asked to self-contemplate, 'provoking awareness of and reflection on their own act of perception' (2018: p.173).

Measuring the heterotopic effect of theatre is challenging as all research with audiences and actors is subjective and does not lend itself easily to quantifiable outcomes. Whilst feedback can and is often sought at the end of performances there is a very real possibility that the deeper impacts of the production may be felt more keenly after some time for reflection. Changes in perception and opinion may never be entirely attributable to a single theatre production but the combined life experiences of which the performance may be one amongst many. Walmsley asserts that:

> Audience research is inherently and inevitably cross-disciplinary. This is because any deep and rigorous understanding of audiences' experiences of the performing arts needs to draw on a range of complimentary methods drawn from different theoretical and empirical traditions and perspectives.
>
> (2019: p.111)

He also acknowledges that 'audience studies [struggles] to cohere around a set of agreed methods and approaches' which he believes is needed for 'greater credibility' (2019: p.112). Reports such as *Key Research Findings: The case for cultural learning* (Cultural learning Alliance, 2017) provide statistical evidence of the benefits of cultural and creative engagement. Assessing and understanding the direct impact on audiences and performers is a field which continues to grow but currently remains embryonic.

Demarcated spaces

This section draws on examples of marginalized performers through case studies of Out of Character, Firebird Theatre and Acting Up! theatre companies as well as Flute Theatre where professional actors and learning-disabled children perform together. I will also touch upon relaxed performances designed for marginalized audiences performed by non-marginalized actors. With marginalized performers, the heterotopia is a more conscious one, encouraging the audience to overcome their potential perceptions about the limitations of those with learning disabilities or mental health issues to perform text-based work. These perceived limitations often preclude the idea that a marginalized group could tackle the complexity of Shakespeare's language. However, by making the performance their own these theatre companies demonstrate that he does not belong only to the economically or intellectually elite but to any who choose to engage with his themes and narratives. Performing or watching Shakespeare within a demarcated theatre space adds a validation to the experience especially for those usually marginalized; they too can take ownership of recognized cultural capital in a location filled with theatrical signifiers.

Out of Character

There have been multiple campaigns over recent decades to tackle the stigma of mental illness, confirming the continued reticence for people to speak up about mental ill-health. Out of Character, a York based company founded in 2009, comprised entirely of performers who have been mental health service users, specifically challenges perceptions and stigma related to this topic. They perform locally but also tour NHS events and academic institutions to provoke discussions about mental illness and service provision. They work with a combination of devised and textual pieces and are perhaps most famous for their productions which engage directly with service users' experiences.

In 2014 they created a pastiche of Shakespearean characters within a mental asylum entitled *Disturbing Shakespeare* with the aim of using the concept to explore mental health from an unusual perspective. I published an article in *Shakespeare Studies* (Mackenzie, 2019) on the heterotopic qualities of this production which I will summarize here as it is pertinent to the chapter. The constructed space of the play was 'Bedlam'; the infamous psychiatric hospital during Shakespeare's era and to which the audience were transported through a combination of disparate beings muttering to themselves in the opening moments, Jaques's direct references to the place and the inhabitants' evident madness throughout the production. Artistic Director, Paul Birch assumed audiences would be familiar with Ophelia's descent into madness (4.5.1–73), Lady Macbeth's 'come you spirits' (1.5.40–54) and King Lear's tirade 'blow winds and crack your cheeks' (3.2.1–24), amongst others. These familiar lines in an unfamiliar setting created a heterotopia through the way in which the stage-play world of the archetypal mental institution of Bedlam echoed with Shakespearean lines. Hearing classic lines associated with the theatre-going experience but portrayed in this production as the ramblings of psychiatric patients was designed to have the effect of making the audience realize that mental ill-health is not something 'other', to be locked away in hospitals. Instead, it is an intrinsic part of society much as Shakespeare is, affecting individuals from all elements of the social strata. As Birch explains, Shakespeare created 'convincing and empathetic figures struggling with ill health' (blog, 2015).

The play made social comment on the contentious issue of restraint of mental health patients through the gagging and physical removal of Bottom. A literal enactment of Titania's line 'tie up my love's tongue, bring him silently' (3.1.194) saw him bound, gagged and dragged from the stage. The *Mental Health Crisis Care* report documented over 100 instances of physical injury following mental health related restraint in England in 2012 (MIND, 2013) and this inversion of the traditionally comic love scene in the forest into one of physical restraint within a secure hospital was jarring and powerful. The magical world of the besotted lover was reimagined into the constrained world of Bedlam making the audience aware of the tangible and borderline-brutal effects of physical restraint within the mental health system.

This production toured a number of universities and included a post-show talk back session where the audience had the opportunity to discuss the performance with the cast, encouraging consideration of the changes of perspective brought about by the show's heterotopic nature. This was the case regardless of the venue used for the performance as it was the combination of the theatre company and Shakespeare's works which created the heterotopia. Anecdotal feedback during the eighteen-month production run was 'extremely warm' (Birch – blog, 2015) although unfortunately no formal feedback was gathered. The cast were initially nervous of performing Shakespeare as they felt it was going to be difficult and only two of the actors had previous experience of his work (Furnell – interview, 2016). If they felt that Shakespeare would be challenging for them then it seems reasonable to extrapolate that audiences may have felt Shakespeare to be too demanding for a theatre company of mental health service users.

However, they took a 'deeply personal approach' (Birch – blog, 2015) to Shakespeare, augmenting the selected scenes with material written by the company to give an unexpected twist to the work, including a fervent defense of Richard III penned by one actor who is also an avid Plantagenet enthusiast. The company's approach is always to take mental health as the starting point but to push the work in unexpected directions, as they did with this pastiche and with their more recent *Fresh Visions* trilogy. *Fresh Visions* uses a science fiction paradigm to move away from the constraints of reality and demonstrate 'both values and criticism of different social models to demonstrate that healthcare is a lot more challenging and contradictory than we might think' (Birch, 2019). The importance of engaging audiences in meaningful dialogue is summarized eloquently by one actor who explained:

> When people watch one of our performances and interact with the characters, the meaning behind the story goes on and makes change over time. The dialogue that comes from the play about important and complex issues in society is just as important as the play itself.
> (People's Health Trust, 2019)

The change he refers to is in relation to perceptions the audience and the wider public have about those with mental health issues. Misconceptions about mental health issues abound and the stigmatization of mental ill-health continues (as the MHFA and other websites document); Out of Character proactively tries to combat these problems of public perceptions through theatre. Quantifying this change is difficult but Birch and the actors feel that each performance has a ripple effect which spreads the word that mental illness does not preclude artistic achievement (Birch – interview, 2016).

Acting Up!

Acting Up! youth theatre company rehearses and performs in the same theatre-space specifically to minimize any sensory issues of relocating for the performances as 'some of the actors need consistency of space' (Goodspeed – interview, 2016). Their performances are attended only by families and caregivers but it is an opportunity for them to see these young people working together positively, interacting with others, using their imaginations and performing. A large percentage of the group have autism spectrum disorder (ASD), although many have multiple Special Educational Needs (SEN) with ASD being only one of them. *Educating Children with Autism* documents that 'shared symbolic play […] involves capacities for social attention, orientation, and knowledge, which are areas of difficulty for children with autism' (Lord & Magee, 2001). The Social Communication, Emotional Regulation and Transactional Support (SCERTS) educational model was developed in response to this publication and focuses on enabling children to become 'confident and competent social communicators' (SCERTS website). Many of the indicators they identify resonate with my research into the beneficial effects of Shakespeare with learning-disabled participants, such as building trusting relationships, emotional expression and regulation and enhanced communication skills. It has been argued that focus should be on:

> broader and more dynamic measures, such as degree of success in communicative exchange, related dimensions of emotional expression and regulation, social-communicative motivation, social competence, peer relationships, and the child's competence and active participation in natural activities and environments.
> (Prizant et al., 2003: p.313)

These act as appropriate measures for the effects of drama with the notable exception that demarcated spaces are not the child's natural environment, despite in this instance Goodspeed's attempts to normalize the space through repeated usage. However, the expectation is that the skills fostered within this demarcated space will enable ongoing enhanced participation outside of the theatrical space. Andy Kempe draws on the SCERTS model by highlighting the benefits of 'joint attention' in relation to the group dynamic and interactive role of the audience and performers in drama (2014: p.264). He also notes that 'given that drama is a social art form. ... active engagement in dramatic activity can facilitate positive social outcomes such as a sense of belonging to a group' (2011: p.165).

During Acting Up!'s performances of *The Tempest* anecdotal audience feedback included comments on how much the participants enjoyed the weekly rehearsals, the effort they put into learning lines and how great it was to see them being creative (verbal feedback, 2016). Goodspeed described that the actors 'got really excited about the characters and the story and found the language less of an issue than people thought' (interview, 2016). Whilst the heterotopic potential of these performances was limited by the restricted number of attendees, to hear the young people speaking Shakespeare's words was something their loved ones had not experienced previously which impacted on the families' perceptions of their abilities and the limitations placed on them by their disabilities and by society's expectations. Goodspeed expressed pride that:

> many of them involved are amazing actors, partly because they have none of the self-consciousness that many adults have – they are able to get involved and express themselves without worrying if people will laugh etc.
>
> (interview, 2016)

Flute Theatre

With Flute Theatre's work SEN children are both audience and participants for the sessions held in theatre venues, watched by their parents or school staff. The UK productions at The Orange Tree Theatre were discreet interventions, where participants often knew no one other than their caregiver. As Children and Adolescent Mental Health Services (CAMHS) notes on their website if 'a young person does not know what will be happening …. this can lead to uncertainty and make them feel extremely anxious' (CAMHS, 2017). In contrast, the performance at the Teatre Lliure, Barcelona provided more familiarity as three workshops preceded the performance so upon arrival at the theatre the children knew each other and the actors.

Robert Shaughnessy has written extensively on the work of Flute Theatre with an interest which combines academia with a personal connection through his autistic son, Gabriel. In *This Rough Magic*, Shaughnessy questions 'how much of this is about Gabriel, and how much about me?' as well as 'how much of this is about Shakespeare?' (2020: pp.2 & 10) which he concludes is less relevant than the fact that it has a positive impact on his own child and others. This raises a question of whether there is some intrinsic benefit from using Shakespeare's work or whether the benefit of Shakespeare is the 'cultural authority' (Shaughnessy, 2020: p.11) it bestows upon the observers. Whilst it is difficult to evidence that there is some specificity in the use of Shakespeare when the play has been reduced to such tiny snippets of scenes, perhaps the reason it is Shakespeare and not another playwright is that it was his work which inspired Hunter and which encourages caregivers and schools to attend. The rhythm and metre of iambic pentameter echo the human heartbeat upon which the games are based. As scientific studies demonstrate, there is evidence that rhythm has a beneficial impact on those with ASD and can help with sensorimotor regulation (LaGasse & Welde-Hardy, 2013).

The focus in this chapter is the Barcelona performance in which the same children had engaged in workshops prior to the performance (as discussed in the previous chapter). When they entered the theatre space with its painted floor-cloth and dimmed lighting the children immediately sought out 'their actor', taking confidence from the familiar in a space which was not. The appropriated space of rehearsal had been replaced with the demarcated space for the performance which initially seemed to unsettle the children as they seemed unsure what to expect. During the opening games there were some glances back to the audience, as if seeking reassurance from their families, but this seemed to fall away as they became drawn into the action. The demarcated theatre space allowed for the lighting to be subtle and focus attention within the circle, encouraging the 'joint attention' which Kempe describes as being a key measure of success within the SCERTS model (2014: p.263). Only the circle was lit, encouraging the children to engage with the actors and other children rather than their families. It was subtle yet effective and only made possible by the professional lighting of the theatre.

One extremely powerful moment came towards the end of the show where the twin brother of one of the children involved chose to join the circle. This boy is more profoundly disabled than his twin and had previously shown no interest in engaging in games. He is non-verbal autistic and his parents were amazed when he slipped from his seat in the darkness and entered the circle to join actor Quim Avila's group of children. He simply sat down and Avila immediately included him in the final game 'M'en Viag! Volante!' ('I'm free!') where Prospero spun each child around holding hands as they were released from their servitude as Ariel. This game was not truly Shakespearean but gave what *The Guardian* described as 'a tingle of real joy' (Gardner, 2016). This eleven-year-old boy felt so enthralled by the games being played that he chose to enter a circle of strangers so that he could share in the activities. Understandably this major change in his behaviour provoked tears from his parents who were delighted by his proactive response, reportedly the first in his lifetime.

He remained in the circle as the games were brought to their customary close with the heartbeat circle bidding 'adieu' to reduce the energy levels to calmness, before a quiet round of applause from the participants and then from those in the 'outer circle'. As the house lights came up, emotions were evident as parents, children and actors shed tears over the intensity of the show. The families seemed amazed at the extent to which the children had integrated with the group and actively engaged in activities which would usually be challenging for them. I was not able to gather written feedback in Barcelona but the feedback from The Orange Tree Theatre performances (where I was able to gather post-performance data) confirmed this view, with one parent stating:

> it was fabulous how many children blossomed – starting off they were withdrawn, quiet and looked slightly worried/uncomfortable but they really impressed me how they gradually got involved, performed with more & more conviction and beamed. It was fabulous to see the true personalities of so many of the young people – each character type was accepted, praised & nurtured from the most exuberant to the most shy.
> (feedback, 2016)

The games derived from *The Tempest* allowed the children to expand their engagement with the external world and to respond positively to new experiences, a phenomenon that often eludes those with complex learning disabilities. Hunter requested prior to the performances that the actors 'tuned into each other, using the musicality of Shakespeare and the theatre' (2017) which was evident in their creation of a fantasy world the children became absorbed in, focusing not on their limitations but on what they could do. In this sense, the heterotopia was two-fold; affecting both the children (albeit they may not have consciously realized this change in themselves) and their caregivers who saw them behave with fewer constraints than normal life may often allow. The sharing of this change in their behaviour allowed the caregivers to see some 'glimpse of a somewhere where things are otherwise' (Shaughnessy, 2020: p.14) and to perhaps see their abilities in a different light for a time. Whilst the 'performance' lasted less than two hours the memory of their children actively engaging with relative strangers to make eye contact, share joint attention and welcome physical contact would have stayed with the parents and guardians much longer. The images of them owning a domain usually reserved for professional actors is one which continues to have an impact on me years later and to their families this effect would have been even more profound. One parent noted their child 'quickly realised that no-one was comparing or judging her' and another commended the emotional nature of 'seeing everyone's story become entwined' (questionnaire, 2016), evidencing the heterotopic potential from playing these theatre games.

Firebird Theatre

Firebird Theatre company in Bristol is a learning-disabled theatre company who described themselves as 'a family of actors with a job to do' (Fiebird Theatre – programme, 2010) and that role was to bring theatre to as many people as they could. Following the death of their Director, Jane Sallis, in 2018 the company ceased to operate for a period of time but recent online activity confirms that they plan to reconvene under the auspices of Andy Harris (website, 2021). Sallis embodied Bree Hadley's description of an 'ally' (2020: p.178), supporting the efforts of disabled theatre-makers whilst she herself was able-bodied. Firebird Theatre used *The Tempest* as a basis to develop a series of artistic events: an adapted performance at Bristol Old Vic (2010), a poetry reading – *The Nine Lessons of Caliban* (2011) and a series of episodic relaxed performances entitled *Prospero, Duke of Milan* (2014). Their starting point for this collection of works was 'taking Shakespeare's story and making it more accessible for all' whilst 'considering Caliban not as a monster but as a shunned victim' (Sallis – interview, 2016). They consciously chose a play on the current school syllabus to ensure young people would attend, opening up different perspectives of Shakespeare's narrative through their interpretation. Performing at the Old Vic gave cultural credence to their work and meant that it was likely to be considered serious theatre by the local schools they wished to attract. Social geographer Edward Hall affirms that:

> through theatre performances in high profile venues, and the self-confidence gained through such performances, learning disabled

actors strengthen their individual and collective identities, making engagement with the challenging mainstream world more possible and satisfying.

(2010: p.281)

In an appropriated space, they would not have this additional element of taking possession of a theatre space and they would have also engaged with the 'mainstream world' differently, not benefitting from the cachet the Old Vic added to their productions.

Their focus, during their adaptation of *The Tempest*, on Caliban – 'the names he's been called, we've been called similar' (cast interview, 2016) – led them to search for suggestions within Shakespeare of his more human traits. They focused on the early friendship between Caliban and Miranda which they developed into a consensual relationship stopped by the father who 'wanted better things for his daughter' (programme, 2010: p.3) and who enslaved Caliban as a result. The cast described how 'people were very moved by Caliban, very sympathetic', in a similar vein to many post-colonial readings of the play. Ania Loomba, in her conclusion to *Shakespeare, Race and Colonialism,* charts the development of colonial and post-colonial academic discourse in relation to the play and her description of the refusal from the 1980s onwards to view 'Caliban as monstrosity without humanity' (2002: p.161) resonates strongly with the portrayal of him in Firebird's production.

Firebird Theatre's heterotopic inversion of the audiences' expectations about *The Tempest* began from the opening moment as a widening pinprick of light revealed an ostracized, pregnant Sycorax being marooned ashore a desert island and resolving 'I will be strong' (Sallis – script, 2010: p.1). The theatre lighting was essential to centralize Sycorax and emphasize her loss; an appropriated place would not have facilitated the same visual opening effects and would have lost much of the heterotopic impact that the play started from this central theme of maternal displacement. Sycorax's eventual demise was narrated by the isolated, bereft Caliban who 'dug her grave with [his] bare hands' (Sallis – script, 2010: p.7) and who was delighted when Prospero and Miranda appeared. When they taught him to speak Miranda wanted him to call Prospero father but Prospero insisted he call him 'master' (Sallis – script, 2010: p.9) in an attempt to subjugate him even as a child. The audience saw an intimacy develop between the two youngsters as they progressed from friendship to a desire to 'know each other skin to skin' which Prospero found abhorrent, decrying the boy as 'a monster' (Sallis – script, 2010: p.13).

Drunken Stephano and Trinculo acknowledge the damage of such labels when they tell him:

> you behave like a monster because you are treated like one. Remember? When you get called a name enough you get to think it is right, you cannot get away from it. Names can hurt and harm you inside.
>
> (Sallis – script, 2010: p.27)

The cast spoke of how this resonated on a personal level as many had been subjected to name-calling for their disabilities, which enabled them to identify with the emotional and psychological damage caused by Prospero's hurtful treatment. The production reviews evidence that this portrayal came across clearly as Katy Austin described how they articulated 'Shakespeare's themes of human suffering, love and the wielding of power against those ostracized by a judgmental society' (Firebird website). Sue Wheldon commented 'the epilogue says it all: "One day they might see me as I really am. One day they may respect the difference and see the man"' (Firebird website). This encapsulated the heterotopic quality of the production; they used the themes and narrative of *The Tempest* but devised their own interpretation to focus the gaze of the audience more sympathetically on Caliban, not as a symbol of colonial oppression but a modern youth cast out for his *otherness*, emphasized from the opening moment by the banishment of his mother.

Firebird also created a relaxed performance series; *Prospero, Duke of Milan*, specifically for learning-disabled schoolchildren, an opportunity for these disabled actors to teach learning-disabled children about Shakespeare and also to use the work to teach them that they do not need to be restricted by the limitations society imposes on them. Relaxed or sensory adapted productions utilize muted lighting and acoustics to avoid distress and with fewer expectations of what Sedgman terms 'reasonable audience' (2018: p.2) behaviour and it is important to understand the context of these generally before considering Firebird's contribution to this trope.

Relaxed performances are often simply specified performances of an existing production where explicit changes are made to the front of house to reduce stress levels for those attending and where audience silence during the performance is not expected. Andy Kempe argues that 'one of the main aims of a relaxed performance is to make as few changes to the actual show as possible' (2016: p.60) and whilst this is the case for some productions the fluidity of the term means that it also encompasses specifically designed productions such as *Prospero, Duke of Milan*.

The *Relaxed Performance Project* aimed to 'develop a model of best practice for dissemination' (Potter, 2013: p.4) and to widen accessibility to the theatre through modified performances of eight existing productions at large public theatres across the UK. Attendees were issued visual guides in advance and lighting and sound effects were softened to avoid discomfort. The data gathered across all eight productions demonstrated a 'positive impact upon audience members' confidence and self-esteem' (Potter, 2013: p.22) although there was no differentiation made between the individual productions in the conclusion of the report. The productions were not shortened but ticket prices were reduced or free and staff received specialist training prior to the events. It seems likely that the plays were selected as they were in the current season at the participating theatres rather than being specifically chosen for their appeal to a learning-disabled audience. The Globe *Romeo and Juliet* was part of their Playing Shakespeare season and one audience member enthused:

> One of my children, who is severely Autistic, can quote Shakespeare, *Hamlet, Romeo and Juliet,* and helped draw stick men pictures for a stop-go animation for his *Romeo and Juliet* project, he really enjoyed it!
> (feedback – The Globe website)

Sue Jennings advocates using *Romeo and Juliet* in Dramatherapy as she sees great therapeutic benefit in considering 'the destructiveness of what happens when people don't get on and they disagree' (interview, 2016). These themes may well resonate with those with learning disabilities, especially autism which is a 'lifelong developmental disability that affects how a person communicates with, and relates to, other people' (National Autistic

Society website); however, I am not aware that those themes were highlighted or explored as the choice of play for inclusion in the *Project* was entirely circumstantial. Those involved in the *Project* had ASD and a further understanding of their reception of *Romeo and Juliet* would have helped when assessing the effectiveness of using Shakespeare in this context, where the performance was relaxed but there were no specific follow-up activities to help those watching to explore the emotions and themes of the narrative. Audience feedback from the event was positive and it was noted that the 'visual story was amazingly helpful' to ensure that people could follow the plot. Through interventions such as these it is possible to appeal to a wider range of audience members than would perhaps be attracted to a mainstream theatre production. The National Theatre and other venues now subdivide their performances into relaxed performances, which allow 'for noise and movement in the auditorium', and sensory adapted performances, which include 'technical adjustments to light and sound effects, for those with sensory sensitivities' (National Theatre website).

Firebird addressed both of these adjustments under the banner of *relaxed performance*. They created a series of four fifteen-minute productions designed to introduce children from three local SEN schools to the theatre. The facilities of the theatre were essential for these productions; appropriated space would not have allowed them to control the sound and lighting as required. Each attendee was provided with a visual handbook which explained every step from their initial arrival at the theatre and who would greet them. The cast were introduced to the audience in order of appearance complete with photographs of them in character and a brief synopsis of each episode of the play to enable the children to engage with the story before attending (Sallis – guidance booklet, 2014). For example, one section provided information which enabled the teachers to explore the relationships of Prospero's family before they watched the performance and made it explicit that Prospero loved his daughter and also the brother who would go on to betray him. Many profoundly disabled people struggle with expressing and recognizing emotions so Firebird Theatre felt it was important that they were told of this love, rather than being expected to glean it themselves. The description of Prospero was very humanizing (in contrast with their depiction of him in *The Tempest*) to encourage empathy and understanding of his actions.

The company were committed to engaging the younger generation and making their work accessible to those who are 'wary of visiting the theatre for fear of disrupting the performance and/or other audience members' (Potter, 2013: p.11). This acknowledgement of the fear of visiting a theatre is emblematic of the embedded signifiers of a demarcated theatre space and how these can create an expectation of behaviour which some find overwhelming or unachievable. Sedgman and Reason's guest edited edition of *Participations* considered 'what constitutes acceptable modes of audience behaviour' (Sedgman, 2015: p.123) and the way in which societally accepted norms can be used to stifle and inhibit those who react differently. Relaxed or sensory adapted performances explicitly advertise the relaxation of these social conventions to remove a barrier which may otherwise preclude the attendance of neurodiverse audiences. The demarcated space adds both an element of validation of the authenticity of the theatrical experience and the ability to control stage lighting and sound, to avoid attendees being overwhelmed by theatrical practice, but without explicit labelling as a relaxed performance the idea of attending may be off-putting.

Performances within these demarcated theatrical spaces drew on the inherent cultural signifiers of the locations in creating their heterotopic experiences, using the theatre itself to lend weight to the other elements. The combination of a marginalized audience or cast whom the 'challenging mainstream world' (Hall, 2010: p.281) would expect to be limited in their ability to enjoy the theatre and Shakespeare is a powerful one in any setting. With the added layer of meaning from a professional theatre location this becomes even more compelling. These elements provoke society to realize that people from marginalized groups can and will use Shakespeare to communicate positively and proactively. As the 2020 Spectra Report describes, for:

> the most marginalised in society there is a feeling that an absence of critical engagement with artistic output both reflects and compounds this – and conversely that an improvement in critical engagement could help to bring wider societal change.
> (Todd, 2020: p.7)

Whilst this refers specifically to learning-disabled theatre, the argument can be extrapolated to encompass other marginalized groups. This challenging of the refusal of critics to engage is partly addressed by the usage of Shakespeare or other canonical works and partly by performing in spaces traditionally belonging to professional actors and is considered further in Chapter 5. There are a limited number of examples of 'theatres' existing or being temporarily created within unexpected locations such as prisons. For example, the women's facility where Shakespeare in Prison works in Huron Valley features an auditorium with a proscenium arch and raked seating but almost all prisons and institutions rely on appropriation of other spaces for performances. Pimlico Opera who work within one English prison each year, bringing in West End actors to work alongside inmates for eight weeks before a week of public performances, transform the prison location through the addition of professional sets and seating – creating a unique world where a prison gym feels like a theatre. This was the case when I saw their production of *Hairspray* in HMP Bronzefield in March 2020.

Appropriated spaces

Whilst the additional benefits of demarcated spaces cannot be overestimated, there are different nuances within spaces temporarily repurposed for performance. In these locations there are none of the expectations linked to a theatre with either positive or negative overtones. Instead there will be embedded signifiers linked to the primary purpose of the space such as a hall or chapel, which need to be mentally put aside to allow it to be experienced as a theatre, albeit temporarily. This transience of purpose of location links to the way in which space is altered by the activities which take place within it, explored in Chapter 2, and the interchangeability between space and place, dependent on permanence. Appropriation of space is usually led by practicalities, within the context of the groups I work with, rather than a desire to create site-specific interventions. However, this temporary repurposing can deliver heterotopic experiences for the audiences, many of whom may not be regular theatre goers.

Appropriated spaces are normal within psychiatric hospitals and the criminal justice estate, where space is at a premium and the locations used are familiar to those incarcerated, often with emotional baggage relating to their primary use. Audiences for productions often include a mixture of peers, families, staff and external visitors and for each of these (admittedly non-homogeneous) groups the space and the heterotopia are likely to be experienced differently. The heterotopia within an appropriated space often allows those marginalized to become central to the theatrical experience, 'to really change what is possible and inspire a desire to achieve more' (Rob, 2019). It invites self-reflection to be altered and the perceptions of others to shift positively as these productions 'open doors into what appeared to be a world of elitism' (Michael, 2019) and show that Shakespeare can be appropriated by anyone. Across all groups though there is a likelihood that attendance may not be primarily driven by a love of theatre. The patients/inmates are often seeking any break in the monotony of daily regime, staff are likely rostered to attend or are there in a support function, families want to share whatever part of their loved ones' lives they can and visitors are either there to support the work and/or for academic research. Performances in appropriated spaces often have significant logistical and spatial constraints in contrast to the demarcated space productions which use the location of a theatre to endorse the cultural capital of their work.

Broadmoor Hospital

Between 1989 and 1991 a number of Shakespeare plays were performed in Broadmoor, one of the UK's three high-security psychiatric hospitals, about which *Shakespeare Comes to Broadmoor* (Cox, 1992) was written. The book details a range of perspectives on the project including a chapter dedicated to 'The Set and Stage Management' (written by Ian Bayne, a nurse in the Creative Department), which provides an in-depth consideration of the practicalities of staging a production within this heavily controlled environment, including seating, props and lighting as well as staff attendance at the performances. This is one of the few such published analyses of the constraints and additional considerations of operating within an institution and much of this resonated with my own experiences in prisons where performances are partially informed by theatrical design and partly by security requirements and the continued functioning of the institutional regime. As Bayne writes, 'these preparations may seem mundane to the polished professional' (1992: p.120) but within the context of appropriated spaces inside the secure estate they are necessary and inform the spatial ambience of the work.

The four performances in Broadmoor were each attended by circa 100 patients whose requests to do so were approved by the hospital administration. Mark Rylance comments on the 'small room' of the Central Hall and that it 'was very shocking to turn to someone no further away than you are and speak to them and see all their faces'(1992: pp.28, 40). Whilst Rylance judged the appropriated space as confined in comparison to the professional theatres he usually performed in, Bayne viewed the location as more than adequate for the annual performances of the in-house theatre group – the Broadhumoorists. Ron Daniels who directed *Hamlet* commented that it 'was very clear ... that the smallness of the space in which we performed was critically important' (1992: p.86). He likened it to the run-throughs in rehearsal rooms where the 'raw emotion' was not diluted by the spectacle of performance with its theatrical trappings. The directors and actors spoke of being unsure if the productions would engage the audience who may not be theatre-aficionados and a delight that they appeared transfixed throughout. In this environment the heterotopic impact appeared to be more prevalent in the context of the theatre companies than the audience. Their anticipated spectator reticence failed to materialize; instead they were met with 'not an audience but an important part of the action' (Cox, 1992: p.149) who actively engaged with the characters and themes portrayed.

Shakespeare Comes to Broadmoor focuses primarily on the perspective of the theatre makers and staff, with less detailed consideration on the effect for the patients. This may be due to a myriad of factors, including perhaps limited abilities to coherently discuss the effect on themselves and in some instances a lack of capacity to externalize the inner emotions generated in an analytical manner. This is similar to the difficulties of gathering meaningful qualitative responses from those with profound learning disabilities. Much of the patient impact is narrated through the staff or theatre makers; this recounting of impact through a secondary lens is not uncommon for marginalized groups such as those incarcerated or with complex learning or mental health needs although it does further entrench their marginalized position. Within this institutional context, to which Cox draws attention in the opening statement of ethics, there is a pertinent need for confidentiality to protect the patients and those connected with victims of the patients, where a reignition of past narratives could cause emotional and mental harm. Sue Jennings writes the final chapter of the book describing the 'powerful therapeutic affect' which brought 'everyone in a very raw way into contact with their extreme fears and fantasies' (1992: p.248). However, she does acknowledge an awareness of the 'major changes it has brought about for staff and actors' (p.248) rather than for the patients. The book was published over a decade after the events to 'set on record certain crucial events which transpired when two worlds met' (Cox, 1992: p.xv).

It is not possible to understand the extent to which a heteropia was created for the audience as their pre-performance expectations remain largely unknown. Daniels made the value judgement that 'for the patients in the audience it was a terribly special event' (1992: p.88) but this was not substantiated through primary evidence. His response, and those of others in the companies, by contrast, speak of their own preconceptions being altered through 'confronting the myth that they were monsters and finding instead people who were just ordinary' (1992: p.89). The project appears to have initiated a dialogue between two disparate groups of people which focused on a shared humanity rather than their expected differences. Rob Ferris's insight into the way that these productions enabled the staff to objectively consider patients they have worked with for many years also suggested a reframing of reality. He documented that what may have seemed to Daniels 'an entirely natural and ordinary thing' (1992: p.90) when a patient hugged the director for revealing autobiographical elements to his interpretation of *Hamlet* was 'extraordinary'. Ferris acknowledged that psychiatrists focus on the differences between the lives of the patients and their own experiences but that the 'process of identification' the theatre companies undertook minimised the 'gulf' (1992: p.90) between them. The published text makes it difficult to ascertain the precise elements which contributed to this change but it seems likely that the performing of these plays was the catalyst for these conversations and subsequent realignments of opinion.

Donmar trilogy

The Donmar version of *The Tempest* (set in a women's prison with Harriet Walters as a female Prospero) was performed in the gym at HMP New Hall as well as in external theatre spaces. Reason published on his qualitative research with the incarcerated audience, describing how 'this audience was particularly implicated; watching a version of themselves on stage, filtered and projected through the lens and language of Shakespearean drama' (2019: p.86). Reason's article focuses predominantly on moments of resonance with their own experience as many elements provoked a consensus of emotional engagement and he acknowledges Peter Holland's nuanced consideration that 'Shakespeare is not universal – always and everywhere the same – but is everywhere different and that is why we keep going to it' (conference, 2018). This richness of Shakespeare's appeal extended beyond the theatrical devices of the production and meant that the women identified with Prospero's parental concerns as strongly as the first night incarceration scene and the urine tests Lloyd included to signify prison-life. Reason draws on Anna Harpin's conceptualization of the verbalization of trauma when he describes:

> Tension between the 'impossibility of telling' (which would entail a return to the trauma) and the 'impossible silence' (which would entail a neglect or erasure of the trauma). For the women in the prison audience it was into this place that *The Tempest* inserted itself – able to speak of and about and for them without being the thing itself.
>
> (Reason, 2019: p.101)

It is perhaps this ability for Shakespeare's work to be used to articulate trauma when words may be otherwise elusive which imbues it with much of its power. This production interwove Shakespeare with the realities of prison for incarcerated women to bring this to a general theatre audience as well as those in HMP New Hall, who may have seen themselves differently through the lens of performance. The appropriated space of the prison gym developed the heterotopia in potentially unexpected ways as there are none of the signifiers of theatre but the arrival of professional actors to stage a performance would have been a significant event in the prison regime.

In contrast with these examples of performing for marginalized audiences, the final two case studies demonstrate the heterotopic impact when incarcerated actors perform full-length plays within the English prison estate. These case-studies reveals much of the multi-faceted heterotopic capabilities, using Shakespeare as a communication method and form of cultural validation.

The Gallowfield Players – *The Merchant*

The Gallowfield Players' adaptation of *The Merchant* (which won a Silver Koestler Award for the performance) featured a Shylock ostracized, not for his religion, but for having a life sentence. The play opened as Officers discharged him through the prison gates and he soliloquized that:

SHYLOCK
    Too many years have passed me by.
    Too many losses made me wonder why?
    To reflect on my actions and their cost.
    Photos on a wall reminders of all I'd lost,
    The price to pay far too high.
    Yet I pay only the least part of it,
    Those left outside take the biggest hit;
    They suffer the most, they pay the real cost.
    Children's tears as they sit on visits,
    Each one a sad memory elicits.
    Scarring my heart, searing my soul,
    A souvenier of my part in the sorrow I have caused.
    A painful reminder to be a better man, a better dad.
    A new start?
    I doubt it, the baggage I carry sits heavy on my shoulders,
    An invisible label more apparent as I get older.
    Becoming seen by all and set apart, I am now an ex-con.
    A man with no future, simply abandoned
    By the institutions which placed this lodestone around my neck.
    But for the sake of redemption I must,

I must resist the temptation to seek revenge,
Or to walk the same path as I once did.
Instead I need to bask in the love a child bears for their father,
Try harder, do better, go farther
Than who goes furthest to prove I deserve such a love.
I must move forward no matter what the load,
No matter what burden is laid or title bestowed,
I shall begin anew.

(*The Merchant*: Prologue)

The production repurposed Shakespeare's plot and characters to a modern setting where Jessica's bitterness grew from her father's physical and emotional absence during her childhood. Portia, a wealthy, philanthropic heiress, asked each suitor to deliver a gift to demonstrate their feelings towards her, choosing Bassanio who 'showed those others to be poor' (*The Merchant* 2.7.85) with his simple flower. Humour was injected through numerous references to prison life – shrunken clothes, inside loyalties and quips about weight gain as well as the addition of the dead parrot scene from Monty Python, albeit he became a 'Venetian Blue' (2.6.63) in keeping with the play. The court scene was re-engineered to enable Portia to highlight the legalities, warning him 'this course of action breaches your parole' (4.1.83) and that 'conspiracy to commit such an act' (4.1.95) would be sufficient to return Shylock and his accomplice Tubbs to prison under their license conditions. In the final scene Shylock sat alone, contemplating the reality of being 'so hated, so despised' (5.1.1) and writing a farewell letter to his daughter as he planned his suicide, accepting that 'no excuses or platitudes will | Ever put right the wrongs I've done' (5.1.29–30). Portia remonstrated with him for such self-pity and pointed out that she had interceded to prevent the taking of Antonio's pound of flesh because Shylock's return to prison would have devastated Jessica. An emotional reunion with his estranged daughter ended the production with Shylock's affirmation that 'with this chance I'll do all I can to make amends'(5.1.144).

There were two performances: one in the chapel for circa forty inmates, a few external guests and staff-members and one in the Visits Hall for the actors' loved ones and invited attendees; both performances were commended for the 'pride, passion and dedication' (feedback, 2020) of the actors. I will consider first the response from those in the chapel. Ron Daniels commented in the context of Broadmoor that the incarcerated were not experienced with theatre (Daniels – Cox, 1992: p.86), which is a somewhat reductionist assessment of the spectrum of cultural exposure those incarcerated possess. However, it is true that many of the inmates were unfamiliar with Shakespeare and had been invited as a result of friendships or to ease their social isolation. Attendee feedback included 'first Shakespeare play seen', 'I know little of Shakespeare' and 'at school I found Shakespeare a bit dry and unrelatable' (feedback, 2020). Whilst the audience were being assembled (a time-consuming process within prison) our pianist played, accompanying relaxed chatting. Shylock's entrance escorted by two uniformed officers and carrying his belongings in a HMP property bag resulted in immediate silence from the audience as they saw not a Shakespeare character but a peer of theirs. This silence prevailed throughout the performance, punctuated only by laughter at the comedic elements.

The inmates found humour in the prison jokes and references to the previous production, *Julius Caesar*, which many of them had seen. Several staff commented on how 'engaged and enthralled the men were' and the 'respect they had for the actors' (feedback, 2020) which, whilst it may seem normal to many, is often an alien concept in a prison environment which is noisy and chaotic with continuous challenging undertones. Attention was riveted throughout the 90 minutes of the performance (punctuated by a ten-minute interval) and the men evidently followed the narrative of the tale. Feedback included 'just for a couple of hours I was out of the normal constraints of being a prisoner and felt so relieved to be able to just enjoy myself freely' and 'helped to escape from prison for 2 hours' (feedback, 2020). There was not a single comment about disliking Shakespeare or finding the language difficult to understand and many commented that they understood the play more than they anticipated.

The chapel was not a neutral space – religion is incredibly powerful at creating communities in some instances but can also cause significant divisions within society, and has similar effects within the prison estate. Many prisoners turn to faith to help them with their sentences and 'in discussing the role of religion ..... prisoners often made direct reference to sanity and survival' (Crewe et al., 2019: p.174). Religion tends to instigate strong feelings whether of a positive or negative nature amongst inmates and for every person who seeks solace in the multi-faith chapel there is another who feels abhorrence for organized religion. So, the actors and the audience would have felt these conflicting emotions in relation to the location of the performance and as one jokingly put it, 'I expect the thunderbolt to strike me down while I'm in there' (Sam, 2020). Wayne, who had not previously discussed his religion within the group, invited his Mormon chaplains to attend the performance. They spoke with me before the event about the benefits he attributed to being part of The Gallowfield Players and that they felt it was 'marvellous, builds self-esteem and belief in a person' (Shepherd – conversation, 2020).

The production scenery was minimal due to a combination of prison restrictions, lack of stage and budgetary constraints, as the project received little funding. So, the audience were not transported into a professional set with raked seating and painted flats as they are for the in-prison productions organized by Pimlico Opera. Instead they saw a relatively bare chapel with regular seating and minimal attempts to differentiate the locations within the play. The changing of a painted cardboard sign above a doorway crafted from cardboard tubes and garden canes denoted whether the scene was taking place in Portia's home, the 'Parrot and Welshmen' pub or Shylock's office. A simple cardboard desk-sign differentiated HMP Gallowfield of Shylock's custodial sentence from Antonio's office. Yet this lack of attempt to create a realistic theatre set had little impact on the way in which the audience engaged with the performance which created 'great memories' and 'took me away from this place' (feedback, 2020). Whilst the chapel was not physically changed for the performance it was altered mentally through the shift of intention for the room during the time of the production. Many felt that it temporarily transcended the constraints of the prison; this feeling was generated not by any physical alterations to the chapel but by the power of the adaptation of Shakespeare's work which both utilized the cultural capital of his plays and showed the audience that it was for them, imbued with prison references they could identify with. Shylock's famous soliloquy was adapted and spoken directly to the audience:

There is not so much difference between myself and you;
Indeed, do we not eat the very same food?
Breathe the same air?

> Feel the same breeze that blows through our hair?
> If you prick me do I not bleed?
> If you tickle me do I not laugh?
> If you poisoned me would I not die?
> Well then tell me, pray tell me why
> You think that the revenge you would surely seek
> If you were wronged should not be the same for me?
> (*The Merchant*, 3.1.67–76)

This asked a fundamental question: does our underlying humanity differ based on our actions and mistakes? This embodied the heterotopic impact of the performance: adapted famous Shakespearean lines delivered directly to the audience by a man serving a life sentence for a violent crime, this 'audience-addressed soliloquy establish[ed] an overt relationship'(Hirsh, 2003: p.14). The audience were 'invited to participate in the dramatic action … as the fictional world of the character and the world of the playgoers overlap[ped]' (2003: p.14) by being asked to consider if their similarities to him outweighed their differences from him. This was powerful with other inmates who seemed to take from it a sense that their underlying humanity may have been affected by their crime but remained alive in some form, however deeply buried. One inmate wrote

> You're on your own as a prisoner in every sense of the word, you are actively discouraged from building relationships because you are simply not trusted [...] but this – acting, being open and honest, not being frightened to express yourself without fear of consequence is vital.
> (feedback, 2020)

One of the deepest resonances with the inmates appeared to come from the final scene where Shylock wrote to his estranged daughter while contemplating suicide, before an emotional reunion. *The Grapevine* (in-prison magazine) wrote 'the final scene meant so much to everyone' (2020; p.6) and the statistics on prison self-harm and suicide which ended the play evidenced the stark reality of longer sentencing and poor mental health amongst prisoners with escalating incidents of self-harm.

Liebling and Ludlow's research provides a solid foundational analysis of the issues of self-harm and suicide within the prison estate as well as identifying that there are 'few systematic attempts to investigate which aspects of the prison experience might be most relevant to suicide and suicide attempts' (2016: p.226). Peter Clarke, Her Majesty's Chief Inspector of Prisons, affirmed that 'where hope is absent everything goes in the wrong direction' (keynote, 2020), in the context of self-harm within custody. A number of inmates identified that they felt the play highlighted issues of importance and relevance to them and that they identified with Shylock. Two of them showed me their scars from cutting themselves, which they had used to deal with pain and emotional trauma. They said that to bring such a generally taboo issue into the open made them feel more able to speak about it and helped to reduce the stigma they felt (both were referred for additional support via their Keyworker). One of the psychologists praised the work for 'demonstrating that it's ok to talk about issues' whilst another stated that 'The Gallowfield Players give hope' (feedback, 2020). The use of Shakespeare's play, adapted to reflect their own experiences had allowed them to feel that they were less isolated and that their hidden issues could be more publicly discussed, as Reason articulated 'able to speak of and about and for them without being the thing itself' (2019: p.101). The performance in the chapel created a heterotopia which united them with others across the estate and those beyond the walls, utilizing Shakespeare as a means of creating a dialogue of solidarity rarely experienced between those incarcerated and those not.

Following the performance there was an opportunity for cast, inmates, staff and external guests to speak informally which they did, breaking down the perceived barriers which would usually exist. The Lord Mayor of Leicester was effusive in her praise as she spoke to the actors, enthusing that 'it was absolutely wonderful' (Byrne, 2020), and asking that she be invited for all future productions. Fionnula Gordon, Criminology Lecturer and ex-HM Prisons Inspectorate reflected:

> the exchanges between Jessica and Shylock were very emotional, dealing with leaving kids on the outside and showed how difficult it is to repair the harm between a father and his child.
> (2020)

The interweaving of Shakespeare and the criminal justice system resonated not only with those with lived experience of prison but those who were watching the play from more emotionally distanced positions. A Library Assistant commented on the 'rawness' which 'brought everyone together, a platform for both prisoners and staff' which was 'so needed' (feedback, 2020). This sense of unification between staff and inmates is rare within the prison estate on a group-scale. Two officers played cameo roles to facilitate Shylock's release from the prison and Lancelot Gobbo enlisted members of the audience to represent his conscience and the fiend, borrowing heavily from the Globe's 2015 production (Munby – director, 2015). The involvement of staff and guests as equals with the actors was a powerful way of breaking down some of the barriers which exist between those incarcerated and wider society. Lloyd's trilogy, which included *The Tempest* examined earlier in this chapter, cast two Clean Break actresses (with lived experience of incarceration) in relatively minor roles alongside the professional actors (Lloyd – director, 2016). The Gallowfield Players production inverted that balance with the significant roles played by the Company and cameo roles for staff. A Psychotherapist in the audience commented that this 'enabled a shift both inside and outside for the men' (Feedback, 2020), allowing them the opportunity to be the ones revered for a brief period, an experience felt profoundly by the inmates and their families in the second performance.

The second performance was part of a Family Day, an extended and slightly more informal visit. The Ministry of Justice's *Strengthening Prisoner's Family Ties Policy Framework* identifies that Family Days 'help to improve positive relationships between prisoners and [...] family members' (MoJ, 2019: p.10). Prison Rule 35 entitles convicted prisoners 'to receive a visit twice in every period of four weeks' (rule 35.2(b)) and family days are in addition to this allowance. The *Framework* cites:

> growing evidence that family support and maintaining family ties is not only important for the well-being of prisoners, but may also aid reintegration into the community following release from prison, and reduce reoffending.
>
> (MoJ, 2019: p.5)

However, as Laura Piacentini acknowledges 'prison is a problematic space in the context of the family' (2020) with familial relationships often fractured by incarceration. Eight actors invited relatives who arrived to a Visits Hall which had been reconfigured to create a thrust-stage and seating. Around the room, the cast and families shared lunch (standard prison fayre). The six without family attendance and myself ate in a group. Ben commented 'this feels like normal life, having food with your mates outside' (2020) and the atmosphere felt distinctly different to the usual prison environment. The cast were keen to introduce their fellow actors to their families. Normal visits involve inmates sitting one side of their allotted table and visitors the other, a clear demarcation which must not be breached and there is no opportunity to interact with other inmates and their visitors. Rob's Aunt wrote to me afterwards, saying that seeing 'a loved one engaging with and relaxed with other prisoners was a magical experience' (personal correspondence, 2020) which allayed her fears over how he was coping and who he was interacting with during his long sentence. Crewe et al. dedicate a section of their book to 'reforming a social world in prison' where they map the changing nature of inmate friendships from largely superficial during early years of sentences to ones involving 'mutual disclosure and trust' (2019: p.237) in later years. There is usually a sense that these friendships remain separate from external contacts but this opportunity allowed the actors to bring their families and inmate friends together positively.

Michael, who wrote the adaptation of *The Merchant* (which earned him a Koestler Commended Award for the script) 'as a love letter to [his] children' (programme, 2020), played Shylock and this was the first of The Gallowfield Players' performances he invited visitors to. His children were unable to attend but he invited Eleanor, the lady he classes as his mother. Whilst Michael was collecting lunch she initiated the following conversation:

ELEANOR
    Thankyou
ROWAN
    What for?
ELEANOR
    For giving me back my son. I haven't seen him for many years, long before he came in here. And now he's back and that's all thanks to you and the work you do (feedback, 2020).

She told me that their telephone calls are about The Gallowfield Players and that it has given him focus as he serves his sentence. As

Shelley Tracey notes in her 2017 study 'the connections between interventions and rehabilitation are complex and not easily articulated' (2017: p.15), but to be seen by a mother as returning her son to her was powerful testimony of the changes this in-prison theatre company enabled.

A number of invited guests arrived after lunch for the performance, including Jeremy Wilkinson of Opus Arte who was unsure what to expect from this, his first prison visit. He commented that his 'first impression was the warmth, everyone chatting and you couldn't tell staff, visitors and inmates apart, the cast made me feel so welcome' (feedback, 2020). Professionally printed programmes were distributed to the audience to enhance the feeling of this being an authentic theatre production, allow the actors to share some of the behind-the-scenes experience and provide a memento. The audience took their seats as the prologue began. Watching Shylock's poignant soliloquy about the years behind bars and how his love for his family had kept him going was even more emotional performed in front of those very families who sustain the inmates throughout their sentences. The visits hall ceiling was too low to accommodate the constructed doorway so Malcolm (our Stage Manager as well as playing minor roles) improvised by propping the hand-painted signs in one of the high windows to signify the change of locations. The performance did not benefit from stage-lighting, proper scenery or even a backstage area, but despite that Martin's wife commented 'it was as though I was watching it elsewhere (not in prison)' (feedback, 2020). Those who had previously seen a Gallowfield Players production 'expected to see greatness' while those unfamiliar with the company 'didn't know what to expect with limited resources' but all agreed they were 'blown away' (feedback, 2020).

For those in the audience who were not related to the cast the performance delivered a heterotopia through using the combination of Shakespeare, adapted and spoken by inmates serving life sentences. For some, who had not spent time with inmates before, this had the effect of showing them as people rather than prisoners, much as Daniels noted when he met the patients in Broadmoor. Kevin Wright from the Royal Shakespeare Company attended and afterwards commented that 'rarely has a piece of theatre resonated in my mind the way this did' (feedback, 2020). An Independent Monitoring Board (IMB) representative praised the work for 'demonstrating that it is ok to talk about issues' including self-harm and family estrangement (feedback, 2020). This was done through the lens of 'dramatic distancing' (Jennings, 1992: p.17) which drew on Shakespeare's iconic characters to highlight much less palatable topics in a way which allowed a diverse audience to engage with them. Whilst much prison creative art encourages inmates to tell their own stories, this can at times be seen by some as solipsistic as it:

> encourages a level of self-obsession from people with no assistance for moving forward. [...] this reiterates the internal dialogue and leads the person to believe this to be true. The pathways in the brain are strengthened. [...] This can be damaging rather than helpful.
>
> (Bridge – interview, 2016)

Bridge takes the rather controversial view that re-telling of 'same-old series of personal stories' (2016: p.52) encourages introspection and stifles the possibility of building a positive narrative for the future. I refute this as there are undoubtedly therapeutic benefits in discussing one's personal experiences; however, care needs to be taken to ensure that the dialogue does not become entirely introspective and retrospective but opens up avenues for development. There are many people who would have little sympathy for hearing the fears of a prisoner about their treatment upon release, taking the view that they have brought this on themselves by their crimes. Sensationalist newspaper headlines and social media stories help to develop and perpetuate a stigmatization of those incarcerated, reducing them 'from a whole and usual person to a discounted one' (Goffman, 1963: p.3) and often inciting public disgust at any positive interventions provided. Warr, a criminologist with lived experience of prison acknowledges 'the impact of prison stigma is all-pervasive' (2016: p.600) and societal opinion of the formerly incarcerated is to reduce them to *other*, somehow different from those casting judgement.

Michael and Rob specifically chose *The Merchant of Venice* for the way an adaptation would allow them to tackle this stigma by placing Shylock in the position of having a life sentence. Rob told the group 'it's the thing that keeps me awake at night, knowing how society will hate me when I do get out' (2019), sobering honesty from an intelligent, articulate man who will not be considered for parole for over two decades. Using Shylock to voice those concerns added a cultural validity which lifted the message from being self-pitying and individual-focused to being a sociological reflection on the experiences and concerns of the estimated 11 million people incarcerated globally (Walmsley, 2018). Shylock was not created as a one-dimensional figure of pity but drew on Shakespeare's character to create a complex, irritable man whose human failings were evident, a man difficult to love but also difficult to dismiss. A number of visitors suggested that the production should be shown more widely across the prison estate 'to show that being in prison is not the end of life' (feedback, 2020) and that it should be shared with outside groups such as local colleges, schools and drama groups. The Gallowfield Players are keen to 'leave a lasting legacy that will change lives, help people and show that [they] are more than a label' (Michael, 2020).

For the families it created a heterotopia by making them forget they were 'visiting a prison, it felt like a theatre' (feedback, 2020) and allowing them a few hours of seeing their loved ones being applauded for their skills. It is worth quoting at length from Rob's rehearsal diary for that day:

> I actually had butterflies in my stomach, it was the first time I can remember really feeling that sensation. My Mum, Nan and Aunt came to watch the performance and knowing they were watching seemed to exaggerate how nervous I was feeling. Retrospectively, I think it was the pressure that this was something I could do to make them proud of me. This isn't something we ever really have the opportunity for in here, we can achieve things and tell family/loved ones about it but I can't think of anything else I have been able to share, something special like that, with them. It's the sort of thing that weighs heavily on me. Today was such a powerfully positive experience.
>
> (2020)

Crewe et al.'s research evidences that 'the impact of separation from deeply embedded familial relations was, for the majority of prisoners, both agonising and enduring' (2019: p.214), which goes some way to explaining Rob's nervousness prior to performing. His desire to physically share an experience of pride with his family rather than telling them of the event afterwards was significant; it would allow him and his family to experience positive emotions together in a way which had been impossible since his arrest. The standing ovation and visitors openly weeping as the production ended affirmed to the actors that they were being hailed as actors not judged as prisoners. Wayne wrote 'all I want is for my family to be proud and this production made that happen, it's the best day I ever had in prison' (Wayne – rehearsal diary, 2020). The Gallowfield Players' adaptation of Shakespeare's play enabled them to communicate parts of themselves which they may not have been able to find the words for previously, in ways which resonated with inmates, staff, families and external visitors alike, using the cultural capital of Shakespeare to speak with impactful clarity and deep honesty. Michael's summation of the 'elation, joy, pride, happiness at the way everyone pulled together' (rehearsal diary, 2020) perfectly articulates the supportive community-spirit of the group.

Emergency Shakespeare – *Macbeth*

The inaugural production of Emergency Shakespeare in September 2019 very consciously engaged with the concept of space with a modern adaptation of *Macbeth*. The company rehearsed and performed in the Visits Hall, a large well-lit space with high ceilings and numerous windows. The set was designed by Brody, who discovered his artistic talent whilst in prison and has since commenced an undergraduate Art degree. This adaptation set the play in a modern theatre company rehearsing the Scottish play.

Extract from Emergency Shakespeare's *Macbeth* – Act 4, Scene 1
Rehearsal workshop – enter Director, Producer and Stage Manager, they are the first to arrive

DIRECTOR
    Ok, as the production team I feel like we ought to address the elephant in the room. With two deaths in the company what on earth is our insurance premium looking like?

PRODUCER
: {groans}Urrrggghhh ... don't even. I'm not sure we're going to have enough cast left to open at this rate

STAGE MANAGER
: Isn't that a bit heartless?

PRODUCER
: I've got all of my assets tied up in this company, macabre humor is all I've got left.

DIRECTOR
: They do say *Macbeth* carries a curse

STAGE MANAGER
: Well that's gone and done it. Well done!

[Director winces as he's realized what he's done]

PRODUCER
: Never speak the play's title aloud in the theatre you're performing!

DIRECTOR
: Life is imitating art a little too closely for me at the moment

STAGE MANAGER
: What would that make us then? The witches?

[Director, Producer and Stage Manager start clearing up remnants of the party, throwing them in the bin. Stage manager comes across three witches hats and passes them out]

DIRECTOR
: Round about the cauldron go

PRODUCER
: In the poisoned entrails throw

STAGE MANAGER
: Eye of newt and toe of frog

A relative newcomer to the company, Wade, overheard the Stage Manager, Director and Producer (who parodically self-identified as the witches) prophesying greatness in his future which drove him and his partner to devise the plan of pouring a potion into Duncan's drink rendering him temporarily ill, allowing Wade to step up from understudy to leading man (*Macbeth: Adapted*, 2019). However, their scheme triggered a fatal heart attack for Duncan and from there the adapted plot of *Macbeth* ensued with Banquo pushed down the stairs and McDuff's family burnt in a house-fire before Wade was arrested, having just heard the news of his partner's suicide. The play

FIGURE 5 *Emergency Shakespeare*, Macbeth, *The Visits Hall, HMP Stafford (17 September 2019). Photo: George Vuckovic Photography.*

within a play concept incorporated famous Shakespeare lines with modern text and staff playing cameo roles. One of the most powerful components of the heterotopia they created in this production was the concept of things spiralling out of control; Wade did not intentionally set out to kill Duncan but his ambition overruled his sense of right and wrong. The actors were keen that he should not appear as a depraved individual from the outset but a man whose flaws initiated his downfall whilst possessing redemptive qualities too. Their attempt at an Aristotelian tragedy figure was created to challenge the often-held assumptions that those convicted of sexual offences are 'recidivistic, untreatable predators' (King & Roberts, 2015: p.71), a view fuelled by the media despite evidence to the contrary in terms of recidivism, which shows that 'compared with all offender types other than those convicted of fraud, sex offenders have lower conviction rates' (Mann – Crewe et al., 2016: p.247).

The Visits Hall had a number of pillars which Brody's design incorporated by using green prison sheets strung between four of them to create a proscenium stage into which the audience looked from their chairs arranged in gently curved rows. What began as doodling in his rehearsal diary during an early session which frustrated him for being 'too unproductive, digressive and interrupted' formed the basis for the staging of the play (Brody – rehearsal diary, 2019). Prison sheets were used as they were in plentiful supply, making the set practical and inexpensive. The creation of a cube, enclosed on three sides by sheets was intended by Brody to 'give the audience the feeling at once of being enclosed in the action and apart from it' (conversation, 2019), emulating the way that prison visitors are both temporarily enclosed within the prison and very much external, seeing only a limited glimpse. Free-standing display boards were repurposed as flats across the rear of the stage, forming central entrances and allowing for the changing of the location through a series of different room-scapes. The Art Department painted these to Brody's design, providing a rehearsal room, a public house and a living room. These were pinned onto the boards and flipped by members of the cast between scenes. We utilized the concept of the audience witnessing rehearsals to make the scene changes part of the play rather than a separate activity, echoing Boal's assertion that for the oppressed 'their theatre will be the rehearsal not the finished spectacle' (Boal, 2008: p.120).

Props, including a cardboard bar with working beer pumps, a props box and numerous smaller items, were created within the prison. The morning before the performances was a full run-through and the men remained out of their cells over lunchtime (a rare occurrence within the regime) to create the set, allowing a dress rehearsal in the afternoon. The painted sheets arrived that day and it became apparent that somewhere a miscommunication had occurred, resulting in them being painted on the material with the wrong orientation. Given that this was Brody's set design, which he had put a lot of effort into, and a history of bad feeling between himself and the art teacher, I anticipated an angry outburst from him. However, his emotional resilience and coping mechanisms, developed partly through being a member of the company, meant he simply shrugged, gave a wry smile and commented 'oh well, it'll be alright, we'll work it out' (Brody – conversation, 2019). This self-control would have been beyond comprehension a few months earlier but with a little creativity of approach the set was indeed 'alright'.

The space was altered significantly and the actors commented that 'the stage made a huge difference, it felt like we were in a totally

FIGURE 6 *Brody's initial sketch of the set design, completed during rehearsals in his Rehearsal Diary (June 2019). Courtesy of Brody.*

different room' and 'the set made it feel like I wasn't in jail' (cast debrief, 2019). Feedback questionnaires were handed out as the audience arrived but a number of the residents declined to complete one which surprised me as the population was usually very compliant with prison requests. Ray explained that many of these men were functionally illiterate – '62 per cent of people entering prison were assessed as having a reading age of 11 or lower' (Bromley Briefings, 2019: p.15) – but were embarrassed to admit this.

'Work, Intimacy and Prison Masculinities' examines the complexities and often contradictory natures of masculine facades as a survival mechanism, challenging 'the presentation of male prisoners as "hypermasculine"' but acknowledging that prison 'generates defensive responses' (Morey & Crewe – Maycock & Hunt, 2019: p.38). From the atmosphere in the room it seemed to me likely that there were reservations about coming to see a Shakespeare play as well as thinking it reputationally detrimental to display excitement about such an activity in the presence of their peers. Regardless of their expectations the atmosphere throughout was engaged and they evidently enjoyed the performance. The buzz at the end as they came to speak to the cast was palpable and many of them congratulated the company on the overall quality of the work. This evidently continued on the wings as when we held a further performance the following week the chapel was filled to capacity both with individual attendees and teachers bringing their classes to see it. One inmate commented that the play 'has encouraged me to read some of [Shakespeare's] work, which is not something I would normally read' (feedback, 2019), affirming that the performance changed perspectives and made Shakespeare accessible to men who perhaps felt it was not for them.

In the latest HMIP Inspection Report for this prison it was noted that

> Relationships between prisoners and staff were good, 85 per cent of prisoners said that staff treated them with respect and 84 per cent said that there was a member of staff they could turn to if they had a problem.
>
> (Clarke, 2016: p.27)

However, there were areas for improvement identified, such as staff addressing prisoners by their first name and a requirement for supplementary anti-conditioning training for staff. The performance of cameo roles within the play by a Custody Manager and the Governing Governor was welcomed by the residents, one of whom commented that 'staff involvement was surprising and positive' (feedback, 2019). Whilst the heterotopic potential I had envisaged for the performance was more in relation to changing the inmates' perspectives of Shakespeare, this feedback demonstrated the incremental shift in staff-prisoner relations which can be created by such initiatives. As a result of the positivity surrounding staff involvement, a Senior Officer (SO) became involved in the scratch performance of *Shakespeare is Disturbed!* we created as part of the Talent Unlocked Festival in November 2019. The SO then went on to play the role of Slender in *The Merry Wives of Windsor* which was due for performance in April 2020 but cancelled due to the Covid-19 pandemic. Alison Frater, Chair of the National Criminal Justice Arts Alliance, attended the second performance of *Macbeth* and described it as 'an excellent model for other prisons' while another guest commented on 'how great to see staff involved' (feedback, 2019). Staff involvement has become an important part of my model for in-prison theatre companies, helping to break down barriers in communication between the two groups, through shared exploration of Shakespeare.

Whilst these positive steps may seem small to those not familiar with the prison estate they are considerable when viewed in context. A Dramatherapist working in the prison volunteered with the group for the *Macbeth* production, performing the role of Director in the triumvirate. Despite having worked with the men for a period of time she noticeably only ever addressed them as Mr. Xxxx, rather than their first name. When she and I discussed this privately she told me that she felt it important to keep boundaries of respect and differentiation which being on first name terms would transgress, a decision I disagreed with but which I respected. She continued to adhere to this personal boundary until the dress rehearsal where she began to call them by their given names. Afterwards she told me that her perception had altered and she saw that although the inmates and I were all on first name terms the respect between us remained high and our philosophy was founded on an equality within the company. The SO who performed with the company gave them explicit permission to call him by his given name during rehearsals, although he was strictly known by the more formal 'Mr'

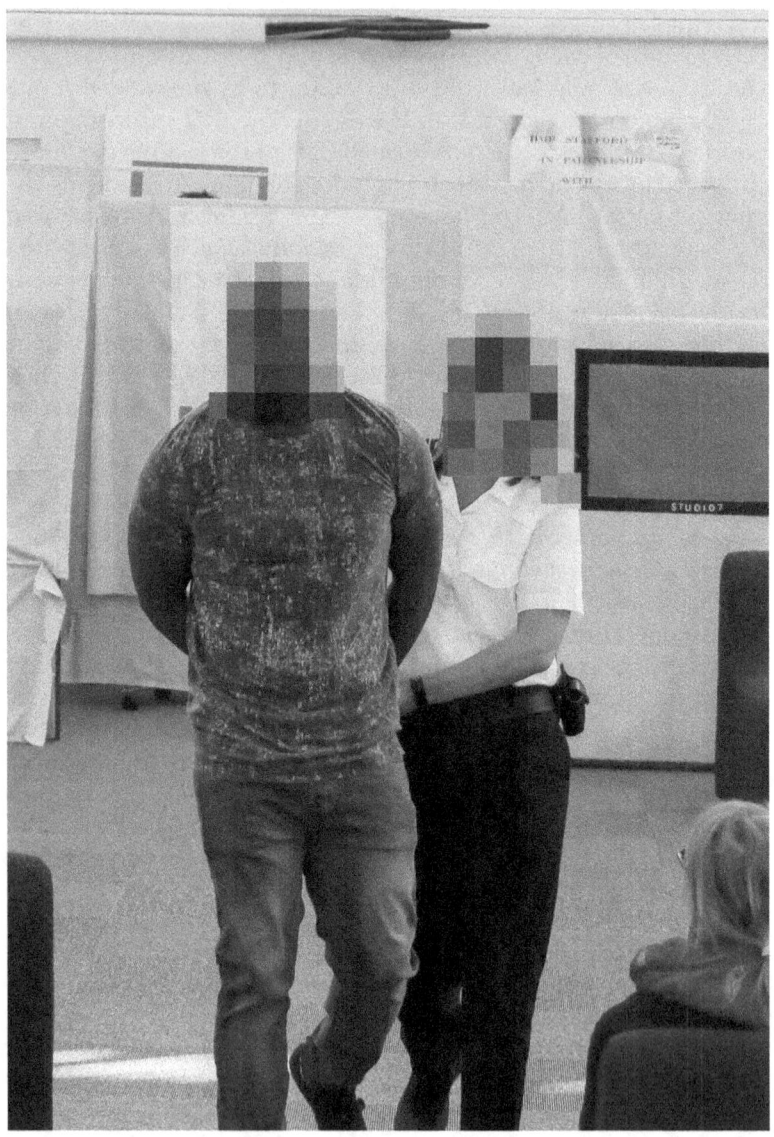

FIGURE 7 *Wade (played by Mark) being arrested by HMPPS Custody Manager, Emergency Shakespeare,* Macbeth *(17 September 2019).* Photo: George Vuckovic Photography.

address outside of those three hours each week. This is indicative of the way in which the dynamics of the group, whilst working towards a common goal of performance, broke down barriers and allowed everyone to feel they had equality of input and their views were given validity and consideration.

The other key element of heterotopia within these performances was the feeling of pride that the actors had of their endeavours, similar to that described earlier within The Gallowfield Players. Richard Tewkesbury describes sex offenders as 'the most despised and publicly discussed social deviants' (2012: p.607) in the opening to his article on the stigmatization of those convicted of sexual offences, a view prevalent across the Western world. When I retweeted HMP Stafford's response to the Covid-19 pandemic of repurposing their sewing workshop to make scrubs for the NHS, one negative reply was 'given that HMP Stafford only houses sex offenders I really don't think fabulous is appropriate in any context that involves those animals' (tweet, 2020). John Braithwaite theorized the shaming of those who have committed an offence as being either reintegrative (temporary censure with an aim to reintegrate the offender back into the community) or disintegrative (which causes societal division and creates outcasts) (1989: p.104). For many the stigma of being convicted of a sexual offence results in disintegrative shaming both within the penal system (if held within a Vulnerable Prisoner Unit rather than a sex offender prison) and upon release, impacting significantly on mental health and confidence. Criminologist Ruth Mann acknowledged that 'sex offenders face considerable public hostility' as 'the harmful, indeed shocking, nature of sex offending dominates public discourse about the people who have committed this type of crime' (2016: pp.260–1) and this prejudicial opinion often erodes any level of personal confidence and self-worth these individuals may have had.

The men within the company were very mindful of how they would be judged by society for their offences and Mark in particular spoke with me at length about his fears of hatred by society and the impact on his own self esteem. He is a young man with very supportive familial ties and three of his relatives attended the performance. His mother gave feedback that Emergency Shakespeare 'helps them feel free and normal again' while his sister wrote 'amazing way to showcase talent, talent they didn't know they had, bravo, 100 out of 10!!!!' (feedback, 2019). In the debrief Mark spoke of the way his family 'were so proud and you don't expect someone to be proud of you when you're in prison' (debrief, 2019). Brody's parents commented that they were 'immeasurably proud and moved' by watching him perform in a way which meant they 'saw Shakespeare in a totally different light – Stratford will never be the same!' (feedback, 2019). As psychotherapist James Gilligan describes

> the basic psychological motive, or cause, of violent behaviour is the wish to ward off or eliminate the feeling of shame and humiliation – a feeling that is painful, and can even be intolerable and overwhelming – and the goal of those who feel shame is to replace [shame] with its opposite, the feeling of pride.
> (2001: p.29)

Often this manifests itself through interpersonal violence but this can instead be channelled positively, such as through theatrical performance.

This production offered an opportunity to share their 'extraordinary talent; the play was clever, funny, dramatic; it told a great many stories' (feedback, 2019). The pride on the faces of family and friends was evident and the actors hearing them marvelling at the 'hugely impressive, professional performance' (feedback, 2019) had such a positive impact. Brody wrote that it was 'a massive confidence boost and made me so happy that we have created something that people have enjoyed' (rehearsal diary, 2019). Others explained how they were 'absolutely buzzing after the first production and can't wait for many more' and 'great reaction, it's been a journey and we are going to do it all again – love it!' (Batu & Callum – rehearsal diaries, 2019). This validation through the pride of external visitors was a powerful 'boost to self-esteem and confidence' (Paul – letter to author, 2019) as they appropriated the cultural capital of Shakespeare and shaped it into their own creation, demonstrating to their loved ones that they are more than their offences and that they have much to offer of which they can be proud. The two residents released shortly after this production both planned to attempt to join local drama groups as a way of negotiating their reintegration to society and seeking positive activities where they felt their self-esteem could be rebuilt and which provided the 'vital community spirit' (feedback, 2019) shared within Emergency Shakespeare.

Conclusion

The enacting of Shakespeare with marginalized groups, as performers or audience, elicits heterotopic opportunities as the juxtaposition of the constructed play-world and the abstracted concept of the cultural capital of Shakespeare shows the world to have unexpected possibilities. The demarcated spaces of theatres add gravitas to performances and draw upon the cultural signifiers codified within the architecture of the space. This can add an additional layer of validity; performing words from the most iconic playwright in the canon within a professional theatre evidences that marginalized people are able to assert their rights to access culture. They cannot only *access* the cultural capital of Shakespeare but appropriate it as their own and use it to share their experiences in ways which society can, and often will, choose to engage with. Performances within demarcated spaces allow the opportunity for professional lighting and sound needed for the sensory-aware approach of relaxed performances for those who may find traditional theatre productions overwhelming. They attract a wider audience of mainstream society, including school parties and the general public, allowing the heterotopia to permeate society to some extent. What may have begun as an interest in seeing a marginalized performance out of curiosity can develop into a more profound experience where they 'leave the theatre in a different "headspace"' (Lutterbie, 2020: p.101).

In contrast, the appropriated spaces used by those without access to a theatre may often draw an audience for reasons other than a desire to see a performance: boredom, familial loyalty and rostered work all being major drivers. Initially, the engagement may be less consciously with a piece of theatre-making but the opportunity to allow the unexpected to flourish is significant. The reframing of perceptions, both of self and of others, was a key heterotopic effect of the performances examined. The professional actors who went into Broadmoor realized that the men they were performing for were not the monsters they had previously believed them to be. Inmates in the audience for prison theatre company performances saw their peers using Shakespeare as a bridge between those incarcerated and wider society whilst families and performers often felt shared pride for the first time in years.

Bourdieu's notion of cultural capital permeates the use of Shakespeare with marginalized groups across all types of spaces but nowhere does it resonate more strongly than within performative locations. This is the pinnacle of the outward possession of cultural capital, when those dispossessed by society, and often disenfranchised as a result, are able to actively engage with Shakespeare as a way of demonstrating their ability and their right to access culture often denied to them. John Guillory argues that 'everyone has a right of access to cultural works, to the means of both their production and their consumption' (1993: p.54) but too often the reality is that this is denied through social and cultural exclusion. Involvement in Shakespearean productions, whether as audience or performer, enables many from marginalized groups to take ownership of the spaces in which they are performed, legitimatizing their endeavours through his work. Everyone does have a right to access cultural works and for many the performing of Shakespeare is a way of laying claim to that right which is societally acceptable and in doing so causes a paradigm shift through creating a heterotopia which shows the world to be different to how it appeared previously. These changes may be subtle rather than seismic but they resonate outwards and each performance, perhaps, gives a little more credence to the rights of all to access cultural works.

4

Reflective spaces

In contrast with public performance is the private reflection on Shakespeare which often takes place when people are isolated or dislocated from their community. This chapter considers the use of Shakespeare in a reflective context within three types of space: the physical (inside internment camps or prison cells), the conceptual (the reading of Shakespeare and exercising of imagination) and the social (using Bourdieu's concept of 'habitus' to articulate how Shakespeare can help people transcend their physical restrictions by a sense of belonging within a longer tradition) (1977). The chapter is divided into two sections: individual reflections and reflections on group dynamics – the former being people engaging in a personal capacity with Shakespeare and the latter being those engaged within group activity but reflecting on those activities outside of the sessions. The theoretical framework for this chapter is drawn from Foucault's concept of mirrors as heterotopias, Lefebvre's work on reflection and Deleuze's assertion that difference is a crucial element of individuation as well as Said's reflections on exile. People in traumatic, stressful situations have often used the reflective properties of Shakespeare to develop emotional and intellectual resilience. In this context *reflective* describes how someone uses Shakespeare on an individual basis and how that engagement may lead them to consider themselves and their own experiences in connection to the work they are reading, allowing them to examine their personal circumstances and develop resilience. Historian Anne Dutlinger wrote of the Second World War:

> Individual identity could be reclaimed – albeit momentarily – through art. Art, music and performance transformed fear

into freedom. The act of making art suspended the collective nightmare [...] it helped to sustain hope, a sense of self, and the will to live.

(2001: p.5)

Shakespeare, particularly, offers those experiencing isolation a methodology for reflecting their current circumstances but also engaging with something which has a cultural history strong enough to offer comfort that life will continue beyond their current experiences. Cultural history is an elusive term to define, with Alessandro Arcangeli acknowledging 'there is no agreement [...] upon the definition' (2011: p.3) but my interpretation is that it connects the concepts of place within society with the longevity of historical context. Shakespeare's influence on philosophers, academics, authors and thinkers is widely known and disseminated but there is little literature considering the way in which Shakespeare is used as a mechanism for private reflection with those from marginalized echelons of society. Through reflecting on Shakespeare's characters and narratives many individuals are able to connect with humanity at times when circumstances and practicalities may render interpersonal connections difficult or impossible.

Reflective uses of Shakespeare can provide solace, self-contemplation and a source of external strength during challenging times and whilst people are contained within liminal spaces. His work also allowed people to develop a sense of personal agency through their engagement with this cultural capital whilst they were oppressed by circumstances. A number of those whose experiences are examined in this chapter appeared to draw core strength from the connection with this canonical literature which their marginalization did not preclude. Whilst their physical freedom was restricted, there is a sense that Shakespeare allowed them mental freedom and formed a way for them to link with an ongoing narrative outside of their situation. This helped to locate them socially along a temporal continuum which would continue beyond their circumstances. This was a way of combatting the temporal vertigo which can often arise in such situations, a sense of time distorting and disorientating reality. I will consider both those for whom societal dislocation is a temporary yet instantaneous event, such as prisoners of war and those for whom marginalization and ostracization from mainstream society are an ongoing issue, such as those incarcerated or with mental health issues (albeit many people with mental health issues may not self-identify as marginalized).

Foucault describes mirrors as heterotopic: their physical existence 'exerts a sort of counteraction on the position that I occupy' (1984). During periods of solitude Shakespeare's work can function as both a mirror in which personal experiences are reflected and also a focal point into which the attention of the individual is diverted in considered contemplation. This mirrored image engages the brain in consideration of narratives and circumstances outside of the immediate situation, allowing people to develop resilience through reframing their situation as temporarily to be endured. Lefebvre asserts that:

> reflection pierces the surface and penetrates the depth of the relationship between repetition and difference .... When the mirror is 'real' as is constantly the case in the realm of objects, the space in the mirror is imaginary .... In a living body, on the other hand, where the mirror of reflection is imaginary, the *effect* is real.
>
> (1991: p.182)

Drawing on this concept, I argue that reflections on Shakespeare can be used to pierce the surface of *otherness* and to allow penetration of the relationship between self and society. I develop Lefebvre's argument that a real mirror produces an illusory reflection whilst the imaginary mirror of reflection that we, as humans, use to consider the world we see produces a perceptible effect. Often the use of Shakespeare by someone who is marginalized allows them to effect tangible changes to their own perceptions of their relationship to society. Reflecting on one's currently restricted space but reading through the lens of Shakespeare allows people to reassess their conceptual space and their sense of self. David Schalkwyk described this in relation to the passages selected by inmates on Robben Island:

> these people, at a particular point, saw in Shakespeare's words some kind of mirror of themselves. So, you're sitting in your prison

cell, you read the play and it seems to speak to you. Thirty years later, under a completely different set of circumstances, you're no longer the same person, and so, you don't see yourself in the mirror of the words that you've actually chosen. A fascinating reflection on the nature of human identity.

(podcast, 2014)

I believe that reflection also allows contemplation of difference and similarity. Deleuze argues that difference is an intrinsic part of individuation and that far from being a judgement of how one thing does not resemble another, difference is a productive and essential part of individuation (1994: p.28). The argument that it is through difference that beings, species and objects create their identity is particularly significant for those marginalized by society. The opportunity to use Shakespeare in a reflective capacity allows individuals to consider similarities and differences between themselves and characters but also wider humanity, enabling them to draw emotional sustenance from the narratives. This can form the basis of developing resilience which allows their difference to become a part of their individuation whilst also allowing them to contextualize themselves amongst the long tradition of those who have engaged with Shakespeare.

Literary scholar Edward W. Said describes exile as 'the unhealable rift forced between a human being and a native place' (2000: p.173) and explores the association between nationalism (with its overriding notions of belonging) and exile, its diametric opposite (a displacement which cannot be easily reconciled). As Rehnuma Sazzad articulates both Said and Foucault were exiles to some degree but their reaction to this phenomenon was very different: Foucault saw the potential for emancipation through his 'exilic intellectualism' whilst Said spoke out 'against imprisoning ideologies in a decisive and articulate way' (2008: p.4). Said links exile to Bourdieu's notion of '*habitus,* the coherent amalgam of practices linking habit with inhabitance' (2008: p.176) in the sense that habitus is the embodiment of achieved nationalism, the antithesis of exile, a deep sense of belonging. I build on this to argue that the emotional dislocation embodied by exile, in many ways shares significant similarities with those marginalized within society. Said's description that 'in a very acute sense exile is a solitude experienced outside the group' (2008: p.177) reflects the experiences of those who are rejected by mainstream society whether through mental ill-health, learning disabilities, other reasons for ostracization or the physical separation from their familial group as a result of incarceration. Said asserts that:

> The literature about exile objectifies an anguish and a predicament most people rarely experience first-hand; but to think of the exile informing this literature as beneficially humanistic is to banalize its mutilations, the losses it inflicts on those who suffer them, the muteness with which it responds to any attempt to understand it as "good for us".
>
> (2008: p.174)

Shakespeare can be an alternative language of communication for those unable to find words to describe their isolation and dislocation from society.

Reflective engagements with Shakespeare are, by their nature, difficult to capture and are reliant upon the individual's sharing of the impacts, complete with the intrinsic vagaries and nuances that entails. I have divided the contemplative activities within this chapter into two sub-sections as each is subtly different; those where the reflection is individualistic in nature and those where it is intrinsically linked to a larger group dynamic. In the former the individual may be using Shakespeare as a way of occupying their mind, passing time, making sense of the world or exercising their creative impulses, largely on an individual basis, although these explorations may be shared with others when possible. I will also consider those who engage with Shakespeare in a group setting then reflect on that in their own time, combining the characters, narrative and language of Shakespeare with their perceptions of the wider programme they are involved in. The demarcation between these two ways of using Shakespeare reflectively is important, as in the first the engagement is largely individualistic whilst the latter reflects not just on Shakespeare but on the wider social aspects.

Theatre in places and times of conflict has attracted increased interest over recent years, stemming from Augusto Boal's work in 1970s civil-war ridden Argentina where he developed his Theatre of the Oppressed principles to engender conflict resolution (Boal, 2008). Boal writes that:

> *Empathy* is the emotional relationship which is established between the character and the spectator and which provokes, fundamentally, a delegation of power on the part of the spectator, who becomes an object in relation to the character: whatever happens to the latter, happens vicariously to the spectator.
> (2008: p.84)

He contrasted the unidirectional nature of professional theatre where the audience passively receives from the actors with the dialogic nature of spectators who may intervene as well as observing. I believe that in addition to this, empathetic power can exist between an individual and the text when there is no performative or theatrical element involved. Returned citizen, Michael Shortt commented that 'it is people in prison who really have time to sit with the text and focus on it' (Shortt – interview, 2020), recalling his own engagement with Shakespeare during his custodial sentence. I think this *sitting with* and reflecting on the text on a personal basis is extremely powerful, often in a different but no lesser way than engaging in rehearsals or watching a performance.

James Thompson, founder of 'In Place of War' which researches and funds arts programmes in conflict zones, is influenced by Boal's work, asserting that he himself is 'a practitioner who writes not a theoretician who practices' (Thompson, 2005: p.8). He articulates the complexity of the ethical considerations of external practitioners working 'with vulnerable communities' and that the 'digging up of stories' (Thompson, 2005: p.39) is exploitative and oppressive more often than liberating and affirmative. His nuanced and pragmatic approach to the ethics of working with marginalized communities has been influential on my own work as a practitioner. I consciously try to avoid imposing my own cultural references on those I work with and strive to ensure the development of each group happens organically and is not facilitator-led. Thompson examines the concepts of 'discipline and play' and the extent to which discipline (frequently seen as a form of subjugation as a result of Foucault's work) is often offered as a positive in the context of the 'discipline of learning the arts' in places 'where there has been intense disruption' (Thompson, 2005: p.173).

Individual Reflections

Internment camps

Ton Hoenselaars's archival research demonstrates that Shakespeare featured relatively widely across the first and second world wars within refugee, internment and prisoner of war camps throughout Europe, and it is reasonable to assume that this engagement spread even more widely with many instances not recorded. Hoenselaars primarily focuses on performances but acknowledges the 'more personal, private engagement' of George Beringer, W.E. Swale and Countess Karolina Lanckorońska (2019: p.15). Lanckorońska wrote detailed diaries of her time in exile as a prisoner of war during the Second World War and the challenges and dispensations her social standing as Polish nobility afforded her. She gained her PhD in 1936 in the History of Art and acknowledges in her diary that she had read Shakespeare before internment but the impact it had during her imprisonment was profound, 'it [was] as though [she] had never before heard of Shakespeare' (2005: p.168). Deleuze's theory that repetition is impossible as each time we experience something we ourselves are different, is evidenced succinctly here. In Lanckorońska's prologue, written in 1998, the Countess described the diaries to be 'a report and only a report of what I witnessed' and she was commended for her 'dispassionate objectivity, intelligence and restraint' (Anonymous review, 2006: p.272). In direct contravention of Said's claim that 'willfulness, exaggeration, overstatement [...] are characteristic styles of being an exile' (2000: p.182), dispassionate objectivity is a hallmark of her diaries. She intended publication posthumously, although she finally consented to it during her final year of life. She documents the atrocities committed against her fellow prisoners, and her stoic commitment to expose the murders of Lwow professors, with calmness and lucidity (Yones, 2004: p.96). However, that objectivity seems to be put aside when she enthuses that her 'sensitivity to an artistic masterpiece has decidedly increased' (2005: p.168) and she quotes lines of Shakespeare which she relates to her circumstances and frame of mind, as outlined later.

In Lacki Street Prison, Lanckorońska was imprisoned in 'total, absolute isolation' (2005: p.165) for many months with the exception of her weekly trips to the showers where she struck up an exchange of knowledge with Tymon (the water-controller); she gave him scholarly knowledge and in return he passed on the political news he gleaned from others. During the isolation a combination of her religious faith and her intellectual interests appeared to have sustained her and she used the time to read Shakespeare and other canonical works and to begin her planned monograph on Michelangelo. Returning to Lefebvre's quotation from the start of the chapter that 'reflection pierces the surface and penetrates the depth of the relationship between repetition and difference' (1991: p.182), Lanckorońska used Shakespeare in this way during her internment. Her memoirs quote directly from the only exercise book of her notes which survived until her liberation. She often began her entry with a literary quotation upon which she reflected, the first being Richard II's speech 'I have been studying how I may compare| This prison where I live unto the world' and 'no thought is contented' (2005: pp.161–2 quoting *Richard II* 5.5.1–2, 5.5.11). These were the first lines written yet she dismissed their relevance as she 'cannot say that they apply to [her] own thoughts. Many thoughts of [hers *were*] *contented*' (2005: p.162). The choice of prison metaphor was an obvious one given her solitary confinement but she used Shakespeare's words to consciously frame her own positivity that 'a period of forced meditation and concentration has begun' (Lanckorońska, 2005: p.162). She specifically selected this passage as the first words of the book, against which to consider her feelings, suggesting that she was comparing the two in order to highlight and substantiate the difference. Her usage of Shakespeare appears to have enabled her to reflect on both her cultural experiences prior to internment and also her currently restricted existence.

She had received the complete works of Shakespeare a week prior and found the experience of reading it to be significant, liberally peppering her diary with quotations. Although she wrote that she had read several other works during this period (she was allowed to order books in acknowledgement of her nobility), it is to Shakespeare she returned frequently, quoting from *Richard II*, *Julius Caesar* and *King Lear*. The morning after she had heard the brutalization of the Jewish women by Schutzstaffel (SS) officers, an aural cacophony of 'shrieks and wails from the women and children. ... laughter and wild bellowing from the SS' (2005: p.167), she quoted Edgar's line 'What, in ill-thoughts again'. This line, written in large letters and doubly underlined for emphasis, was followed by Martial's *Epigrams* 10.47*'supremum nec metuas diem nec optes'* (neither fear death nor desire it the highest) and the explanation that she feared not death but she loved life more intensely than previously. No explicit rationale was given for this opinion but it appears that the fragility of life she witnessed reinforced her desire to survive the atrocities she was enduring and to continue to live her life, once freed in the future. She ended this very short diary entry with Caesar's speech:

> Of all the wonders that I have yet heard
> It seems to me most strange that men should fear
> Seeing that death, a necessary end
> Will come when it will come.
>
> *(Julius Caesar* 2.2.34–7)

In contrast with Schalkwyk's theory that one may see oneself in the mirror of Shakespeare during isolation but thirty years later the circumstances would have altered (Shalkwyk – podcast, 2014) and the mirror changed, Lanckorońska faithfully recollected these images in her memoirs published almost 60 years later.

It seems reasonable to assume that she chose those two quotations and her snippet of commentary about the preciousness of life in direct response to the abuse she had heard the previous night. She avoided sentimentalism about the atrocities and made no further mention of the abuse suffered that night by the 'Jew-girls' (2005: p.167) but she seemed to use Shakespeare's words to express what she struggled to articulate herself about the bleakness of her thoughts but the extent to which this had made life more tangibly precious. As van der Kolk explains, 'even years later traumatised people often have enormous difficulty telling other people what has happened to them [...], [their] feelings are almost impossible to articulate' (2015: p.43). Shakespeare often provides a way for people to find the words to express themselves when they are otherwise struggling, a voice they can speak when their own is too traumatized. Lanckorońska's marginalization was the direct result of her internment although she personally did not lack communication in the sense of her intellect and educational level. Hoenselaars writes 'Lanckorońska started a culture not only of reading and re-inventing Shakespeare, but also of quoting Shakespeare, to reflect the situation she was in' (2011: p.92). Whilst it may not be strictly accurate that she *started* a culture, which can be traced back to the Romantics who frequently quoted Shakespeare as a way of defending their 'human sympathy' (Ortiz, 2013: p.112), it is true that she continued the tradition throughout her internment.

Hoenselaars describes Lanckorońska as 'countering the barbarism of the day with daily quotations from a deified author' (Hoenselaars et al. – Maxwell & Rumbold, 2018: p.174), which is something of an exaggeration of the frequency of the quotations and imbues Shakespeare with a centrality to Lanckorońska's mental survival which is insufficiently evidenced. There is no doubt that she drew on Shakespeare regularly but not in exclusivity and she did not quote his works daily. During her time at Ravensbrück a 'great delight' arrived at the camp – an English language *Complete Works of Shakespeare*, brought from Auschwitz – which she quickly claimed as her own, secreting it in her mattress and loaning it out as required, although it is unclear how many interned women could read English. Her assertion that even on days when she lacked time or energy to read the volume 'for us the mere awareness that *King Lear* or *Richard II* was with us was proof that the world still existed' (2005: p.269) demonstrates the inherent value she placed in these works. *King Lear* and *Richard II* have exile and estrangement as central themes whilst *Julius Caesar* focuses on political turmoil and all three deal 'with issues of freedom, the fall of dictatorships and the horrors of war' (Seller, 2001: p.136) which seems to explain their regular appearances in her diary.

She described 'one great source of strength, which constantly gained intensity – that was the ever growing need to escape into the realm of intellectual riches' (2005: p.269), citing the ability she and her fellow prisoners felt to draw sustenance from Shakespeare and other works to support their mental resilience. In many ways it appears that Lanckorońska used the sharing of Shakespeare and other topics on which she delivered lectures as a coping mechanism to allow her to develop an element of personal agency in a world where she possessed so little control. Van der Kolk argues that 'resilience is the product of agency: knowing that what you do can make a difference' (2015: p.355) and I believe that the ability to share 'intellectual riches' acted as a coping mechanism for the Countess. She acknowledged that her reception of Shakespeare was not a repetition of her previous reading of it, as she herself comments 'it [was] as though [she] had never before heard of Shakespeare' (2005: p.168). She does not explain this changed reading of Shakespeare but it seems logical that her exposure to extreme violence and deprivation enabled her to identify more deeply with those characters she quoted, who themselves experienced severe political turmoil and exile from their own habitus.

This changed interpretation of reading Shakespeare is also mentioned by actors in The Gallowfield Players who comment 'when it comes to Shakespeare I can truly say I am like a wide-eyed child despite having looked at his works at school and college' (Michael, 2019) and 'I never fully understood the words of Macbeth until now' (Miguel, 2018). As reading reflects personal experiences it is logical that when we live through extreme circumstances our perceptions alter. The emotional dislocation of Lanckoroñska's exile was intense and underscored by the abuse she witnessed of her peer group, yet she used Shakespeare and other texts in an almost-religious sense to sustain her and to give her words when she was unable to find them. She describes the appearance of a copy of the text as a 'miracle' and muses that 'the whole world is probably created so as to enable genius to interact with creation' (2005: p.168), using language evocative of images of the Old Testament Book of Genesis' story of creation. These words formed a record in her diary, leaving a legacy to ensure the suffering endured did not remain unacknowledged.

Robben Island

Shakespeare was also read by political prisoners on Robben Island, South Africa. The claims regarding the centrality of the 'Robben Island Bible' (a Complete Works of Shakespeare) to the mental survival of the political prisoners are widespread but partially contested. As David Schalkwyk explores in *Hamlet's Dreams*, the truth was somewhat more complex and the widespread nature of Shakespearean appreciation less prevalent than some assert (Shalkwyk, 2012). Sonny Venkatrathnam owned a copy of *The Complete Works of Shakespeare* during his time in the prison and shortly before his departure he asked a number of prisoners to each sign beside a passage they felt was relevant to them. Schalkwyk challenges the claims of Anders Hallengren, Anthony Sampson and Tom Lodge about the extent to which Shakespeare was the 'common culture and text' (2012: p.13) within the prison given that evidence of circulation extended only to a few dozen prisoners. There is an evident desire to predicate the narrative that Shakespeare was the common cultural currency within the prison although evidence suggests engagement with his work was in reality more individual and less commonplace.

Ashwin Desai's *Reading Revolution* was endorsed by Verne Harris of the Nelson Mandela Foundation as 'troubling dominant narratives about Robben Island in this magisterial work' (2014). It utilized the lens that Shakespeare was an important bastion of political commentary used throughout their incarceration and upon release, focusing on the signatures in Venkatrathnam's text, described as 'chosen hauntingly' and 'point[ing] to a deeper understanding' (Desai, 2014: pp.21–2). Neville Alexander is quoted as saying:

> 'When to the sessions of sweet silent thought, I summon up remembrance of things past' – when you look at a sonnet like that, it is exactly what you are doing in prison all the time. You are constantly reflecting on your life, on what's happened and of course you couldn't say it more beautifully in a sense, you couldn't describe that act of remembering more beautifully than Shakespeare.
>
> (2014: p.103)

Alexander is consciously using Shakespeare as a tool to reflect on the life he had experienced prior to imprisonment and how Shakespeare provided eloquent language for remembrance of the past. This aligns with my theory that Shakespeare can provide a way of enduring hardship through drawing on sense of permanence provided by the cultural capital. The physical space of confinement was tempered by using Shakespeare to reflect on the situation but also the social space to which he connected them.

It is evident that for some, including Venkatrathnam and Kathrada, Shakespeare was a way of escaping from the monotonous hardships of prison and of reflecting their political opinions. Schalkwyk argues that some 'found in Shakespeare a source of vitality, reflection, creativity and personal identity' (2012: p.16). That it brought solace to Venkatrathnam seems evident and he himself signed the title page of the book, demonstrating his ownership of the entire volume. In an interview with Matthew Hahn, Venkatrathnam chose Lady Macbeth's speech 'all the perfumes of Arabia will not sweeten this little hand' to reflect that:

> Apartheid is done to the people of South Africa and just like Lady Macbeth this system cannot be purified [...] It means that the damage that is done by the system of apartheid cannot be repaid.
>
> (Vetter – TV, 2014)

His choice was intended to enable people to understand a set of oppressive political constraints which would otherwise be unfathomable to many who had not endured the regime.

Much has been made of Venkatrathnam's openly acknowledged interest in Shakespeare, including his text twice being displayed in England. The Royal Shakespeare Company advertised one of these exhibitions, stating that:

> The 'Bible' was passed between inmates during the 1970s, all of whom treasured the book and each signed their favourite passages with initials and a date. The book was signed a total of 32 times by prisoners, who highlighted passages and quotes that they found meaningful and profound. They now offer us an insight into how the words of Shakespeare resonated with these men who were imprisoned for campaigning for an equal South Africa.
>
> (RSC website)

Hahn's play *The Robben Island Shakespeare* also endorses this view through its specific focus on the role of Shakespeare during their time on the island and is based on interviews with survivors, but heavily influenced by Hahn's desire to create a work which centralized Shakespeare (Hahn, 2017).

Kseniya Filinova-Bruton, Educape Managing Director, described that 'as far as we know prisoners were discussing Shakespeare, discussing the plays and sonnets, reciting it'

(Mtongana – producer, 2014). Whilst his plays, characters and narratives do feature in accounts of the apartheid years, it is evident that these were not widespread communal activities but a relatively few individuals who drew on his words as a way of reflecting on the 'rightness, wrongness, beauty and ugliness of our actions' (Williams-Smith & Somers-Hall, 2012: p.36) whilst they were imprisoned in a terrible exile within their own country. The memoirs of Nelson Mandela, Robert Sobukwe and Ahmed Kathrada make mention of Shakespeare but do not suggest his works were central to life on the island. Whilst Desai's book draws heavily on the Shakespearean connection for the title, the text describes the wider educational initiatives amongst the prisoners, which earned the prison the description 'Our University' following the inmates successfully taking the prison to court over their right to education (Desai, 2014: p.56). Marcus Soloman acknowledged 'Shakespeare was important at the time because his writings covered such a wide range of experiences and emotions' (Desai, 2014: p.58) through which readers could reflect their own experiences, but it is important to note that he includes a much broader selection of writers including Tolstoy, Zola and Shirer; Shakespeare was one source of intellectual stimulation but certainly not the sole source.

The 'Robben Island Bible' with its famous signatures is less significant as a cultural icon within the history of apartheid than it may appear. The signatures were added at the request of Venkatrathnam prior to his leaving the island, not some deeply thought out response to the impact of Shakespeare but a memento for him to take with him as he left the prison. A number of the signatories later claimed they remembered no importance in the passages they signed, and Kathrada spoke in a news article of the inaccuracy of the claims of its centrality to life on the island during the struggles (Schalkwyk, 2012: pp.19–20). So, whilst some may have encouraged the perception that Shakespeare was a communal activity in the prison, it is likely it was a more individualistic, personal contemplation on their situation. As Collette Gordon documents 'the story of the Robben Island Bible writes itself [...] it suited the mood and intellectual agenda of the Mbeki years'(Gordon – Sullivan & Prescott, 2015: p.210), suggesting that memories are flawed and often constructed retrospectively, refracting reality to align with current opinions.

English prisons during Covid-19

The global pandemic of Covid-19 had a significant impact on prison regimes within the UK and many other countries. The Public Health England response to the outbreak led to the issuance of a HMPPS Instruction on 24 March 2020 which stated that all visits, education and the majority of activities were to be suspended to minimize the risk of infection within a prison estate which was at 97 per cent capacity at the start of the pandemic (Moore, 2020). This was part of a series of measures designed to curtail the spread and which also included the introduction of regime changes to enable 2 metre social-distancing (as far as possible), Protective Isolation Units (PIUs) for those who were symptomatic, Shielding Units (SUs) for those identified as vulnerable and Reverse Cohorting Units (RCUs) to quarantine new receptions or inter-prison transfer cases (albeit transfers were suspended where possible). The Government announced that this was to be combined with the release of 4,000 prisoners who were nearing the end of their sentences and assessed to be low risk against stringent risk assessment criteria (automatically excluded were those sentenced for violent or sexual offences), in order to create additional space to facilitate the requisite distancing measures (MoJ, 2020). In a well-publicized failure to achieve this, only thirty-three individuals were released in the first six weeks of the lockdown period, with the plans suspended due to six prisoners being wrongly released (all of whom returned compliantly to custody). This saw the Howard League and Penal Reform Trust implement the Pre-action Protocol for Judicial Review although they later ceased this action as a result of their satisfaction with the Government response (*Judicial Review*, 2020). The end-of-custody temporary release scheme (ECTR) was then reinstated temporarily but permanently suspended in August having released only 275 people (MoJ, August 2020). The population of 80,827 incarcerated individuals in England and Wales (as of 1 May 2020 – *Prison Population Figures*) were spending upwards of twenty-three hours per day in their cells, unlocked only for food, showers, limited exercise and access to phones in a concerted effort to limit the transference of Covid-19.

This against a backdrop of already rapidly increasing instances of self-harm (61,461 incidents September 2018 to September 2019, an increase of 16 per cent on the previous twelve months) and the knowledge that family connections and purposeful activity are key tenets of mental well-being for many whilst incarcerated (MoJ *Safer Custody Statistics*, 2020). Prisons faced staffing issues as frontline workers were forced to self-isolate if they or household members displayed symptoms or advised to shield if they were vulnerable. Third sector organizations working within the prison estate suffered uncertainty around suspended services and delayed contract decisions. Many sectors including the arts industry were significantly impacted by the pandemic and the decision to close theatres, music venues and galleries, and prohibit public gatherings meant for many creatives their sources of income shrunk significantly or ceased completely; artists and facilitators faced an uncertain period.

The suspension of my physical presence in prisons prompted me to consider how I might continue the work remotely with those in the theatre companies, through written communication. These correspondence activities would not be solely a reflection on Shakespeare for the actors but also their emotional connection to the group and will be considered later in the chapter. These activities led me to create Activity Packs for the wider prison population aimed at encouraging people to engage with Shakespeare as an individualistic activity, and which are analysed here. The packs were designed for people who may have had no prior experience of Shakespeare and used the narratives of the plays as a base from which to encourage creative responses. Creating materials for such large volumes of people I did not know was very different to the tailored work with the theatre companies where the activities were nuanced to account for personal strengths and preferences. The assumption had to be that many receiving Activity Packs would not be familiar with Shakespeare and would simply be seeking something to occupy their mind for a period of time. The materials were shared across all UK prisons through the central Quantum system and inclusion within the Prisoner Learning Alliance In-Cell Activity Hub. Through word-of-mouth recommendation these were also made available to other organizations supporting groups of society including but not limited to, social services, children separated from their birth families, youth custody services, Violence Reduction Units and community library services. I was also asked by Central Safer Custody Services to work collaboratively with them to contribute to their weekly newsletter for the prison estate, producing a one-page activity aligned with their chosen weekly topic which included subjects such as knowledge, healthy relationships and inner peace.

The Activity Packs were created at three levels to account for differing literacy and proficiency with English as a written language. 62% of people entering prison are assessed as having a reading age of eleven or below, based on the last comprehensive study, whilst foreign national prisoners account for 11% of the population, although there are no publicly available statistics on the number for whom English is not their primary language (Department for Business Innovation and Skills, 2012; The Bell Foundation, 2019). The packs were not calibrated to any formal educational development tool but broadly speaking attempted to address the needs of inmates across the spectrum, using my own knowledge from years of working in prisons.

- Level 1 used simple single or double-syllable words only, short sentences and stories summarized in typically six–eight sentences, inviting a combination of creative, artistic responses such as drawing video game characters and cartoon strips with the opportunity for some simple written answers (such as text message responses).

FIGURE 8 *Richard's illustration of the two Dromios for inclusion in* The Comedy of Errors *Activity Packs during Covid-19 (May 2020). Courtesy of Richard.*

- Level 2 was aimed broadly at those whose literacy levels would allow them to read a newspaper or similar; the synopses were slightly more detailed and the activities invited creative visual and written responses, including creating newspaper articles, short dialogue exchanges and insult generators.
- Level 3 was aimed at those with higher levels of literacy and encouraged participants to engage with Shakespeare's language through creating their own modern translations, writing poetry and a range of other written activities.

The first of the Safer Custody newsletters included an introduction from me and guidance on the differing types of packs so that inmates could self-select the appropriate level.

I received a limited amount of inmate feedback (which was to be expected given the circumstances) along with anecdotal feedback from prison staff. The staff feedback was positive with responses such as 'I got goosebumps reading them, could work to express internal dialogue, very, very clever' and 'thank you so much for your support and creativity on behalf of our men' (emails from various prisons, 2020). The Prisoners' Education Trust requested permission to use my materials based on *The Tempest* as their contribution to *Inside Times,* which has an estimated circulation of 60,000 inmates, as they felt it was 'the perfect fit' for the needs of prisoners during this period (Walker – email, 2020).

The activities were designed to encourage participants to engage in a wide range of activities, linking Shakespeare's characters and narratives to external interests they may already have, such as electronic gaming, technology and puzzles. Shakespeare's language was used sparingly, being mindful of Guy Cook's pedagogy that 'when presented within the spirit of the play, we can tolerate and indeed enjoy ambiguous and unusual language' (Cook – Winston, 2015: p.78) which is borne out in rehearsal room techniques but less true with stand-alone activities. It was also important to strike a balance between encouraging them to use Shakespeare reflectively whilst not instigating any emotional triggers which they would be unequipped to deal with during the restricted regime. During group activities it has been possible to address deeper-seated emotional issues within the supportive framework of the

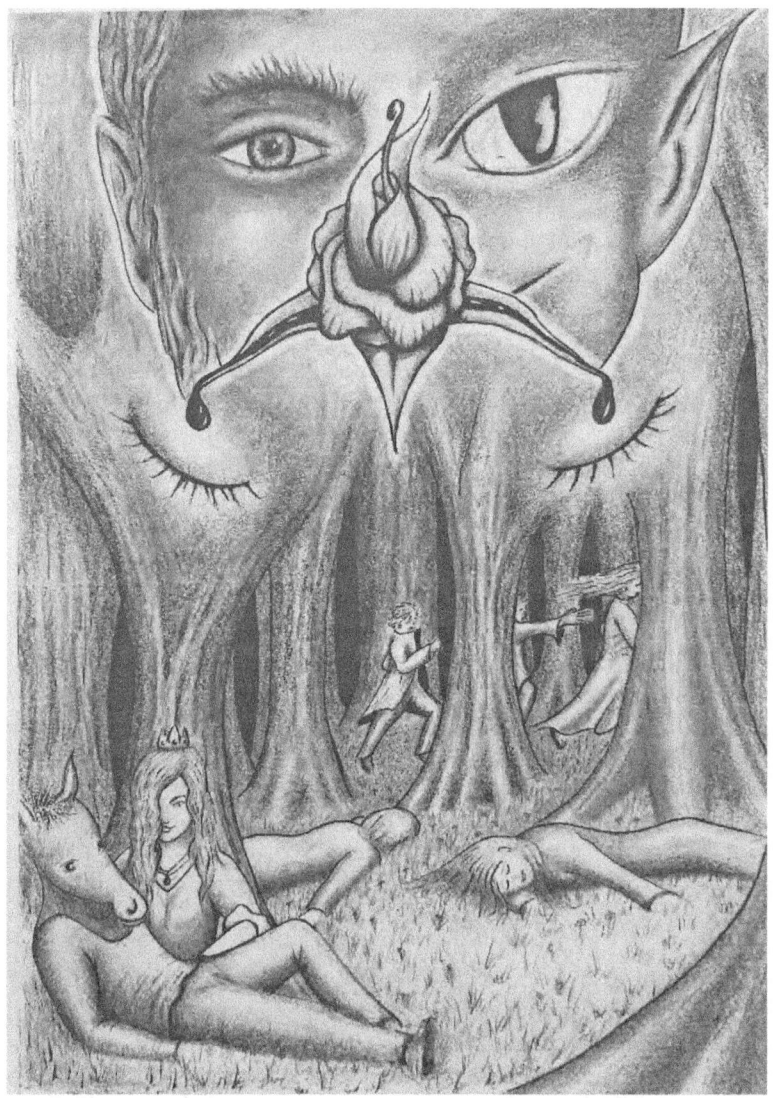

FIGURE 9 Brody's illustration of A Midsummer Night's Dream *for inclusion in the Activity Packs during Covid-19 (April 2020), which won him a Koestler Commended Award, 2020. Courtesy of Brody.*

company but whilst people were isolated it was important to avoid any inadvertent triggers, a topic I discussed with Occupational Therapist Deborah Murphy in relation to how to deal with the theme of suicide in *Romeo and Juliet* (Murphy – email, 2020). The *Romeo and Juliet* packs focused not on death but on the elements of love, families and friendship alliances. Many activities across various plays encouraged participants to think about the feelings and perceptions of multiple characters to develop their empathy and ability to understand the views of others, for example; how did Rosalind and her father feel when they were reunited and how did Desdemona and Othello respectively experience their journey to Cyprus as separated newly weds? There were also activities which asked for reflection on times when they have been asked to do something they were uncomfortable with and the emotional turmoil this engendered; for example, using Cassio's being pressured by Iago to drink more than he wanted prior to the altercation with Roderigo.

Activities within the packs such as writing newspaper articles enabled them to explore the extent to which the media determines the perspective through which events are refracted, a topic many of them have personal experience of from their own arrest and sentencing. This subject was initially raised during a Gallowfield Players rehearsal where the actors explained the extent to which they felt inaccurate portrayal around the time of their arrest and sentencing had adversely impacted their loved ones. This was not quantified or explored for legitimacy but was a noting of their perception and was incorporated into *Sycorax's Storm* (a prequel to *The Tempest,* written by Michael specifically for The Gallowfield Player's) where the prologue proclaims:

> The stories we know are only chapters within much larger tales, wheels within wheels, part of something more or indeed something less. What we think we know is often shrouded by a cloak of disinformation and half- truths, recorded by those with an agenda. The subtext to a larger story or a completely different narrative. A sequel to what we believe to be written in stone or the prequel to an established tale.
>
> The malicious intent visited upon the wretched Caliban, itself, is only one chapter of his story. Prospera would have us believe his servitude is justified but if we draw back from the tale of

Prospera's deliverance a more complex, broader narrative can be seen. Ages old perspectives then questioned when a hero can be seen as a villain and a villain vindicated.

Join us as we open a different set of pages in the twisted tale of Prospera and Caliban.

(Michael, 2020)

Within the Activity Packs, the focus on characters provided 'dramatic distancing' (Jennings, 1992: p.17), preventing the reflection being insistently personal; they could choose to complete the activity at a fictional level or to consider the similarities to their own lives, depending on their willingness to engage with self-reflection. This has been evidenced strongly in rehearsals which provide 'the opportunity to express ourselves in ways that are safe' (Michael, 2019) but the packs were created bearing in mind there was no support network available during the pandemic lockdown and that the packs were being made available across the prison estate for men and women I did not know.

As an Alumnus from the Shakespeare Prison Project explains of the process of exploring a role, 'you begin by examining the emotional needs of the characters using the script and then start to extrapolate that back to your own life' and this same approach is used with the actors in my theatre companies and which the Activity Packs were designed to replicate, albeit to a more superficial degree (Williams – interview, 2020). Feedback from inmates about the packs suggests this was achieved as they explained 'it allowed me to be somewhere else' and 'I focused on other things and relaxed' (inmate feedback, 2020). As van der Kolk writes:

Projecting your inner world into the three-dimensional space of a structure enables you to see what's happening in the theatre of your mind and gives you a much clearer perspective on your reactions to people and events in the past.

(2015: p.299)

These activities utilized not the three-dimensional space of the physical world but the infinite dimensions of the play-world where the characters can help to provide perspective and to allow exploration of alternative thought-processes and opinions without participants having to commit themselves to making them personal.

FIGURE 10 *Richard's illustration of Henry V for inclusion in the* Henry V *Activity Packs during Covid-19 (June 2020). Courtesy of Richard.*

Whilst feedback was limited it came from a variety of prisons with differing demographics of prisoner and therefore provided a useful insight into the effectiveness of the packs. Extrapolation of this feedback, combined with the deeper analysis of how others have engaged with prolonged theatre activities, suggests that there is significant benefit in the Activity Packs, allowing participants to connect with the world outside of their cell in a meaningful way. The measure of success in this work was providing a creative outlet which enabled the participant to cope more productively with the regime, which was evidenced through feedback such as 'I enjoy creative writing and this really helped' (inmate feedback, 2020). However, for some it went beyond a pleasant diversion from the monotony of their cell with reports of men in shared cells working collaboratively with their cell mates, giving them the opportunity to find some common ground and develop shared interests. Another reported 'I spoke to my son about it, which was nice' (inmate feedback, 2020); family connections are a powerful support function for those incarcerated. During the extraordinary regime all visits were suspended and phone calls restricted so enabling of positive connections with a child was significant. To this end a number of prisons have stated their intention to stock these Packs in the Visits Hall and to signpost families to them for this specific purpose. The theatre company actors have 'frequent conversations' (Wayne's family – conversation, 2020) with their families, sharing detail about the work while Michael described with jocularity 'oh how the mighty do fall – an anti-establishment punk to a Shakespeare nerd' (correspondence, 2020), recounting the teasing from his children for requesting Shakespeare books for his birthday. The Activity Packs offered an opportunity for strengthening familial connections during a time of intense isolation and uncertainty.

One inmate commented that it was a positive reminder of school which supports my belief that Shakespeare can be used to engage those who may otherwise be unwilling to engage with formal educational programmes. This type of activity encouraged personal agency in the most challenging of prison regimes and it was significant that individuals used these to reflect on their own lives and think about the value education could bring.

The potential benefits of materials which encourage people to reflect on their place in cultural history and to exercise their creativity

FIGURE 11 *Brody's illustration for inclusion in the* Julius Caesar *Activity Packs (May 2020). Courtesy of Brody.*

FIGURE 12 *Richard's illustration of Titania and Bottom for inclusion in the* A Midsummer Night's Dream *Activity Packs (May 2020). Courtesy of Richard.*

are evidenced through the scant feedback gathered and the prisons' continued engagement throughout the period. Research was the secondary goal of this project; my primary goal was sustaining those behind their cell doors for upwards of twenty-three hours per day during the pandemic. As Liebling and Ludlow articulate in their work on 'Suicide, distress and the quality of prison life', inmates' ability to avoid suicide or self-harm depends on their 'coping skills and resources' (2016: p.229). Between 23 March and 28 May 2020 there were sixteen recorded suicides in prisons in England and Wales, a dramatic rise linked to the 'anxiety and psychological distress' (Gulatti et al., 2020) of prison during the pandemic. This was a significant concern for all those working within the system and significant resources were mobilized to provide activities in an attempt to curb self-harm and self-inflicted deaths. Recorded instances of self-harm within the estate fell during the pandemic, with 55,542 instances recorded during 2020 (Safety in Custody statistics, 2021), potentially due to lower levels of violence and

FIGURE 13 *Brody's illustration of Banquo's ghost at the banquet in* Macbeth, *part of a comic book version he created during the pandemic (September 2020). Courtesy of Brody.*

drugs combined with 'a more proactive approach among all staff to identify and support prisoners at risk of mental distress' (Hewson et al., 2020). This is typical of the *honeymoon period* often seen in the general population following national disasters. Sustainability of these lower levels of reported incidents is not anticipated by academics or practitioners and Peter Clarke declared 'serious concerns about what the scrutiny visits are revealing' (keynote, 2020). During this period of enforced isolation the Shakespeare packs, for some at least, provided a positive distraction from the monotony of the regime, allowing people to engage with characters and narratives with which they could reframe their own confinement to some extent.

The final example in this section contrasts with the shorter-term response to Covid-19; it examines the beneficial effect on mental resilience where the reflections are developed over a protracted period of isolation. US practitioner and academic Laura Bates worked for many years with Larry Newton, a man held in solitary confinement in Wabash Valley Correctional Facility. Bates's work spans both the individualized reflections of engaging with Shakespeare as a solitary activity but also the additional impacts of group endeavours. Bates's detailed analysis of her work evidences the impact it had on Newton in both her own and his words. Bates has worked within prisons for many years and cites influences from Geese Theatre and Tofteland but says that her work:

> Attempted to go one step further: rather than attempting to turn inexperienced and often semi-illiterate inmates into Shakespearean actors, I encouraged my students to rewrite Shakespeare's text into their own words, to engage in both linguistic and cultural translation.
> (Bates – Davies, 2003: p.152)

Ten Years with the Bard (2013) documents the work she and Larry did, which resulted in his creation of *The Prisoner's Guide to the Complete Works of Shakespeare*. She describes her own trajectory and the years of working with prisoners who, despite being in solitary confinement, wrote their own creative responses to the tragedies, as well as her 'individual session[s] with Newton [who] was not allowed to join the group given his history' (2013: p.26). After stabbing other inmates and an officer he was detained in solitary confinement for over a decade. Interaction between inmates in the solitary confinement cells was limited to shouting messages through cell doors, as described when Newton and another inmate, Green, debated the potential for 'predetermination' encompassed by Richard II's phrase 'Fortune's slaves' (Bates, 2013: p.28). Bates writes candidly about the challenging behaviour displayed at times by inmates but declared the programme was a success and extended her tenure there as a volunteer, far beyond her initially planned twelve months.

She specifically chose *Hamlet, Othello,* and other plays she felt the men would connect with, asking them to read aloud and ensure they understood each word before they began to debate the themes and then write their own adaptations ensuring reflection was an intrinsic part of the work. This is an explicit exploration of the way in which Shakespeare 'pierces the surface and penetrates the depth of the relationship between repetition and difference' (Lefebvre, 1991: p.182) between personal experiences and those of Shakespeare's tragedians. She asked them to consider how their own experiences were repetitions of Hamlet's description of being 'bounded in a nutshell', encouraging them to liken their own experience to Hamlet's. Their analysis of his visions of the ghost drew strongly on their experiences of long periods of solitary confinement, where they actively engaged in the creation of fantasies so realistic that they could 'feel the sensations, smell the food, feel the dampness of the rain' (Bates, 2013: p.119). Their reflections on Shakespeare were individualistic at the outset as interaction with other inmates was prohibited. Despite mental engagement with others during Bates's class they remained physically isolated and conducted their conversations on their knees, peering through the slots used to affix handcuffs. Newton and others expended significant efforts working on Shakespeare and writing versions of multiple plays, including full adaptations written in their cells and a communal work entitled *To Revenge or Not to Revenge* in which Newton challenged them that 'Hamlet should choose *not* to kill' (Bates, 2013: p.132).

Her transcripts of conversations with Larry 'present a powerful portrayal of one prisoner's analysis of Shakespeare's criminal tragedies and his own process of criminal development which could have ended as tragically' (Bates – Shailor, 2011: p.41), a claim evidenced by the lucidity and honesty of Newton's self-reflection.

He directly attributes his own change of mindset to 'trying to figure out what motivated Macbeth' which meant he:

> had to ask [himself] what motivated [him] and came face to face with the realisation that [he] was fake, motivated by external appearances and garnering approbation from others instead of considering his own core values.
> (Bates – Shailor, 2011: p.41)

He described this revelation, directly prompted by his reflections on Macbeth, as liberating; allowing him to analyse his psyche and begin to consciously control his motivations.

Each of these case studies of isolated reflection on Shakespeare has demonstrated the way this practice allowed people to mentally escape their physical location through a combination of conceptual and social space they accessed through Shakespeare's plays, in some instances directly through reading the text, in other cases through accessing the Activity Packs created using his themes and characters.

Reflections on group dynamics

Now the focus shifts to the way in which individuals reflect on the work of Shakespeare but with the additional lens of their involvement in prison theatre companies. The actors' reflections are refracted through the emotional connections embedded within the group dynamic. This section is subdivided into two, the first exploring rehearsal-diaries written during normal times and the second on how the work was adapted in response to the implementation of the emergency regime instigated by Covid-19. The consideration of the two sets of circumstances with the same group of individuals reveals the depth of the emotional connections developed during the work and how those connections can effectively bolster resilience.

Prison is a challenging and complex environment for inmates to navigate at any time and the loss they feel is much more than the deprivation of liberty which forms their sentence; many report feelings of loss of humanity, self-worth and their relevance within society (Gallowfield Players rehearsal, 2019). Yvonne Jewkes describes that the 'loss of autonomy in prison is usually total. ... as the prisoner is

FIGURE 14 *Sketch completed by Brody during Emergency Shakespeare rehearsals for* Macbeth, *HMP Stafford (2 June 2019). Courtesy of Brody.*

reduced to the weak, helpless, dependent status of a child' (2002: p.17). For the inmates engaged in our collaborative theatre companies 'these trends are reversed' within the group as they 'are treated as equals, as people' (Michael, 2019) and this remains fundamental in the process of autonomous change we created together. This group dynamic and sense of autonomy feature heavily in their diaries which document reflections on the work done both collectively and alone in their cells. Within the theatre companies, I encourage the actors to keep rehearsal diaries which document their experience of the process, although as expected some engage enthusiastically whilst others are reticent to do so. The quantity and depth of reflection on the work contained within the diaries vary significantly, from some who write multiple notebooks for each production to others who are willing to write a few-page summary at the end.

The extent to which Shakespeare allows them to reflect on themselves as individuals yet within a wider continuum of humanity, to develop resilience and find their voices, was borne out in the diaries. One such example within The Gallowfield Players is this extract in which Wayne reflected on a line by line walkthrough of *Julius Caesar*, early in rehearsals, to encourage depth of characterization.

> We talked about the seriousness of the play because it is a tragic story. I can relate it to my crime in a way, the feelings of indescribable regret and remorse is very real for me. But it also helped me because it told me I am human and I'd never wish death upon anybody.
>
> (2019)

Wayne spoke to me privately in February 2019 in some detail about his crime and the impact of it on himself and his family; it was evident that the work done on *Julius Caesar* was the catalyst to his initiation of this self-reflection. He told me that the work we had done together had enabled him to objectively examine the details of his index offence and the chain of events which triggered it. When he joined the group, he appeared an immature individual, focused exclusively on his own needs rather than considering others but he used the characterization work to reflect on his own circumstances and those of his loved ones. He wrote in his diary 'today was probably the most helpful session yet, not only for the play, but for my life' (Wayne, 2019). Shortly after this he began to speak about the possibility of entering the therapy regime within the prison's Therapeutic Community, which another actor had successfully completed. This intervention is 'a 25-bed, high-intensity offending behaviour programme for prisoners with long-standing emotional and relationship difficulties that had led to their violent offending' (Clarke, 2018: p.50). The Community was assessed as 'very effective in giving eligible prisoners opportunities to address their risk factors' (Clarke, 2018: p.18) and Wayne felt that he was emotionally and mentally able to commit to this, a fact he attributed to his inclusion in The Gallowfield Players. He moved into the Community following the performance of *The Merchant,* on the agreement that he could play a cameo role in productions, whilst daily therapy excluded him from rehearsals, and he could return to the group upon completion of the intervention.

Throughout his diaries Wayne reflected on the resilience he developed within the group, noting in June 2019 'I'm proud to say my identity has changed from being a Gallowfield Player'. However, this trajectory to a more mature, resilient individual was not linear and he also catalogued the difficulties experienced during the process. I wrote earlier about his outburst when people were not taking the rehearsals seriously enough and his conversation with Michael and myself which subsequently led to a mature, considered apology. He reflected on this in his diary, both his building feeling of 'wanting to quit, feeling small, little, incompetent' (Wayne, 2019) in the preceding weeks and then the incident and subsequent feeling of relief. He wrote of his concerns about how he was perceived in prison generally and that to mitigate this he 'tried to take on a persona that felt unnatural' (Wayne, 2019) which resulted in escalating frustration. He noted long-standing feelings of being unable to be himself in prison, thoughts echoed widely by others including Ben who described that 'prison often feels like a bad soap opera, a lot of lying and overacting' (2019). Wayne's diary-entry of the conversation with Michael and myself was focused on the way 'we all support each other' (2019), rather than the specific use of theatre, but it was through Shakespeare's work that those bonds were created and strengthened over a significant period. Later in the diary he wrote an apology for a joke he worried had offended me (no offence was intended or taken) and acknowledged 'I find it really hard to forgive myself as I do with a lot of things I've done in life, that's one of the reasons I'm leaving for therapy and why I love this group; I'm accepted despite my flaws' (2019). He explained that by 'thinking as the characters I saw different sides of the same situation and then I realized it showed me the different sides of my own life too' (2019). This usage of Shakespeare to consider and understand elements of his own personality which may have been too troubling for him to confront directly charts Wayne's maturation as an individual and the way in which it enabled him to develop communication skills which seemed previously elusive to him.

Rob wrote on several occasions about the additional rehearsal work done both alone in his cell or in small groups with other actors on the wing. He wrote of a Saturday where they had spent their association time 'in mine doing a rehearsal and as we were doing the reading we discussed the emotions and motivations behind what the characters were saying. I think Ben found this really beneficial' (Rob, 2019). In prison, unprompted discussions about emotions and vulnerabilities are rare; however, Shakespeare provided the catalyst for this and for the development of friendships between men who had barely known each other prior to joining the company. This development of an emotionally intelligent vocabulary which they gained the confidence to use with each other and myself was one of the tangible ways in which they reflected their own lives within Shakespeare but also reflected Shakespeare back into the carceral environment. Outside of rehearsals Rob arranged to review early drafts of the script Michael wrote for *The Merchant* and his diary documents his thoughts on this, including an awareness of the need to avoid Shylock 'playing into public perceptions of criminals' (Rob, 2019). He was one of the actors who initiated the choice of play and wanted to address 'how society will judge me when I finish my sentence, it scares me' (Rob, 2019) which was the reason that Shylock was developed as an ostracized man convicted of serious crime. Rob's self-awareness of the importance of making Shylock a believable yet not unsympathetic character continued throughout rehearsals and was considered in detail regarding the ending of the play where some called for him to commit suicide whilst others challenged this as playing to stereotypes that suggest the cycle of criminality can be broken only by death.

Rob reflected on this regularly in his diary and it was clear that getting his viewpoint across to the audience in a manner which was

FIGURE 15 *Richard's drawing of the cast of* The Merchant *wearing masks, drawn during the Covid-19 lockdown and inspired by a cast photograph taken at the Family Day performance (illustration – May 2020). Courtesy of Richard.*

authentic but allowed them to show this man in a non-stereotyped way was very important to him and dominated his thoughts. Early in the rehearsal schedule Rob was nominated by the group to take this role and his diary documented his attempts to compare his own life experiences to those of Shylock. He found difficulty in reconciling the two as he felt 'Shylock should be older and very much more rough around the edges' (Rob, 2019). He directly contrasted himself with the character and felt that he was ill-equipped to play the role as he was not a father himself and so, whilst he was a vociferous advocate of the play, he was pleased when Michael agreed to take the lead role. Rob was keen to take a larger role than in his first production but his primary objective was for the play to have heterotopic impact; to that end he was 'happy to relinquish the role' to Michael as he felt 'him to be a better Shylock' (Rob, 2019). He felt that Bassanio's role was 'a better fit' for himself and throughout the rehearsal process he commented numerous times verbally and in his diary about the role reflecting him more closely (2019). He

FIGURE 16 Richard's illustration of Shylock, Portia and Antonio for inclusion in The Merchant of Venice *Activity Packs (July 2020). Courtesy of Richard.*

likened rehearsal feedback about the lyricism of his verse speaking to family memories where he was told that his attempts at French speaking sounded like singing, demonstrating the way that this linked his current and pre-prison life.

During the rehearsal process for *The Merchant* there was also the additional complication of Michael's hunger strike. He documented the impact of the strike on his mental and physical well-being in his diary, as did others within the group. The level of compassion and support demonstrated during this period was testament to the way the group had bonded. Rob wrote 'I am concerned for Michael, I put my hand on his shoulder and could feel how weak he was' (2019), and during this period they would escort him around the prison, carrying his bag and ensuring that he didn't collapse. Michael's own diaries from that period describe 'feeling rough but drama always brightens things up' (2019). Much of his focused reflection in the diaries was on the practicalities of learning a significant line-load such as Shylock as whilst in prison he suffered some degree of brain damage from severe meningitis. He also reflected how the group had inspired him to find his inner creativity once more, he wrote

'Rowan has given me confidence, given me hope, given me a voice once more and without her I think I'd still be struggling to cope with the brain damage' (2019). After the peaceful conclusion of his hunger strike he reflected that The Gallowfield Players:

> Is a gift that keeps on giving –
> I see it save my friends,
> I see it bring families together,
> I see it draw people out of their shells,
> I see it being inclusive, beautiful, caring, communal,
> I see it getting people out of bed,
> I see it do so many things,
> And it reminds me daily that I need to be a better person,
> That I can be a better person (2019).

Shortly before performing *The Merchant*, Michael had a sentencing appeal rejected and he acknowledged the emotional impact of denial of early release but he wrote 'all I've been focusing on is the play – such is the hold it has over us that nothing else seems to be of importance right now' (2020). Over time the resilience they drew from Shakespeare's characters and the resilience from the emotionally supportive environment we had created began to merge. As Ben reflected, 'in our humble drama group we've found a sense of living life again, not just doing *life*' (2019), and just as spaces are permeated and altered by the activities which take place within them so Shakespeare became intrinsically linked with the community of The Gallowfield Players. Keith reflected that when he joined the group

> reading and understanding Shakespeare was a skill I was yet to acquire but by being part of this creation the deeper meanings slowly began to take shape and I began to grasp 'what all the fuss is about'.
>
> (2019)

However, as time went on they focused more on the overall experience: the combination of Shakespeare, the emotional support function of the group and their desire to share the work with a wider audience to create a positive legacy. The interweaving of these elements means that it is difficult, if not impossible, to separate what benefit they took from using Shakespeare to develop their resilience and reflect on their own lives compared to the effect of being part of an autonomous group. Regardless of the delineation of where the benefits accrued the impact was significant enough that Ben wrote:

> I can honestly say that during our second performance to our loved ones I forgot I was in prison, forgot I was a prisoner, so much so that when it was over and I stepped back into the main prison it felt like my first day back in prison – the noise, the atmosphere, the distant coldness, it left me with an empty feeling.
> (2019)

To have emotionally and mentally freed someone from the confinement of prison for even a few hours was immensely powerful.

Shakespeare was the medium which enabled me to ask these inmates to develop trust with me and with each other; it was an important element of the richly complex community we created. For many of the actors the work included 'moments of intense cognitive or emotional epiphany' (Crewe et al., 2019: p.145) which criminologists acknowledge are a crucial part of coping with prison. Michael articulated 'there is such a magic in these plays, every time we talk about it, hold onto these moments we get the excitement, the buzz, it's addictive, it's powerful' (2019) and their passion for discovering more about Shakespeare grew exponentially as they continued to develop the group. He described *The Merchant* as 'a love letter to [his] children [...] a chance to say that [he] understands their hardships' (Michael, 2020) and that he had drawn heavily on his own life, in conjunction with the original text to create this adaptation. The interweaving of Shakespeare and his personal journey was so powerful that many of the audience wept. Through Shakespeare the actors were able to find their voice and develop resilience which helped them to cope during the time they were alone in their cells and when the loneliness of prison life was particularly difficult to endure.

This development of emotional resilience from the in-prison theatre companies was also evidenced in Emergency Shakespeare where a number of the men documented in their diaries the positive impact of the work we did together. Brody's complex mental health situation was explored in Chapter 2 and during rehearsals for *Macbeth* he began to comprehend that he could 'use the spectrum of emotions that I have struggled with for years' (2019) in a positive

FIGURE 17 Brody's illustration of The Tempest *for inclusion in the Activity Packs (April 2020). Courtesy of Brody.*

creative outlet. He wrote of watching a DVD of a production to 'help put the text into context and show the emotions' (2019) which then informed his own Banquo. Navigating the desire for appropriation from many in the company, who saw the filmed version as *the way they should play a role,* was a delicate balance to be negotiated as I encouraged men such as Batu, who struggled to find their own interpretation of the character, to make the role their own and not simply a reconstruction of the recording. Batu self-identified that he struggled to 'portray enough emotion' (2019) during rehearsals as Macduff, but by reflecting on feedback from myself and others he was able to overcome this challenge prior to performance. His self-reflection that his autism affected his way of processing emotions seemed to unlock his ability to communicate them more freely than previously. Following the productions of *Macbeth* he chose to share with the cast that 'expressing emotions' (2019) was the skill he had most developed, and this admission in a group setting demonstrated significant progression for someone who was previously extremely guarded with his conduct.

The final subsection of this chapter considers the effect on the work within the two theatre companies during Covid-19. During my final rehearsal within each prison prior to lockdown we discussed the likely implications of the pandemic and I made the commitment that I would endeavor to maintain contact in some form whilst unable to be physically present. Initially I was unsure what form this communication would take and the logistical practicalities but both prisons were supportive of maintaining contact and agreed to be the conduit for correspondence, which I was immensely grateful for. The first correspondence was distributed before the next rehearsal was due to take place. I wrote them a weekly letter and included approximately three hours of activities, suggesting that where possible we all completed the activities at the usual rehearsal time as that would mean that everyone was focusing on Shakespeare at the same time. I envisaged this to offer them a semblance of normality, as far as possible, given that they were behind their cell doors.

The letters aimed to provide a sense of continuity and combined enquiries about their physical and mental health and that of their loved ones (many of whom I have met at performances) with topical comments such as we would exchange at the start of rehearsals.

The Gallowfield Players were at the stage of script-editing *Sycorax's Storm*, a prequel to *The Tempest* because 'the stories we know are only chapters within much larger tales' (Michael, 2020). Michael had drafted the play so editing continued (albeit somewhat more slowly than intended as his handwritten work was posted to me for typing and amendments). The activities sent to the group included analysis of the characters in the adaptation (which featured a female Prospera, the addition of Prospera's partner Lucilius, and a male Sycorax), the relationships and how these develop during the play.

Extracts from The Gallowfield Players' *Sycorax's Storm*

Act 1 Scene 2

NARRATOR
Prospera begins to tell the tale to Miranda of times past and the woeful narrative of her exile by the King of Naples.

PROSPERA
Daughter, you were but a babe in arms
When upon this strange shore we landed
Too young to remember all the trials
And the tribulations we were handed
This black place stole so much of who we once were,
And its more than a blessing that you cannot
Recall the desperate hunger we endured.

The painful desolation that we suffered
Dignity was not all that we buried
In the fight to construct this paltry life
While we scavenged this cruel land to ease our strife
And find any morsel to sustain us.

Such pains sank deep roots in the caverns of my mind
Not easily forgotten nor forgiven
Are those who orchestrated our agonies
Despite the unmarked seasons marching relentlessly
Despite praying to deaf Gods for mercy
All we received was further torment
No matter which Devil I had to extract

You will never again go hungry,
Never again shall we struggle to eat.

I played by their rules, I played their games
Followed all the customs in old Milan
But for no reason than perfidious greed
We were exiled, cast into the sea.
A pair of ruthless and wicked siblings
Who undermined my standing with the King
Whispered wounding words in Alonso's ear
The rightful ruler who once held me dear.

In response to the accusations of witchcraft made by her treacherous brother Antonio Prospera defends her innocence.

PROSPERA
Of course this indictment is not true
That laid before you is not even proof
Those books are beyond my understanding
But my liege they were gifts from you given
Your honour to save I will not fight this case.
Remember how on this day you were played
What can I say, but that which I must
Contradicts this accusation and
The testimony which I would give would
Scarce back to me to say I'm not guilty
Counted as falsehood my integrity
And as I express it the powers divine
Keep us within the aspect of this gaze
And behold these, our human actions
Innocence, my innocence still make
False accusations blush and tyranny tremble
My life as I prize it, I would spare it
And in doing so spare you all the grief
Of such injustice for honour
Tis a derivative from me to mine
And only that I stand for. I appeal
To your conscience my Lord
If one jot beyond the bounds of honour
Or in act or will those are inclined

Hardened be the hearts of all who hear
Let my nearest kin cry fie upon my grave.
I have been but your loyal servant
And now my life in unsafe balance hangs
Such threats of death I fear them not
For if you are to steal my honour then
My life already as good as forfeit be
What blessing do I have here alive
That I should fear to die, therefore proceed.

It's gender and not law that condemns me
Your honour – refer me to the oracle
And then let Apollo be my judge.
As for you my beloved brother
Shackled by ghosts of memories unremembered
Our futures were set in stone, predetermined
Destiny has now let you write your own story
But when others read of your treachery
You will be judged, judged most poorly.
You shall be forever destined surely
To repeat your cycles of destruction
Destined to always feel the same frustrations.
Hope that our paths do not cross again
Before my final breath is taken.

My lord, my King, do as you will
Despite the twisted motives of those two I bear you no ill
The punishment for those guilty of witchcraft
Is to be burnt but I would ask
That you consider my loyalty, my service
And perhaps give me a kinder death.

A plot outline for *The Tempest* and character descriptions sent to the actors helped to ensure a foundation for understanding the play. A degree of hot-seating of characters produced varied results with some producing copious, emotionally detailed notes about the trajectories of each character whilst others 'struggled as I really don't understand *The Tempest*' (Leigh, 2020). Whilst this could be easily addressed with a conversation in rehearsals it posed more of a challenge whilst working remotely and led to me adapting the work to encompass more creative activities such as translating modern

REFLECTIVE SPACES

FIGURE 18 *Richard's cartoon of* Sycorax's Storm *(July 2020). Courtesy of Richard.*

songs into Shakespearean language or creating cartoon panels depicting plays we had worked on. I gained agreement from artists Charlie Mackesy and Mya Gosling to include some of their work in the packs to engage visually with those who preferred pictorial to written materials. It was important the actors continued to feel connected with the work and several of them wrote to explain the importance of it in their mental wellbeing – 'This is an incredibly tough time but having a reminder each week that we are part of something incredible carries on giving us hope' (Leigh, 2020). Will commented that the packs were 'distracting and entertaining' (2020) whilst he coped with the fact he may not see his overseas family for a considerable time.

This sense of continuity as a collective group helped them to cope with the prolonged isolation of the restricted regime. I was very concerned about the mental health impacts and many admitted that they found it hard, with some of them having days when it was difficult to summon the energy and enthusiasm to get out of bed. However, they wrote of proactively trying to follow some form of routine, which included the activities. Many of them elected to use the time to work on educational initiatives such as Open University courses, read books they had previously not had time to start or develop their artistic skills. Richard wrote to thank me for including the Good Tickle Brain comic-strips stating 'it's inspired me to have a go at cartoons myself' (2020). His artwork had already been featured in posters and programmes for The Gallowfield Players and during lockdown I liaised with him, via the prison, to begin producing illustrations of Shakespeare's plays which were included in the Activity Packs for general circulation across the carceral estate. He had developed an intense interest in Shakespeare during the time we had worked together and proudly told me of the *Complete Works of Shakespeare* his parents bought him for his birthday (Richard, 2019). As well as the illustrations for the Activity Packs, in mid-June a package of costume designs for *Sycorax's Storm* arrived which he and Michael had worked on collaboratively. He wrote 'Michael and I have spent much of the last week working out the details of costumes and looks for the characters to get the visuals right' (Richard, 2020). Their continued focus on the next production even during lockdown and the mental stress of the pandemic demonstrated how central it had become to

REFLECTIVE SPACES

FIGURE 19 *Richard's pastiche of Shakespeare characters in* Sir John Falstaff in Looking for Love *(July 2020). Courtesy of Richard.*

their sense of identity and Michael asked me to share my thoughts on the designs, adding 'I just wish I could see your face with some of them' (Michael, 2020).

Despite rehearsals having been suspended for many months their commitment to the work remained high, with requests for additional reading materials, texts for plays Michael wanted to adapt for future productions and origami instructions to assist Malcolm with props and set design plans. The emotional strength the actors drew from the connection to The Gallowfield Players and to the work they embarked on as a collective was evident and even actors who had shown less interest in the text previously engaged more during this time. Christian is an older, dyslexic gentleman who had previously shown little interest beyond participating in the weekly rehearsals, but he expressed an interest in 'rewriting *Caesar*' (Michael, 2020) which we performed in 2019, although to date he has not actioned this plan. One letter from Michael included an affirmation that 'I'm tired of letting fear prevent me from doing things I once enjoyed, so I am trying to fix all the broken bits in my head' (Michael, 2020).

Additionally, Michael was also keen to help with the preparation for the additional group, which was being planned. The prison intended to commission me for the work with The Gallowfield Players and an additional session (three hours) each week where myself and three to four of the actors would work with a group of ten to twelve inmates who had not previously engaged with the company. The proposal was that the group worked together for three months putting together a number of short scenes which would be showcased at an internal sharing event. During the course of the year this would enable up to forty-eight additional inmates to engage with Shakespeare and staff were keen that this would 'get people involved who might be challenging in other activities or be isolated' (Head of Reducing Reoffending, 2020). Michael was delighted to hear that this had been formally ratified and he wrote of 'wanting to sit and talk about how we best make this group effective' (2020). He was keen to create a legacy and to use his own life experiences and the experiences within The Gallowfield Players to help others to build their resilience. Following the easing of the pandemic regime this has begun to take place, albeit on a smaller scale than initially planned – myself and Ben are working with smaller groups of men for four-week programmes, exploring themes from Shakespeare's plays.

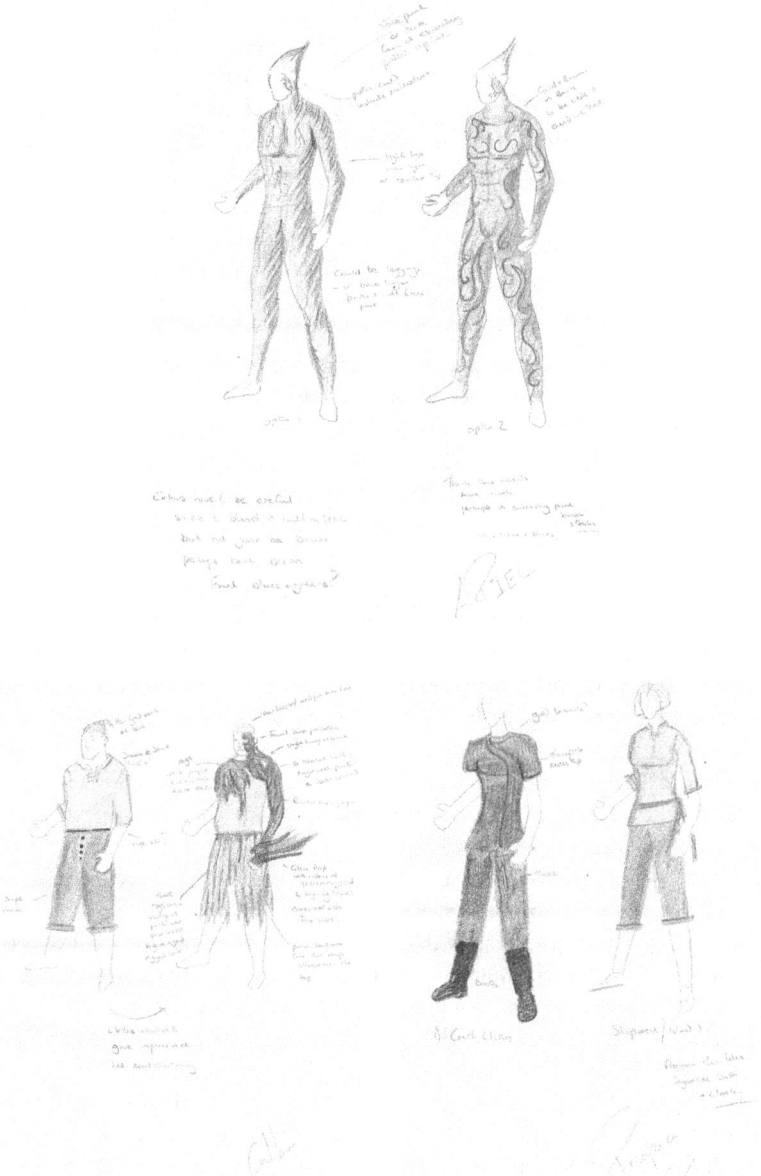

FIGURE 20 *Richard and Michael's sketches for costumes for* Sycorax's Storm *(July 2020). Courtesy of The Gallowfield Players.*

Another pertinent example of this desire to improve the lives of others was demonstrated by Brody in Emergency Shakespeare who worked prolifically during the pandemic to create artistic depictions of the plays to illustrate the Activity Packs. He began drawing whilst in prison and during the course of our work together had grown in confidence sufficiently to begin an undergraduate degree in Fine Art (kindly funded by Prisoners' Education Trust). He articulated to a member of staff who was sending the materials to me that 'it makes me feel good about myself that my drawings bring other people pleasure' (Brody, 2020). This desire to bring pleasure to others was demonstrated through his ready agreement to support the initiative and his dedication to meeting deadlines for the artwork. These responses from the actors during the pandemic evidenced emotional development and that they were able to demonstrate resilience during this challenging time. They continued to feel connected to the social space we had created through Shakespeare's work and the dynamics of the group which acted as sustenance whilst rehearsals were indefinitely halted. Alice Mills and Kathleen Kendall concur that 'prisons are hostile environments where people experience fear, intimidation, psychological and physical damage' (Mills & Kendall – Jewkes et al., 2016: p.187) so it is unsurprising that many inmates mask their emotions and vulnerabilities and shut off from the world. For many of the actors this had previously been the case but the pandemic clearly demonstrated that this was no longer their reality, instead they continue to be connected to a community even though circumstances meant the community was physically fragmented for over a year. They draw strength from a sense of belonging, whether this was the strength for them to 'continue to pull through the dark times with my family, friends and the group in mind' (Leigh, 2020) or whether they were actively contributing to activities to help others find creativity in isolation. For individuals serving long sentences for violent crimes to agree to share their creative efforts (drawings, reflections on plays, activities) with the wider prison population and open themselves up to potential criticism and ridicule is a significant act. Their confidence in themselves, their trust in me and their passion for using Shakespeare as a form of human connection were all evidenced by these instances of proactivity.

FIGURE 21 *Brody's illustration of* King Lear *which he and I agreed was too macabre for inclusion in the Activity Packs (June 2020). Courtesy of Brody.*

Conclusion

Whether people are dislocated from society on a temporary or a more permanent basis, their reflections on Shakespeare can offer them the chance to develop a resilience which comes from knowing that they are working with characters which speak to contemporary life just as eloquently as they did to Elizabethan and Jacobean experiences. This invokes Bourdieu's sense of habitus, of belonging to the wider humanity which can help them with dealing with the challenges facing them during the period of isolation. Using Shakespeare to hold up a mirror to themselves and to society can help individuals to calibrate the similarities and differences between the characters, themselves and the wider community. This placing of oneself in the continuum of history provides a vital and powerful sense of autonomy that oppression and social control cannot eradicate. Some are separated from their loved ones and communities for short periods, some for long spells and others for an indefinite period of time, but for all people this induces feelings of vulnerability, fear and loss, the feelings Liebling and Ludlow ascribe as the primary motivations for suicide in custody (2016: p.229). The provision of activities and material which can counteract these emotions is a powerful antidote and when these are in the form of canonical works such as Shakespeare this effect is heightened. They allow people to engage with a world which is not bounded in the realm of their restricted, isolated reality but allow them to find a deeper internal resilience which allows them to survive the negative impacts of their exile from their established network.

REFLECTIVE SPACES

FIGURE 22 Brody's cartoon-strip of Othello, Acts 1 & 2, drawn for inclusion in the programme for Emergency Shakespeare's production of the play, planned for 2021 (September 2020). Courtesy of Brody.

5

Mediated spaces

Most people's knowledge of applied Shakespeare is refracted through the lens of the media, delivered in easily accessible formats but fraught with embedded agendas. For a majority of the public their entire sphere of reference for these marginalized groups may be through media representation, endorsing the phenomenon of 'mediachosis' (Osborne – Kidd & Osborne, 1995: p.37) – the unconscious and unquestioning acceptance of information portrayed through electronic media. This chapter examines the impact of media patronization, theories of media impact and the cruciality of authenticity of voice, using examples along a spectrum of mediation, categorized by the closeness of the mediating voice to the origination of the work. Whilst the ethics of applied theatre are complex and challenging to navigate, as any practitioner will agree, the additional step of then preparing this work in a mediated format for consumption by the general public makes those ethics additionally problematic. Even when a practitioner is mindful of the dangers of intrusion and consciously attempts to avoid this, there is a likelihood that the mediated portrayal will have an embedded narrative which may be patronizing and play into perceptions of marginalized people as incapable of cultural or intellectual achievements. As Barnes describes, the reality of applied theatre is complicated and to some extent reliant on privilege which plays into a neoliberal agenda where emotional development is seen as being given through what Nicholson terms the 'gift of theater' (Barnes, 2020: p.3). Barnes's judgement that the films he critiques 'depict philanthropic practices that risk being perceived as patronising intrusions' (2020: p.3) partially articulates the core of the issue in media coverage of these types of projects. However, there is a further issue in that it may be the media itself which is the patronizing intrusion and which may at times obscure and distort the truth of the work taking place.

'Patronizing' has the duality of being both to offer support as a patron but also to behave in a condescending manner, which is important to media portrayals of marginalized communities. The purpose of media coverage of projects involving marginalized communities is usually to engage support (with the notable exception of tabloid coverage of prison projects) from a wider community who may otherwise be unaware of the initiatives. However, there is a very real danger that this support is offered from a place of social superiority which becomes derogatorily patronizing. A danger that those who create the media play into stereotypes of marginalization in their portrayal of the redemptive qualities of Shakespeare, as if to achieve the ability to orate Shakespeare adds meaning which was previously lacking in people's lives. It is a precarious balance between showcasing the way in which Shakespeare can offer people an opportunity to have their voices heard and the risk that this becomes a neatly packaged *product* which encourages the audience to feel socially, economically, intellectually or physically superior to those they are watching. This danger exists with physical interactions too but is exacerbated by the fact that audiences consuming the media are not in direct contact with the participants and so some degree of humanity is lost from the experience. My research into this double-edged sword of media-coverage has been fundamental in my work as a practitioner. I attempt to ensure that the voices given centrality are those of the community to minimize the potential of patronizing intrusion from non-marginalized perspectives.

Society has become accustomed to the infiltration of media and social media into almost every aspect of our lives, and for many it is a primary gateway for engagement with the world. Although from 1961, Lefebvre's description in *Critique of Everyday Life: Volume II*, provides a relevant starting point:

> Radio and television do not penetrate the everyday solely in terms of the viewer. They go looking for it at its source: personalised (but superficial) anecdotes, trivial incidents, familiar family events. They set out an explicit principle: 'everything [...] can become interesting and even enthralling, provided that it is *presented* ie *present*'.
>
> (Lefebvre, 2002: p.370)

Whilst media forms have diversified and the impact on lives has intensified his argument that if an event is *presented* it will become engaging to media consumers, prevails in modern society. The concept that any everyday topic can be interesting if it is *presented* and shown to be of the *present* (relevant in the immediate moment) via the media is one which has been borne out by the rise of reality TV over recent decades. I build on Lefebvre's theory and refer to *presenting* and *presentation* which are linked to *presented* and *present*. Presenting in this context is a combination of the act of showing something and the immediacy of the time frame within which it is shown, layering the physical and the temporal. It is this act of *presenting* which stokes interest in the media coverage of the artistic endeavors of marginalized people.

Presentation is the act of portrayal of a specific event or series of events with a time-bound qualification – the reception of the media is dependent upon the time in which it is given to the public; it either reinforces or challenges the current social framework. Set against the backdrop of cultural and sociological concerns of the moment, these media creations provide a representation of reality which is somewhat distorted – it cannot be an exact replication of the event which took place. There is a natural mediation effect when an event is recorded; the reality is transmuted from objectivity into subjectivity, driven by where the focus is directed and the context within which the media content is set. This chapter is not a critique of the prevalence and influence of mass media but an examination of how this society-wide phenomenon is utilized in the creation of narratives about Shakespeare and marginalized people, sharing the work with a wider audience. Mediated representations of those from marginalized sectors of society engaging with Shakespeare are embodiments of the explicit principle of *presentation* which defines audiences' receptions, bringing their perceptions into alignment with the pre-determined agenda. Whilst the majority of these agendas are designed to be supportive of the examples they showcase there is, as Barnes articulates, the risk that they are 'as exploitative, as manipulative and as commercial as reality television' (2020: p.14). They are often created with the intention of encouraging endorsement and funding of the initiative but this, at times, becomes warped by the sociological desire for what Ian Wilhelm terms 'charity TV – that make doing good – or the appearance of doing good – a key part of their audience appeal' (2007: p.24).

The media's influence on the opinion of the individual has vacillated between the 'magic bullet theory' (that media has immediate, pervasive effects on those targeted) and claims of minimal impact, with the reality being more nuanced and complex than either extremity of theoretical opinion (Neuman & Guggenheim, 2011: pp.171–2). There can be little debate that media has the ability to take a story and to present this in such a way as to fulfil the agenda of those creating the material. As Lefebvre argued, 'the art of presenting the everyday by taking it from its context, emphasizing it, making it appear unusual or picturesque and overloading it with meaning has become highly skillful' (1961: p.370); the intention of media is always to make things engaging and, where necessary, manipulating them to do so. This principle of things becoming 'enthralling' is intrinsic to broadcasting; the underpinning foundation of all media is that it must attract attention in order to be able to disseminate the content.

Neuman and Guggenheim coordinate communication effects into six themes: theories of persuasion, new media, social context, societal and media theories, active audience and interpretive effects (Neuman & Guggenheim, 2011: pp.177–8) with the latter two of particular relevance in this context. Active audience theories consider the way in which information received is influenced by the recipients' existing psychological orientations and opinions of the world – 'the motivations and psychological orientations of audience members' (2011: pp.177–8). The interpretive effects theories, in contrast, 'include [...] agenda-setting, priming and framing theories', focused on the messages being encoded during production and the way in which the media 'may influence salience of, interpretation of and cognitive organisation of information and opinions to which individuals are exposed' (2011: pp.177–8). These are not binary theories; meaning is created symbiotically between the producer of content and the consumer of it, particularly within the social context of the moment of production. To some degree, the media construct the messages being broadcast but in today's society those messages are also driven by public perception and demand. As Jose Van Dijck confirms, 'social media platforms have unquestionably altered the nature of private and public communication' (2013: p.7). The exponential rise of campaigns such as Black Lives Matter, in response to incidents of police brutality in the United States, demonstrates the power of social media as a platform upon which to engage and organize protesters. The days of media as a one-way, omnipotent disseminator of information (if it ever existed in that form) have long been replaced by a more complex structure of influence which operates bilaterally.

Alongside the developments in media studies there has also been a recent rise in digital Shakespeare. Sarah Olive's article on 'televised teaching and learning Shakespeare' (2016) focused specifically on the rise of reality television depicting educational Shakespeare, frequently for 'hard-to-reach groups' from financially impoverished backgrounds, building on the sub-genre begun by the 1994 documentary *Shakespeare on the Estate* directed by Penny Woolcock. Woolcock describes how filming this altered her perception as:

> instead of imagining a post-industrial vacuum populated by victims [she] started piecing together a picture of a thriving marginal economy with an alternative system for keeping order.
> (Woolcock – website)

This sub-genre has developed further with more examples of what Bottinelli termed 'substance-based reality television' being created in the past two decades, satisfying a demand for the combination of 'real experiences of learning and performing communicated through techniques common to reality television with a subject culturally constructed as heavyweight' (Bottinelli, 2005: p.308).

The global Covid-19 pandemic had a devastating effect on live theatre and almost all work produced in 2020 had to be adapted into a digital format. The long-term economic impacts on the sector are not yet fully known but many institutions have been forced to announce redundancies and some have closed altogether. The Government created a £1.57 billion Culture Recovery Fund to offer some degree of support to artists, practitioners and venues but it is highly likely that the impact of Covid-19 will have permanently altered the landscape of performative arts. Digital theatre will have a more prominent presence in the future which brings with it both opportunities for widening access but also challenges regarding financial sustainability and the way this alters the concept of live theatre. On this basis the importance of mediated spaces will become increasingly central to theatre studies, whilst at the same time in some ways it poses additional divisions. The lack of technology within prisons, and amongst many economically deprived sectors of society, means that access is being increased for the general public but with some notable exclusions which exacerbates issues of exclusion and marginalization.

This chapter focuses on the ways in which the media play into the psychological expectations of audiences and also frame narratives about the appropriation of Shakespeare by marginalized people in quite specific ways. In the context of media representations of Shakespeare with excluded communities, the event is never unmediated even if it is spontaneously captured in the moment and location of occurrence. This is true regardless of whether the media chooses to portray such an intervention in a positive light (as is often the case for learning disabled theatre companies) or a negative one (frequently applicable to tabloid headlines relating to prison creativity). There is always a strong underlying subtext to any such reportage, based partly on society's pre-existing opinions and partly on the way in which the story is mediated through the communication of it. However, as Greenhalgh counsels, these broadcasts 'are never neutral documentations but rather transcode performance into the conventions of broadcast narrative and presentation' (2019: p.77). These are not unmediated recordings of reality, they are carefully constructed in order to present a specific version of a reality into which many would not otherwise glimpse. This raises challenging ethical questions about who controls the messages which are constructed and to what extent such media productions play into existing narratives of marginalization and this concept of 'redemptive performance' (Barnes, 2020: p.2). The importance of centralizing the voices of the marginalized and their 'allies' (Hadley, 2020: p.178) when the media *presents* Shakespearean engagement from marginalized and underrepresented communities cannot be underestimated.

Barnes argues that the logic of 'Shakespearean charity' documentaries is that 'marginalised communities are composed of self-defeating, self-marginalizing, failed individuals and families who, through the power of the arts, might be better interpellated into healthy national cultures' (2020: p.24). Whilst this is a seemingly harsh accusation there appears to be an element of truth in this perspective, borne out by the narratives delivered by many media examples. Yet this is a simplistic view of those marginalized and suggests a level of homogeneity which does not exist and also casts value judgements on those who are different for whatever reason. Whether the mediation and presentation of the work are done by those internal to the project (ie the practitioner facilitating the work, often with input from the community themselves) or by an external observer, whether academic or news reporter, influences the perspective but the reportage never depicts neutrality. All stories told are mediated to some degree, focused more on certain aspects than on others and contextualized in a specific manner which influences the way meaning is derived from the narrative. The narrative of 'the Robben Island Bible' exemplifies this point: the media portrayal of the book's centrality to the 'communal and individual unconscious' of the political prisoners of Robben Island far surpasses the evidence to substantiate this claimed importance (Shalkwyk – podcast, 2014). Whilst it was signed by a number of the men, the importance it held for those other than Venkatrathnam is unclear yet the media have continued to make much of the connection between Shakespeare's text and Mandela. It appears connecting these two cultural icons was deemed significant enough that factual details were overlooked as the narrative was moulded to produce the story the media felt 'suited the mood and intellectual agenda of the Mbeki years' (Gordon, 2015: p.210).

There is a spectrum of mediation, from the simplest: the protagonist recounting or sharing their version of an event, to the production of a theatre-programme (playbill), to coordinated narration by the facilitator, to the critical analysis of the researcher, to the much-removed perspective of the journalist. Although items such as theatre-programmes would not usually be classified as media, more as merchandise, I have included them in this chapter as they allow those closest to the work, the participants and facilitators, to create a media presence. The chapter begins with the most removed from the specific work and culminates in media created by the artists themselves. I have excluded articles and books whether written by academics, practitioners or, occasionally, co-authored with marginalized participants, as the primary focus of such works is academic research rather than media creation. Within the context of Shakespeare with marginalized people, this spectrum helps to understand and categorize the media representations, focusing on the key concept of whose voice is the one being heard and who controls the power of the narrative. Power is given to the individual or entity who is able to direct the portrayal in line with their agenda, influencing the audience reception in their chosen way.

Scott Magelssen's argument regarding cultural rights and the authenticity of voice (Magelssen – Woodson & Underiner, 2018: pp.223–33) is extremely relevant regarding marginalized communities engaging with Shakespeare; who is best able to articulate the benefits and restrictions of this type of social initiative? Logic dictates that it should always be the participants themselves, but this simplistic line of thinking does not take account of the practicalities that some individuals may be unable to do this or lack a frame of reference against which to assess the experience. Additionally, participants in a project are usually keen to please those supporting the initiative and to conform to the expected outcomes, seeking validation and 'saying what they think you want to hear' (Conlon – interview, 2019). In a world where outcomes are crucial for funding applications both arts practitioners and participants are keen to expound the virtues of involvement in such a project. The Arts Council England reported receipt of 13,688 applications for emergency funding in a three-week period during the early months of the pandemic, compared to a typical annualized figure of 14,000 grant applications, demonstrating the significant and immediate need for funding as a result of Covid-19 and of which theatre applications accounted for 15 per cent. Against a backdrop of such competitively sought funding it is understandable that facilitators want to present the best representation of their work possible to encourage financial support.

It is important to understand whose voice is being heard through the narration and to understand that this is a more complex issue than simply who may be speaking or being quoted. Very rarely is the media brief owned or defined by the marginalized people themselves, even if they are involved in producing the mediated content. Sheila Preston describes how 'representations of the disenfranchised can so easily become a problematic commodity' (2009: p.68) and this commodification is a difficult yet pertinent issue which cannot be ignored. Media productions such as documentaries (even those created with input from the participants) tend to have clearly defined objectives from the outset, to which they are bound in order to comply with the requirements of those who commissioned or are funding the media, meaning that messages are pre-determined and the recording needs to adhere to these rather than developing organically. Further removed along this spectrum are media portrayals of these interventions, those chronicled and analysed by external observers, frequently for either the creation of a documentary or funded academic research. Their perspective is based on their time spent with a project or the performance they were privy to, but as discussed in Chapter 2 it is difficult for an external individual to genuinely experience the dynamic of a group as it is naturally altered by their own temporary inclusion.

As an additional layer of complexity in the fabric of the construction of mediated narratives, observers frequently form some kind of emotional connection with the group, influencing their role as an objective observer, with one such academic writing 'little did I know that going to prison would be the most important and enlightening experience of my adult life' (Scott-Douglas, 2007: p.x). Those who are sufficiently removed to avoid such a potential emotional connection are likely to be too distanced to understand the nuances of the dynamic within such a collective, making their analysis relatively superficial. Without in-depth knowledge of such a complex community it is difficult to avoid talismanic concepts of how Shakespeare offers opportunities for marginalized individuals. The criticality of whose narrative is being verbalized is central to this chapter and forms the basis for my own practice-based research. A large proportion of media aims to provide a behind-the-scenes view where the purpose is not the final production, or not *only* the final production, but the way in which the group develops through the process (Jessop, 2015; Rogerson, 2005). Navigating the line between the aesthetic and the social judgement of the creative practice of marginalized communities is challenging. This chapter aims to isolate the key elements which allow for a successful balance to be struck: true ally-ship from non-marginalized counterparts and control of the narrative taken by marginalized people but in a physical, social and mental space where they are able to express themselves authentically and eloquently.

Journalism

Journalistic articles and podcasts are perhaps the form of media most widely seen by the general public, a piece in the local or national news is likely to attract attention from readers who may not otherwise have an awareness of the topic. These are usually short, human interest pieces, based on soundbites from practitioners and participants and perhaps observation of a performance or, less frequently, a single rehearsal. They are designed to give a glimpse of this work, not an immersion into the detailed workings. As Ray Surette observed,

> People use knowledge they obtain from the media to construct a picture of the world, an image of reality on which they base their actions. This process [is] sometimes called 'the social construction of reality'.
>
> (1997: p.1)

These are also the media examples at the furthest remove from those involved. They can, broadly speaking, be divided into those which are supportive of the work and those which seek to incite 'moral panic' (McRobbie & Thornton, 1995: p.559). News coverage of theatre companies working with those with learning disabilities tends to be supportive in nature although focused on the therapeutic rather than the artistic aspects of the process. The presentation of these initiatives often relies heavily on the framing of the narrative as one of social inclusion and participatory benefits with the artistic qualities deemed secondary.

Blue Apple has been featured with some regularity in *The Hampshire Chronicle*; charting their collaboration with the University of Winchester, several production reviews and their innovative responses to Covid-19. The news articles are designed to offer a brief overview of positive initiatives with a feel-good element and usually feature soundbites from the company themselves. There is a sense that the newspaper has built a sense of local pride about this charity with the editorial team knowing the motivational impacts on their audience of such features. For example, Sam Hatherley wrote about their collaboration with the University of Winchester's D@rwin Dance Company, which Noyale Colin described as contributing to 'a more diverse programme of repertoire of dance in terms of representation, abilities and accessibility' (Hatherley, February 2020). The article also quoted dance student Lydia, Blue Apple actor Lawrie Morris and Blue Apple Manager Simon Morris encompassing all of their perspectives in this piece extolling the benefits of this newly formed collaboration.

In contrast, in July 2019, the University of Winchester published a news article for the first anniversary of Blue Apple's residency on-site which was written in support of the work but notably excluded the voices of the actors. The article briefly outlined the context of the five-year residency, providing quotations from Alec Charles (Dean of the Faculty of Arts) and Simon Morris. Both of them spoke positively about the opportunity this afforded to both Blue Apple participants and university students, although interestingly the unnamed reporter chose not to include direct comments from participants. Whilst this may not have been a conscious decision, or could have been due to time or logistics, this omission of the voices of the marginalized people about whom the article was written was noticeable and suggested commodification, which happens so easily. This was compounded by the two images used, one of which featured the Chair of the Board surrounded by seven of the actors, with no caption provided for identification purposes. The other was of five adults, four of whom were identified in the caption beneath the picture, but with the notable exclusion of actor James Elsworthy. Given the context of this article was about the way in which differently abled performers were integrated within the university community this lack of acknowledgement of the actors' identity gave the very distinct impression that they were further marginalized within this piece. This could have been an ideal opportunity to allow their opinions on the work to be shared with an academic audience but this was not the case, instead reinforcing the sense of exclusion. The actors were offered as a voiceless commodity to be utilized by the university as publicity, rather than being treated as equals who have a right to articulate the benefits of the collaboration in their own words.

News coverage of programmes within prisons is divided into two distinct sectors: those which endorse the humanitarian benefits of the initiatives and those which aim to incite outrage about the supposedly *easy conditions* of prison sentences. With both there is a tendency to commoditize and fetishize the criminality of participant – the worst of an individual's lived experience is provided as the lens through which the work should be viewed. One such example being 'Act V' in *This American Life* which focuses on Agnes Wilcox's work in prison. Whilst often viewed as a supportive piece Jack Hitt's focus throughout the podcast is on the interpersonal politics and previous crimes of the participants rather than their work as an ensemble tackling Shakespeare (Hitt, 2002). Almost all new stories and documentaries insist on divulging the nature of inmates' convictions as a key component in the narrative, whether to evidence the redemptive qualities of the Shakespeare intervention or to elicit anger about creative outlets for those dehumanized by their past actions. In the former are articles such as those written by Anthony Field and Darren Raymond. Field, former Finance Director of the Arts Council, attended the The Shakespeare Prison Project production of *King Lear*, at Racine Correctional Institution and wrote an article affirming his previous arguments that carceral arts projects should be funded by the prison system not arts organizations. This article typified Ashley Lucas's assessment that

> Popular news pieces on prison theatre tend not to analyse the production for its artistry, directing, acting or production values but instead provide a profile of the program in question and sing the praises of its uses for rehabilitation or healing.
>
> (2020: p.11)

There was a sense that Field was using the actors as a commodity to argue his political standpoint rather than honouring the validity of their contribution to the artistic community. He wrote of the 'standing ovation' which followed this performance and his article included quotes from some of the actors, identified only by their characters in order to preserve anonymity. However, the language used drew heavily on the trope of redemptive narratives, presenting the material in a way intended to invite emotional responses. He wrote of the crimes of the 'actor-prisoners' (Field, 2005) including murder, kidnap and sexual offences, closely juxtaposed with personal details about the emotional outlet from the programme. Whilst these were no doubt part of the journey these men had undertaken there was not a single comment on the artistry produced in their performance. There was no review of the process or the production, instead the focus was on the opportunity to 'vent out [...] sadness and frustration', making no mention of the quality of the work being showcased. The Shakespeare Prison Project productions evidence significant artistic ability, hard work, commitment, passion for nuanced portrayal of the characters and creation of impactful performances. Whilst there is nothing negative written in Field's article, the omission of any detail of the quality of the work suggests in his view it was secondary to the emotional impact and, for a publication such as *The Stage*, this manipulates the reader into questioning whether the work was of insufficient quality to be reviewed on its own merit. Shepherd-Bates does, however, question whether it is possible to review a prison performance through such a critical lens and makes the valid point that 'quality is so subjective' (interview, 2022), making it difficult to compare the austere surroundings and limited rehearsals with a professional production.

Raymond published about his own redemptive journey, begun in a prison session 'led by this overtly camp, extravagant man' (Raymond, 2015), which inspired a desire to become better acquainted with Shakespeare after a disastrous encounter at secondary school. Although Raymond makes no secret of his criminal record the article is focused on the theatre work rather than this and, in contrast to Field's piece, there is no inclusion of florid details of crimes. The narrative then charts his post-release journey as an actor and then director before he founded Intermission Youth Theatre (IYT), which works 'with young people from London's inner-city boroughs who were at risk of offending or lacked opportunity' (Raymond, 2015). He documents his process of encouraging them to 'use their own words in replacement for the original text' and of the ownership this gives them, inviting them to actively engage with the story and encouraging them to seek further knowledge. His assertion that 'the key to unlocking Shakespeare is to believe you own it' acknowledges the intrinsic challenges of the language but the potential for leveraging the intrinsic cultural capital from engagement with his plays.

London Theatre Reviews have written media critiques of a number of IYT's adaptations. They describe the adapted narrative, the process by which the company 'unpacked and reassembled the play' and the quality of the artistic endeavours along with 'simply infectious' (Ferrouti, 2018) energy. Their adaptation of *The Comedy of Errors* was applauded for 'skilfully [moving] the action from ancient Greece to contemporary United Kingdom where refugees are no longer welcome' (Eastham, 2017) and offsetting Shakespearean and contemporary street language in a 'truly inspired artistic touch', which used the two to illustrate the cultural differences between the twins. These reviews centralized the quality of the theatre rather than the backgrounds of the actors. This connects with Hayhow and Palmer's desire for a 'new aesthetic' (2008: p.31) in the search for equality, and whilst they wrote this in the context of learning disabilities it resonates with all marginalized groups. This aspirational equality has not yet been achieved but the media has a significant influence over the journey towards this, whether positively (as in these reviews) or negatively (whether obliquely through marginalization of the artistic or more definably through the negativity some reports incite).

For some members of the public tabloid newspapers' inflammatory declamations of the injustice of interventions to 'boost lags' morale' (Moynes, 2018) may be the only information on this type of work to which they have exposure. They utilize the prejudice many of their readership have against those who have committed crimes in their creation of an agenda of anger. When *The Sun* published an account of a Pimlico Opera production, they quoted criticism from Conservative MP David Morris because 'prisons should be preparing offenders for release back into the community by training them for proper jobs or giving them skills' (Moynes, 2018), seemingly ignoring the skills that creative arts develop and which are directly transferable into the modern labour market (confidence, public speaking, teamwork and many more). There is a sense that the journalist sought to validate the fury he wished to incite in the readership through affirmation from a member of parliament and the article used derogatory, sensationalist terms such as 'lags' and 'drug-plagued', citing former inmates such as high-profile paedophile Gary Glitter to encourage a sense of moral outrage. This type of presenting goes beyond the description of patronizing; it is dehumanizing and as Jewkes writes, such journalists do not 'engage in dispassionate analysis but precisely the opposite – passionate engagement for the purposes of exercising moral sentiment' (2005: p.26). Ex-Prison Governor and academic Jamie Bennett draws on the research of R. Freeman when he argues that 'it has also been demonstrated that coverage of both prisoners and prison staff is more likely to be negative than positive' (2006: p.99) and this is borne out by the sensationalism with which the tabloids commodify those connected with the penal system.

The response of the tabloid press to *Mickey B*, Educational Shakespeare Company's (ESC) adaptation of *Macbeth*, filmed within Maghaberry Prison was negative in extremis. This groundbreaking filmic adaptation featured serving prisoners within a maximum-security establishment. The contextualization of the penal setting and the deep-rooted violence during the political turmoil of Northern Ireland's Troubles were provided by the two short films which featured alongside the performance on the DVD – 'Category A, *Mickey B*' and 'Growing Up With Violence'. The project experienced severe logistical problems during filming with prison staff described as 'appearing either blatantly apathetic or downrightly hostile' (Magill & Marquiss-Muradaz – Jennings, 2009: p.110). Wray described the project as 'a test case for the significance of specificity in prison Shakespeare' (Wray, 2009: p.344) and the Arts Council of Northern Ireland funded the development of an educational resource entitled *Unlocking Shakespeare* to accompany the film. Despite receiving Arts Council support, winning the Roger Graef Award for Outstanding Achievement in Film at the 2008 Koestler Awards and being translated into seven languages, the initial media reaction was negative.

The absconsion of a cast member during permitted compassionate leave stirred up coverage of his original convictions and 'the gutter press ran sensationalist stories saying [the] makeup girl was impregnated' and guns and ammunition had been smuggled into the prison by the crew as they indulged in 'a sick twisted "Driller Killer" flick with murderers playing murderers' (Magill & Marquiss-Muradaz – Jennings, 2009: p.111). Magill's own story is one of 'transformation through arts education that began in prison' (Magill – email, 2017) but, following the controversy encountered both inside the prison and in the media in relation to *Mickey B* he ceased prison work in 2009 and now focuses on projects associated with mental health. The trailer on ESC's website revels in the notoriety the film provoked, blood red lettering proclaiming 'Made By Prisoners', 'Censored by the State', 'Imagine being known for the worst thing you have ever done', 'should this film ever have been made' and 'Northern Ireland's Hardest Men' against a powerful drumbeat and atmospheric shots of close ups of their faces. Johnny McDevitt's article in *The Guardian* in 2009 offers a balanced perspective on the news coverage of 'the close-to-the-bone nature of the project, some of which centred around the decision to film one of the more macabre of Shakespeare plays' (McDevitt, 2009) and the time-delay of release for public viewing due to laws relating to prisoner anonymity. The project has a positive legacy and now that the tabloid furore has died down the film and associated documentaries provide evidence of an event described by one inmate as 'the most important thing I've ever done' (McClane – McDevitt, 2009). The relative distance of journalists from the reality of the projects analysed means their media coverage will always be somewhat detached from the participants' experience but their versions of the narrative are often the only ones known by mainstream society. This distancing should allow for objectivity but there is frequently the sense that there is a predetermined agenda being pushed which counteracts this possibility.

Documentaries

Documentaries are able to provide a more detailed and, at times, more nuanced portrayal of the work; it is, however, important to be mindful of who is defining the narrative even if the voices speaking are those from the marginalized community. Filmed presentations of marginalized communities can offer a deeper insight into the artistic work being undertaken but often the packaged product is heavily influenced by funding requirements and participants are encouraged to labour the emotional element of their involvement to the potential detriment of the aesthetics. My interest lies in those documentaries which feature marginalized people and specifically those created by, or with significant input from, the facilitators of the projects. Notable examples are *Shakespeare Behind Bars*, narrating the story of the US prison project of the same name, and *Growing Up Downs*, which featured the work of Blue Apple Theatre Company.

Shakespeare Behind Bars was founded in the United States in 1995 by Curt Tofteland and continues to deliver projects with incarcerated, released and at-risk adults and youth, forming 'circles of trust' (Tofteland – TedX, 2013) in which the participants are encouraged to reflect and to develop. Tofteland has written and spoken extensively about his work, as well as being a co-founder of the Shakespeare in Prisons Conference which draws together practitioners, academics and alumni of such programmes from the international community. In 2005 Hank Rogerson directed a documentary about creating a production of *The Tempest* in Luther

Luckett Correctional Facility. It has become one of the best known of this genre and was partially funded by an ITVS Open Call grant secured during production. Whilst there are several large funds such as this one, the average success rate for applications is below 2 per cent for the ITVS Open Call (Lees, 2012: p.215); however, Rogerson and Spitzmiller's application successfully met the criteria.

The 93-minute documentary opens with three men standing in the open air reciting a speech from *The Tempest* before the camera pans back to reveal a prison watch tower and miles of razor wire fences. It continues in this vein, interspersing rehearsal room techniques and scenes of Tofteland's 'interventions typically urging the actors towards finding "truth" through emotionally charged performance' (Greenhalgh, 2019: p.81) with reportage of the mundanity of prison regime; a seemingly endless cycle of headcounts, mealtimes and cleaning. The grant application stipulated the way in which the documentary was to be framed:

> The words of Shakespeare act as a vehicle to transport this group of incarcerated men to a potentially better place in their hearts and minds […] They have the support and encouragement needed in order to examine their darkest selves, and to shed light on how they might find healing and redemption.
> (Rogerson & Spitzmiller – Lees, 2012: p.226)

The transportation metaphor suggests a passivity to the men's experience with the programme and that they will arrive at a destination somehow altered from their original state, but with someone else having provided the impetus for the transition. The concept of redemption through their involvement in the production and documentary is suggestive of the emotional labour of which Arlie Russell Hochschild writes and that 'institutional purposes are now tied to the [individual's] psychological arts' (1985: p.185). As a practitioner I can attest to the emotional journey undertaken and driven by those incarcerated who have become co-owners of the theatre companies we collectively run and this documentary explicitly focuses on the concept of redemptive development. The extent to which this grant application relies on the 'close up visceral experience' (Rogerson & Spitzmiller – Lees, 2012: p.227) of the emotions of the incarcerated actors probes beyond the artistic and makes social discourse a central tenet of the film.

The actors featured are predominantly 'experienced members of the project from previous years' (Greenhalgh, 2019: p.80) and yet they are invited by the filmmakers to lay bare their past lives, regrets and details of their crimes for consumption by the film's audience. This embodies the *presentation* element of media: personal admissions made within trusted support networks of the theatre project are then reconstituted for audience perusal. The timeline of the project is subverted and 'their past acts will be revealed gradually over the course of the film to build dramatic tension' (Rogerson & Spitzmiller – Lees, 2012: p.226) when in actuality these details had been shared with the group and Tofteland prior to the grant application submission. Sammie Byron's emotional account of his troubled childhood and explosive relationship which culminated in the murder of his mistress is not included for the sake of his psychological processing or the production of *The Tempest* but for the viewers to see this moment of reflection as being of the instant the film was made. Tofteland explicitly references the concepts of 'habilitation', Shakespeare and the redemptive narrative in his statement that 'Shakespeare would adore this group, we are very true to Shakespeare, theatre people were seen as pickpockets, rapists and murderers' (Tofteland, 2005). Whilst people associated with the theatre in the Jacobean and Elizabethan periods were treated with mistrust and often seen as petty criminals (Laoutaris, 2014: pp.183–8) there is nothing to suggest players were deemed to have committed violent or sexual offences. Tofteland's comment has the effect of suggesting Shakespearean patronage and validity for the work being done by the project, placing it within the lineal history of Shakespeare's legacy. Osborne's phenomenon of 'mediachosis' (1995: p.37) means that for many viewers Tofteland's words will assume the status of fact through their portrayal in digital media, when the reality is much more nuanced.

The construction of this piece of media affords centrality to the voices of Tofteland and Rogerson and whilst the viewer may feel they hear mainly from the 'characters', the entire documentary is carefully arranged to convey specific messages. The cast are 'not your ordinary stereotypical prisoners' (Rogerson & Spitzmiller – Lees, 2012: p.228) but have exemplary behavioural records within the penal system (which is a requirement for involvement in such a project within the US penal system). Whilst Harriet Walters claims that 'theatre is the antithesis of prison, it gives you a voice'

(Walters – documentary, 2019), within media spaces that voice may not be your own; instead, the actors are the mouthpiece for the documentary makers. The grant application documents the aspiration that 'public television and this programme will be a perfect match-up', allowing the wide-spread dissemination of 'vital issues that deserve more public discourse and consideration' (Rogerson & Spitzmiller – Lees, 2012: p.234) as the US prison population continues to rise exponentially. The aims of the film-project were laudable and sought to open up national and international dialogue about the potential solutions to crime, claiming appeal to people in a 'wide range of disciplines' (2012: p.234). As Greenhalgh notes this documentary is 'the best-known example of the genre and also the one most used in teaching' (2019: p.82), which suggests that to some degree the aims of the project were successfully realized. However, to some extent the men involved are asked to perform emotional labour in order to convey the aims of the project to the audience with authenticity. The final scene of the documentary, a montage of exultant images from the final production, is evidently crafted as an uplifting end to the process of the project but a bitter irony pervades in that they remain incarcerated and the release offered by the theatre is but a temporary interlude in the monotony of their sentences.

William Jessop's 60-minute documentary *Growing up Down's* charts the work of Blue Apple Theatre as they rehearsed and toured a greatly abridged version of *Hamlet*. The familial connection is immediately established as Jessop introduces himself as the brother of Tommy (who plays the lead role in the performance and the documentary) and son of Jane (founder of Blue Apple Theatre in 2005). The focus of the programme, the edited result 'of hundreds of hours of amazing footage' (*Growing Up Downs* website), foregrounded the social aspect of the work of the learning-disabled actors more than the artistic result of the production. The reportage-style film followed Tommy, Katy, Lawrie and James through the process of rehearsal and touring of the show in what Greenhalgh describes as 'the rights of passage these young people undergo as they embark on adult life with Down's syndrome' (Greenhalgh, 2019: p.83). Down's syndrome has a significant impact on the mental age of the individual with 'independence and social lives noticeably more restricted' (Carr, 1995: p.170) than neurotypical individuals so there is basis for Greenhalgh's assessment, fueled by the fact that much of the airtime is focused on friendships, relationships and love, both requited and unrequited. William Jessop is cited as saying that 'the actor's learning disabilities mean that they are to some extent still going through their teenage years' (Jessop – Wright, 2014), although the situation was more complex in that James (aged thirty-two) does not have Down's syndrome and is instead likely to be on the Autism spectrum whilst Katy lives independently.

The opening sequence – Tommy climbing onstage before delivering lines from Hamlet's 'to be or not to be' soliloquy – establishes the artistic context of the work at the outset, in what William describes as a visual 'taking of this space' (Jessop – interview, 2020). However, much of the focus is on the personal development of the individuals with many intimate scenes of the actors at home and in social situations. In the context of what Neuman and Guggenheim describe as 'interpretive effects theory', the framing of this media is more predominantly social than artistic. The viewer is invited to witness extremely personal conversations, tears and frustrations as Lawrie confesses his love for Tommy, Katy reveals the photograph kept beneath her pillow, Jane describes her depression following the Doctor's prognosis that Tommy 'would never develop' and James has police contact. Disability Arts Online described it as 'a compelling documentary made with honesty and integrity that gives a truly refreshing slice of life in the world of learning disability arts' (Hambrook, 2014). The honesty of the filming is evident and William Jessop comments on how 'powerful' the footage of Tommy and Katy's break-up is just before the tour commences (Wright, 2014). However, at times this level of emotional intimacy with the actors borders on intrusive, such as when the couple are about to share what appears to be their first kiss. The inclusion of this type of deeply personal footage (and that of Lawrie's response to their relationship) appears intended to stimulate empathy from the viewer as a result of what Hochschild terms 'sincere display' (1985: p.185). This sincere display is an engagement tool utilized in media to invoke an emotional response from a social perspective. From an artistic angle however, it begins to hint at the commodification which Preston warned is so often intrinsic in applied theatre.

This raises a fundamental question of intention and reception with this documentary. William Jessop explained 'you're not tuning in to watch a deconstruction of working practice – you're tuning in for an emotional rollercoaster' (interview, 2020) and this is evident in the way the documentary is edited, with far more emphasis on the social than the artistic. From speaking with William it is clear that he feels deep emotional attachment to all of them, not just Tommy, and he attempted to convey this through cinematic images and evocative music, his attempt to 'bottle the essence and make it come to light, a new way of showing people with learning disabilities' (2020). As he explains

> With film-making you can't step outside of yourself and be objective, it's always filtered. People that are in that film look at it and see a version of themselves – they may not always recognise themselves.
>
> (2020)

This explicit acknowledgement of the effect of media presentation of reality is insightful and, in many ways, provides the link between intention and reception; the act of mediating a story naturally leads to some degree of distortion.

As Greenhalgh notes 'very little camera time is given to the director, Peter Clerke' (2019: p.83) and the appearances he does make seem removed from the main narrative of the documentary. His first comment in the film, 'the worst that could happen is it's a crap show, got to be sure they're not put in a position they can't cope with' (*Growing Up Downs*, 2014), seems to deny them active agency and infantilize them to some degree. His director's notes discuss using *Hamlet* as a way of articulating themes before it is too late, 'too late to speak of people who are marginalised or disenfranchised because they don't "fit in"' (Clerke – blog, 2012), but his role in the documentary is marginal. The editing of his involvement does not present him in an overly positive light: one of his rare directorial moments in front of the camera shows him giving Tommy the note 'you've got to stop stuttering on your lines' (*Growing Up Downs*, 2014), not something that those who have any form of speech impediment are able to influence in that manner. However, William was keen to explain that the reason for Clerke's relatively marginal screen-time was a desire to keep the focus on the actors and that to view it otherwise is a 'slightly unfair interpretation' (Jessop – interview, 2020). William spoke warmly of Clerke's contribution to the company and the sense of professionalism he brought to what was previously, essentially, a community theatre, so it is clear that the portrayal in the documentary can be interpreted differently from the way he meant Clerke to be viewed.

The focus of the lens, and therefore of the viewer's attention, is the interpersonal relationships and the emotional development of the central four actors. I would question Greenhalgh's claim that 'the majority of sequences deal with the rehearsal process' (2019: p.83) as very few scenes focus on the process of rehearsing the play. The footage in the rehearsal space features little about the artistic process, focusing instead on the friendships and tensions within the group. Bishop argues the 'necessity of sustaining a tension between artistic and social critiques' (2012: p.277) in the context of socially engaged participatory-art. However, the mediated depiction of Blue Apple's work in this documentary veers decisively towards the social, leaving the artistic critique largely unexplored except for relatively fleeting glimpses of rehearsal activities and audience feedback on the 'stunning' production. Even that is counterbalanced by Katy's closing thoughts on the touring project which focus on the personal impact above the professional or artistic as she states happily 'we're famous and I can't believe it for my life' (*Growing Up Downs*, 2014).

Low-budget media

In contrast to professionally produced documentaries are the pieces of low/no budget media produced by the theatre companies themselves. These are the ones most closely connected to the participants and facilitators and offer perhaps the most authentic version of mediation, although it cannot be forgotten that they too will have an agenda of how they wish to be perceived by the public. The voices of Blue Apple actors were heard loud and clear in their Covid-19 inspired 'newly discovered Polonius' speech' (Blue Apple Theatre, 2020) which they filmed during the first lockdown of the pandemic. They created a YouTube recording in which they interlaced Shakespearean lines with advice about dealing with Covid-19, in what Artistic Director, Richard Conlon described as them having 'some fun with what Shakespeare might have to say about the pandemic' (Conlon – newsletter, 2020). The script was written by

Conlon and incorporated well-known lines and references from multiple plays such as 'neither a borrower nor a lender be' (*Hamlet* 1.3.75), 'slings and arrows' (*Hamlet* 3.1.58), 'households – alike in dignity or not' (*Romeo and Juliet* Prologue.1) and 'rotten boats, not rigged, no tackle, sail, no mast'(*The Tempest* 1.2.146–47). This was interspersed with snippets from the multitude of Government and Public Health guidance which had been disseminated via media and social media during the pandemic, relating to keeping 2 metres apart, washing hands, the creation of 'social bubbles' and the enforcement of localized lockdown measures in Leicester. The impact of the suspension of rehearsals for Blue Apple was significant to the participants, many of whom have multiple, complex learning disabilities and the staff were concerned about them experiencing feelings of isolation (Morris – correspondence, 2020). As Debanjan Banerjee and Mayank Rai describe in their article on the social impacts of Covid-19, 'the modern world has rarely been so isolated and restricted' (2020), citing a number of studies which document the feelings of loneliness this situation has generated and the negative effects on mental and physical wellbeing. Those with learning disabilities already have generally more isolated lives with smaller social networks and 77 per cent of those surveyed aged eighteen to thirty-four reported feeling lonely, prior to the pandemic, which it was anticipated would exacerbate the situation (Cox Commission, 2017).

Blue Apple Theatre responded to these challenging circumstances by initiating weekly Zoom meetings, an opportunity for the members to engage and to speak about their experiences. It was from these sessions that Conlon developed the concept of drawing on Blue Apple's long engagement with Shakespeare to create a short media clip to showcase their work to a wider audience as 'the digital format means it can be shared with lots of people' (Benfield – Zoom discussion, 2020). Those who were involved in the previous Shakespeare productions (a promenade-version of *A Midsummer Night's Dream* 2010, *Hamlet* 2012 and *The Tempest+* 2019) speak with pride about these performances and it is evident that they hold them to be in some ways more of an achievement than their many other successful productions. Conlon harnessed this pride and created a comic pastiche of Shakespeare and Government guidance which linked their past connection with Shakespeare to the current concerns and often confusing information about how to actualize social-distancing. Although social and artistic agendas rarely merge in the context of media coverage of applied theatre, this is one where I think to some degree this fusion is achieved. The script was written by Conlon, as few of the actors would have had the capacity to write something like that unaided, but the wording was designed to draw together Shakespeare, Covid-19 language patterns and the abilities and personalities of the actors for whom the speech was written.

Written media

Written media is another important mechanism for community theatres to publicize their work and does not have large-budget funding requirements to fulfil. Acting On Impulse is a Manchester-based performance charity which aims to 'develop the acting skills of people with experience of homelessness', enabling them to 'share their stories with a wider audience on screen and stage' (Acting on Impulse website). They provide professionally run acting workshops over a period of time, culminating in the creation of short feature films which they make available on-line to challenge perceptions of those who have experienced homelessness and to promote the acting talents of those involved, actively seeking agent representation for them. This focus on employment opportunities and agents suggests that the organization actively prioritizes the artistic agenda rather than the social one, or at least gives each equal priority. However, in the programme which Director Lauren Tomlinson wrote for their 2010 *Dream on the Streets,* the focus appeared to have been more on the social aspects. This was their first live performance and Tomlinson wrote that this was a 'new challenge' she had elected to set for them, alongside tackling Shakespeare for the first time as his 'stories can be told in any setting and era' (unpublished programme, 2010). The play was set in a fictional location with Theseus and Hippolyta employed at The Mustard Tree Law Firm whilst Titania and Oberon were patrons of the Hilton Day Centre for the Homeless, all details documented in the programme. The production made a significant feature out of being set in the world of which the actors have lived experience, using Shakespeare to bring these issues to the attention of a wider audience. Homelessness is a significant yet often overlooked issue which is estimated to affect over 280,000 people in England alone (Shelter, 2019: p.6). However, Tomlinson chose not to use the scale of the issue as a framing mechanism, instead focusing more on the individual plights of the actors.

The programme provided a combination of background on the work of Acting on Impulse, headshots and short bios of the actors, a synopsis of their adaptation and acknowledgements of support, along with a plea for further funding. The fact that their own voices were not heard directly in this programme shifted the emphasis in a subtle yet powerful way; the narration heard was that of Tomlinson as facilitator. The only direct quotation from an actor was in relation to Tomlinson being 'forcibly told by one of the actors "It's hard to learn your lines when you're sleeping under the arches!"'(programme, p.2). The exclusion of their reactions to the process of producing a live production or tackling Shakespeare, in what appears to be their first foray into his work within the theatre, suggests that the media of the programme was more focused on their previous or current experience of homelessness than their standing as artists. The artist biographies included professional headshots taken by a local photographer whilst the text documented their relationship with rough sleeping as well as their involvement in previous Acting on Impulse films, giving equal weighting to the two issues. The multi-coloured flyers produced for the performance (which were used to generate publicity and encourage ticket sales) also centralized the headline-issue of homelessness and gave information on the organization. The overall narrative of the media surrounding this adaptation and the staging itself was much more orientated towards telling the reality of life on the streets (although not referencing the widespread and growing nature of the problem which saw homelessness affect 1 in 200 people in the first quarter of 2019 compared to 1 in 213 people in Q2 2016) (Shelter, 2019: p.7) through the medium of Shakespeare. The lack of the voices of the participants was noticeable and led to a lack of clarity regarding their own opinions about the work they produced.

Media creates opportunities to promote visibility to a wider audience than would otherwise be possible, encouraging societal awareness of this work and the benefits it can offer. However, often these narratives play into 'active audience theories' (Neuman & Guggenheim, 2011: p.177), foregrounding the social over the aesthetic and not challenging people to see this work as truly artistic. There is a clear need for marginalized artists to be given centrality in defining the presentation of media and for 'ally-ship' (Hadley, 2020: p.178) from non-marginalized collaborators which I have incorporated as a blue-print into my own practice. To illustrate this, I will consider two examples from The Gallowfield Players: articles included in *The Grapevine* (the in-prison magazine written and produced by inmates for inmates) and the programme for *The Merchant*. *The Grapevine* has reported on each production to date and several inmate-journalists have written about the work of The Gallowfield Players, covering reviews of the performances as well as interviews with the cast and attendance at rehearsals to generate some *behind the scenes* insight for the wider prison population. The reviews always lauded the company with praise but highlighted any issues with performances such as 'the one who giggled his way through his monologue of the soon-to-be-vanquished Banquo' in *Macbeth* (Walter, January 2019: p.19). The magazine demonstrates the active audience theory, selecting content for the appeal to its readers. Over the years the column space dedicated to the company grew, increasing from one page to two to a six-page spread on *The Merchant*, with the editor explaining that this was due to the theatre company becoming an ever more prominent part of life in Gartree and a burgeoning good news story which inmates wanted to read about.

The review of *The Merchant* included reviews from invited guests including the Mayor of Leicester who enthused 'it was absolutely wonderful, I really enjoyed myself' (Byrne, 2020). It appears that the inclusion of complimentary feedback from external visitors was seen as a more powerful validation than similar enthusiasm from peers. In the context of whose voices are being heard and who controls the dialogue this raises a complex issue. *The Grapevine* is written and edited by inmates with only a final check by staff prior to printing to ensure that nothing inappropriate is included. The intention is that it speaks to inmates in the voices of their peers, not those of staff or external agencies. The magazine features interviews with senior management, articles of interest such as the in-prison industries, book and music reviews, puzzles and recipes and is notable in that in the more than two dozen editions I have read, none features quotes from people external to the prison. It seemed that the editors wanted to evidence that the invited guests (including those from Royal Shakespeare Company, Opus Arte, other theatre companies and academics) felt the performance to be high caliber, in some way affirming the success of the work, in the context of the artistic agenda which has become increasingly a focus for The Gallowfield Players. The editor added his own judgements on the 'talented theatre company' whose performance 'meant so much to everyone' and then concluded the article with a quotation from the programme in which the actors described the personal connections they had formed with the theatre company (*The Grapevine*, 2020).

Will, one of the actors, was invited to write a guest article for the magazine following the *Julius Caesar* production, which he did, acknowledging 'as one of the performers, I find it difficult to write about the play as I was obviously not looking on, but performing was great fun' (2019: p.14). He framed the article as a reflection on the progress made from the outset as he was one of the very first to join, a fact in which he demonstrates ongoing pride. He affirmed, 'we've come a long way' (2019: p.14), citing the extent to which the company is an integral part of the prison community with twice yearly performances. The choice of language used, such as 'community', 'supportive', 'impressed' and 'family feel' (2019: pp.14–15), suggests a desire for The Gallowfield Players to be seen as a crucial part of the positive elements of the prison regime and offering benefits for all concerned. The way in which the narrative is positioned within media coverage is evident in this short article. Will, although a conscientious attender of rehearsals, was frequently frustrated by what he saw as others' lack of seriousness about the work. His rehearsal diary documented annoyance at others' perceived flippancy towards the production, noting 'what a wash out! Felt like a wasted morning' only four weeks before the performance of *Julius Caesar* and that he had been enlisting the support of other actors during their gym session to agree with his perspective in the 'hope we can make it all a bit more serious' (rehearsal diary, 2019).

However, his article reflected none of these frustrations and presented an image of rehearsals as 'a place to relax and have a laugh, for these hours every week we can forget that we are in jail' (2019: p.15). He and I discussed his annoyance when others were in his estimation 'messing around' and he acknowledged that he finds group settings difficult and feels unable to participate in the banter which abounds. During the time we have worked together he has made some progress with regards to joining in with communal jokes but still often remains on the fringes during comedic interludes. However, his allegiance to the company meant that he would not publicly air his personal gripes and instead portrayed a unified image in the magazine article, evidencing 'interpretive effects theory' (Neuman & Guggenheim, 2011: p.172) through his conscious use of framing and agenda setting to project an image of unity beyond even the solid basis which exists in reality. He described his response to the group dynamic in a reflective piece he wrote after *The Merchant* as:

> for someone like myself who is not the most social of animals, this group can be challenging, bouts of banter in large groups can overwhelm me, so the Gallowfield Players do not only produce plays there are aspects of social therapy too.
>
> (2020: p.4)

The Gallowfield Players also produced a theatre-programme for their 2020 production of *The Merchant,* having raised the concept during a Production Meeting organized and chaired by Michael. The theatre company felt it was a way of providing a meaningful memento of the performance for families to cherish and a promotional item for invited guests, to share a little more of the ethos and culture embedded within the group. A unanimous vote approved the concept and, after securing confirmation of prison permission to issue them to families, the actors began to create the content. Leigh took overall ownership as she was prohibited from attending rehearsals for a period of time following anonymous threats made as a result of her transgender identity. During this period of suspension from rehearsals I visited her weekly for half an hour before or after rehearsals to ensure she continued to feel part of the group dynamic and responsibility for the programme content helped to ensure this on a tangible level. My research around the media representation of marginalized groups had highlighted the importance of whose voice is being heard and I was keen that the ownership, creation and editing belonged in totality to the actors, not mediated by myself or the prison. This meant that the actors had the opportunity to promote their perspective of The Gallowfield Players in the professionally printed programme for *The Merchant.* The creation was driven by a conscious focus on the reception it would receive; there were two clearly different intended audiences and the actors were keen to balance these contrasting requirements. Interestingly for many of them the priority was to generate publicity for the company and evidence our professionalism to invited guests. They were also keen for their families to have a memento but felt that they would be proud to receive content suited to a semi-professional theatre company programme.

Whilst frequently the social element of media narratives on applied Shakespeare takes precedence over the artistic, the actors were keen to avoid this being the case. They wanted to evidence their abilities as a theatre company not as *a theatre company of prisoners*, or any other label society may have accorded them since their arrest, although there was a desire to use the programme and the content-matter of the play to explore the challenges of those who have a life sentence. They 'did not want to sugar-coat the reality of the situation people face and the impact on their loved ones, friends and family' (programme, p.3) and were keen to use this as a way of showing themselves as artists exploring a complex topic of which they had lived experience. They asked me to provide examples of programmes from professional theatre companies upon which they modelled the layout. The programme consisted of articles from myself as Artistic Director and Michael as scriptwriter, a timeline for the adaptation, interviews with the cast as actors and as characters, a thankyou page and details for mental health support for anyone experiencing difficulties, as well as a biography section on the actors' previous roles for the company. Understandably they were unable to include headshots of the cast and had to restrict

FIGURE 23 *Motif of The Gallowfield Players in character for* The Merchant, *drawn by Richard (January 2020). Courtesy of Richard.*

identities to first names only for the purposes of relative anonymity as the programmes would be taken away by visitors, but a cleverly drawn caricature image of the cast was included.

Two quotations were highlighted within my article: 'we are, I believe, the first UK theatre company to be co-owned by me and a number of serving prisoners' and 'I was asked if this group had become what I thought it would. The simple answer is no – it has far surpassed my expectations, my hopes and my aspirations' (Programme, 2020: pp.4–5). Michael's article described the process of script writing as an 'undeniable opportunity to say something of worth' whilst acknowledging that 'writing to suit a disparate group is difficult' (Programme, 2020: p.8). Michael is open about his dyslexia within the prison but chose not to include this in the programme as he wanted the focus of the piece of media to be the achievements of the theatre company. He described the script as 'a love letter to [his] children [...] something that would last beyond a prison sentence, something that will endure' (Programme, 2020: p.9). This concept of creating a legacy is something which has motivated him from the formation of The Gallowfield Players and is a trait evidenced from research with those serving life sentences (Crewe – book launch, 2020). In pursuit of that aim Michael has been a driving force behind many of the decisions taken, including the creation of programmes, a request to explore the possibility of publication of scripts and a fund-raising programme which saw him organizing the actors to send out dozens of letters to potential benefactors. This initiative resulted in financial donations (which were paid into a separate bank account within the prison to fund costumes and props) and significant donations of DVDs of productions and books on relevant topics allowing The Gallowfield Players to compile a specialized library of resources which they can borrow to enhance their learning.

The two cast interviews (one in character and one as the actors themselves) were designed by the group as a methodology to ensure all voices were heard and that the ensemble nature and genuine warmth of the company as a whole were portrayed. The equality and collaborative nature of the work was subtly yet importantly conveyed through the way in which throughout the programme my name was shortened to first name only and initialized when others were and that the 'interviews' were facilitated by the narrator Liam with my responses treated equally to those of other cast members

(Programme, 2020: pp.14–18, 20–4). This piece of media was genuinely owned and designed by the actors, enabling them to own the space it occupied and for their voices to be the ones heard. It was not mediated by anyone external as the editing was owned entirely by Richard, Leigh and Michael, but they were rigorous in ensuring that the image it presented conformed to their desire to be taken seriously as a theatre company. Obviously they would have operated their own internal censorship as they did not wish to cause any issues with the content which may have impacted on the company's future.

They used the concepts of active audience theory but instead of playing into the pre-existing beliefs of the audience they wanted to challenge them, delivering a theatrical experience of far greater artistic quality than expected. They elected to follow the conventions of traditional theatre publicity in order to invite assessment as a theatre company, choosing to ask for judgement of the play's artistic merits rather than as theatre made by a marginalized group. Whilst they have expounded the personal and community benefits of the group in their diaries, in letters seeking financial support and in interviews, they felt keenly that they wanted to avoid the way in which the 'benefits of participation are highlighted far more than the resulting aesthetic product' (Goodley & Moore, 2002: p.5) for the creation of this media to accompany the production. They wanted the programme to serve as a piece of theatre memorabilia not as an exploration of their marginalized status and it was they who controlled the narrative of this media.

Shakespeare Behind Bars (SBB) produce very similar style materials where Hal Cobb (a founding actor in SBB Kentucky) 'who works in the prison print shop, lays out the playbill and then has it printed in color' (Tofteland & Wallace – email, 2020). The playbill for their recent production of *King Lear* included a endorsement from Warden Scott Jordan who acknowledged 'the pride taken in the preparation, production and performance of this programme shows the dedication of everyone involved' (Playbill, 2019: p.4). The actors each had a half-page where they articulated their own involvement in the initiative and the personal connections they felt with the character they played, as well as a selection of images from rehearsals. Hal Cobb who played the title role wrote that 'I knew to properly take on the role I would have to look at dark corners of my soul long avoided and bring to the surface residual issues in need of healing' (Playbill, 2019: p.10). Matt Wallace, Keith McGill and Brian Hinds as facilitators each have a half-page resume written in the third-person, as does Holly Stone (Communications) and Donna Lawrence-Downs (Costumes) whilst Tofteland's resume spans two full pages.

It is evident that those creating the playbill for SBB Kentucky understand the importance of framing the media they present to portray their messages. There is balance between the artistic achievements of the company with its long history of productions listed in full, the 'professorial patronage' (Playbill, 2019: p.31) and a traditional style plot synopsis with the social elements of the process. Many of the actors make personal dedications to family whilst a past participant is quoted as saying 'the play's not always the thing' (Playbill, 2019: p.15) and a detailed Ensemble History lists all those who have been associated with the programme as well as whether they remain incarcerated, have been paroled, released or are now deceased. Bishop's argument that the social and the artistic discourses of participatory art are binary and cannot be reconciled (2012: pp.275–7) has many points of validity on a macro-structural level. However, it seems to be less applicable when considering the work of companies such as Shakespeare Behind Bars and The Gallowfield Players which harness the two in tandem and invite audience engagement on multiple levels. They utilize small-scale media such as programmes to offer their artistic work as a creative commodity which they temper with their position as prisoners, excluded from mainstream society by the crimes of which they have been convicted. The underlying message to the audience is 'there is not so much difference between myself and you' (*The Merchant*, 2020: 3.1.67) and that they hope the shared humanity which exists adds resonance to their artistic endeavours.

Conclusion

Media consciously and subconsciously frames and articulates the narrative when depicting the engagement of marginalized communities with the cultural capital of Shakespeare. The recipient of the mediated messaging is not presented dispassionately with facts from which to formulate their own objective opinion, instead they are invited to engage with an initiative carefully packaged in a specific way. This act of presenting the material as being current and relevant, combining the physical and temporal, is deliberately designed to attract the attention of the viewer. It is in this way that such media allows those defining the strategy to influence the response of those who engage with the content. Bishop argues that in the context of politically and socially engaged theatre, 'social and artistic judgements do not easily merge' (2012: p.275) and for many media portrayals of applied Shakespeare the dominant focus of the narrative is the social rather than artistic. Matt Hargrave writes of 'the underlying tension between theatre as a mechanism for social emancipation and theatre as an art form' (2015: p.21) and although his study is specifically concerned with 'disability arts' the read-across to other forms of applied theatre is strong. As Hughes and Nicholson acknowledge, applied theatre contains 'complex networks of power' (2016: p.5) and this complexity is multiplied by the addition of media with its own multi-layered infrastructure of influence. Frequently, media representation works with the psychological motivation of the recipients, as is the case in examples such as the Hampshire Chronicle's supportive coverage of Blue Apple Theatre and 'the opportunity to be shocked and outraged' (Jewkes, 2002: p.26) by tabloid coverage of prison initiatives. In contrast, it can seek to challenge or subvert widely held opinions (and prejudices) such as in the theatre programmes produced by The Gallowfield Players and Shakespeare Behind Bars. Understanding the motivation and acknowledging the active agency of the audience enables those mediating the messaging to do so in a way which frames the narrative for maximum receptive impact.

Barnes's judgement of the 'patronizing intrusions' (2020: p.3) such interventions can be within a community remains a cautionary tale which any practitioner would do well to heed. The presence of the media can be and often is a noticeably patronizing intrusion which can have the effect of dehumanizing the very group whom the story depicts, such as the University of Winchester's article which failed to name or include views from the Blue Apple actors. Even those media explorations which heavily involve the facilitator and participants will often divert the focus from the aesthetic towards the social. This refraction can marginalize the importance and quality of the artistry by centralizing the redemptive qualities for the participants in preference to the quality of the performances.

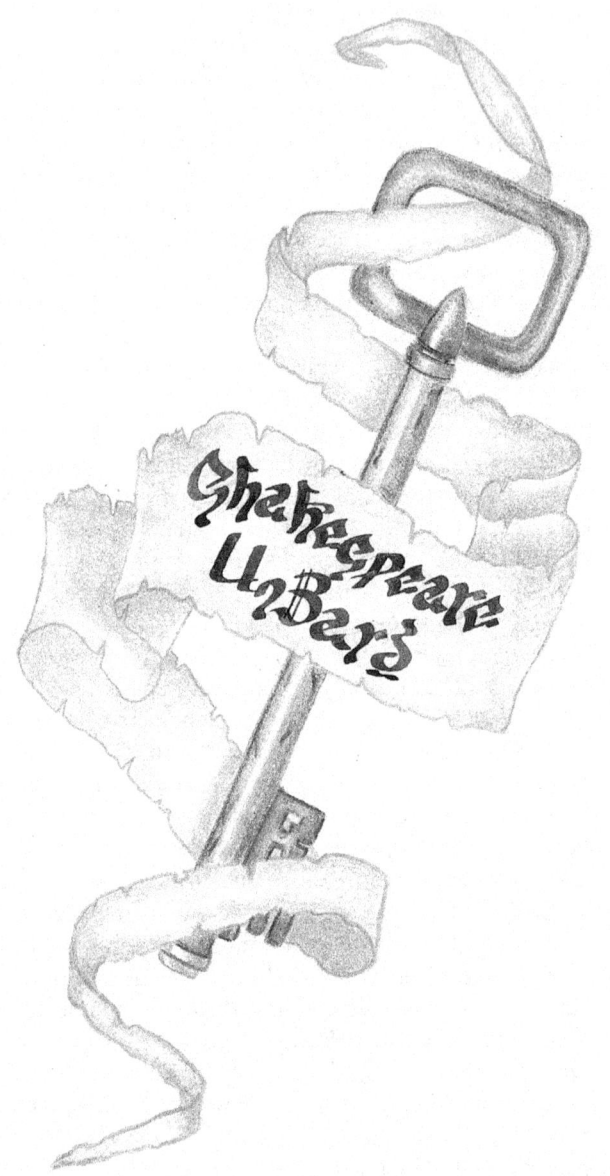

FIGURE 24 *The logo for Shakespeare UnBard, designed and drawn by Michael, The Gallowfield Players (August 2020). Courtesy of Michael.*

There is no simple solution to this quandary as the seemingly logical answer of always centralizing the voices of those marginalized continues to be fraught with pitfalls and complications. There are occasions where this approach is appropriate and where they are able to represent their own work with authenticity and authority. There are other instances where it would not be within their capabilities to do so, whether physically, intellectually, emotionally or logistically. Even where a marginalized group is able to create and edit their own media we need to remain mindful of the complexity of this infrastructure of influence and that nothing mediated is ever neutral. Media is weighted with meanings, signifiers and codes.

Conclusion

This book has developed lines of interdisciplinary enquiry across fields which have traditionally been considered separate, drawing together research from multiple marginalized sectors of society: people with learning disabilities, people with mental health issues, incarcerated people and people who have experienced homelessness. Given the significant overlap between these groups, this cross-fertilization of consideration is necessary when analysing communication methodologies through Shakespeare and the aspiration is that this will open up new avenues for academic dialogue. In many ways Shakespeare's work and marginalized people are at opposite ends of a spectrum – Shakespeare deemed the epitome of culture, internationally revered, with a rich cultural history, and people frequently ostracized, facing judgement and prejudice from wider society. Yet the combination of the two can bring about paradigm shifts as Shakespeare is appropriated and used as a method of communication for those often previously silenced or ignored. This field of academic research is rapidly expanding but predominantly continues to focus on the benefits of theatre for a singular type of marginalized person, not taking account of the intersectionality which exists in this sphere. The beneficial impacts of the arts are widely documented and acknowledged, with a growing desire to ensure that such interventions do not become an 'unwelcome intrusion' (Nicholson, 2015: p.166) and instead facilitate personal growth through 'allyship' (Hadley, 2020: p.178) not patronage.

Shakespeare enables the alteration of spatial constraints for those who feel imprisoned (either physically or metaphorically) through allowing them to speak and to be heard by others in ways which may have been previously inaccessible. 'Shakespeare contributes to present day psychological understanding of the dynamic processes which activate an individual's feelings, thoughts and actions' (Cox & Thielgaard, 1994: p.388), which, combined with the intrinsic cultural capital of his canonical works, means Shakespeare opens up alternative opportunities which may otherwise remain closed to those who are marginalized within society. His characters offer people an opportunity to consider the world from a myriad of perspectives, considering the choices and decisions the characters face and the factors influential in those decisions. As Michael explains 'Shakespeare has allowed us to reinvent ourselves as human once more, through his works and his creativity we are inspired' (2020), a positive affirmation of Shakespeare's power from a man who initially argued against what he saw as an unjustified deifying of the Bard. Reader response theory (Fish, 1976) suggests that meaning is constructed through the two-way interaction between the author and the reader and this applies here: Shakespeare and the marginalized individual or community create a meaning which may differ from the mainstream interpretations of his works. 'Dramatic distancing' (Jennings, 1992: p.17) allows people to choose the level of personal reflection they engage in when they encounter a Shakespearean character – these creations at once are like them and not like them, allowing the mirror of reflection to be held at a comfortable distance. Tom Magill described Shakespeare as 'a safe environment through the mask of classical theatre' (Magill – Landy & Montgomery, 2012: p.155) when discussing *Mickey B* and this is equally applicable across other projects utilizing Shakespeare with those who are marginalized.

Focusing on spaces rather than marginalization markers enabled the superordinate themes of communication (both verbal and non-verbal), resilience, emotional growth and positive autonomy to be explored. People who are marginalized have often suffered trauma in one form or another, so my work follows the principles that guide a trauma-informed approach: developing safety, trustworthiness and transparency, peer support, collaboration and mutuality, empowerment and choice, and addressing cultural, historical and gender issues. Making these a central element of my own practice-based research enabled me to 'be aware of power, control and interpersonal boundary issues' (Freeman – Harri & Fallot, 2001: p.75), which are critical to successful implementation of this approach, whilst providing environments which offered safe places within which to work and to develop.

My own positioning as both practitioner and academic has enabled me to carry out ethnographic research from a position of relative inclusion, witnessing first-hand the changes such interventions are able to engender both for those who are marginalized and for wider society's opinions of them. Working alongside marginalized people for prolonged periods of time gave me a unique integration into the fabric of the theatre companies and developed deep levels of reciprocal trust that yielded at times painfully honest insights into the transformative effects of the work. This transformation was symbiotic – affecting both those involved and those who saw the work. I was mindful to consciously avoid:

> the social dynamic in which the normals feel pity for the stigmatized and express their good intentions and well wishes – in other words, their disavowal of stigma – through charity, or at least through a charitable attitude which often comes across as patronizing.
>
> (Wilson, 2017)

My own participatory practice aimed to centralize the voices and opinions of those marginalized, not as stigmatized people but as talented artists with important messages to express.

The creative spaces of rehearsals allowed ideas to be formulated, explored and refined without the gaze of an audience and those projects with temporal longevity provided the opportunity for the spaces to become influenced by the activities being undertaken. The relative permanence of theatre companies allowed the time for development of more deeply supportive communities amongst those participating, encouraging friendships to form and communication both inside and outside of the rehearsal spaces to flourish. The spaces in which the creative processes took place became 'felicitous spaces' (Bachelard, 1964: p.27) embedded with comforting memories of using Shakespeare in a safe corner of a world which is often intimidating or overwhelming. The imprinting of these memories within spaces altered the participants' perceptions of the locations not just during rehearsals but on an ongoing basis. In this sense the felicitous spaces created often became portable as even outside of rehearsal locations the feeling of safety and community continued to flourish amongst those involved. Considering the central tenets of trauma-informed methodologies – safety, transparency and trust, peer support, collaboration and mutuality, empowerment and choice, cultural, historical and gender issues – permanent theatre companies allow these to develop in ways which short-term interventions are unable to. They encourage participants to experience emotional growth through the positive autonomy of owning the work being created, the prolonged interaction with Shakespeare's characters, and the depth of trust in themselves and each other which challenges their marginalized position. Michael described that:

> To change a space is to change a mindset – to alter the way the physical body operates within it, to remove longstanding attitudinal barriers and change perceptions, but it is not only physical, it is philosophical, altering images of space within the mind, changing purposes of space changes people. By doing this [the Gallowfield Players] the mind can be opened to a series of psychological possibilities, a re-wiring of long-standing beliefs and a rethinking of misconceptions.
>
> (Michael, 2020)

These philosophical changes to belief systems have a significant effect on people's lives and although they take time to germinate, once they do begin to flourish they are powerful and can leave a lasting sense of autonomy and self-belief which can alter perceptions of the future.

Within performances marginalized communities can harness Shakespeare to create heterotopias which challenge not only their own perceptions but those of the wider public. Using as a foundation Tompkins's theory that a heterotopia is created by the juxtaposition of two seemingly contradictory states (the constructed space of the theatre and the abstracted space of the performance) (2014), I assimilated this within the context of Shakespeare with marginalized people. The constructed space of the theatre assumes differing qualities depending on whether the production is performed in a demarcated theatre space or an appropriated space. Juxtaposing the embedded cultural signifiers of a production of classical theatre with a group society typically ostracized for being different creates a heterotopia through which social and aesthetic expectations are challenged.

Through inversion of the cultural capital of Shakespeare, and the attached concepts of it as being elitist and exclusionary in many ways, it is possible to 'disrupt the very fundamentals of theatre' (Reason – Hadley & McDonald, 2018: p.173). This can be taken further, to disrupt the fundamentals of society's perception of marginalized people as evidenced by the professional actors' reassessment of their previous opinions of the patients at Broadmoor Hospital and The Gallowfield Players' proud feedback that 'performing for family and friends is so inspiring, it's so good for them to share in what we do, to feel pride for what we can do' (Wayne, 2020). The performances impacted on the actors' self-perception (these perceptions of self can often be highly critical and the most resistant to change) and on audience perceptions, both external audiences and those connected to the performers, through familial bonds or working relationships.

In contrast to performances, Shakespeare also offers a reflective lens through which individuals can consider themselves and their own experiences during periods of isolation or dislocation from the community. There are notable examples of Shakespeare providing cultural sustenance during difficult times, invoking a sense of habitus, social belonging, connection to something more durable than their present isolation and a place in the wider history which Shakespeare's work represents. Dutlinger's explanation of the transformative power of performance and the way it enables at least temporary reclamation of 'individual identity' (2001: p.5) was evident. The critical distancing afforded by Shakespeare's work allowed people to reassess their situation through the characters of the plays in an almost analytical way, not objectively because it related to their subjective experience, but using dramatic distancing which allowed for a greater variety of viewpoints for exploration of their problems and potential ways of dealing with those problems.

The outbreak of Covid-19 provided the opportunity to explore Shakespeare as a source of reflection and resilience with the theatre companies formed as part of my practice-based research and also the wider prison population. The extraordinary regime implemented across the estate to contain the risk of infection meant that those incarcerated in the UK were kept in virtual isolation from March 2020. For some, the Activity Packs I provided would have been their first exploration of Shakespeare and offered them an opportunity to creatively engage with themes and stories outside of their own currently restricted existence, allowing them to discuss topics with their cell-mates or families and encouraging them to consider educational opportunities for the future. For those within the theatre companies the pre-existing interconnections blurred the lines between Shakespeare and the support network of the group and myself, with Brody writing 'the return to Shakespeare Sundays can't come soon enough, I'm looking forward to that more than I am the prospect of a new job (hopefully!) or the return of my course' (correspondence, 2020). Dean is a relatively new member of The Gallowfield Players, with a significant resistance to any form of authority and discipline, so the arrival of correspondence from him contemplating his view of reflection as 'taking the time to ponder the task and how it can be improved, understanding characters and researching previous productions is vital in building a worthy product' (correspondence, 2020) was unexpected and poignant. Consistency of connectivity was crucially important to the theatre companies throughout the lockdown period and this epitomized the need for trauma-informed work to be ongoing and collaborative.

In the context of all work with marginalized communities it is important to heed Barnes's warnings about the perils of intrusion and seemingly charitable efforts which patronize rather than support those with whom the work is facilitated, and perhaps nowhere more so within media portrayals. Media is central to contemporary communication, meaning that it often forms the basis of peoples' perceptions and with this level of influence comes both benefits and potential concerns. There is no longer (if indeed there ever was) a top-down dissemination of information; instead influence flows in both directions and whilst difficult to capture, especially given the ever-changing nature and exponential growth of social media, this is the reality into which narratives of Shakespeare with marginalized people are released.

There are no unmediated stories; every narrative shared takes a particular perspective, whether conscious or not, shaping the way in which messages are conveyed and received. Accepting this enables us to focus on who is shaping the narrative and whose voice is really being heard. Often the voice being heard is not the one speaking, particularly with marginalized people; it may be the facilitator, the funding body or someone else entirely who is articulating the way in which the reality should be mediated for public consumption. Ironically, one of the significant benefits of

Shakespeare is the opportunity for enhanced communication, yet when the story is being shared often this is subsumed by other competing voices. Informed by the existing body of media, the intention was that media content created by The Gallowfield Players' and Emergency Shakespeare would offer centrality of voice to those involved, not modulated by my own thoughts and perceptions. The actors in those particular companies are the ones best placed to articulate their own reality and the work we have done using Shakespeare's texts has given them the vocabulary and the confidence with which to speak directly to society, asking them 'to look beyond the labels, see behind the stigma and see something more' (Keith, 2019). Michael's aspiration that we 'hope to be seen as torchbearers for another viewpoint, the group who made people think differently about the humans behind the label of criminal' (2020) both evidences his pride in his achievements so far and his plans to continue building a future legacy.

Across each of these spaces it was evident that Shakespeare's characters and narratives did not *give* people the methods of communication they needed – to do so would have been a passive act. What Shakespeare's characters and narratives did was to inspire and to enable people to develop their own methods of communication, allowing them to create the mental and physical space and capacity to do so. So, for people often pushed to the sidelines of society, Shakespeare can be used as a lens to reflect on their own underlying humanity and to see their differences not as a negative but as an intrinsic part of their individuation. Whilst other playwrights have created characters which can be used similarly, the inherent cultural capital and sense of achievement from appropriating Shakespeare for oneself cannot be underestimated.

Navigating a pathway through being an advocate of using Shakespeare in this way and extolling the benefits of this for people, both marginalized and otherwise, is complex. It requires avoidance of being patronizing or inflicting value judgements which are inappropriate or prejudiced. This research and my own practice brought this question to the forefront of my consciousness and there is no singular right way to facilitate Shakespeare or any creativity but there are a number of ways which, in my view, should be avoided. The social conventions of encouraging anyone who is different in society to conform to social norms and a missionary-like zealousness to impose culture as a panacea are damaging. As Atkins and Duckworth write:

> Social justice researchers are transparent about the values that researchers should adhere to, most notably, democratic values: concern for marginalised and minority rights and dignity, commitment to the common good, conviction in the power of individuals to have agency, belief in the importance of dialogic engagement and the transparent stream of ideas, reflexivity and the central premise of individual and collective responsibility for others.
>
> (2019: p.119)

I have attempted to structure my own work in this way, being respectful of those I worked with and openly acknowledging that learning and enrichment flows in both directions.

Trauma-informed methodologies are becoming more prevalent across pedagogical, therapeutic and carceral settings as this knowledge becomes more widely embedded and the implications of underlying trauma are becoming better understood. From my own research, those interventions which use these principles as their core operating structure demonstrate a more collaborative approach to Shakespeare, to creativity and to those marginalized than those which seek to impose a concept of Shakespeare as a 'treatment' (Loftis, 2019: p.265) which in some way will cure our differences. Those differences are what makes each person unique and, whilst enabling people to find their voice and the confidence to use that voice is important, we need to move towards a society which does not seek to homogenize each individual, instead celebrating everyone's differences and the richness they can bring. The power of Shakespeare can be double-edged; for many marginalized people (including a high proportion of inmates and people who have experienced homelessness) it may have been used to highlight their academic failings during formal education or denied them due to them being neuro-divergent or as a result of socio-economic barriers. This same power can be realized positively if people are able to then access Shakespeare, not to learn his work in some purely academic sense but to interweave Shakespeare and their own reality. For in the telling of those tales we may see more revealed about Shakespeare and about their own lives than we know today, indeed, if we choose to look into the mirror of these tales we may see more of our own personal reality reflected too.

Funding for the arts has been put under continual pressure for decades and against the economic impact of Covid-19 the situation looks even more bleak than before, with many institutions announcing redundancies to reduce costs. In contrast to this, the costs of the criminal justice system, mental health services, special educational facilities and work with those experiencing homelessness continue to escalate. The 2018/19 cost per annum for prisons in England and Wales was £3.4 billion (an increase of £22 million from the previous year) (MoJ Accounts, 2019). In 2007 the NHS, social and informal care costs of mental ill-health were £22.5 billion and wider costs to society were £77 billion; these costs are estimated to increase by 45 per cent by 2026 (National Mental Health Development Unit, 2009). Attributing a figure to the costs of SEN schooling is difficult as funding in this area is complex and disparate, split into differing 'blocks'. SEN children account for 14.6 per cent of school populations in England and there is an estimated shortfall of SEN funding in 2021 of £1.2-£1.6 billion (House of Commons Education Committee, 2019: p.33) and this figure was before the impact of Covid-19 on teaching. Councils are reported to spend over £1.1 billion per annum in temporary accommodation for those experiencing homelessness, without factoring in the costs of trying to permanently alleviate the homelessness (Shelter, 2019). The Institute for Public Policy Research (IPPR) estimated that a further 1,100,000 people in the UK would face poverty as a result of Covid-19 (McNeil et al., 2020) and that those worst affected are from ethnic minorities (Patel et al., 2020). None of these costs quoted remain static; they rise exponentially each year. Comparative costs on a global scale are not readily available but the estimated cost of incarceration alone in the United States is over $182 billion per annum (Prison Policy Initiative, 2017) while the global cost of poor mental health is estimated to be $2.5 trillion per annum, expected to reach $6 trillion per annum by 2030 (Horton, 2020). These costs relate to those marginalized, causing a continual resentment from many non-marginalized people about where money from taxes is spent. Perhaps in order to alleviate some of the root causes of this marginalization and effect a more integrated society for the future, creative alternatives need to become more than *nice to haves* as they are often seen today. Quantifying individual change is difficult

FIGURE 25 *The Gallowfield Players, crown from* Macbeth, *created from cardboard and silver paper by an inmate who is cell-bound due to age and ill-health. This has become symbolic of the work of The Gallowfield Players (October 2018). Photo: Rowan Mackenzie.*

however, the intention is that this book lays the foundations for further explorations both nationally and internationally and opens up dialogue between practitioners, academics and people with lived experience of marginalization. Spaces for these changes to happen are important but as Dean counsels 'any space can be used to facilitate our work as it is the willingness and support of the group that makes the foundation the end result is built on' (2020).

REFERENCES

Films and documentaries

Bloomstein, Rex (dir.) 2019. *A Second Chance* (The Timpson Foundation)
Davies, John Howard (dir.) 1969. *Monty Python's Flying Circus: Dead Parrot* (BBC)
Hitt, Jack. 2002. *This American Life Act V* (podcast)
Jessop, William. 2014. quoted by Jeremy Wright, 'Growing Up Downs: Tommy's Got Talent', *The Independent* (21 January)
Jessop, William (dir.) 2015. *Growing Up Down's* (Maverick Productions)
Lloyd, Phyllida (dir.) 2019. *Donmar Theatre Shakespeare Trilogy* (Opus Arte)
Magill, Tom (dir.) 2005. *Mickey B* (ESC Ltd), Education pack also includes additional footage – 30-minute documentary on the making of the film, *Category A, Mickey B* and *Growing Up with Violence*
Munby, Jonathan (dir.) 2015. *The Merchant of Venice*, The Globe Theatre (Opus Arte)
Rogerson, Hank (dir.) 2005. *Shakespeare behind Bars* (Philomath films)
Rogerson, Hank (dir.) 2006. *Shakespeare behind Bars* (Philomath Films)
Tofteland, Curt. 2005. *Speaking in Shakespeare behind Bars*. Hank Rogerson (dir)
Tomlinson, Lauren (dir.) 2010. *Dream on the Streets* (Acting on Impulse)
Woolcock, Penny (dir.) 1994. *Shakespeare on the Estate* (BBC)

Government and institutional policy documentation and data

Arts Council England. 2016. *Analysis of Theatre in England* (London: BOP Consulting), https://www.artscouncil.org.uk/sites/default/files/download-file/Analysis_theatre_England_16112016.pdf
Arts Council England. 2018. *Arts Council National Lottery Project Grants*, https://www.artscouncil.org.uk/sites/default/files/download-file/Information_sheets_Repeat_projects_Project_grants.pdf

Arts Council England. 2020. *Data Report: Emergency Response Funds for Individuals and Organisations Outside of the National Portfolio*, https://www.artscouncil.org.uk/sites/default/files/download-file/Data%20report%20-%20Emergency%20Response%20Funds%20for%20Individuals%20and%20Organisations%20outside%20the%20National%20Portfolio.pdf

The Bell Foundation. 2019. *Improving Language, Improving Lives: Supporting ESOL in the Secure Estate*, https://www.bell-foundation.org.uk/app/uploads/2019/09/Improving-Langauge-Report-2019-FV.pdf

Coates, Dame Sally. 2016. *Unlocking Potential: A Review of Education in Prison* (Ministry of Justice), https://assets.publishing.service.gov.uk/government/uploads/system/uploads/attachment_data/file/524013/education-review-report.pdf Contains public sector information licensed under the Open Government Licence v3.0

Dattani, Saloni, Hannah Ritchie and Max Roder. 2018. *Mental Health* (Our World in Data), https://ourworldindata.org/mental-health

Department for Business Innovation and Skills. 2012. *The 2011 Skills for Life Survey: A Survey of Literacy, Numeracy and ICT Levels in England*, https://www.gov.uk/government/publications/2011-skills-for-life-survey Contains public sector information licensed under the Open Government Licence v3.0

Department for Education. 2018. *FE Data Library—OLASS English and Maths Assessments: Participation 2017/18* (London: SFA), https://www.gov.uk/government/statistical-data-sets/fe-data-library-education-and-training Contains public sector information licensed under the Open Government Licence v3.0

Fair, Helen and Roy Walmsley. 2021. *World Prison Population List*, Institute for Crime and Justice Policy Research, 1 December, https://www.prisonstudies.org/sites/default/files/resources/downloads/world_prison_population_list_13th_edition.pdf Contains public sector information licensed under the Open Government Licence v3.0

Garton Grimwwood, Gabriella Garton. 2015. *Categorisation of Prisoners in the UK: Briefing Paper Number 07437* (London: House of Common Library)

Government. 2020. *Culture Recovery Fund*, https://www.gov.uk/government/groups/culture-recovery-board Contains public sector information licensed under the Open Government Licence v3.0

Halliday, Matthew. 2019. *Bromley Briefings Prison Factfile: Winter 2019* (Prison Reform Trust), http://www.prisonreformtrust.org.uk/Portals/0/Documents/Bromley%20Briefings/Winter%202019%20Factfile%20web.pdf

HMP Wakefield. 2020. Staff Induction Training (undertaken on-site, January)

House of Commons Education Committee. 2019. *A Ten-year Plan for School and College Funding*, https://publications.parliament.uk/pa/

cm201719/cmselect/cmeduc/969/969.pdf Contains public sector information licensed under the Open Government Licence v3.0

MIND. 2013. *Mental Health Crisis Care: Physical Restraint in Crisis – A Report on Physical Restraint in Hospitals in England*, (foreword Dr. S.P. Sashidharan), https://www.mind.org.uk/media-a/4378/physical_restraint_final_web_version.pdf

Ministry of Justice. 2018. *Education and Employment Strategy*, https://assets.publishing.service.gov.uk/government/uploads/system/uploads/attachment_data/file/710406/education-and-employment-strategy-2018.pdf Contains public sector information licensed under the Open Government Licence v3.0

Ministry of Justice. 2019. *Costs Per Place and Costs Per Prisoner by Individual Prison, HM Prison and Probation Service Annual Report and Accounts 2018–19 Management Information Addendum*, https://assets.publishing.service.gov.uk/government/uploads/system/uploads/attachment_data/file/841948/costs-per-place-costs-per-prisoner-2018-2019.pdf Contains public sector information licensed under the Open Government Licence v3.0

Ministry of Justice. 2019. *Strengthening Prisoner's Family Ties Policy Framework*, https://assets.publishing.service.gov.uk/government/uploads/system/uploads/attachment_data/file/863606/strengthening-family-ties-pf.pdf Contains public sector information licensed under the Open Government Licence v3.0

Ministry of Justice. 2019. *Youth Justice Statistics 2018/19*, https://assets.publishing.service.gov.uk/government/uploads/system/uploads/attachment_data/file/862078/youth-justice-statistics-bulletin-march-2019.pdf Contains public sector information licensed under the Open Government Licence v3.0

Ministry of Justice. 2020. *COVID-19 Operational Guidance – Exceptional Regime and Service Delivery*, Version 3.0, 3 April, https://howardleague.org/wp-content/uploads/2020/05/1.-Exceptional-regime-and-service-delivery-27.03.20_Redacted.pdf Contains public sector information licensed under the Open Government Licence v3.0

Ministry of Justice. 2020. *End of Custody Temporary Release Document: Effective from 07 April 2020*, 24 April, https://assets.publishing.service.gov.uk/government/uploads/system/uploads/attachment_data/file/881061/end-custody-temporary-release.pdf Contains public sector information licensed under the Open Government Licence v3.0

Ministry of Justice. 2020. *Prison Population Figures: 2020*, https://www.gov.uk/government/statistics/prison-population-figures-2020 Contains public sector information licensed under the Open Government Licence v3.0

Ministry of Justice. 2020. *Safety Custody Statistics – England and Wales: Deaths in Prison Custody to December 2019 Assaults and*

Self-harm to September 2019, Ministry of Justice, 30 January, https://assets.publishing.service.gov.uk/government/uploads/system/uploads/attachment_data/file/861732/safety-in-custody-q3-2019.pdf Contains public sector information licensed under the Open Government Licence v3.0

Ministry of Justice. 2021. *Safety Custody Statistics – England and Wales: Deaths in Prison Custody to December 2019 Assaults and Self-harm to December 2020*, Ministry of Justice, 30 April, https://www.gov.uk/government/statistics/safety-in-custody-quarterly-update-to-december-2020/safety-in-custody-statistics-england-and-wales-deaths-in-prison-custody-to-march-2021-assaults-and-self-harm-to-december-2020 Contains public sector information licensed under the Open Government Licence v3.0

National Mental Health Development Unit. 2009. *Factfile 3: The Costs of Mental Ill Health*, https://www.networks.nhs.uk/nhs-networks/regional-mental-health-workshop-mids-east/documents/supporting-materials/nmhdu-factfile-3.pdf Contains public sector information licensed under the Open Government Licence v3.0

OfSTED School Inspection Handbook. 2019. https://assets.publishing.service.gov.uk/government/uploads/system/uploads/attachment_data/file/843108/School_inspection_handbook_-_section_5.pdf Contains public sector information licensed under the Open Government Licence v3.0

O'Moore, Eamonn. 2020. Ministry of Justice, *Briefing paper: Interim assessment of impact of various population management strategies in prisons in response to COVID-19 pandemic in England*, 24 April, https://assets.publishing.service.gov.uk/government/uploads/system/uploads/attachment_data/file/882622/COVID-19-population-management-strategy-prisons.pdf Contains public sector information licensed under the Open Government Licence v3.0

Organisation for Economic Co-operation and Development. 2020. *Policy Responses to Coronavirus (COVID-19), Culture Shock: COVID-19 and the Cultural and Creative Sectors*, 7 September, https://www.oecd.org/coronavirus/policy-responses/culture-shock-COVID-19-and-the-cultural-and-creative-sectors-08da9e0e/ Contains public sector information licensed under the Open Government Licence v3.0

Prison Policy Initiative, https://www.prisonpolicy.org/data/

Prison Policy Initiative. 2017. *Following the Money of Mass Incarceration*. https://www.prisonpolicy.org/reports/money.html

Prison Reform Trust. 2019. *Prison: The Facts – The Bromley Briefings*, http://www.prisonreformtrust.org.uk/Portals/0/Documents/Bromley%20Briefings/Prison%20the%20facts%20Summer%202019.pdf

Sentencing Council. 2020. *Sentencing Offenders with Mental Disorders, Developmental Disorders, or Neurological Impairments*, 1 October, https://www.sentencingcouncil.org.uk/overarching-guides/magistrates-court/item/sentencing-offenders-with-mental-disorders-developmental-disorders-or-neurological-impairments/ Contains public sector information licensed under the Open Government Licence v3.0

Singleton, M., H. Meltzer and R. Gatward. 1998. *Psychiatric Morbidity among Prisoners* (London: Office of National Statistics)

Statutory Instruments. 1999. *The Prison Rules 1999, No 728*, http://www.legislation.gov.uk/uksi/1999/728/made

Sturge, Georgina. 2020. *UK Prison Population Statistics: Briefing Paper Number CBP – 04334* (London: House of Commons Library), https://commonslibrary.parliament.uk/research-briefings/sn04334/ Contains public sector information licensed under the Open Government Licence v3.0

Substance Abuse and Mental Health Services Administration, U.S. 2014. *SAMHSA's Concept of Trauma and Guidance for a Trauma-Informed Approach* (Rockville, MD), https://www.cdc.gov/cpr/infographics/6_principles_trauma_info.htm

Walmsley, Roy. 2018. *World Prison Population List: Twelfth Edition* (Institute for Criminal Policy Research), https://www.prisonstudies.org/sites/default/files/resources/downloads/wppl_12.pdf

Her Majesty's Inspectorate of Prisons Reports

Clarke, Peter. 2016. *Report of an Unannounced Inspection of HMP Stafford by HM Chief Inspector of Prisons, 8–19 February 2016* (London: Her Majesty's Inspectorate of Prisons) Contains public sector information licensed under the Open Government Licence v3.0

Clarke, Peter. 2018. *Report on Announced Inspection of HMP and YOI Nottingham by HM Inspector of Prisons 11–12 December 2017 and 8–11 January 2018* (London: Her Majesty's Inspectorate of Prisons) Contains public sector information licensed under the Open Government Licence v3.0

Clarke, Peter. 2018. *Report on Unannounced Inspection of HMP Gartree by HM Inspector of Prisons 13–23 November 2017* (London: Her Majesty's Inspectorate of Prisons) Contains public sector information licensed under the Open Government Licence v3.0

Clarke, Peter. 2018. *Report of an Unannounced Inspection of HMP Leicester by HM Chief Inspector of Prisons, 8–19 January 2018* (London: Her Majesty's Inspectorate of Prisons) Contains public sector information licensed under the Open Government Licence v3.0

Clarke, Peter. 2018. *Report of an Unannounced Inspection of HMP Birmingham by HM Chief Inspector of Prisons, 30 July – 9 August 2018* (London: Her Majesty's Inspectorate of Prisons) Contains public sector information licensed under the Open Government Licence v3.0

Clarke, Peter. 2019. *HM Chief Inspector of Prisons for England and Wales, Annual Report 2018–19* (London: Crown Copyright), https://www.justiceinspectorates.gov.uk/hmiprisons/wp-content/uploads/sites/4/2019/07/6.5563_HMI-Prisons-AR_2018-19_WEB_FINAL_040719.pdf Contains public sector information licensed under the Open Government Licence v3.0

Stacey, Glenys and Peter Clarke. 2016. *An Inspection of through the Gate Resettlement Services for Short-Term Prisoners: A Joint Inspection by HM Inspectorate of Probation and HM Inspectorate of Prisons* (London: Her Majesty's Inspectorate of Probation), https://www.justiceinspectorates.gov.uk/cjji/wp-content/uploads/sites/2/2016/09/Through-the-Gate.pdf Contains public sector information licensed under the Open Government Licence v3.0

Stacey, Dame Glenys and Peter Coates. 2017. *An Inspection of through the Gate Resettlement Services for Prisoners Serving 12 Months or More* (HM Inspectorate of Prisons, June), 8

Taylor, Charlie and Amanda Spielman. 2022. *Prison Education: A Review of Reading Education in Prisons* (Her Majesty's Inspectorate of Prisons), https://www.gov.uk/government/publications/prison-education-a-review-of-reading-education-in-prisons/prison-education-a-review-of-reading-education-in-prisons#print-or-save-to-pdf Contains public sector information licensed under the Open Government Licence v3.0

Performance publicity content

Acting on Impulse. 2010. *Dream on the Streets Programme*
Acting on Impulse. 2010. *Dream on the Streets Flyer*
Emergency Shakespeare. 2019. *Macbeth Programme*
Firebird Theatre. 2010. *The Tempest Programme*
Firebird Theatre. 2014. *Prospero: Duke of Milan* guidance booklet
The Gallowfield Players. 2020. *The Merchant Programme*
Shakespeare Behind Bars. 2019. *King Lear Playbill*

Productions

Acting on Impulse. 2010. *Dream on the Streets,* The Hub, Altrincham (May)
Acting Up! 2016. *The Tempest,* Friargate Theatre, York (October)
Blue Apple Theatre. 2019. *The Tempest+,* Winchester Royal Theatre (June)
Blue Apple Theatre. 2020. *Polonius Speech Reimagined,* Zoom (June)
Emergency Shakespeare. 2019. *Macbeth,* HMP Stafford (September)
Firebird Theatre. 2010. *The Tempest,* Bristol Old Vic
Firebird Theatre. 2011. *Nine Lessons of Caliban,* Bristol Old Vic
Firebird Theatre. 2014. *Prospero: Duke of Milan,* Bristol Old Vic
Flute Theatre. 2016. *The Tempest,* Orange Tree Theatre (25–26 October)
Flute Theatre and Kompanyia Lliure. 2017. *The Tempest,* Teatre Lliure (26 March)
The Gallowfield Players. 2018. *Macbeth,* HMP Gartree (October)
The Gallowfield Players. 2019. *Julius Caesar,* HMP Gartree (June)
The Gallowfield Players. 2020. *The Merchant,* HMP Gartree (January)
Lloyd, Phyllida (dir.). 2016. *The Donmar Shakespeare Trilogy* (Donmar Pop-Up Theatre, London)
Munby, Jonathan (dir.). 2015. *The Merchant of Venice* (The Globe Theatre)
The Shakespeare Prison Project. 2017. *The Merchant of Venice,* Racine Correctional Institution (June)

Rehearsals and workshops

1623 Theatre. 2019. *A Midsummer Night's Dream,* Fountaindale SEN School (March)
1623 Theatre. 2019. *The Tempest,* Fountaindale SEN School (March)
Acting Up!. 2016. Rehearsals for *The Tempest,* Friargate Theatre, York (April–October)
Blue Apple Theatre. 2019. *The Tempest+,* Winchester (January, February and April)
Emergency Shakespeare. 2019. *Macbeth* rehearsals (March-September)
Emergency Shakespeare. 2019–20. *The Merry Wives of Windsor* rehearsals (October 2019–March 2020)
Emergency Shakespeare. 2020. *Othello* rehearsals (September)
Flute Theatre and Kompanyia Lliure. 2017. *The Tempest,* Centre d'Educacio Especial Montserrat Montero (March)

The Gallowfield Players. 2018. *Macbeth* rehearsals (March–October)
The Gallowfield Players. 2018–19. *Julius Caesar* rehearsals (December 2018–June 2019)
The Gallowfield Players. 2019–20. *The Merchant* rehearsals (July 2019–January 2020)
The Gallowfield Players. 2020. *Sycorax's Storm* rehearsals (February–March)
The Gallowfield Players. 2019–20. Production Meetings
HMP Leicester. 2017. *Othello* (October)
HMP Leicester. 2018. *Macbeth* (June)
HMP Leicester. 2018. *Romeo and Juliet* project (September)
Kelvin Goodspeed, during rehearsals for *The Tempest*, Friargate Theatre, York (May 2016)
Spiller, Ben. Artistic Director 1623 Theatre, Tweeting after attending a rehearsal for *The Merchant*, HMP Gartree (22 November 2019)
Wayne. 2019. Rehearsal diary for *The Merchant* (20 September)

Shakespeare texts

Brooks, Harold F. (ed.). 1979. *A Midsummer Night's Dream* (London: Arden Shakespeare 2nd series)
Brown, John Russell (ed.). 1955. *The Merchant of Venice* (London: Arden Shakespeare 2nd series)
Daniell, David (ed.). 1998. *Julius Caesar* (London: Arden Shakespeare 3rd series)
Foakes, R. A. (ed.). 1997. *King Lear* (London: Arden Shakespeare 3rd series)
Jenkins, Harold (ed.). 1982. *Hamlet* (London: Arden Shakespeare 2nd series)
Honigman, E. A. J. (ed.). 1996. *Othello* (London: Arden Shakespeare 3rd series)
Mason Vaughan, Virginia and Alden T. Vaughan (eds). 1999. *The Tempest* (London: Arden Shakespeare 3rd series)
Muir, Kenneth (ed.). 1951. *Macbeth* (London: Arden Shakespeare 3rd series)
Siemon, James E. (ed.). 2009. *Richard III* (London: Arden Shakespeare 3rd series)
Weis, Rene (ed.). 2012. *Romeo and Juliet* (London: Arden Shakespeare 3rd series)

Unpublished Interviews

Acting Up!. 2016. Verbal feedback from audience following performances *The Tempest* (October)
Birch, Paul. 2016. York (18 April)
Bloomstein, Rex. 2019. London (28 November)
Blue Apple Theatre. 2019. Interviews with various cast members, University of Winchester (April 2019)
Blue Apple Theatre. 2020. Interview with Core Company, Zoom (21 July)
Bridge, Gillian, 2016. Surrey (13 September)
Conlon, Richard. 2019. University of Winchester (19 January)
Conlon, Richard. Interview (12 February 2019)
Derek. 2018. HMP Leicester (various conversations)
Emergency Shakespeare. 2019. Post-performance cast debrief for *Macbeth*, HMP Stafford
Firebird Theatre Company. 2016. cast interview, Bristol (3 October)
The Gallowfield Players. 2018. Post-performance cast debrief for *Macbeth*, HMP Gartree
The Gallowfield Players. 2019. Post-performance cast debrief for *Julius Caesar*, HMP Gartree
The Gallowfield Players. 2020. Post-performance cast debrief for *The Merchant*, HMP Gartree
Goodspeed, Kelvin. 2016. York (5 June)
Hunter, Kelly. 2016. Teddington (5 September)
Jackson, Adrian. 2016. London (16 December)
Jennings, Sue. 2016. Wells, Somerset (19 October)
Jessop, William. 2020. Telephone (11 September)
Keehan, Bridget. 2016. Birmingham (12 April)
Michael, Rehearsal Diary entry (30 January 2020)
Out of Character cast. 2016. York (16 June)
Peer Mentor. 2018. HMP Gartree (April)
Sallis, Jane. 2016. Bristol (3 October)
Shepherd-Bates, Frannie. 2022. Detroit (3 January)
Shortt, Michael. 2020. Zoom (24 May)
Spiller, Ben. 2019. Derby (6 March)
Verbal feedback from Lord Mayor of Leicester, Annette Byrne, 27 January 2020
Wilkinson, Jeremy. 2020. Telephone conversation with the author (4 February)
Williams, Haisan. 2020. Zoom (5 May)

Unpublished written content

Acting Up! 2016. Debrief drawings, *The Tempest*
Batu, Emergency Shakespeare, Rehearsal diary *Macbeth* (unpublished, July 2019)
Beech, Elizabeth. 2020. Email correspondence, various dates
Ben. 2019. The Gallowfield Players, *No Drama: A Reflection on The Gallowfield Players*
Birch, Paul. 2014. *Disturbing Shakespeare* Script
Brody, Emergency Shakespeare, Rehearsal diary *Macbeth* (unpublished, June 2019)
Conlon, Richard. 2019. *The Tempest – New Scenes* Script
Conlon, Richard. 2020. *Polonius Speech Reimagined* Script
Dean. 2020. The Gallowfield Players, *Reflections*
Dean. 2020. The Gallowfield Players, *Creative Spaces* (unpublished, August)
Emergency Shakespeare. 2019. *Macbeth: An Adaptation* Script
Emergency Shakespeare. 2019. Rehearsal Diaries for *Macbeth*, multiple notebooks
Emergency Shakespeare. 2019. Feedback forms completed by families and external guests attending performance of *Macbeth*
Emergency Shakespeare. 2019. Feedback forms completed by inmates attending performance of *Macbeth*
Emergency Shakespeare. 2019. Feedback forms completed by staff attending performance of *Macbeth*
Emergency Shakespeare. 2019. Self-assessment questionnaires
Emergency Shakespeare. 2020. Correspondence during COVID-19
Firebird Theatre
Flute Theatre. 2016. Feedback gathered from adults who attended *The Tempest* (Orange Tree Theatre)
The Gallowfield Players. 2018. Feedback forms completed by inmates attending performance of *Macbeth*
The Gallowfield Players. 2018. Feedback forms completed by staff attending performance of *Macbeth*
The Gallowfield Players. 2018. *Macbeth: An Adaptation* Script
The Gallowfield Players. 2018. Self-assessment questionnaires
The Gallowfield Players. 2019. *Julius Caesar: An Adaptation* Script
The Gallowfield Players. 2019. Feedback forms completed by families and external guests attending performance of *Julius Caesar*
The Gallowfield Players. 2019. Feedback forms completed by inmates attending performance of *Julius Caesar*
The Gallowfield Players. 2019. Feedback forms completed by staff attending performance of *Julius Caesar*

The Gallowfield Players. 2019. Rehearsal Diaries for *Julius Caesar*, multiple notebooks
The Gallowfield Players. 2020. Correspondence during Covid-19
The Gallowfield Players. 2020. Feedback forms completed by families and external guests attending performance of *The Merchant*
The Gallowfield Players. 2020. Feedback forms completed by inmates attending performance of *The Merchant*
The Gallowfield Players. 2020. Feedback forms completed by staff attending performance of *The Merchant*
The Gallowfield Players. 2020. Rehearsal Diaries for *The Merchant*, multiple notebooks
The Grapevine. 2018–20. HMP Gartree in-prison magazine, various editions including 'Gartree players give Macbeth the treatment' (January 2019); 'Gallowfield Players take an audience to Rome' (July 2019); 'The Gallowfield Players proudly present *The Merchant*' (February 2020)
The Grapevine, HMP Gartree in-prison magazine (unpublished, February 2020)
Goodspeed, Kelvin. 2016. Acting Up! *The Tempest* Script
Hack, Helen. 2020. Email correspondence, various dates
Her Majesty's Prison and Probation Service (HMPPS) National Research Committee approval. 14 March 2018. Reference 2018-065
HMP Leicester. 2017. *Othello* script rewrites.
HMP Leicester. 2018. *Macbeth* script rewrites
HMP Leicester. 2018. *Romeo and Juliet* project outputs.
HMP Leicester. 2017. Self-assessment questionnaires
HMP. 2019. Stafford's mission statement
Jennings, Sue. 1999. *Romeo and Juliet: The Nurse's Story* Script
Keith. The Gallowfield Players, *Rehearsal Diary – Julius Caesar* (unpublished, 2019)
Leigh. Correspondence with the author (May 2020)
Magill, Tom. 2017. Email correspondence (25 October)
Mark. Emergency Shakespeare, conversation with the author (29 September 2019)
Martin. 2020. The Gallowfield Players, *Reflections on Creative Space in HMP Gartree*
Michael. 2019. The Gallowfield Players, *Experiencing Freedom within the High Security Estate*
Michael. 2019. The Gallowfield Players, *Reflections on the Rehearsal Process*
Michael. 2019. The Gallowfield Players, *Shakespeare and Perception of Space*
Michael. 2019. The Gallowfield Players, *A Sense of Freedom*
Michael. 2019. The Gallowfield Players, *The Merchant* Script

Michael. 2019. Verbal Feedback
Michael. 2020. The Gallowfield Players, *Reflections on Creative Space in HMP Gartree*
Michael. 2020. The Gallowfield Players, *Reflections on Creative Space* (unpublished, August), p. 6
Michael. 2020. The Gallowfield Players, *Sycorax's Storm* Script
Michael. 2020. The Gallowfield Players, *Thoughts on Reflective Space*
Michael. 2020. The Gallowfield Players, *Reflections on Media Space*
Michael. 2020. 'Late Nights and Friday Mornings', *The Merchant Programme* (unpublished, January), pp. 5–7, p. 7
Miguel. 2018. The Gallowfield Players, post-performance debrief *Macbeth* (19 October)
Morris, Simon. 2020. Email correspondence, various dates
Murphy, Deborah. 2020. Email correspondence, various dates
Reynolds, Rosie. 2019. Email communication (June)
Rob. 2020. The Gallowfield Players, *Reflections on Creative Space in HMP Gartree*
Rob. 2019. The Gallowfield Players, *Reflections on Performing Julius Caesar*
Rob. 2019. Rehearsal diary for *The Merchant* (27 July)
Rob's Aunt. 2020. Personal correspondence with the author (17 February)
Sam, Gallowfield Players, HMP Gartree comment made during rehearsal for *The Merchant* (January 2020)
Sallis, Jane. 2010. *The Tempest: An Adaptation* Script
Sallis, Jane. 2014. *Prospero: Duke of Milan* Script
Tofteland, Curt. 2020. Email correspondence (11 August)
Tom, verbal comment during Acting Up! debrief session, Friargate Theatre, York (October 2016)
Ron Daniels interviewed by Rob Ferris in *Shakespeare Comes to Broadmoor*, p. 88
Walker, Callum. 2020. Email correspondence, various dates
Wallace, Matt. 2020 Email correspondence (11 August)
Wayne, The Gallowfield Players, Rehearsal Diary – *Julius Caesar* (unpublished, 2019)
Wayne. 2020. The Gallowfield Players, *Thinking about Creative Space*
Wayne. 2020. The Gallowfield Players, *Thinking about Creative Space* (unpublished, August)
Wilkinson, Jeremy. 2020. Email correspondence, various dates
Wilkinson, Paula. 2020. Email correspondence, various dates
Will. 2020. The Gallowfield Players, *The Gallowfield Players: A 24 Month Journey so far*
Will. 'Gallowfield Players take an audience to Rome, *The Grapevine*, (July 2019), 14–17 (pp. 14)

Academic publications

Aldridge, Jo. 2016. *Participatory Research: Working with Vulnerable Groups in Research and Practice* (Bristol and Chicago: Policy Press)
Anonymous. 2006. 'Those Who Trespass against Us: One Woman's War against the Nazis Review', *Contemporary Review*, 288, 1681, https://search-proquest-com.ezproxy.bham.ac.uk/docview/204956761?accountid=8630&rfr_id=info%3Axri%2Fsid%3Aprimo
Arcangeli, Alessandro. 2011. *Cultural History: A Concise Introduction* (London: Taylor & Francis)
Atkins, Liz and Vicky Duckworth. 2019. *Research Methods for Social Justice and Equity in Education* (London: Bloomsbury Research Methods for Education)
Bachelard, Gaston. 1964. *The Poetics of Space*, trans. by Maria Jolas (London: Penguin)
Bailey, F. Y. and D. C. Hale (eds). 1998. *Popular Culture, Crime and Justice* (Wadsworth: Belmont)
Bailey, Ruth.2014. 'What Is Disability Theatre?', *Disability Arts Online*, http://www.disabilityartsonline.org.uk/disability-theatre
Balfour, Michael (ed.). 2001. *Theatre and War 1033–1945: Performance in Extremis* (New York: Berghahn Books)
Balfour, Michael (ed.). 2004. *Theatre in Prison: Theory and Practice* (Bristol: Intellect)
Banerjee, Debanjan and Mayank Rai. 2020. 'Social Isolation in COVID-19: The Impact of Loneliness', *International Journal of Social Psychiatry*, https://doi.org/10.1177/0020764020922269
Banks, Fiona (ed.). 2019. *Shakespeare: Actors and Audiences* (London: Bloomsbury)
Barker, Howard. 1993. *Arguments for a Theatre* 2nd edition (Manchester: Manchester University Press)
Barnes, Todd Landon. 2020. *Shakespearean Charity and the Perils of Redemptive Performance* (Cambridge: Cambridge University Press)
Barthes, Roland. 1977. *Image, Music, Text* trans. by Stephen Heath (New York: Hill and Wang), 146
Bates, Laura. 2013. *Shakespeare Saved My Life: Ten Years in Solitary with the Bard* (Naperville: Sourcebooks)
Bauer, Raymond A. 1964. 'The Obstinate Audience: The Influence Process from the Point of View of Social Communication', *American Psychologist*, 19:5, 319–28, https://psycnet.apa.org/record/1965-01631-001
Bayne, Ian. 1992. 'The Set and Stage Management', in *Shakespeare Comes to Broadmoor*, 114–125, 120

Bennett, Jamie. 2006. 'The Good, the Bad and the Ugly: The Media in Prison Films,' *The Howard Journal*, 45:2, 97–115

Bennett, Susan. 1997. *Theatre Audiences: A Theory of Production and Reception*, 2nd edition (London: Routledge)

Bennett, Tony, Mike Savage et al. 2009. *Culture, Class, Distinction* (London: Routledge)

Bilby, Charlotte, Laura Caulfield and Louise Ridley. 2013. *Re-imagining Futures: Exploring Arts Interventions and the Process of Desistance* (London: The Arts Alliance), http://www.artsevidence.org.uk/media/uploads/re-imagining-futures-research-report-final.pdf

Bishop, Claire. 2012. *Artificial Hells: Participatory Art and the Politics of Spectatorship* (London: Verso)

Blythe-La Gasse, A. and Michelle Welde-Hardy. 2013. 'Considering Rhythm for Sensorimotor Regulation in Children with Autism Spectrum Disorder', *Music Therapy Perspectives*, 31:1, 67–77

Boal, Augusto. 2008. *Theatre of the Oppressed*, trans. by A. Charles, Maria-Odilia Leal McBride and Emily Fryer (London: Pluto Press)

Bottinelli, J. 2005. '"This is Reality. Right Now, Right Here. So Be Real": Reality Television and the Amish "other"', *Western Folklore*, 64, 305–22

Bourdieu, Pierre. 1973. 'Cultural Reproduction and Social Reproduction', in *Knowledge, Education and Cultural Change: Papers in the Sociology of Education*, ed. by Richard Brown (Tavistock: Routledge), 487–511

Bourdieu, Pierre. 1977. *Outline of a Theory of Practice*, trans. by Richard Nice (Cambridge: Cambridge University Press)

Bourdieu, Pierre. 1986. 'The Forms of Capital', trans. by Richard Nice, in *Handbook of Theory and Research for the Sociology of Education*, ed. by J Richardson (Westport: Greenwood), 241–58

Bourdieu, Pierre. 1987. *Distinction: A Social Critique of the Judgement of Taste*, trans. by Richard Nice (Massachusetts: Harvard University Press)

Braithwaite, John. 1989. *Crime, Shame and Reintegration* (Cambridge: Cambridge University Press)

Bridge, Gillian. 2016. *The Significance Delusion* (Carmarthen: Crown House Publishing Ltd)

Bristol, Michael D. 1996. *Big-time Shakespeare* (London: Routledge)

Brook, Peter. 1998. *Evoking and Forgetting Shakespeare* (London: Nick Hern Books)

Brook, Peter. 2008. *The Empty Space* (London: Penguin Classics)

Brooker, Catherine, Julie Repper, Catherine Beverley, Mike Ferriter Nicola Brewer. 2002. *Mental Health Services and Prisons* (Sheffield: University of Sheffield School of Health and Related Research), http://www.ohrn.nhs.uk/resource/Research/MHSysRevIntro.pdf

Car, Janet. 1995. *Down's Syndrome: Children Growing up* (Cambridge: Cambridge University Press)

Carey, Lois (ed.). 2006. *Expressive and Creative Arts Methods for Trauma Survivors* (London: Jessica Kingsley Publishers)

Carlson, Marvin. 1990. *Theatre Semiotics: Signs of Life* (Bloomington: Indiana University Press)

Carlson, Marvin 2001. *The Haunted Stage: The Theatre as Memory Machine* (Ann Arbor: The University of Michigan Press)

Carlson, Marvin. 2003. *The Haunted Stage: The Theatre as a Memory Machine* (Michigan: University of Michigan), 11

Collard, Michelle. 2019. *Blue Apple Community Drama and Dance Projects Evaluation Report*, https://static1.squarespace.com/static/55f7cab7e4b0c173c6bf223c/t/5e149d5ef98bf1711b3bbbf1/1578409312124/Blue+Apple+Evaluation+Final+Report+-+August+2019.pdf

Carson, Christie and Peter Kirwan (eds). 2014. *Shakespeare and the Digital World: Redefining Scholarship and Practice* (Cambridge: Cambridge University Press)

Corbett, Blythe A., Joan R. Gunther, Dan Comins, Jenifer Price et al. 2011. 'Brief Report: Theatre as Therapy for Children with Autism Spectrum Disorder', *Journal of Autism and Developmental Disorders*, 41, 505–11, doi:10.1007/s10803-010-1064-1

Corbett, Blythe A., Alexandra P. Key, Lydia Qualls, Steohanie Fectau, Cassandra Newsome, Catherine Coke, Paul Yoder et al. 2016. 'Improvement in Social Competence Using a Randomized Trial of a Theatre Intervention for Children with Autism Spectrum Disorder', *Journal of Autism and Developmental Disorders*, 46, 658–72, doi:10.1007/s10803-015-2600-9

Cox, Murray. 1988. *Structuring the Therapeutic Process: Compromise with Chaos* (London: Jessica Kingsley Publishers)

Cox, Murray (ed.). 1992. *Shakespeare Comes to Broadmoor: The Actors Are Come Hither* (London: Jessica Kingsley Publishers)

Cox, Murray and Alice Thielgaard. 1994. *Shakespeare as Prompter: The Amending Imagination and the Therapeutic Process* (London: Jessica Kingsley Publishers)

Cox, Murray and Alice Thielgaard. 1997. *Mutative Metaphors in Psychotherapy: The Aeolian Mode* (London: Jessica Kingsley Publishers)

Crewe, Ben. 2014. 'Not Looking Hard Enough: Masculinity, Emotion and Prison Work', *Qualitative Inquiry*, 20:4, 392–403

Crewe, Ben, Susie Hulley and Serena Wright. 2019. *Life Imprisonment from Young Adulthood: Adaptation, Identity and Time* (London: Palgrave Macmillan)

Crimmens, Paula. 2006. *Dramatherapy and Story Making in Special Education* (London: Jessica Kingsley Publishers)

Croy, Ilone, Helen Geide, Martin Paulus, Kerstin Weidner and Hakan Olausson. 2016. 'Affective Touch Awareness in Mental Health and Disease Relates to Autistic Traits: An Explorative Neurophysiological Exploration', *Psychiatry Research*, 245, 491–6

Cultural Learning Alliance. 2017. *Key Research Findings: The Case for Cultural Learning*, https://culturallearningalliance.org.uk/wp-content/uploads/2017/08/CLA-key-findings-2017.pdf

Davies, Lloyd. 2003. *Shakespeare Matters: History, Teaching, Performance* (London: Associated University Presses)

Del Aguila, Mark, Ensiyeh Ghavampour and Brenda Vale. 2019. 'Theory of Place in Public Space', *Urban Planning*, 4:2, 249–59

Deleuze, Gilles. 1994. *Difference et Repetition*, trans. by Paul Patton (New York: Columbia University Press)

Delgado, Maria M. and Caridad Svich (eds). 2002. *Theatre in Crisis? Performance Manifestos for a New Century* (Manchester: Manchester University Press)

Desai, Ashwin. 2014. *Reading Revolution: Shakespeare on Robben Island* (Chicago: Haymarket Books)

Dobson, Michael. 2004. 'Shakespeare Performances in England, 2003', in *Shakespeare Survey (57): Macbeth and Its Afterlife*, ed. by Peter Holland (Cambridge: Cambridge University Press), 258–89, 272

Dobson, Michael. 2007. 'Shakespeare Performances in England, 2006', in *Shakespeare Survey (60): Theatres for Shakespeare*, ed. by Peter Holland (Cambridge: Cambridge University Press), 284–319, 314

Dobson, Michael. 2011. *Shakespeare and Amateur Performance: A Cultural History* (Cambridge: Cambridge University Press)

Dreir, Jenna. 2019. 'From Apprentice to Master: Casting Men to Play Shakespeare's Women in Prison', *Humanities*, 8:123, https://www.mdpi.com/2076-0787/8/3/123/htm

Dustagheer, Sarah. 2013. 'Shakespeare and the Spatial Turn', *Literary Compass*, 10:17, 570–81

Dutlinger, Anne. 2001. *Art, Music and Education as a Strategy for Survival: 1941–1945* (New York: Herodias)

Elam, Kier. 2002. *The Semiotics of Theatre and Drama* (London: Methuen)

Etheridge Woodson, Stephani and Tamara Underiner (eds). 2018. *Theatre, Performance and Change* (London: Palgrave Macmillan)

Felitti, Vincent J., Robert F. Anda, Dale Nordenberg, David F. Williamson, Alison M. Spitz, Valerie Edwards, Mary P. Koss, James S. Marks. 1998. 'Relationship of Childhood Abuse and Household Dysfunction to Many of the Leading Causes of Death in Adults: The Adverse Childhood Experiences (ACE) Study', *American Journal of Preventive Medicine*, 14:4, 245–58, https://doi.org/10.1016/S0749-3797_98_00017-8

Fish, Stanley E. 1976. 'Interpreting the Variorum', *Critical Enquiry*, 2:3, 465–73, https://www.journals.uchicago.edu/doi/abs/10.1086/447852

Fisher-Grant, Kyle, Frannie Shepherd-Bates and Matthew Van Meter. 2019. *Shakespeare in Prison: Case Study* Report, *https://static1.squarespace.com/static/558ccb03e4b0750606e2a303/t/5cec0a9dec 212dc60a54826a/1558973086714/Shakespeare+in+Prison_2016-17+Study+Write+Up+copy.pdf*

Fisher-Lichte, Erika and Benjamin Wihstutz (eds). 2013. *Performance and the Politics of Space: Theatre and Topology* (New York: Routledge)

Fletcher-Watson, Ben and Shaun May. 2018. 'Enhancing Relaxed Performance: Evaluating the Autism Arts Festival', *Research in Drama Education*, 23:3, 406–20

Foucault, Michel. 1991. *Discipline and Punish: The Birth of the Prison*, trans. by Alan Sheridan (New York: Penguin Modern Classics), 252

Foucault, Michel. 1977. *Discipline and Punish: The Birth of the Prison*, trans. by Alan Sheridan (London: Penguin)

Foucault, Michel. 1984. 'Of Other Spaces: Utopias and Heterotopias', in *Architecture/Mouvement/Continuite*, trans. by Jay Miskowiec, https://web.mit.edu/allanmc/www/foucault1.pdf

Gilligan, James. 2001. *Preventing Violence: Prospects for Tomorrow* (New York: Thames and Hudson)

Goffman, Ervin. 1963. *Stigma: On the Measurement of Spoiled Identity* (New Jersey: Prentice Hall)

Goodley, D. and M. Moore. 2002. *Disability Arts against Exclusion: People with Learning Difficulties and Their Performing Arts* (Kidderminster: British Institute of Learning Disabilities)

Gordon, Collette. 2015. '"Mind the Gap": Globalism, Postcolonialism and Making Up Africa in the Cultural Olympiad', in *Shakespeare on the Global Stage: Performance and Festivity in the Olympic Year*, ed. by Erin Sullivan and Paul Prescott (London: Arden Shakespeare), 191–226, 210

Greenhalgh, Susanne. 2019. 'A World Elsewhere: Documentary Representations of Social Shakespeare', *Critical Survey: Special Issue: Applying Shakespeare*, 31:4, 77–87

Guillory, John. 1993. *Cultural Capital* (Chicago: University of Chicago Press)

Gulatti, G., C. P. Dunne and B. D. Kelly. 2020. 'Prisons and the COVID-19 Pandemic', *Public Health Emergency Collection*, 27 May, https://www.ncbi.nlm.nih.gov/pmc/articles/PMC7294073/

Hadley, Bree and Donna McDonald (eds). 2018. *The Routledge Handbook of Disability Arts, Culture and Media* (London: Taylor and Francis)

Hadley, Bree. 2020. 'Allyship in Disability Arts Roles, Relationships and Practices', *Research in Drama Education: The Journal of Applied Theatre and Performance*, 25:2, 178–94, https://doi.org/10.1080/1356 9783.2020.1729716

Hahn, Matthew. 2017. *The Robben Island Shakespeare* (London: Bloomsbury)

Hall, Edward. 2010. 'Spaces of Wellbeing for People with Learning Disabilities', *Scottish Geographical Journal* 126:4, 275–84

Hallengren, Anders. 2004. *Nobel Laureates in Search of Identity & Integrity: Voices of Different Culture* (Singapore: World Scientific)

Hambrook, Colin. 'Growing Up Downs: Blue Apple Theatre Documentary on BBC3' (6 February 2014), https://www.disabilityartsonline.org.uk/growing-up-downs-blue-apple-theatre-bbc3, [accessed 23 August 2020]

Haney, Craig, Curtis Banks and Philip Zimbardo. 2004. 'A Study of Prisoners and Guards in a Simulated Prison', in *Theatre in Prison: Theory and Practice* ed. by Michael Balfour (Bristol: Intellect), 19–33

Hargrave, Matt. 2015. *Theatres of Learning Disability: Good, Bad or Plain Ugly?* (London: Palgrave)

Harpin, Ann. 2011. 'Intolerable Acts', *Performance Research*, 16:1, 102–11

Harpin, Anna and Helen Nicholson (eds). 2017. *Performance Participation: Practices, Audiences, Politics* (London: Palgrave Macmillan)

Harris, Maxine and Roger D. Fallot (eds). 2001. *Using Trauma Theory to Design Service Systems* (San Francisco: Jossey-Bass)

Hasemand, Brad and Eva Osterlind. 2014. 'A Lost Opportunity: A Review of *Art for Art's Sake? The Impact of Arts Education*,' *Research in Drama Education*, 19:4, 409–13

Heim, Caroline. 2015. *Audience as Performer: The Changing Role of Theatre Audiences in the Twenty-First Century* (London: Routledge)

Hernandez, Kevin and Tony Roberts. 2018. *Leaving No One behind in a Digital World* (Brighton: K4D Emerging Issues Report), https://assets.publishing.service.gov.uk/media/5c178371ed915d0b8a31a404/Emerging_Issues_LNOBDW_final.pdf

Herold, Neils. 2014. *Prison Shakespeare and the Purpose of Performance: Repentance Rituals and the Early Modern* (Basingstoke: Palgrave Macmillan)

Herrity, Kate. 2019. '"Some People Can't Hear So They Have to Feel … " Exploring Sensory Experience and Collapsing Distance in Prisons Research', https://www.researchgate.net/publication/337391906_Some_people_can-t_hear_so_they_have_to_feel_exploring_sensory_experience_and_collapsing_distance_in_prisons_research

Hetherington, Kevin. 1997. *The Badlands of Modernity: Heterotopia and Social Ordering* (London: Routledge)

Hewson, Thomas, Russell Green, Andrew Shepherd, Jake Hard and Jennifer Shaw. 2020. 'The Effects of COVID-19 on Self-harm in UK Prisons', *BJPsych Bulletin*, July, https://www.cambridge.org/core/journals/bjpsych-bulletin/article/effects-of-covid19-on-selfharm-in-uk-prisons/2E6B81CF52D64878FE0517F29726812F,

Hirsh, James. 2003. *Shakespeare and the History of Soliloquies* (London: Associated University Presses)

Hochschild, Arlie Russell. 1985. *The Managed Heart: Commercialization of Human Feeling* (Berkeley: University of California Press)

Hoenselaars, Ton. 2011. 'The Company of Shakespeare in Exile: Towards a Reading of Internment Camp Culture', *Atlantis: Journal of the Spanish Association of Anglo-American Studies*, 33:2, 89–103, https://www.academia.edu/4385502/THE_COMPANY_OF_SHAKESPEARE_IN_EXILE_TOWARDS_A_READING_OF_INTERNMENT_CAMP_CULTURESThe_Memorial_production_of_Julius_Caesar_that_premiered_on_15_April_1941_directed

Hoenselaars, Ton. 2019. 'Shakespearean Explorations in Captivity', *New Faces Essay Collection*, HALSHS Archive (May 2019), https://halshs.archives-ouvertes.fr/halshs-02145014/document

Holden, John. 2010. *Culture and Class* (Counterpoint, British Council Thinktank), http://www.bluedrum.ie/documents/CultureAndClassStandard.pdf

Holdsworth, Nadine. 2014. 'Citizenship: The Ethics of Inclusion', in *Performance Studies: Key Words, Concepts and Theories*, ed. by Brian Reynolds (London and New York: Palgrave Macmillan), 133–41, 135.

Holland, Peter (ed.). 2004. *Shakespeare Survey (57): Macbeth and Its Afterlife* (Cambridge: Cambridge University Press)

Holland, Peter (ed.). 2007. *Shakespeare Survey (60): Theatres for Shakespeare* (Cambridge: Cambridge University Press)

Horton, Richard. 2020. 'Editorial', *The Lancet*, 8:11, https://doi.org/10.1016/S2214-109X(20)30432-0

Howard, Jean. 2007. *Theater of a City: The Places of London Comedy, 1598–1642* (Philadelphia: University of Pennsylvania Press)

Hughes, Jenny and Helen Nicholson (eds). 2016. *Critical Perspectives on Applied Theatre* (Cambridge: Cambridge University Press)

Hughes, Joe. 2009. *Deleuze's 'Difference and Repetition': A Reader's Guide* (London: Continuum)

Hunter, Kelly. 2015. *Shakespeare's Heartbeat: Drama Games for Children with Autism* (London: Routledge)

Hus, Vanessa and Catherine Lord. 2014. 'The Autism Diagnostic Observation Schedule, Module 4: Revised Algorithm and Standardized

Severity Scores', *Journal of Autistic Development Disorder*, 44:8, https://www.ncbi.nlm.nih.gov/pmc/articles/PMC4104252/#:~:text=Autism%20Diagnostic%20Observation%20Schedule%20(ADOS),diagnosis%20of%20autism%20spectrum%20disorders

Iveson, Mandy and Flora Cornish. 2016. 'Rebuilding Bridges: Homeless People's Views on the Role of Vocational and Educational Activities in Their Everyday Lives', *Journal of Community and Applied Social Psychology*, 26:3, 253–67

Jenkyns, Marina. 1996. *The Play's the Thing: Exploring Text in Drama and Therapy* (London: Routledge)

Jennings, Patricia. 2019. *The Trauma-Sensitive Classroom* (New York: W. W. Norton)

Jennings, Sue. 1987. *Dramatherapy: Theory and Practice Volume 1* (London: Routledge)

Jennings, Sue. 1990. *Dramatherapy with Families, Groups and Individuals: Waiting in the Wings* (London: Jessica Kingsley Publishers)

Jennings, Sue. 1992. *Dramatherapy: Theory and Practice Volume 2* (London: Routledge)

Jennings, Sue. 1997. *Introduction to Drama Therapy* (London: Jessica Kingsley Publishers)

Jennings, Sue. 1997. *Dramatherapy: Theory and Practice Volume 3* (London: Routledge)

Jennings, Sue. 2007. *Dramatherapy and Social Theatre: Necessary Dialogues* (London: Routledge)

Jennings, Sue, Ann Cattanach, Steve Mitchell, Anna Chesner, Brenda Meldrum. 1993. *The Handbook of Dramatherapy* (London: Routledge)

Jewkes, Yvonne. 2002. *Captive Audience: Media, Masculinity and Power in Prisons* (Collumpton: Willan Publishing)

Jewkes, Yvonne. 2005. 'Prisoners and the Press', *Criminal Justice Matters*, 59:26–7, 26, https://www.tandfonline.com/doi/abs/10.1080/09627250508553038

Jewkes, Yvonne, Jamie Bennett and Ben Crewe (eds). 2016. *Handbook on Prisons: Second Edition* (London: Routledge)

Kathrada, Ahmed. 2008. *Memoirs* (Cape Town: Zebra)

Kay, Christopher. 2020. 'Rethinking Social Capital in the Desistance Process: The "Artful Dodger" Complex', *European Journal of Criminology*, https://journals.sagepub.com/doi/full/10.1177/1477370820960615

Kempe, Andy. 2011. 'Drama and the Education of Young People with Special Needs', in *Key Concepts in Theatre/Drama Education*, ed. by S. Schonmann (Rotterdam: Sense Publishers), 165–9, 165

Kempe, Andy. 2013. *Drama, Disability and Education* (London: Routledge)

Kempe, Andy. 2014. 'Developing Social Skills in Autistic Children through Relaxed Performances', *Support for Learning*, 29:3, 261–74, https://doi-org.ezproxye.bham.ac.uk/10.1111/1467-9604.12062

Kempe, Andy. 2015. 'Widening Participation in Theatre through "Relaxed Performances"', *New Theatre Quarterly*, 31:1, 59–69, http://dx.doi.org/10.1017/S0266464X15000068

Kidd, D and R. Osborne (eds). 1995. *Crime and the Media: The Postmodern Spectacle* (London: Pluto Press)

King, Laura L. and Jennifer J. Roberts. 2015. 'The Complexity of Public Attitudes towards Sex Crimes', *Victims and Offenders*, 12:1, 71–89, doi:10.1080/15564886.2015.1005266

King, Sam. 2014. *Desistance Transitions and the Impact of Probation* (London: Routledge)

Kingsley-Smith, Jane. 2003. *Shakespeare's Drama of Exile* (Houndsmills: Palgrave Macmillan)

Lanckorońska, Karolina. 2005. *Those Who Trespass against Us, One Woman's War against the Nazis*, trans. by Noel Clark (London: Pimlico)

Landy, Robert J. and David T. Montgomery. 2012. *Theatre for Change: Education, Social Action and Therapy* (Basingstoke: Palgrave Macmillan)

Laoutaris, Chris. 2014. *Shakespeare and the Countess* (London: Penguin)

Lees, Nicola. 2012. *Give Me the Money and I'll Shoot!* (London: Bloomsbury Publishing)

Lefebvre, Henri. 1991. *The Production of Space*, ed. by Donald Nicholson-Smith (Oxford: Blackwell)

Lefebvre, Henri. 2002. *Critique of Everyday Life: The One Volume Edition: Volume II*, trans. by John Moore (London and New York: Verso Publishing), 370

Lefebvre, Henri. 2014. *Critique of Everyday Life: The One-Volume Edition*, trans. by John Moore (Volumes 1 and 2) and Gregory Elliott (Volume 3) (London: Verso)

Letherby, Gayle. 2003. *Feminist Research in Theory and Practice* (Buckingham and Philadelphia: Open University Press)

Liebling, Alison and Amy Ludlow. 2016. 'Suicide Distress and the Quality of Prison Life', in *Handbook on Prisons: Second Edition*, ed. by Yvonne Jewkes, Jamie Bennett and Ben Crewe (London and New York: Routledge), 224–45, 226

Lodge, Tom. 2006. *Mandela: A Critical Life* (New York: Oxford University Press)

Loftis, Sonya Freeman. 2019. 'Autistic Culture, Shakespeare Therapy and the Hunter Heartbeat Method', *Shakespeare Survey*, 72, 256–67, doi:10.1080/23297018.2016.1207202

Loomba, Ania. 2002. *Shakespeare, Race and Colonialism* (Oxford: Oxford University Press)

Lord, Catherine and James P. Magee (eds). 2001. *Educating Children with Autism* (London: National Research Council: Consensus Study Report), https://www.nap.edu/catalog/10017/educating-children-with-autism

Loucks, Nancy. 2008. *No One Knows: Offenders with Learning Difficulties and Learning Disabilities* (London: Prison Reform Trust), http://www.prisonreformtrust.org.uk/uploads/documents/noknl.pdf

Lucas, Ashley E. 2020. *Prison Theatre and the Global Crisis of Incarceration* (London: Methuen Drama)

Lutterbie, John. 2020. *An Introduction to Theatre, Performance and the Cognitive Sciences* (London: Methuen Drama)

Mackey, Sally. 2016. 'Performing Location: Place and Applied Theatre', in *Critical Perspectives on Applied Theatre*, ed. by Jenny Hughes and Helen Nicholson (Cambridge: Cambridge University Press), 107–26, 109

Magill, Tom and Jennifer Marquiss-Muradaz. 2009. 'The Making of Mickey B: A Modern Adaptation of Macbeth Filmed in a Maximum-Security Prison in Northern Island', in *Dramatherapy and Social Theatre*, ed. by Sue Jennings, 109–16, 110

Mann, Ruth E. 2016. 'Sex Offenders in Prison', in *Handbook on Prisons: Second Edition*, ed. by Yvonne Jewkes, Jamie Bennett and Ben Crewe (London and New York: Routledge), 246–64, 260–1

McAulay, Gay. 1999. *Space in Performance: Making Meaning in the Theatre* (Michigan: Michigan University Press)

McCartan, Kieran. 2020. 'Trauma-informed Practice', *Her Majesty's Inspectorate of Probation: Academic Insights 2020/05*, https://www.justiceinspectorates.gov.uk/hmiprobation/wp-content/uploads/sites/5/2020/07/Academic-Insights-McCartan.pdf

McConachie, Bruce. 2008. *Engaging Audiences: A Cognitive Approach to Spectating in the Theatre* (New York: Palgrave Macmillan)

McDougall, Cynthia, A. Dominic, S. Pearson, David J. Torgeson and Maria Garcia -Reyes. 2017. 'The Effect of Digital Technology on Prisoner Behaviour and Reoffending: A Natural Stepped-wedge Design', *Journal of Experimental Criminology*, 13, 455–82, https://link-springer-com.ezproxye.bham.ac.uk/article/10.1007/s11292-017-9303-5

McEvoy, William. 2006. 'Writing, Texts and Site- Specific Performance in the Recent Work of Deborah Warner', *Textual Practice* 20:4,

591–614, https://www-tandfonline-com.ezproxyd.bham.ac.uk/doi/full/10.1080/09502360601058821

McGinn, Colin. 2006. *Shakespeare's Philosophers, Discovering the Meanings behind the Plays* (New York: HarperCollins)

Mackenzie, Rowan. 2019. 'Producing Space for Shakespeare', *Critical Survey*, 31:4 (New York: Berghan Journals, 2019), 65–76

Mackenzie, Rowan. 2019. 'Disturbing Shakespeare and Challenging the Preconceptions', *Shakespeare Studies*, 40:7, 49–60 (Plainsboro, NJ: Rosemont Publishing)

Mackenzie, Rowan. 2020. 'Action Is Eloquence: Creating Space for Shakespeare in HMP Gartree', *Drama Research*, 11:1, https://www.nationaldrama.org.uk/journal/

Mackenzie, Rowan 2020. '*The Tempest+* from Blue Apple Theatre Company', *Drama*, 26:1, 25–31

Mackenzie, Rowan 2022. 'Shakespeare Unbarred', in *International Handbook of Therapeutic Stories and Storytelling*, ed. by Clive Holmwood, Sue Jennings and Sharon Jacksties (London: Routledge)

Mackesy, Charlie. 2019. *The Boy, the Mole, the Fox and the Horse* (London: Ebury Publishing)

McNaughton Nicholls, Carol and Stephen Webster. 2018. *The Separated Location of Prisoners with Sexual Convictions: Research on the Benefits and Risks* (HMPPS Analytical Summary), https://assets.publishing.service.gov.uk/government/uploads/system/uploads/attachment_data/file/749149/separated-location-prisoners-with-sexual-convictions-report.pdf

NcNeil, Clare, Henry Parkes, David Wastell and Robin Harvey. 2020. '1.1 Million More People Face Poverty at the End of 2020 as a Result of Coronavirus Pandemic, Finds IPPR' (London: IPPR The Progressive Policy Think Tank), https://www.ippr.org/news-and-media/press-releases/1-1-million-more-people-face-poverty-at-end-of-2020-as-a-result-of-coronavirus-pandemic-finds-ippr

McRobbie, Angela and Sarah L. Thornton. 1995. 'Rethinking "Moral panic" for Multi-mediated Social Worlds', *The British Journal of Sociology*, 46:4, 559–74

Maguire, Mike, Emma Disley, Mark Liddle, Rosie Meek and Nina Burrowes. 2019. *Developing a Toolkit to Measure Intermediate Outcomes to Reduce Reoffending from Arts and Mentoring Interventions* (Ministry of Justice Analytical Series), https://www.gov.uk/government/publications/developing-a-toolkit-to-measure-intermediate-outcomes-to-reduce-reoffending-from-arts-and-mentoring-interventions

Mandela, Nelson. 1995. *Long Walk to Freedom* (London: Abacus Books)

Mantoan, Lindsey. 2018. *War as Performance: Conflicts in Iraq and Political Theatricality* (Cham, Switzerland: Palgrave Macmillan)

Marin, Louis. 1974. *Utopics: The Semiological Play of Textual Spaces*, trans. by R. A. Vollrath (New York: Humanity Books)

Marti, Josep. 2001. 'Music and Ethnicity in Barcelona', *The World of Music*, 43:2, 183–92

Massai, Sonya. 2020. *Shakespeare's Accents: Voicing Identity in Performance* (Cambridge: Cambridge University Press)

Massey, Doreen. 2005. *For Space* (Los Angeles & London: Sage Publishing)

Matheson, Kimberley, Mindi D. Foster, Amy Bombay, Robyn J. McQuaid and Hymie Anisan. 2019. 'Traumatic Experiences, Perceived Discrimination and Psychological Distress among Members of Various Socially Marginalised Groups', *Frontiers in Psychology*, https://doi.org/10.3389/fpsyg.2019.00416

Maxwell, Julie and Kate Rumbold (eds). 2018. *Shakespeare and Quotation* (Cambridge: Cambridge University Press)

Maycock, Matthew and Kate Hunt (eds). 2019. *New Perspectives on Prison Masculinities* (Cham: Palgrave Macmillan)

Mehling, Margaret H., Marc J. Tasse and Robin Root. 2017. 'Shakespeare and Autism: An Exploratory Evaluation of the Hunter Heartbeat Method', *Research and Practice on Intellectual and Development Difficulties*, 4:2, 107–20, doi:10.1080/23297018.2016.1207202

Moran, Dominique. 2015. *Carceral Geography: Spaces and Practices of Incarceration* (Farnham: Ashgate)

Moran, Dominique and Anna Schliele. 2017. *Carceral Spatiality: Dialogues between Geography and Criminology* (London: Palgrave Macmillan)

Muñoz-Bellerin, Manuel and Nuria Cordero-Ramos. 2020. 'The Role of Applied Theatre in Social Work: Creative Interventions with Homeless Individuals', *British Journal of Social Work*, 50, 1611–29

Murray, Susan and Laurie Ouelette (eds). 2009. *Reality TV: Remaking Television Culture: Second Edition* (New York: New York University Press)

Muskett, Coral. 2013. 'Trauma-Informed Care in In-patient Mental Health Settings: A Review of the Literature', *International Journal of Mental Health Nursing*, https://www.psykiatri-regionh.dk/centre-og-social-tilbud/Psykiatriske-centre/Psykiatrisk-Center-Sct.-Hans/forskning/Nationalt-TBT-Center/Artikler/Documents/Muskett-%20Trauma-informed%20care%20in%20-%202013.pdf

Neuman, W. Russell and Lauren Guggenheim. 2011. 'The Evolution of Media Effects Theory: A Six-Stage Model of Cumulative Research', *Communication Theory*, 21, 169–96, https://academic-oup-com.ezproxye.bham.ac.uk/ct/article/21/2/169/4085678

Nicholson, Helen. 2011. *Theatre, Education and Performance: The Map and The Story* (London: Palgrave Macmillan)

Nicholson, Helen. 2015. *Applied Drama: The Gift of Theatre* (London: Macmillan Education UK)

Nochaiwong, Surapon, Chidchanok Ruengorn, Kednapa Thavorn, Biran Hutton, Ratanaporn Awiphan, Chabapai Phosuya, Yongyuth Ruanta, Nahathai Wongpakaran and Tinakon Wongpakaran. 2021. 'Global Prevalence of Mental Health Issues among the General Population during the Coronavirus Disease-2019 Pandemic: A Systematic Review and Meta-analysis', *Scientific Reports*, 11, https://www.nature.com/articles/s41598-021-89700-8

Oakes, Peter M. and Ros C. Davis. 2008. 'Intellectual Disability in Homeless Adults: A Prevalence Study', *Journal of Intellectual Disabilities*, 12:4 (Los Angeles: Sage Publications), 325–34

Oglethorpe, Katy, Amand Deweale and Gino Campenaerts. 2019. *Citizens Inside: A Guide to Creating Active Participation in Prisons*, https://www.prisonerseducation.org.uk/wp-content/uploads/2019/11/Citizens-Inside-A-guide-to-creating-active-participation-in-prisons.pdf

Olive, Sarah. 2013. 'Representations of Shakespeare's Humanity and Iconicity: Incidental Appropriations in Four British Television Broadcasts', *Borrowers and Lenders*, 8:1, https://search-proquest-com.ezproxye.bham.ac.uk/docview/1458231920?accountid=8630&rfr_id=info%3Axri%2Fsid%3Aprimo

Olive, Sarah. 2016. '"In Shape and Mind Transformed"? Televised Teaching and Learning Shakespeare', *Palgrave Communications 2*, https://www.nature.com/articles/palcomms20168

Ortiz, Joseph M. (ed.). 2013. *Shakespeare and the Culture of Romanticism* (Farnham: Ashgate)

Palmer, Emma, Ruth M. Hatcher and Matthew J. Tonkin. 2020. *Evaluation of Digital Technology in Prisons* (Ministry of Justice Analytical Series), https://assets.publishing.service.gov.uk/government/uploads/system/uploads/attachment_data/file/899942/evaluation-digital-technology-prisons-report.PDF

Palmer, Jon and Richard Hayhow. 2008. *Learning Disability and Contemporary Theatre* (Huddersfield: Full Body and the Voice)

Patel, Parth, Alba Kapoor and Nick Treloar. 2020. 'Ethnic Inequalities in COVID-19 Are Playing Out Again – How Can We Stop Them?' (London: IPPR The Progressive Policy Think Tank and The Runnymede Trust), https://www.ippr.org/blog/ethnic-inequalities-in-COVID-19-are-playing-out-again-how-can-we-stop-them

Paterson-Young, Claire, Richard Hazenburg and Meanu Bajwa-Patel. 2019. *The Social Impact of Custody on Young People in the Criminal Justice System* (London: Palgrave Macmillan)

Paul Prescott and Katie Steele Brokaw. 'Shakespearean Environmentalism and Ecology: Shakespeare in Yosemite', *Shakespeare beyond Borders Alliance Equality Shakespeare Festival* (June 2022) Online event

Payne, Helen (ed.). 1993. *Handbook of Inquiry in the Arts Therapies: One River, Many Currents* (London: Jessica Kingsley Publishers)

Pensalfini, Rob. 2016. *Prison Shakespeare: For These Deep Shames and Great Indignities* (Basingstoke: Palgrave Macmillan)

Phillips, Jake. 2016. 'Myopia and Misrecognition: The Impact of Managerialism on the Management of Compliance', *Criminology and Criminal Justice*, 16:1, https://journals.sagepub.com/doi/abs/10.1177/1748895815594664

Plant, Jessica and Dora Dixon. 2019. *Enhancing Arts and Culture in the Criminal Justice System: A Partnership Approach* (National Criminal Justice Arts Alliance, Clinks), https://www.artsincriminaljustice.org.uk/wp-content/uploads/2019/06/Enhancing-arts-and-culture-in-the-criminal-justice-system.pdf

Pogrund, Benjamin. 1990. *Robert Subokwe: How Can Man Die Better* (Johannesburg: Jonathan Ball Publishers)

Potter, Susan. 2013. *Relaxed Performance Project Evaluation Report 2012/13*, https://lemosandcrane.co.uk/resources/SOLT%20Relaxed%20Performance%20Evaluation.pdf

Prentki, Tim and Sheila Preston. 2009. *The Applied Theatre Reader* (London: Routledge)

Prizant, Barry M., Amy M. Wetherby, Emily Rubin and Emily C. Laurent. 2003. 'The SCERTS Model a Transactional, Family-Centered Approach to Enhancing Communication and Socioemotional Abilities of Children with Autism Spectrum Disorder', *Infants and Young Children,* 16:4, 296–316, 313

Reason, Matthew. 2018. 'Ways of Watching: Five Aesthetics of Learning Disability Theatre', in *The Routledge Handbook of Disability Arts, Culture and Media*, ed. by Bree Hadley and Donna McDonald (London: Taylor and Francis), 163–75, 164

Reason, Matthew. 2019. 'A Prison Audience: Women Prisoners, Shakespeare and Spectatorship', *Cultural Trends*, 28:2, 86–102, https://Doi.org/10.1080/09548963.2019.1617929

Reeves, Scott, Jennifer Peller, et al. 2013. 'Ethnography in Qualitative Educational Research: AMEE Guide No.80', *Medical Teacher*, 35, 1365–79

Relaxed Performance Project Conference: Executive Summary. 2013, http://www.includearts.com/wp-content/uploads/2015/10/Relaxed-Performance-Pilot-Project-Executive-Summary-September-2013.pdf

Reynolds, Brian (ed.). 2014. *Performance Studies: Key Words, Concepts and Theories* (London: Palgrave Macmillan)

Ricon, Tsameret, Rachel Sorek and Batya Engel Yeger. 2017. 'Association between Sensory Processing by Children with High Functioning Autism Spectrum Disorder and Their Daily Routines', *The Open Journal of Occupational Therapy*, 5:4, https://scholarworks-wmich-edu.ezproxyd.bham.ac.uk/cgi/viewcontent.cgi?referer=&httpsredir=1&article=1337&context=ojot

Russell, Alexandra and Adrian Barton. 2018. *Research Report: HMP/YOI Winchester Applied Theatre Pilot* published via National Criminal Justice Arts Alliance on their Evidence Library, http://www.artsevidence.org.uk/media/uploads/181114-bearface.pdf

Rylance, Mark. 1992. 'Interviewed by Rob Ferris', in *Shakespeare Comes to Broadmoor: The Actors Are Come Hither*, ed. by Murray Cox (London and Philadelphia: Jessica Kingsley Publishing), 27–42, 31

Said, Edward W. 2000. *Reflections on Exile: And Other Literary and Cultural Essays* (London: Granta Publications)

Sampson, Anthony. 2000. *Mandela: The Authorized Biography* (New York: Vintage)

Sanders, Angela. 2020. *Leadership in Prison Education: Meeting the Challenges of the New System* (London: The Further Education Trust for Leadership)

Sazzad, Rehnuma. 2008. 'Hatoum, Said and Foucault: Resistance through Revealing the Power-Knowledge Nexus?' *Postcolonial Text*, 4, 3

Scaife, M. and J. S. Bruner. 1975. 'The Capacity for Joint Visual Attention in the Infant', *Nature*, 253, 265–6, https://www.nature.com/articles/253265a0

Schalkwyk, David. 2012. *Hamlet's Dreams: The Robben Island Shakespeare* (London: Arden Shakespeare)

Schonmann, S. (ed.). 2011. *Key Concepts in Theatre/Drama Education* (Rotterdam: Sense Publishers)

Schwartz-Gastine, Isabelle. 2013. 'Performing A Midsummer Night's Dream with the Homeless (and Others) in Paris', *Borrowers and Lenders*, 8:2, https://openjournals.libs.uga.edu/borrowers/article/view/2236

Scott-Douglas, Amy. 2007. *Shakespeare Inside: The Bard behind Bars* (London: Continuum)

Sedgman, Kirsty. 2015. 'Be Reasonable! On Institutions, Values, Voices', *Participations: Journal of Audience and Reception Studies*, 12:1, 123–32

Sedgman, Kirsty 2018. *The Reasonable Audience: Theatre Etiquette, Behaviour Policing, and the Live Performance Experience* (Hampshire: Palgrave Macmillan)

Seller, Maxine. 2001. *We Built Up Our Lives: Education and Community among Jewish Refugees Interned by Britain in World War* (Westport: Greenwood Publications)

Senju, Atsushi and Mark H. Johnson. 2009. 'Atypical Eye Contact in Autism: Models, Mechanisms and Developments', *Neuroscience and Bio-behavioural Reviews*, 33:8, 1204–14

Shailor, Jonathan (ed.). 2011. *Performing New Lives: Prison Theatre* (London: Jessica Kingsley Publishers)

Shaughnessy, Nicola. 2013. 'Imagining Otherwise: Autism, Neuroaesthetics and Contemporary Performance', *Interdisciplinary Science Reviews*, 38:4, 321–34, https://doi.org/10.1179/0308018813Z.00000000062

Shaughnessy, Robert. 2019. *This Rough Magic*, http://www.flutetheatre.co.uk/wp-content/uploads/2017/02/Flute-Tempest-Robert-Shaughnessy-.pdf [accessed 23 February 2020], p. 2 & p. 10

Shelter. 2019. *This Is England: A Picture of Homelessness in 2019: The Numbers behind the Story* (London: Shelter), https://england.shelter.org.uk/__data/assets/pdf_file/0009/1883817/This_is_England_A_picture_of_homelessness_in_2019.pdf

Shimamura, Arthur P. 2011. 'Episodic Retrieval and the Cortical Binding of Relational Activity', *Cognitive, Affective and Behavioural Neuroscience*, 11:3, 277–91

Skelton, Francesca. 2020. *Rethinking Cultural Inclusion and Diversity: A Call to Action for Milton Keynes* (Milton Keynes: Arts and Heritage Alliance)

Smith, Daniel W. and Henry Somers-Hall (eds). 2012. *The Cambridge Companion to Deleuze* (Cambridge: Cambridge University Press)

Soja, Edward J. 1989. *Postmodern Geographies: The Reassertion of Space in Critical Social Theory* (London: Verso)

Soja, Edward J. 1996. *Thirdspace: Journeys to Los Angeles and Other Real-and-Imagined Places* (Oxford: Blackwell)

Souers, Kristin and Pete Hall. 2016. *Fostering Resilient Learners: Strategies for Creating a Trauma-Sensitive Classroom* (Alexandria, VA: Association for Supervision and Curriculum Development)

Stevens, Mark. 2013. *Broadmoor Revealed: Victorian Crime and the Lunatic Asylum* (Barnsley: Pen and Sword)

Stewart, Stanley. 2009. *Shakespeare and Philosophy* (London: Routledge)

Stuart-Fishers, Amanda and James Thompson (eds). 2020. *Performing Care: New Perspectives on Socially Engaged Performance* (Manchester: Manchester University Press)

Sugiura, Motoaki, Nadim J. Shah, Karl Zilles and Gereon R. Fink. 2015. 'Cortical Representations of Personally Familiar Objects and Places: Functional Organization of the Human Posterior Cingulate Cortex', *Journal of Cognitive Neuroscience*, 17:2, 183–98

Sullivan, Erin. 2017. '"The Forms of Things Unknown": Shakespeare and the Rise of the Live Broadcast', *Shakespeare Bulletin*, 35:4, 627–62

Sullivan, Erin and Paul Prescott (eds). 2015. *Shakespeare on the Global Stage: Performance and Festivity in the Olympic Year* (London: Arden Shakespeare)

Surette, Ray. 1997. *Media, Crime and Criminal Justice*, 2nd edition (Wadsworth: Belmont)

Tewkesbury, Richard. 2012. 'Stigmatisation of Sex Offenders', *Deviant Behaviour*, 33, 606–23

Thompson, Ayanna and Laura Turchi. 2016. *Teaching Shakespeare with Purpose: A Student-centred Approach* (London: Arden Shakespeare)

Thompson, James (ed.). 1998. *Prison Theatre: Perspectives and Practices* (London: Jessica Kingsley Publishers)

Thompson, James (ed.). 2005. *Digging up Stories: Applied Theatre, Performance and War* (Manchester: Manchester University Press)

Thompson, James (ed.). 2009. *Performance Affects: Applied Theatre and the End of Effect* (London: Palgrave Macmillan)

Todd, Bella. 2020. *Improving Critical Engagement with Theatre Made by Artists with Learning Disabilities*, Spectra Commissioned Report, https://wearespectra.co.uk/2020/02/09/launch/

Tofteland, Curt and Hal Cobb. 2012. 'Prospero behind Bars', in *Shakespeare Survey*, 65, ed. by Peter Holland (Cambridge: Cambridge University Press)

Tompkins, Joanne. 2014. *Theatre's Heterotopias: Performance and the Cultural Politics of Space* (Basingstoke: Palgrave Macmillan)

Tracey, Shelley. 2017. *Building Foundation for Change through the Arts* (Belfast: Prison Arts Foundation)

Troustine, Jean. 2004. *Shakespeare behind Bars: One Teacher's Story of the Power of Drama in a Women's Prison* (Michigan: University of Michigan Press)

Turner, Jennifer. 2016. *The Prison Boundary: Between Society and Carceral Space* (London: Palgrave Macmillan)

Turner, J. and K. Peters (eds). 2017. *Carceral Mobilities: Interrogating Movement in Incarceration* (Abingdon: Routledge)

Ubersfeld, Anne. 1999. *Reading Theatre*, trans. by Frank Collins (Toronto: University of Toronto Press)

Unwin, Tim, Mark Weber, Meaghan Brugha and David Hollow. 2017. *The Future of Learning and Technology in Deprived Contexts* (London: Save the Children International), https://www.alnap.org/system/files/content/resource/files/main/the_future_of_learning_and_technology.pdf

Van der Kolk, Bessel. 2015. *The Body Keeps Score: Mind, Brain and Body in the Transformation of Trauma* (London: Penguin)

Van Dijck, Jose. 2013. *The Culture of Connectivity: A Critical History of Social Media* (Oxford: Oxford University Press)

Vassen, Robert D. (ed.). 1990. *Letters from Robben Island: A Selection of Ahmed Kathrada's Prison Correspondence, 1964–198* (East Lansing: Michigan State University Press)

Vintner, Luke, Gayle Dillon and Belinda Winder. 2020. '"People don't Like You When You're Different": Exploring the Prison Experiences of Autistic Individuals', *Psychology, Crime & Law*, doi.org./10.1080/1068316X.2020.1781119

Wainwright, Lucy, Paula Harriott and Soruche Saajedi. 2019. *What Do You Need to Make the Best Use of Your Time in Prison?* (London: Prison Reform Trust)

Walmsley, Ben. 2019. *Audience Engagement in the Performing Arts* (Hampshire: Palgrave Macmillan)

Wang, Karen. 2020. 'Autism and Stimming', Child Mind Institute website, https://childmind.org/article/autism-and-stimming/

Warr, Jason. 2016. 'The Prisoner: Inside and out', in *Handbook on Prisons: Second Edition*, ed. by Yvonne Jewkes, Jamie Bennett and Ben Crewe (London and New York: Routledge), 586–604, 593

White, Gareth. 2013. *Audience Participation in Theatre: Aesthetics of the Invitation* (Hampshire: Palgrave Macmillan)

White, Joe. 1998. 'The prisoner's voice', in *Prison Theatre: Perspectives and Practices*, ed. by James Thompson (London: Jessica Kingsley Publishers), 183–96

Wiles, David. 1997. *Tragedy in Athens: Performance Space and Theatrical Meaning* (Cambridge: Cambridge University Press)

Wilhelm, Ian. 2007. 'The Rise of Charity TV', *Chronicle of Philanthropy*, 19:8, https://advance.lexis.com/document/?pdmfid=1519360&crid=69631eb4-25f9-4a22-882d-a774c6e06e2b&pddocfullpath=%2Fshared%2Fdocument%2Fnews%2Furn%3AcontentItem%3A4N5C-RDV0-TX4X-X1VX-00000-00&pdcontentcomponentid=171268&pdteaserkey=sr0&pditab=allpods&ecomp=tb72k&earg=sr0&prid=20b5ee48-bd18-49bf-b0fb-d613a93e9732

Wilson, Jeffery R. 2017. 'The Trouble with Disability in Shakespeare Studies', *Disability Studies Quarterly* 37, https://dsq-sds.org/article/view/5430/4644

Winner, Ellen, Thalia R. Goldstein and Stéphan Vincent- Lancrin. 2013. *Art for Art's Sake? The Impact of Arts Education* (Paris: Organisation for Economic Co-operation and Development Publishing)

Winnicott, Donald W. 1971. *Playing and Reality* (London: Tavistock Publishers)

Winston, Joe. 2015. *Transforming the Teaching of Shakespeare with the Royal Shakespeare Company* (London and New York: Arden Shakespeare)

Wolfburg, Pamela J. 2003. *Peer Play and the Autism Spectrum: The Art of Guiding Children's Socialization and Imagination* (Kansas: Autism Aspergers Publishing Company)

Wray, Ramona. 2011. 'The Morals of *Macbeth* and Peace as Process: Adapting Shakespeare in Northern Island's Maximum Security Prison', *Shakespeare Quarterly*, 62:3, 340–63

Wray, Ramona. *Mickey B Education Pack*, https://esc-film.com/product/mickey-b-education-pack/, [accessed 14 August 2020], p. 344

Yang, Yiying, Yuan Tian, Jing Fang, et al. 2017. 'Trust and Deception in Children with Autism Spectrum Disorders: A Social Learning Perspective', *Journal of Autism*, 47, 615–25

Yones, Eliyahu. 2004. *Smoke in the Sand: The Jews of Lvov in the War Years 1939–1944* (Jerusalem: Geffen Publishing House)

Conference papers and key note speeches

Clarke, Peter. 2 October 2020. Keynote address at *What Good Looks Like Conference: A National Partnership Approach to Supporting Those in Prison at risk of Self-Harm and Suicide* (online)

Haney, Craig. 31 January 2002. 'The Psychological Impact of Incarceration: Implications for Post-prison Adjustment', *National Policy Conference – From Prison to Home: The Effect of Incarceration and Re-entry on Children, Families and Communities* (Washington)

Holland, Peter. March 2018. conference paper given at *Shakespeare in Prisons Conference (*The Old Globe, San Diego)

Hulley, Susie. 30 October 2020. Book launch for *Life Imprisonment from Young Adulthood: Adaptation, Identity and Time* (online)

Ivinson, Gabriella. 6 November 2019. Rethinking Pedagogy', *Prison Learning Academic Network seminar* (Manchester)

Kassarate, Danielle. 15 June 2022. 'MAWA Theatre Company Representing Women of the African diaspora', *Equality Shakespeare Festival* (online)

Lewis, Alexandria. 2 October 2020. 'Autism, Suicide and Self-Harm', *What Good Looks Like Conference: A National Partnership Approach to Supporting Those in Prison at Risk of Self-Harm and Suicide* (online)

McCartan, Kieran. 14 September 2020. 'The Importance of Research in Practice: From Reading to Doing and Back again', *HMPPS Insights Seminar Series* (online)

Mackenzie, Rowan and Blue Apple Theatre. 1 June 2019. '"I do forgive thy rankest fault" Workshop', *Applying Shakespeare II Symposium* (Guildford School of Acting)

Piacentini, Laura. 13 November 2020. Book launch for Cara Jardine's monograph, *Families, Imprisonment and Legitimacy: The Cost of Custodial Penalties*

Prescott, Paul and Steele Brokaw, Katie. 15 June 2022. 'Shakespearean Environmentalism and Ecology' *Equality Shakespeare Festival* (online)

A Second Chance screening and panel discussion. 5 November 2019 (University of Leicester)

Shakespeare in Prisons Conference (the flagship programme of the Shakespeare in Prisons Network), https://shakespeare.nd.edu/service/shakespeare-in-prisons/#:~:text=Shakespeare%20in%20Prisons%20Conference,Notre%20Dame%20by%20Curt%20L.&text=Peter%20Holland%2C%20McMeel%20Family%20Chair,the%20University%20of%20Notre%20Dame.

The Tempest workshops at Centre d'Educacio Especial Montserrat Montero, discussion with Raquel Ferri following the school workshop (21 March 2017)

News articles, journalism and social media posts

Akbar, Arifa. 2020. 'The Next Act: How the Pandemic Is Shaping Online Theatre's Future', *The Guardian*, 21 September, https://www.theguardian.com/stage/2020/sep/21/future-of-live-theatre-online-drama-coronavirus-lockdown

Al-Hassan, Allya. 2016. 'The Tempest, Orange Tree Theatre, 27 October 2016', *BroadwayWorld.Com*, 28 October, http://www.broadwayworld.com/westend/article/THE-TEMPEST-Orange-Tree-Theatre-27-October-2016-20161028

Bates, Erin. 2016. 'Robben Island Prisoner's Epic Autograph Book' (News 24), 25 April, https://www.news24.com/Video/SouthAfrica/News/robben-island-prisoners-epic-autograph-book-20160425

BBC Entertainment and Arts. 2012. 'Nelson Mandela's Shakespeare Edition to Go on Display', 19 June, https://www.bbc.co.uk/news/entertainment-arts-18502371

BBC News. 2020. ' Royal Shakespeare Company: 158 Jobs at Risk', 6 October, https://www.bbc.co.uk/news/uk-england-coventry-warwickshire-54437700#:~:text=The%20RSC%20said%20it%20hoped,upon%2DAvon%2C%20in%20

December.&text=However%2C%20the%20Swan%20Theatre%20
and,until%202022%2C%20the%20company%20said
Birch, Paul. 2015. *Out of Character Blog*, 31 August, http://
outofcharactertheatre.squarespace.com/blog/2015/8/22/disturbing-
shakespeare-is-put-to-rest
Blue Apple Theatre Newsletter. 2020. 'Famous Shakespeare Speech
Reworded to Resonate with Current Times', *Blue Apple Theatre
newsletter*, 30 June, http://blueappletheatre.com/news-1
Bouquet, Tim. 2015. 'Not Shut Up', *The Independent*, 11 April
CAMHS. 2017. 'Introducing Routines for Young People with Learning
Disabilities', https://www.camhsnorthderbyshire.nhs.uk/learning-
disabilities-introducing-routines
Clerke, Peter. 2012. 'Hamlet: The Fundamental Question', blog, http://
blueappletheatre.com/hamlet#hamlet-directors-notes
Dale, Simon. 2020. (@simondale) Tweet, 2 April
Desai, Ashwin. 2019. 'Sonny Venkatrathnam, Anti-Apartheid Crusader
with a Shakespearean "Gita"', *The Wire*, 18 March, https://thewire.
in/world/sonny-venkatrathnam-anti-apartheid-crusader-with-a-
shakespearian-gita
Eastham, Terry. 2017. 'Double Trouble', *London Theatre Reviews*,
11 November, https://www.londontheatre1.com/reviews/review-
intermission-youth-theatres-double-trouble/
Elkin, Susan. 2015. 'Prison Drama Changes Lives', *The Stage*, 22 August
Ferrouti, Christiana. 2018. 'Guilt Trip', *London Theatre Reviews*,
8 November, https://www.londontheatrereviews.co.uk/post.cfm?p=641
Field, Andy. 2008. 'Site-specific Theatre? Please Be More Specific',
The Guardian, 6 February, https://www.theguardian.com/stage/
theatreblog/2008/feb/06/sitespecifictheatrepleasebe
Field, Anthony. 2005. 'Captive Audience: Drama in Prison,' *The Stage*,
29 July
Gardner, Lyn. 2002. 'Thou Ripe bum-bailey: Shakespeare at Pentonville
Prison', *The Guardian*, 18 November
Gardner, Lyn. 2014. 'Belonging Review – Pioneering Use of Spoken,
Physical and Sign Language', *The Guardian*, 17 April, https://
www.theguardian.com/stage/2014/apr/17/belonging-circus-graeae-
roundhouse-review
Gardner, Lyn. 2016. 'The Tempest review – Ground Breaking
Shakespeare for Autistic Audiences', *The Guardian*, 31 October,
https://www.theguardian.com/stage/2016/oct/31/the-tempest-review-
groundbreaking-shakespeare-for-autistic-audiences
Grierson, Jamie. 2020. 'Early Release Scheme for Prisoners in England
and Wales to End', *The Guardian*, 19 August, https://www.
theguardian.com/society/2020/aug/19/prisons-inspector-england-wales-
warns-of-mental-health-problems-from-severe-coronavirus-restrictions

Hambrook, Colin. 2014. 'Growing Up Downs: Blue Apple Theatre Documentary on BBC3', 6 February, https://www.disabilityartsonline.org.uk/growing-up-downs-blue-apple-theatre-bbc3

Hatherley, Sam. 2020. 'University of Winchester Teams up with Blue Apple Theatre,' *Hampshire Chronicle*, 25 February, https://www.hampshirechronicle.co.uk/news/18252307.university-winchester-teams-blue-apple-theatre/

Koestler Awards 2020. 2020. https://www.koestlerarts.org.uk/wp-content/uploads/2020/10/2020-Koestler-Awards-Results-30.10.20.pdf

McDevitt, Johnny. 2009. 'Bard behind Bars', *The Guardian*, 9 January, https://www.theguardian.com/film/2009/jan/09/macbeth-northern-ireland-prison

Mackenzie, Rowan. 2020. 'Shakespeare UnBard: A Creative Writing Activity', *Inside Time*,1 May, https://insidetime.org/shakespeare-unbard-a-creative-writing-activity/

Media Statement. 2020. *Judicial Review: Howard League and Prison Reform Trust issue government with letter before action over its response to coronavirus in prisons*, 17 April, https://howardleague.org/news/judicial-review-howard-league-and-prison-reform-trust-issue-government-with-letter-before-action-over-its-response-to-coronavirus-in-prisons/

Ministry of Justice news. 2020. 'Pause of Prisoner early Release Scheme', 19 August, https://www.gov.uk/government/news/pause-to-prisoner-early-release-scheme

Moynes, Stephen. 2018. 'CELL OUT SHOW Inmates at Drug-ravaged HMP High Down Star in Lavish £70-a-ticket "West End" production of Les Miserables', *The Sun*, 23 April, https://www.thesun.co.uk/news/6117572/hmp-high-down-jail-musical/#comments

Mtongana, Athi. 2014. *Shakespeare Bible Taken to Robben Island* (eNCA.com), April, https://www.youtube.com/watch?v=q_nVI9BBHiU

Nash, Kym. 2019. semi-structured interview, University of Winchester (16 April)

Nash, Kym. 2020. (@nashertv_yt) Tweet (12 January)

People's Health Trust. 2019. 'A Fresh Vision for Mental Health', 4 July, https://www.peopleshealthtrust.org.uk/news/news-stories/fresh-vision-mental-health

Prisoner Learning Alliance. 2020. 'Our Work on Digital Technology', https://prisonerlearningalliance.org.uk/our-work/digital-technology/,

Raymond, Darren. 2015. 'I Found Shakespeare in Prison, and Now I'm Passing Him on,' *The Stage*, 10 November, https://www.thestage.co.uk/opinion/darren-raymond-i-found-shakespeare-in-prison-and-now-im-passing-him-on

Rhys, Tim. 2020. 'Theatres Are Already Closing: The UK Government Needs to Act Now', *The Conversation*, 3 July, https://theconversation.

com/coronavirus-theatres-are-already-closing-the-uk-government-needs-to-act-now-141796

Royal Shakespeare Company News. 2020. 'The Royal Shakespeare Theatre in 2020 and 2021', October, https://www.rsc.org.uk/news/the-royal-shakespeare-theatre-in-2020-and-2021

Sense. 2017. '"Someone cares if I'm not there": Addressing Loneliness in Disabled People' (Jo Cox Commission on Loneliness: Disabled People), https://www.sense.org.uk/support-us/campaign/loneliness/

Shelter. 2019. 'Homeless Crisis Costs Councils over £1bn in Just One Year', November, https://england.shelter.org.uk/media/press_releases/articles/homelessness_crisis_costs_councils_over_1bn_in_just_one_year

Shelter press release. 2019. '280,000 People in England Are Homeless, with Thousands More at Risk', 18 December, https://england.shelter.org.uk/media/press_releases/articles/280,000_people_in_england_are_homeless,_with_thousands_more_at_risk

Spiller, Ben. 2019. (@MxBenSpiller) Tweet, 22 November

Stourbridge News. 2009. 'Drama Group Receives Rave Reviews', *Stourbridge News,* 24 August, https://www.stourbridgenews.co.uk/news/4558887.drama-group-receives-rave-reviews/

Sweney, Mark. 2020. 'Majority of UK Theatres and Music Venues "face permanent shutdown"', *The Guardian,* 9 June, https://www.theguardian.com/culture/2020/jun/09/majority-of-uk-theatres-and-music-venues-face-permanent-shutdown

Treacey, Matt. 2020. 'Coronavius: Learning Disability Theatre Company Moves Online', *BBC News,* 24 May, https://www.bbc.co.uk/news/av/uk-england-hampshire-52752308/coronavirus-learning-disability-theatre-company-moves-online

University of Winchester. 2019. 'Blue Apple Celebration Marks First Year of University of Winchester Residency', University of Winchester Press Centre, 11 July, https://www.winchester.ac.uk/news-and-events/press-centre/media-articles/blue-apple-theatre-celebration-marks-first-year-of-university-of-winchester-residency.php

Vetter, Candice (prod.). 2014. *The Robben Island Bible,* CHVTV, 13 November, https://www.youtube.com/watch?v=HBiLP1yNGNs

Wiegand, Chris. 2020. 'Nuffield Southampton Theatres to Close as UK Arts Crisis Deepens', *The Guardian,* 2 July, https://www.theguardian.com/stage/2020/jul/02/nuffield-southampton-theatres-to-permanently-close-as-uk-arts-crisis-deepens

Williamson, Claire. 2017. 'Review: A Spark and a Beating Heart', *B247,* 16 May, https://www.bristol247.com/culture/theatre/review-a-spark-and-a-beating-heart-trinity-bristol/

Wright, Jeremy. 2014. 'Growing Up Downs: Tommy's Got Talent', *The Independent,* 21 January

Podcasts and public talks

Norris, Kyle. 2013. 'Shakespeare Helps Prisoners Change', Michigan Radio, 28 April, https://www.michiganradio.org/post/shakespeare-helps-prisoners-change

Shalkwyk, David. 2014. *Shakespeare Unlimited Podcast: Episode 1* (Folger Shakespeare Library), https://www.folger.edu/shakespeare-unlimited/robben-island-shakespeare

Tofteland, Curt. 2010. *Interview for One to One*, https://www.pbs.org/video/one-to-one-curt-tofteland-shakespeare-behind-bars/

Tofteland, Curt. 2013. *Ted X* talk (University of Berkeley), https://www.youtube.com/watch?v=CfDBh6LO4qc

Tofteland, Curt. 2017. *The State of Shakespeare* (24 May), http://stateofshakespeare.com/?s=tofteland&searchsubmit=

Websites

1623 Theatre Company, http://www.1623 theatre.co.uk/about/the-company

Acting on Impulse, http://www.actingonimpulse.net/about-us/

Arts and Humanities Research Council (AHRC), https://ahrc.ukri.org/

Arts Council England, https://www.artscouncil.org.uk/

Arts of Festivals website, https://artoffestivals.com/2013/10/20/the-relaxed-performance-project-theatre-for-all/

Blue Apple Theatre, http://blueappletheatre.com/

The British Association of Dramatherapists, https://badth.org.uk/dtherapy

Cardboard Citizens, https://cardboardcitizens.org.uk/who-we-are/theatre-of-the-oppressed/

Charlie Mackesy, https://www.charliemackesy.com/

Clean Break, https://www.cleanbreak.org.uk/about/#:~:text=40%20years%20ago%2C%20Clean%20Break,of%20the%20criminal%20justice%20system

Coronavirus (COVID-19), https://www.gov.uk/coronavirus

COVID-19 and Prisons Appeal http://appeal.org.uk/covid19andprisons

Crisis, https://www.crisis.org.uk/ending-homelessness/about-homelessness/

Deborah Warner, https://www.deborahwarner.com/about

Drum and Brass, http://drumandbrass.co.uk/

Educational Shakespeare Company, *Mickey B*, https://esc-film.com/portfolio-item/mickey-b/

Esme Fairburn Foundation, https://esmeefairbairn.org.uk/arts

Firebird Theatre, http://www.firebird-theatre.com/performances. html#prospero
Foundation for people with learning disabilities, https://www.mentalhealth.org.uk/learning-disabilities/help-information/learning-disability-statistics-/187699
Geese Theatre, http://www.geese.co.uk/about/our-history#:~:text=Since%201987%20the%20company%20has,by%20Clark%20Baim%2C%20in%201987.
Global World Cup Foundation, https://homelessworldcup.org/homelessness-statistics/
The Globe, http://blog.shakespearesglobe.com/post/90658621173/relaxed-performance-of-playing-shakespeare-with
Good Tickle Brain, https://goodticklebrain.com/
Grid Iron, http://www.gridiron.org.uk/
Growing Up Down's Story, https://growingupdowns.co.uk/story/
Intellectual Disability and Health, http://www.intellectualdisability.info/historic-articles/articles/research-evidence-on-the-health-of-people-with-intellectual-disabilities
International Network for Audience Research in Performing Arts (iNARPA), https://audience-research.leeds.ac.uk/
Makaton, https://www.makaton.org/aboutMakaton/
MARCH: Social, Cultural and Community Assets for Mental Health website, https://gtr.ukri.org/projects?ref=ES%2FS002588%2F1
Mental Health, https://www.mentalhealth.org.uk/our-work/campaigns
Mental Health First Aid, https://mhfaengland.org/mhfa-centre/research-and-evaluation/mental-health-statistics/
National Autistic Society, www.autism.org.uk/about-autism/autism-and-aspergers-syndrome-an-introduction/what-is-autism.aspx
National Criminal Justice Arts Alliance, https://www.artsincriminaljustice.org.uk/
National Theatre, https://www.nationaltheatre.org.uk/your-visit/access/relaxed-performances
Out of Character, http://outofcharactertheatre.squarespace.com/about
Penny Woolcock, Shakespeare on the Estate, https://pennywoolcock.com/shakespeareontheestate
Pimlico Opera, https://grangeparkopera.co.uk/prison/
Prisoners Education Trust, https://www.prisonerseducation.org.uk/
Prisoner Learning Alliance In-Cell Activity Hub, https://prisonerlearningalliance.org.uk/our-work/in-cell-activity-hub/
Prison Reform Trust, http://www.prisonreformtrust.org.uk/
Procurement for Prison Education, https://www.gov.uk/government/case-studies/procurement-for-prison-education-dynamic-purchasing-system
Punchdrunk, https://www.punchdrunk.org.uk/project/sleep-no-more/

Rideout, http://www.rideout.org.uk/purpose.aspx
Royal Shakespeare Company, https://www.rsc.org.uk/julius-caesar/past-productions/gregory-doran-production–2012
SCERTS Educational Model, http://scerts.com/the-scerts-model/
Shakespeare behind Bars, www.shakespearebehindbars.org
Shakespeare in Yosemite, https://yosemiteshakes.ucmerced.edu/
Tell Tale Hearts, https://www.telltalehearts.co.uk/downloads/Wave-Social-Story.pdf
Theatre and Performance Research Association (TaPRA), http://tapra.org/working-groups/
Theatre in Prisons and Probation, https://www.tipp.org.uk/
University of Kent, *Imagining Autism*, https://www.kent.ac.uk/50/profiles/impact/imagining-autism.html

INDEX

1623 Theatre 32–4
Acting on Impulse 194–5
Acting Up! 65–7, 77, 80–2
 See also Riding Lights Theatre
adaptation 14, 28, 36, 39, 58, 64, 74, 183
Adverse Childhood Experience Study (ACES) 3
Aeolian Mode 16
Ally-ship 85, 176, 179, 196, 207
anonymization 4, 94, 182
applied theatre 1, 2, 6, 10, 75, 171, 190, 194, 203
appropriation 4, 35, 43, 71, 77, 91, 116, 157, 176, 207
Arts Council 26, 73, 76, 178, 182, 185
Ashley Lucas 21, 182
audience engagement 59–60, 74–5
Augusto Boal 2, 22, 53, 110, 123–4
Autism spectrum disorder (ASD) 29, 33, 40–3, 66–7, 80, 83, 88–9, 190
 See Also Flute Theatre
 1623 Theatre
 Autism Arts Festival 13–14
 within criminal justice system 12, 62–3, 157
Autonomy 20, 53, 63, 147, 149, 168, 210

Bear Face Theatre 38
Bessel van der Kolk 15–16, 27, 44, 63, 127, 128, 139

Blue Apple Theatre 14, 63–5, 180–1, 186, 189–92, 192–4, 203
Broadmoor Hospital 16, 20, 26, 37, 92–4, 98, 104, 117, 211
Bromley Briefings 19, 112

Cardboard Citizens 3, 22–3
Clean Break Theatre 20, 102
colonial 6, 10, 24, 31, 86, 87
The Comedy of Errors 183
commodification 178, 181, 190
communication 208, 213
 development of 7, 35, 47, 51
 enhanced 41, 61
 skills 7
Covid-19 133–45, 157–66, 175, 192–4, 215
 activity packs 134–45, 211
creative playing 28, 51
creativity 18, 22, 28, 30, 42, 57, 141, 153–4
criminal justice system 17–22
 England and Wales prison system 17–18, 215
 global incarceration 17, 215
 men convicted of sexual offences 18, 60–3, 107–17, 133, 182
 US prisons 50, 145–6, 186–9
 youth custody 17, 134, 186
cultural capital 4, 8, 27, 50, 71–2, 74, 82, 92, 99, 107, 116, 130, 183, 208
 inversion of 71, 76, 102, 211

cultural history 9, 120, 128, 130, 141, 207
cultural ownership 34, 85–6, 116, 177, 178, 183
cultural signifiers 29, 72–3, 90, 117, 132, 205, 210
Curt Tofteland 145, 186–9, 201–2

Dame Sally Coates 18, 19, 46, 50, 52
Darren Raymond 182, 183
desistance 12, 50
difference 120, 122, 126
digital poverty 175–6
Digital Shakespeare 175, 193
disability 14, 73, 76, 85–91
dislocation from community 9, 53, 119, 120, 129, 168
Disturbing Shakespeare 78–80
documentaries 53, 175, 176, 178–9, 186–92
Donmar trilogy 95–6, 102, 188–9
dramatherapy 2, 15–16, 20, 88, 113
dramatic distancing 16, 36, 38, 105, 139, 208, 211
drug dependency 11, 37, 44
Drum and Brass 43–7
dual role 1, 6, 124, 209, 213–21

Educational Shakespeare Company (ESC) 184–6
Emergency Shakespeare 7, 17, 60–3, 68, 107–17, 155, 166, 212, 213
empathy 21, 31, 34, 35, 38, 46, 52, 67, 89, 124, 138, 190
emotional connection 8, 37, 54, 134, 179
emotional expression 36, 52, 63, 81, 151
emotional growth 7, 25–6, 46, 55–6, 61, 62, 149, 166, 197–8, 208, 210
emotional labour 187, 189

episodic memory retrieval 8, 32
ethics 94, 124, 171, 176
exile 119, 122–3, 125, 128, 129, 132, 158, 168

families 45–6, 101, 102–4, 106–7, 115–16, 118, 141, 149, 153, 199, 211
  pseudo-families 52, 65, 67, 103, 150, 166
Firebird Theatre 14, 77, 85–91
Flute Theatre 14, 28–32, 38, 39–43, 77, 82–5
funding 173, 178, 186, 194, 200, 212, 215

The Gallowfield Players 48–60, 65, 76, 96–107, 115, 129, 138, 147, 150, 154, 158–65, 196–201, 203, 210, 213
gang dynamics 43–4
Geese Theatre 20, 145
The Globe Theatre 88, 102
The Grapevine 100, 196–8
Grid Iron 74
group dynamics 43–4
Growing Up Downs 189–92

habitus 119, 122, 129, 168, 211
Hamlet 78, 88, 93–4, 146, 189–92, 193
heterotopia 5, 84, 86, 92, 95–6, 106
  mirrors as 119, 121, 215
  theatrical heterotopias 7–8, 25, 71–3, 77, 78, 101, 104, 109, 115, 118, 152, 210,
homelessness 2, 6, 22–4, 194–5, 215, 207, 214
  cognitive impairment 12
  Covid-19 22, 215
  global scale 22
  with those released from custody 12
humour 52, 55, 59, 63, 97–8

Hunter Heartbeat Method 29,
    82–5

identity 22, 28, 51, 59, 119, 122,
    131, 150, 164, 181, 198, 211
improvisational activities 13, 44
Intermediate Outcomes
    Measurement Tool 19
Intermission Youth Theatre 183–4
internment camps 125–9
isolation 9, 98, 119–20, 123,
    125–7, 133, 162, 193, 211

James Thompson 15, 20, 124
Jonathan Shailor 20–1
journalism 179–86, 196
Julius Caesar 15–16, 50, 54, 98,
    126, 127, 128, 149, 197

Karolina Lanckoronska 125–9
King Lear 78, 126–7, 128, 182,
    201
Koestler Awards 96, 103, 185

La Kompanyia Lliure 39–43
language
    difficulties with 27, 31, 35, 81,
        98, 127
    English not first language 35,
        135
    illiteracy 35, 50, 112, 135
    literacy levels 135, 200
Laura Bates 20, 145–7
learning 19, 21, 38, 52, 77, 124,
    141, 175, 200, 214
learning disabilities 11, 13–14, 88,
    189–90
    See also ASD
    disabled professional actors 14,
        63–5, 189–92
    dyslexia 12, 200
    within criminal justice system 12
legacy 16, 60, 106, 129, 164, 186,
    200, 213

Macbeth 36, 37, 38, 60–3, 74, 78,
    107–17, 129, 131, 147, 155,
    157, 184–6, 196
Marin Shakespeare Company 50
Mark Rylance 71
media 10, 138, 171–205, 212
    reception theories 5, 190, 198
    social media 10, 105, 172, 174,
        193, 212
mediachosis 171, 188
mental health issues 3, 11, 15–17,
    78–80, 121, 215
    within criminal justice system
        12, 100–1, 155–7, 199
The Merchant of Venice 56, 58–9,
    96–107, 150, 151, 196
Michel Foucault 21, 26–7, 119,
    121, 122, 124
    See also heterotopia
Michael Balfour 20
Mickey B 184–6, 208
A Midsummer Night's Dream 16,
    29, 79, 193, 194–5
movement 41, 44
Murray Cox 16, 20, 37, 92, 94,
    208
music 18, 40–1, 44, 61, 66–7, 84,
    98, 119, 191

Othello 35–6, 61, 138, 146
otherness 8, 9, 87, 121
out of character 78–80
ownership 22, 34, 40, 42–3, 55–6,
    66, 78, 85, 118, 131, 183,
    198, 200

patronage 10, 172, 188, 202, 207
patronizing 24, 171, 203, 209, 213
peer mentors 43
peer support 7, 54–5, 208
Pimlico Opera 91, 99, 184
positive autonomy 1, 7, 25–7, 39,
    41, 47, 53–4, 56, 68–9, 149,
    208, 210

positive physical contact 52, 67, 85
post–traumatic stress disorder
    (PTSD) 54
power 26–7, 58, 68, 71–2, 87, 95,
    102, 124, 177–8
presentation 172–3, 188, 203
pride 60, 82, 97, 106, 115, 180,
    193, 201, 211, 213
prison chapel 73, 91, 97–9, 101,
    112
prisons
    See also Robben Island
    category B high security prison
        48–60
    category B remand prison 34–9
    category C prison for men
        convicted of sexual offences
        60–3
    closed women's prison 95
    Covid-19 responses 134–5, 211
    journalism 181–2
    metaphors 126
    solitary confinement 20, 126,
        145–6
prisoner-staff relations 102,
    112–13
Prisoners Education Trust (PET)
    19, 59, 136, 166
privilege 171–2
Punch Drunk 74

race 58, 61, 76, 86, 174
redemptive narratives 24, 176,
    182, 187, 188
reflection 9, 53, 76, 92, 106, 121,
    130, 132, 136, 168, 188,
    197, 208, 211–13
rehearsal diaries 48, 116, 147, 149
Relaxed Performance Project 14,
    29–30, 73, 88
religion 96, 98–9
resilience 110, 119, 121, 122, 128,
    145, 147, 150, 154, 168

reader response theory 208
Richard II 126, 128, 146
Richard III 79
ride-out 60, 68
Riding Lights Theatre 65–7, 80–2
    See also Acting Up!
Rob Pensalfini 21
Robben Island 121, 129–32, 177
Romeo and Juliet 43–7, 138, 193
Royal Shakespeare Company 92,
    104, 131, 197

self-harm and suicide 11, 62, 97,
    100–1, 104–5, 108, 133–4,
    138, 144, 151, 168
Shakespeare Behind Bars 145,
    186–9, 201–2, 203
Shakespeare in Prison (Detroit
    Public Theatre) 69, 91
Shakespeare Prison Project 139,
    182–3
Shakespeare in Prisons Conference
    186
Shakespeare in Yosemite 74
shame 115–16
silos-dismantling 12, 207
site specific theatre 74
skills 29, 38, 46, 50
social capital 50, 57
Social Communication
    Emotional Regulation and
    Transactional Support
    (SCERTS) model 81, 83
social injustice 58–9
sounds-disruption 44–5
spaces
    appropriated spaces 8, 33, 40,
        43, 54, 73, 91–117, 210
    carceral spaces 21
    conceived spaces 25, 30, 47,
        121
    demarcated spaces 8, 65–7,
        72–3, 77–91, 210

felicitous spaces 40, 209
institutional spaces 92–3
liminal spaces 120
mediated spaces 10, 171–205
performance spaces 75, 118
reflective spaces 9, 119–68, 209
rehearsal spaces 25–70
representational spaces 33
socially constructed spaces 7, 45, 52, 67
Special Educational Needs (SEN) Schools 29–30, 32–4, 39–43, 80, 89, 215
Stanford University Prison Experiment 20
Sue Jennings 16, 51, 88, 94
Sycorax's Storm 138, 158–60, 162

Talent Unlocked Arts Festival 35
The Tempest 29–32, 32–4, 39–43, 64–5, 65–7, 81, 82–5, 85–91, 94, 138, 160, 186–9, 193

Theatre du Bout du Monde 24
theatre-programmes 198–9
theatrical 'ghosting' 27, 39, 66, 209
therapeutic Community 150
therapeutic outcomes 14, 15, 28, 45, 88, 94, 151
Tom Magill 185, 208
trauma 27, 44, 61, 65, 95
  trauma-informed conversations 54, 95, 101, 127
  trauma-informed pedagogies 3, 27, 47, 52, 66
  trauma-informed principles 3, 27, 69, 208, 210, 214
trust 2, 7, 19, 40–2, 47, 52–3, 59, 155, 166, 209

Visits Hall 60–1, 97, 102–3, 109
vulnerability 35, 51, 155, 166, 168
As You Like It 78

www.ingramcontent.com/pod-product-compliance
Lightning Source LLC
Chambersburg PA
CBHW062124300426
44115CB00012BA/1797